THE
SEA IS
SALT AND
SO AM I

CASSANDRA HARTT

THE SEA IS SALT AND SO AM I

ROARING BROOK PRESS

NEW YORK

Published by Roaring Brook Press
Roaring Brook Press is a division of Holtzbrinck Publishing Holdings
Limited Partnership
120 Broadway, New York, NY 10271 • fiercereads.com

The title of this work is drawn from the poem "The Crystal Lithium" by
James Schuyler, from *Collected Poems* copyright © 1993 by the Estate of
James Schuyler. Reprinted by permission of Farrar, Straus and Giroux.

The author gratefully acknowledges permission to quote from the poem
"The Crystal Lithium" written by James Schuyler. Published by Farrar, Straus
and Giroux. Reprinted by permission of Farrar, Straus and Giroux.

Library of Congress Cataloging-in-Publication Data

Names: Hartt, Cassandra, 1992– author.
Title: The sea is salt and so am I / Cassandra Hartt.
Description: First edition. | New York : Roaring Brook Press, 2021. |
    Audience: Ages 14–18. | Audience: Grades 10–12. | Summary: Twins Ellis
    and Tommy and their classmate Harlow, of West Finch, Maine, face a
    change that will shatter the delicate balance between them as secrets are
    revealed and relationships shift.
Identifiers: LCCN 2020039884 | ISBN 978-1-250-61924-2 (hardcover)
Subjects: CYAC: Friendship—Fiction. | Depression, Mental—Fiction. |
    Brothers—Fiction. | Twins—Fiction. | Family life—Maine—Fiction. |
    Maine—Fiction.
Classification: LCC PZ7.1.H377 Se 2021 | DDC [Fic]—dc23
LC record available at https://lccn.loc.gov/2020039884

Our books may be purchased in bulk for promotional, educational, or
business use. Please contact your local bookseller or the Macmillan Corporate
and Premium Sales Department at (800) 221-7945 ext. 5442 or by email at
MacmillanSpecialMarkets@macmillan.com.

First edition, 2021 • Book design by Aurora Parlagreco

Printed in the United States of America
10 9 8 7 6 5 4 3 2 1

For Mom, Dad, and Marisa

. . . a lapse of waves, balsamic, salty, unexpected:

Hours after swimming, sitting thinking biting at a hangnail

And the taste of the—to your eyes—invisible crystals irradiates
the world

"The sea is salt"

"And so am I"

—James Schuyler, "The Crystal Lithium"

March

March 22

Any other town, it'd be all they could talk about: how much longer until the house on Ocean Drive hurls itself into the sea. But considering it's the second storm this year (and only March), the people of West Finch shrug and say that's just what happens here.

There are more interesting topics for them to discuss. And they do. Over squat mugs of diner coffee and eggs dropped on toast:

Who was spotted trying to return an empty box of condoms to the General Store.

Which Black Bear Elementary second grader stuck both index fingers up another kid's nose during recess.

The high school boy who placed fifth in the mile yesterday. Remember when he used to come in last every race? They always knew he had it in him.

The boy's pale shadow: a girl with wild hair and a habit of fixing one thing only to break another.

The boy's twin (identical, if you can believe it): finally up for air after a year underwater. Crisscrossing town with bags of donations, scruffy dog at his heels. Pressing old artwork between cardboard and tying it off with string.

The trio of college students with Something to Say about wildlife conservation. Eight days they've been sitting on that rocky outcrop, blue-haired and pierced to high heavens, shivering in puffy jackets.

With so much going on, the fate of that house on Ocean Drive is barely worth a mention. The people of West Finch don't need to walk by the place to know its shingles hang like teeth in rotting gums. Its collapse a matter of when, not if. Anyone who thinks different is a few fish short of an aquarium.

They'd consider the girl with the wild hair one such fool. There she is again, huddled by the diner's largest window. Sneakers gritty with sand. Palms cool against her own closed eyelids. She pictures clean cedar planks. Stormproof windows, the factory stickers still intact. A woman at a nearby table touches the girl's arm and asks if she's feeling sick. She's never quiet like this.

Rain starts that night and doesn't let up until late Saturday morning. Power's out in half the town by then, and West Finch is ready with card games and candles. Lobster traps hauled, trash cans stowed, flowerpots snug on indoor welcome mats.

The girl waits out the last whispers of the storm at home. But this Ocean Drive house, it's the only thing on her mind. All week her steps twisted toward its trembling frame. In the morning before school, when the tide was teasingly low. Before dinner, when its eaves glistened with foam. She whispered affirmations:

You are strong and solid.

You have the structural integrity of a fallout bunker.

She convinced him to come with her, once. The boy who runs. With him at her back and the house dead ahead, she had silently promised no one at all that if the house weathered this weekend's storm, she and the boy would come back to step through the naked door frame, climb the stairs, and shine a flashlight through the attic window. Their wishful lighthouse.

But that was then. At home now, on the other side of the storm, the girl pulls on whale-print rain boots and a yellow coat. Perched on the stairs, phone in lap, she's waiting for a bone-like crack of wood. Chewing a hangnail. Hoping for a miracle. And though it's been days since she last visited Ocean Drive, her finger still tastes like it's been pickled.

One
HARLOW

Saturday, March 25

Ellis texts me, asking (1) Did I hear it? The house collapsing just now? And (2) When does he get his ten dollars?

You're going straight to hell, I write back. **Do not pass go, do not collect $200.**

Ellis: after you :)

Yesterday he waved an Alexander Hamilton under my nose and said the Ocean Drive house wouldn't last the weekend. I just about slapped it from his hand. In no universe is it okay to bet on catastrophes, for or against. No matter that no one lives in that house. No matter that I pretty much always want to do whatever Ellis wants.

Me: Wait, pretend I said DMV. I feel like that's worse.
Him: to late! we're going to hell!! get in the car!!!

I blink at that "to" like my phone might locate a second "o" if I wait long enough.

Ellis MacQueen, folks. The boy who beat me on the SATs.

Him: see you in 10?

My whale-print boots and I wade through brown water and wave at neighbors retrieving soggy newspapers. I'm smiling, but I'm picturing the worst. The two-story Cape Codder cracked open like a hinged dollhouse. Ellis saying "Oh wow," trying to sound sad. But the truth is he likes how something as big and sturdy as a house will collapse if you kick it hard enough.

Ellis is already there when I hit the beach. He stands apart from the other onlookers, his navy L.L. Bean windbreaker zipped to his chin. It's too cold for shorts but he's wearing them, so his prosthetic leg is visible below his right knee. Damp, dark hair hangs in his eyes. Without saying anything, I step up next to him and bump the side of my body into his. He bumps me back.

The only surprise: a leash knotted around his fist, and Goose herself at the other end. She's as ugly as ever. If I had to guess her breed, I'd say black Lab–Australian shepherd mix meets hyena. Plus there's her mouthful of snaggleteeth, matted fur no matter how recently she's been groomed, and today the addition of four little booties, one on each paw.

Ellis sees the question on my face and explains, "Tommy asked me to watch her."

Before I can figure out what that means, there's a crash that makes both Goose and me jump. The Ocean Drive house shivers and settles into its most dangerous slant yet.

"Oh wow," Ellis says.

As its foundation buckles, everything the rental's landlord didn't bother putting in storage spills from its open mouth. Soggy seashell-print curtains, red pot holders shaped like lobster claws, all too brightly colored against the gray sea, the taupe sand.

"Is the diner okay?" I say it like *who cares, not me*, but of course I do. His parents' restaurant has one of our town's many unplanned oceanfront views. With the house in front of us becoming driftwood as we speak, MacQueen's Diner is next-closest to shore, and last I checked, his family doesn't have plans to rebuild. They don't have any plans at all.

Ellis's eyes go wide. "Um. I think you should see for yourself."

At once I'm back in a childhood nightmare: standing on the diner's countertop as water surges through the front door, seaweed coiled in the coffeepot, barnacles scarring every surface, stubborn as cement. All this in the two seconds it takes Ellis's face to fall into a lazy, teasing grin.

"You shouldn't joke about that!" I gasp.

He looks down at my hand, which has accidentally grabbed his wrist. I let go. Scowl. His smile stretches across his whole face.

I let him get away with it only because of how pitiful this whole situation is. Figure A: waves swallowing a house and only nine people bored enough to come see it. Figure B: Goose up to her doggie elbows in floodwater, trying to sniff her own butt.

If you've never seen a jetty, walk to the end of Main Street and look for the man-made pile of rocks sticking out into the water, a straight shot for a whole quarter mile.

If you only want to know the important part, it's this: The jetty makes it so the waves don't just break against our shores—they pummel the coastline until it's unrecognizable. Add rising sea levels and we lose several feet of beach each year.

Last month, Maine's governor finally approved funds to tear the jetty down. But it's like the fourth law of physics that every time one problem gets solved, another takes its place.

For West Finch, that looked like the three college kids from California who parked themselves on the rocks last week. After reading about West Finch in environmental studies class, they felt they had a civic duty to save our precious coastal wildlife. Specifically, a bird called the piping plover.

The piping plover's thing is that it lays its eggs right in the sand where anyone can step on them. So of course they're under all these protections and somehow still halfway extinct. West Finch hasn't had plovers in years, but—just in case!—our mayor put the jetty demolition on hold. Dynamite is not ideal egg-laying mood music, apparently. Meanwhile the protestors say they're not leaving until the project's canceled altogether.

I scan the faces of the other Ocean Drive spectators. No sign of the ring-leader's vibrant blue hair, or the dreads or Birkenstocks or hemp-whatever her two co-members are probably sporting. I haven't seen them up close (pretending they don't exist is my protest of their protest), but I'm sure I'd recognize them. I snap a few pictures of the wrecked house with my phone. Maybe if they saw this place, they'd understand their crusade is more complicated than they think.

I follow Ellis to where the house's back door used to be. Water gushes from a rectangular basement window, and with it, a stream of items that point to a richer life than summer holidays. I collect a topless Barbie doll with seaweed threaded through her hair, a bloated paperback with yellowed edges, and a teacup patterned with pink peonies, broken cleanly in two. Ellis comes back with a WORLD'S BEST GRANDPA medal around his neck.

I raise an eyebrow.

"It's because I give out a lot of sweets," he says.

Face full of mischief, he reaches into his jacket pockets and pulls out a whoopie pie in each hand, nestled in plastic sandwich baggies. He offers what looks like the bigger one to me. It doesn't feel entirely appropriate to snack while we wade through thousands of dollars in property damage, but whoopie pies are so much work that Ellis's mom bakes only a couple dozen each day. The sandwich cakes are a dark, sticky chocolate filled with whipped marshmallow fluff.

"So," I say through a glob of frosting. "Are we going to talk about Goose's footwear?"

Because the dog, she is still wearing those booties.

Ellis pushes his hair out of his face with the back of his arm and rolls his eyes. "He wouldn't let us leave without them."

It's no secret Tommy is obsessed with his dog. Nicer to her than he is to most humans (and me especially, his least favorite member of our species). I'm no fan of his, either, but I'm being 100 percent objective when I say the dog looks ridiculous.

I abandon my treasures in the sand and scramble up the boulders stacked along the western side of the yard. I find a dry, flat rock and sit with my knees under my chin. The half-naked Barbie gets yanked out to sea on the next wave, but the heavier teacup and book are dragged along for several minutes before they disappear. I squint at the horizon and don't blink until my eyes water.

It gives me a rash to think we're in any way alike, but besides me, Tommy would appreciate this more than anybody. He thinks he's some kind of artist. Or he used to. Before he got depressed, before he left school for two weeks in January to "get back on track" (doctor's orders), he'd draw whatever you put in front of him. A mountainside prickly with pine trees, Goose making a face only a dog-parent could love, and once a house split down the middle, staring down a wave as tall as itself. It gave me a behind-the-eyes feeling that made me need to hit him. Instead I sent the drawing through a paper shredder and left the skinny strips scattered around his bedroom. I hoped his lungs would freeze in his chest when he saw. I hoped he'd know it was me.

It felt like an appropriate response at the time.

Ellis is running figure eights in the flooded street. His stride's a little awkward without his running blade, but he's still pretty fast. Mud splatters clear up the back of his jacket. Goose chases him unleashed, first in big circles with her different-colored eyes bulging, then zigzags, until she's panting. Ellis will make varsity any day now, so he could keep going if he wanted. But he slows when Goose quits chasing. It's no fun if someone isn't telling him to stop.

We wade north toward the center of town. The ocean pulses to our right some fifty feet away, and Ellis and Goose shield me from most of the spray. In my head I make this week's to-do list: order a better SAT prep book; draft a plan to save West Finch from climate change; etc.

"Listen," Ellis singsongs when I'm quiet for too long. "You can be upset that I'm smarter than you and always have been, or you can be upset about that worthless house. Not both."

"You are *not* smarter than me."

He spreads his arms in a grand shrug. "Who are we to argue with the College Board?"

"Not in this universe." My steps, now stomps, soak my leggings. "Not in any of your pretend universes, either."

"String theory isn't pretend. It's physics."

"Well, whatever it is, enjoy it while you can. I'm doing a retake in May," I say, making a mental note to register.

Ellis and I are both near the top of our class, but my grades are always a little better. It'll be a nonissue soon enough. When he gets recruited for track, the whole well-rounded-student-athlete thing will make our on-paper selves look pretty much identical to elite East Coast deans of admissions. That's The Plan.

My radioactive SAT score is not part of The Plan. But then, neither is Ellis's skipping homework whenever he feels like it and not making varsity yet, so.

I continue. "Saving the diner comes first, though. Plus the rest of West Finch."

"Right. Priorities."

"And you're going to help."

He halts. We're in the middle of the street, no cars, but still. I want to drag him to the safety of the road's shoulder. He shrugs helplessly and points to Goose, who's off-leash and lagging several feet behind. My hands find my hips.

"Ellis."

"Harlow."

"Hurricane season is only three months away. I need your full participation. Put that brilliant mind to work."

He takes his time clipping Goose onto her leash, incorrectly assuming I'd miss him rolling his eyes. But his jaw clenches as he stands. Something behind me catches his eye.

A figure in a black wet suit rocks on his heels at the water's edge. Close enough to hear us if we yelled. Far enough I'd rather not. He even looks around once, but he must not see us from there.

I know Tommy by the bumpy white curve of his shaved head and familiar slope of his shoulders. He quit therapy last month, and according to Ellis, his prescription now consists of antidepressants, exercise, and sunshine. He could swim at the YMCA, like a normal person, but their mom is just happy he's cultivating an interest in something besides sleeping.

The first wave touches his ankles. Next, his knees. The ocean is maybe thirty-six degrees, so how's that wet suit warm enough? Not to mention the current's always strongest after a storm.

"Guess that explains dog duty," I say.

Ellis squints. "Let him freeze his balls off if he wants to. It's a free country."

As far as Ellis is concerned, looking alike is the only thing they have in common. I have to agree. They're identical twins, so mix-ups happen—to other people. To me, the MacQueen boys are different in a million ways, all starting and ending with the fact that Tommy and I are not friends. His hatred of me could fuel several bonfires, and I've fantasized about accidentally closing his fingers in a car window once or twice.

The diner shimmers through the mist at the end of the road. Ellis turns toward it, away from his brother, and tugs on Goose's leash. He's told me Tommy isn't trying that hard to feel better. But if happiness is a switch he can turn on and off, wouldn't he have flipped it already?

When Tommy dives, his form is infuriatingly perfect. Hands stacked. Chin tucked like he's holding a fifty-cent piece against his collarbone, the way they taught us in swim class when we were kids. Me, I scattered at least fifteen dollars in the deep end before our instructor conceded diving might not be my thing.

A wave explodes above the spot where he disappeared. Goose barks once.

I can hold my breath longer than he can. I'm sure of it, even as my eyes fill and my lungs crumple against my spine. The ocean roars like I'm pressing shells to my ears. I count to almost sixty before my breath rips through me. Moments later, his white scalp bobs to the surface, impossibly far out. I knew he could swim but not like this.

A fishhook in my chest tells me to stay, though past experience says later we'll find him curled under a blanket on the couch, and there he'll sleep until dinner, snoring so loudly I sometimes think he's faking.

Ellis and Goose are miniatures halfway down the street. I could squish them between two fingers, or put them in my pocket.

Have fun, I think, sparing one last glance toward the ocean. Then my jacket flares out behind me as I hurry after them.

Two

HARLOW

Goose's tail whacks the backs of our legs as we stomp our boots on the diner's doormats. She shouldn't be in here, but the spot in the grass where Tommy usually ties her up is too wet. Floodwater covers the picnic table seats, and in the surging waves, even the jetty out back looks small.

Ellis's mom pokes her head around the corner. "Is Tommy with you?"

The boys are tall and lean like their dad, but their faces are all their mom, which is why it's so unsettling to watch the thin lips that live in a near-constant smirk on Ellis's face press together in a grimace on Helen Bell's. Low-level annoyance is pretty much her constant state. Owning a restaurant with your ex-husband will do that to you, I guess—especially when that restaurant still goes by your married name.

Ellis and I shake our heads, silently agreeing not to mention we saw Tommy ten minutes ago. Going out in the storm was his bad decision, not ours. And it's like Ellis said: his balls, his business.

Helen's wearing an apron over a heathered-gray MacQueen's T-shirt and jeans, purple-red hair in its signature messy bun. Her pale skin is covered in a fine dusting of flour.

Two lines appear between her eyebrows. "It's rude to stare."

"I'm not," I say automatically.

But I am. Her hair's the same purple-red of the diner's menu sleeves.

Perfect match. Which came first, and does she bring a menu to the salon as a reference for her colorist? I've never been brave enough to find out.

She wrinkles her nose at the eau de wet dog and says, "Your parents are here."

My parents. Coastal oceanographers who know everything about erosion—except how to fix it. A pretty huge knowledge gap, if you ask me. Still, they could draw a timeline of how and when our tiny town will disappear. My parents could probably say down to the day.

Not that I've asked. It's a day that'll never come, if I can help it.

I find them at a table under a section of wall strung with red-and-blue buoys. Mom's mostly gray hair is in a low bun, and the little bald spot on the back of Dad's head winks under the fluorescents. I give them each a one-armed hug and ask how the supply drop went. They report that everyone has power back now, and Dad almost knocks over his iced tea showing me a picture he snapped of a black, oily bird with a hooked bill. I'm just glad it's not a piping plover.

"Where'd you go, sweet pea?" Mom asks.

"We checked out that house on Ocean Drive."

They exchange a look, and Dad takes a long time cleaning his glasses on his shirt. Lately we've had several family discussions about whether my obsession (Dad's word) with the destruction of West Finch is reaching an unhealthy level.

"Chloe said it's halfway gone already." He nods toward Mrs. Samuels, sitting at the counter that runs the length of the room. Ellis has already grabbed us drinks and landed beside her. Now he's chatting with her husband as the old man stares down a mountain of iceberg lettuce, the diner's only low-sodium, heart-healthy anything. Ellis says something that makes Clifford Samuels sweep the grubby red knit cap off his own head and dab his eyes. Then his laugh turns into the kind of cough that makes you want to pull your shirt over your face.

I shrug. "I wouldn't say halfway."

Ellis meets me at our favorite table by the big window, although right now, plywood covers the glass. Goose whines for a few minutes before sighing and sprawling on the floor at Ellis's feet—only to leap up again when his mom brings over a veggie burger cut down the middle and a basket of steaming fries. I give everything a healthy squirt of ketchup.

I'm ready to dig in, but she's still standing there, skewering Ellis with just her eyes.

"Want to tell me what's really going on? Let's start with why you have the dog if your brother's not here."

Ellis takes his time eating a fry in three bites, a move so bold that if I'd done it, I'd be afraid for my life. "He went for a swim."

Her nose twitches, but the rest of her remains eerily still. A few flour motes drift down to join their friends on her shirt. "Did you think, *huh, maybe I should tell him not to swim in the ocean after a nor'easter?*"

His eyes narrow. "Did *you?*"

They glare with the same furious thought: *I shouldn't have to.*

"He didn't pick up when I called home. Go check on him." Big pause. "Please."

"Why me?!" he cries, hands flipping an imaginary table. I picture our burger, fries, everything on the floor, best day of Goose's life.

Helen's face says, *because I said so.*

"It'll take us half an hour to walk there and back. I'm already tired." He props his wet sneakers on the chair next to us for dramatic effect, fidgeting just enough to make his right leg glint.

"I'll go," Mrs. Samuels says behind Helen. Her lavender raincoat threatens to swallow her tiny frame as she slides off the counter stool. "I can drop off Goose while I'm there."

Mrs. Samuels is one of those people who has to be involved in everything. She and Clifford are always butting into stuff, acting like they're the boys' grandparents, and Ellis's parents let them because they've all known each other for decades.

I only like Mrs. Samuels because when we were in her fourth-grade class, she let Ellis and me sit next to each other for two whole months before she moved our seats for talking. Our other teachers gave us one week max.

Mrs. Samuels gets the car keys from her husband and leaves with Goose. I frown at Ellis.

"I'm not in charge of him, okay?" He sucks loudly on his straw.

Like he *wants* me to say something about it.

"Plastic straws never biodegrade. They get caught in sea turtles' noses. Just so you know."

"And just so *you* know, lots of people rely on plastic straws." His damp hair hides one dark eyebrow, but the other shoots up. "So that's a pretty ableist thing to say."

My face burns. "I know that."

When I tear open my own straw and stick it in my pink lemonade (solidarity and all that), he leans back in his seat and cackles.

"Which hippie told you that thing about the sea turtles?" he asks once he's calmed down. "The one with the hair or the pretty one?"

I'm doing the math (three college kids total, so he's left out one; which does he think is pretty?), but that's not the point. "Read it somewhere," I say.

"I'll bet." He's laughing at me again. With me? "Hey, Harlow. Hey."

I take a large bite of dill pickle to show I'm listening. He leans toward me over the table, and despite myself, I do the same.

"On your tenth birthday, what'd you ask for instead of presents?" he asks, brown eyes bright and all too eager.

I drop the pickle in disgust and slump back in my chair.

"No, seriously. I can't remember. Was that the year you said the best gift of all would be a donation to the piping plover foundation? Or was it the year after?"

"It was both years," I snap. I'm sorry I went there about the turtle noses. "I was extremely empathic for my age."

I grab the ketchup bottle, shake hard. I *do* care about those useless birds.

They should be able to build a nest and have consensual bird sex and incubate their eggs in peace. They just need to do so three to five miles away. When I squeeze, the ketchup's top explodes off and disappears into our basket under roughly half the bottle's contents.

Ellis pretends not to notice, though he does carefully use a spoon to scrape some ketchup off a couple fries before he shoves them in his mouth. "Maybe we have to start our own group to fight back."

"Like Correct the Coast?"

He makes a sound that says no, nothing like that. "Correct the Coast is for retired people who like picking up beach trash. Our group will make sure they still have a beach to keep clean."

I must be making a face because he says, "What? Bad idea?"

I shake my head.

"Good idea?"

I kick his chair leg.

"Is that a yes?"

It is.

———

Half a bottle of ketchup later, the bell above the door rings.

In my experience, there are two types of bad situations: the kind you feel coming—prickly neck, oil-slick gut—and the kind that hits you like a tractor trailer coming down a mountain pass, and you weren't checking your rearview mirror.

Mrs. Samuels returns, minus Goose, plus a wake of muddy footprints. The doormat's right there and she hasn't wiped her boots. That's the first clue.

"He wasn't home," she reports. That's the second.

Depending on how you're counting. There's also the determined way Tommy dived, and the fact that it's been, what, half an hour? Thirty minutes is nothing, unless you're in the Atlantic Ocean at the end of March, and then any time is probably too much.

But I knew that already.

He could've gone for a walk after his swim. He could've stopped by the General Store. It's premature to panic, agrees everyone who didn't watch him disappear into thirty-six-degree water.

Jim MacQueen finally emerges from the diner's kitchen. He has the look of a man wild with purpose, though maybe that's just his scruffy winter beard. He goes straight outside and calls Tommy's name for several minutes, circling the diner. Whatever he left on the stove smells like it's burning.

Helen, Clifford, Mrs. Samuels, and now my parents are suggesting other places to check, people to call. They say *just in case* until it means nothing.

When Jim comes back alone, Clifford squats down next to our table, red knit cap in leathery hands.

"Now, no one's going to get in trouble," he says.

His head looks small without his hat. If I didn't know better, I'd assume he was a cute, harmless grandpa.

I glance across the table. Ellis knows how I feel about Clifford Samuels, but he just grips the back of the chair beside him and studies the boarded-up window.

"Where'd he go in?" Clifford looks at each of us in turn. When we don't respond, he tries again. "Can you remember what streets were nearby?"

I watch his hat slowly rotate as he worries the edge with his fingers. A familiar leaky-pipe feeling starts in my chest. Like something is deeply wrong and there's no way to stop it.

"Birch and Ocean." It takes me a second to realize those words, they came from me. I resist the urge to clap a hand over my mouth, and add, "Northeast corner."

I answer the rest of his questions too, telling as much as I dare without saying plainly that we watched Tommy dive into the Atlantic, and no, I guess it didn't look like he'd be back anytime soon. After each answer I leave Ellis an opening to back me up.

His grip on the chairback tightens.

His mouth stays shut.

Clifford Samuels stands up straight and smooths his hat onto his head. "Here's what we're going to do. Mira, you stay with Helen in case he comes here. Chlo, you'll want to go back and check the house again."

"Jim and I can take the beach," Dad offers.

"Good. And I'll go out and take a little ride around," Clifford says. He means on his lobstering boat.

Great. A plan. I like plans. Ellis likes plans too, but across from me, he looks plain bored.

"Why are you being like this?" I don't give a shit about his brother, but my lungs are still doing this whole taking-on-water thing. It makes me want to knock over my chair or shake him, hard, just to make his face move.

"Like what?" He drags his finger through the ketchup and puts it in his mouth, his eyes fixed on the basket. "Don't you think I'd know if something happened to him? He's *fine*. Probably floating on his back and laughing about how worried you all must be."

I want him to be right, but this leaky-pipe feeling, it's telling me otherwise. He didn't know anything was wrong the month before last, when Tommy spent half his weekends asleep. Got skinny like Ellis except he wasn't running eight miles a day. That's when they found out he was failing most of his classes and wasn't on track to pass junior year.

"Is he still not taking his meds?" I ask, my voice low.

His stony gaze lands on me. "Not since you told him they were making him fat."

I didn't say fat. But they were.

"He's a strong swimmer," he says.

For the next twenty minutes I make myself believe him. I take the menu out from where we tucked it behind the napkin holder and read it all, though it hasn't changed since my family moved to West Finch seven years ago. I squint at Jim MacQueen's untidy scrawl on the specials board. Memorize it. Clam chowder with two rolls. Chicken parm. I grab some napkins, wipe away the sweat from our drinks, and finish the pickle spear in our burger basket.

Ellis is on his phone. He scrolls through an endless stream of our classmates enjoying their Saturdays. Doesn't even blink when the diner's landline bleats. Helen grabs it before the second ring.

Her hand covers her mouth.

My mom sits between us in the chair still wet from Ellis's sneakers. She looks at me. Him. I wish for noise-cancelling headphones, earmuffs, a wrench.

"They found him," she says.

I give Ellis time to ask the obvious question.

Any question.

"Who did?" I ask when he won't.

"Cliff."

Ellis and I both have our hands on the table and Mom grabs one of each like we're having a séance, which is how I know Tommy's dead. I yank my hand back. Ellis stands, but Mom won't let him get away that easy.

"He's okay," she says. "Tired but okay. They're on their way back now."

Without a word, he breaks her grip and crosses to the front door. The little bell sings. I don't know what to feel yet except worried for Ellis, and I can't see him through the boarded-up windows. I grab our jackets and follow him outside.

He's sitting on top of the picnic table with his back to me. Still on his phone. He drags his finger and scrolls. Again. I wade through the floodwater, climb up next to him, and sit cross-legged. I loop my arm through his and lean my head on his shoulder, and he lets me stay that way for three whole minutes.

At last Clifford Samuels's lobstering boat drops anchor near the marina a couple streets down. Then a smaller dinghy with two silhouettes against the purple waves, one rowing toward shore. As soon as Tommy's foot hits that dock, Ellis launches himself off the table and lands hard, water splashing.

"Where are you going?" I call. He's already halfway across the parking lot.

"Home. I have shit to do."

Clifford Samuels walks first and Tommy follows, looking tiny wrapped in an oversize towel, head bowed. The pressure in my chest climbs to my throat. At least he won't see Ellis is gone.

They reach the diner's door. The sun hasn't set but the light has changed, and everything is orange and pink except for the ocean, which is the same steel gray as before. Clifford Samuels goes inside. Tommy trails him, almost safe, until just when I think he won't, he looks back at me.

Three

ELLIS

Eject me from this universe and put me back where everything is as it should be.

Give me that quantum theory, multiverse shit from physics class. For every choice or possibility in this world, there's another universe where things went a different way. Your parents didn't get divorced. You never learned to ride a bike. You're aching and covered in salt because the twin connection thing is real, not made-up bullshit to get you to be nice to your brother.

Whatever it takes, I'll do it: Turn and wait with Harlow like she wants me to. Reach my house, then keep walking. Or go inside to check if Goose is still where Mrs. Samuels left her. Just one thing staying where it's supposed to. One damn thing. And she is. She's pacing the kitchen, or staring blankly at her water dish, or getting her hopes up it's not me at the front door.

I go straight upstairs so if there's a note on the counter or stuck to the fridge I don't have to see it. But at the same time, I'm checking everywhere: the calendar on the basement door, every receipt in the junk drawer, the block of sticky notes by the phone. If it's a scrap of paper he may have looked at once, I'm searching it for some instructions on what I'm supposed to do next.

I'm checking my phone. I'm not checking my phone. Definitely not reading my texts.

Harlow: They went inside. Should I follow them?
Harlow: Oh no I did and everyone's crying.
Harlow: Where are you?

I'm face-to-face with his bedroom door, hand testing the knob like I'm inside a burning house. Too dangerous to enter.

All at once I'm messaging anyone not from West Finch, thinking I'll hook up with whoever responds first. Ian says he's free in a few hours. Paige doesn't answer.

I find the hurricane bag Harlow made us last year and eat a protein bar because this feels like an emergency.

Harlow: They're taking him to the hospital.
Harlow: Going home first, though. I said you'll see them there.

Instead of waiting around, maybe I change my clothes and swap out my leg. Running right after a big storm, the sky's pressed in closer than it could ever be in real life. A world of churning clouds and pavement black with rain. A puddle covers most of the road ahead and I charge straight through, soaking the sneaker on my left foot, but somehow it's the curved carbon fiber that feels more, a cold crash of needles below my right knee, on skin that isn't even there.

When we saw Tommy on the beach, I had no clue it was anything but a normal swim. Harlow watched him, though. By the time she caught up with me she was panting. Smiling. That alone should've told me everything I needed to know. If she's smiling it never works out well for him.

Then there are the little things that meant nothing before, everything now. How clean his room got in the last few days. Harlow digging through the garbage while I ate peanut butter from the jar: childhood drawings stacked in crushed shoeboxes, letters from grandparents who died before we knew them. Harlow held up a C-minus from a recent geometry quiz and joked maybe if I tutored him, I could get credit for community service hours.

If I'd told him to stop on the beach today, would he have listened?

In some parallel universe, the car to my left barrels through the stop sign as I cross the intersection. It could happen. Instead I flinch hard at an impact that never comes and land sprawled on the ground, palms full of road. I get up and the driver meets my gaze, a startled but safe ten feet away.

Hot pink shame washes down my spine. I scramble up and surge forward at a self-shattering pace that justifies my heartbeat. In this universe, I put as many miles between me and the ocean as possible. I run until I can't.

Four

HARLOW

Monday, March 27

When Ellis doesn't reply to my messages Saturday night, doesn't show up for pancakes at the diner Sunday, I know I can't mention Tommy unless he does first. That if I try, he'll shut me out completely.

In solidarity, I do a good job not thinking about Tommy the rest of the weekend. Like, I don't think about watching him dive into choppy waves, or when Helen asked me where Ellis went (Right in front of Tommy! Still shivering!). I do think about the boxes I found a couple weeks ago, but only long enough to decide anyone can gather their possessions in containers labeled with their family members' names, and it doesn't necessarily mean they're planning anything bad. It's allowed.

By the time Ellis drives us to school Monday, we're so good at not thinking about it that neither of us glances at the back seat where Tommy would usually sit.

It got cold overnight. The collar of Ellis's winter coat hits halfway up his cheek, and his beanie practically covers his eyebrows, but otherwise he's the same. He cranks up the radio as we fly beyond the West Finch town limits. Doesn't care it's not even music. I suffer through the loudest car commercial in history before my hand darts toward the volume knob.

"Driver's rights!" he yells, swerving but staying in his lane as he knocks my hand away.

"But it's my car!" I shout over the music.

The irony isn't lost on me that I hate cars and yet, of the two of us, I'm the one who has one. It's all part of my parents' campaign to Change Harlow's Mind About Driving. I only got my license because they wouldn't take me to Ellis's track meets anymore. So after I took driver's ed (twice) and passed my driving test (third try), they gifted me their ancient Volvo.

He brakes hard at a yellow light. "And if you ever drive, you can choose the volume."

I'd give it a try, maybe, if school wasn't so far. But West Finch's Black Bear Elementary only covers K-through-5. After that, the district buses us to Seaborough's enormous, consolidated schools twenty minutes inland so we can join Model UN or play football if we want to. Which we don't. I'd be perfectly content riding the bus, but Ellis thinks it's a crime against humanity to have a car and not use it. So every morning I carefully drive the half mile from my house to his, then switch to the passenger seat so he can drive us the rest of the way. I'd rather not let my parents find out he's the primary driver of my car, and in West Finch, nothing stays secret for long.

The light turns green and he guns it, a smile dancing at the edges of his lips. I'm slammed back in my seat, the terrible music humming through my bones, but somehow a laugh bubbles out of me. If I can keep him happy like this it will all be okay.

My parents said I needed to give the MacQueens space after the Tommy incident, and reluctantly I agreed. So I spent yesterday strategizing with Coop. If we're on schedule, by now he's managed to tell most of the school (1) Tommy's gone again, and (2) don't say anything to Ellis.

Coop's leaning against the brick wall near the school's back entrance, grin fixed in place. He's one of only a few people of color at school, and the lone Black kid, so he's not exactly hard to spot. Especially when he starts waving at us, arms wiggling like he's one of those inflatable balloon men you see at car dealerships. It almost gives me a headache to watch. But Coop knows how silly he looks, just like he knows that the watery, skim-milk smile it gets from Ellis is a big deal. If I weren't around, he'd probably be Ellis's closest friend. He knows that too.

"Missed you at Ben's Saturday," Coop says as he thumps Ellis's back.

Mentioning the weekend (or any topic that could lead back to Tommy) is the exact opposite of what we agreed. I glare at Coop. He smiles wider.

"Aw, don't be jealous, Harlow. You know I missed you too," he says with a wink.

Gross. Also, not the point.

I pretend Coop's transparent, like one of those sea pigs, and look through him to the table where student council's selling prom tickets. I'd rather spend an evening picking ticks off Goose than one surrounded by Seaborough High's dullest and drunkest. Thank god Ellis and I already agreed prom is too cringey to consider.

A couple juniors turn away from the table and, prom tickets in hand, sneak glances at Ellis on their way inside. He looks like he wants his winter jacket to swallow him.

Coop barrels onward and says, "Olivia asked about you."

Olivia is a pole vaulter on the track team and, to put it nicely, she's a bit clueless. Like, didn't know the first name of the president when that came up in US History. Olivia is not part of our plan.

Yet Ellis's face changes like I guess Coop knew it would. He loves when people pay attention to him, so he's already hooked up with quite a few girls in our year and a couple boys too. But who's counting?

Nothing distracts him like a fling. I should've thought of this myself.

"She asked me first!" I cut in because, well, let's get this timeline straight. "Last week, she asked if you're dating anyone."

Coop rolls his eyes hard as Ellis focuses on me. "What'd you say?"

"I told her to ask you herself." She also asked twice if I would be okay with it, but I don't mention that.

Operation Let Ellis Make Believe Tommy Didn't Almost Hypothermia Himself to Death goes surprisingly well. All day I intercept condolences for him, gathering our classmates' and teachers' worry so he doesn't have to. But although Coop has spread the basic facts of what happened, that doesn't stop the question I dread from bubbling up. It comes in whispers with weighty looks, puzzled head tilts.

Why?

If I knew, I wouldn't be half as worried about what might happen when Tommy comes home.

When I say everyone does their part, I mean everyone. Sometime between first and last period Olivia finds Ellis. Latches on like a pretty leech. Apparently, they spent most of lunch making out in the math wing until Ms. Wheelock caught them and sent them back to the cafeteria. I was in the computer lab working on my West Finch climate change manifesto (tentative title, *Preparing for the Worst: Coastal Erosion and You*), so I didn't notice.

When I get to US History, Olivia's sitting next to him. In my seat.

"Do you mind, Harlow?" she says.

The desks are pushed together in pairs, arranged in rows. She's leaning so far in his direction she's in danger of falling out of her chair. Meanwhile Ellis doesn't look at me, has no idea how many times I've told the story of his weekend for him today.

I drop into her usual seat behind him.

For the next thirty minutes I re-memorize the whorls and cowlicks in his hair. This whole thing is classic Ellis after catastrophe: Grab the closest person who shows interest and casually date them until the catastrophe resolves itself. He did the same thing in ninth grade, after finishing last in his first-ever cross-country race (Lila Baxter, five days); when Coop got an email from a college recruiter sophomore spring, the first of any track boys in our grade (Paige Michaud, seven days); when Tommy was out of school for two weeks this past January (Ian Taylor, thirteen days).

It gets worse. Mr. Delmonico gives back our quizzes from Friday, and he hands me the wrong one because this has a huge B circled in red pen, except it's my name at the top. I can see the A on Ellis's quiz from here.

Olivia keeps touching his arm.

I fold my quiz into an accordioned paper fan. Mr. Delmonico asks me to pay attention.

If Tommy had half the game Ellis does, he'd be too busy making out to go swimming when he shouldn't, and this wouldn't even be happening.

I refold my quiz into a fortune-teller, leaving all eight inside flaps blank so each time I land on one, I can make up whatever I need to hear.

7—Ask for extra credit and you shall receive.

3—Pole vaulting is the most dangerous of all track-and-field events.

8—Concussions. Impaling.

Mr. Delmonico takes my fortune-teller/quiz away.

I should be nice. One thing Olivia has going for her is her legs seem to go all the way from the floor to her chin.

Still, supposing I put up with her, I don't see her helping measure sand loss or make anti-plover posters. She likely won't last long—and then Ellis will replace her with whoever looks at him next. Which means he's pretty much on a crash course to ruining our summer plans.

It's because of Tommy that Ellis is acting this way. But if Ellis can cheer up just by kissing someone, maybe it can be that easy for Tommy too.

There's only one person I know who's come close to trying.

Ruby Lee and Tommy were pretty friendly fall semester, at least by Tommy's loner standards (they had a couple painting classes together and ate lunch with the other artsy weirdos). But they had a big falling-out in October. Ruby hasn't talked to him since, and her crew followed her lead. The only art kid who's spoken to me today was Ethan. Asked *How'd Tommy do it?* during second-period band and I honked my clarinet at him (B♭, staccato) until he retreated.

Ruby finds me by my locker at the end of the day. Comes right up to me with her shiny black hair, her clear skin. She's wearing purple lipstick and no other makeup, and the white parts of her Vans are graffitied with Sharpie spirals and stars. She leans her head against my open locker door.

"How is he?"

I can tell she's not just asking to be polite, or worse, to get juicy details she can share with her friends later. There's literally nothing to dislike about her, which is why I've been successfully avoiding her for months.

I slowly load up my backpack and describe Saturday in broad strokes. Tommy looked tired. His parents have already visited the hospital twice. We don't know how long he'll be there.

"I'm glad he's getting help," Ruby says when I'm done. "I feel like I should text him or something. Would that be weird?" My mouth gaping open. That thing that happens to pet fish sometimes where they can't close their mouths and they starve. And then the kicker: "This must be really strange for you."

I transform, betta fish to hummingbird. Pulse vibrating. "What do you mean?"

She scrapes the toe of one doodled sneaker against the other. "Ethan told us you were being really intense, but I think it's cool you're not letting people talk shit about him," she says. "I wouldn't wish this on anyone. Even him."

She pats my shoulder, which must mean my face is doing something weird.

It's not like me wrecking the one nice thing Tommy had is what made him depressed.

But it sure didn't help.

———

Ellis asks to eat dinner at my house even though our fridge is a wasteland of oceanwater samples and cold cut turkey. He says he's tired of diner food.

Translation: He doesn't want to spend time anywhere Tommy's absence feels too big.

We take turns telling my parents about school. Ellis ran good times during practice, so hopefully he can set another personal record at his meet next week and bump Coop off the varsity roster. My parents recount their day cataloging West Finch's beach post-storm. All their measurements and sand loss projections have to be updated and shared back with the National Ocean Service. They talk like it's business as usual—as if there aren't three intruders sitting on the jetty even now, tagging their selfies #SavingTheEnvironment and screwing up our plans.

"Don't you feel like if someone promises to blow something up, there shouldn't be any take-backs?" I ask as I twirl spaghetti around my fork.

"Those kids might be right, you know." Dad points at me with the veggie meatball speared on the end of his fork.

Mom nods. "Even we don't know what will happen if the jetty's torn down. It could make things worse."

Ellis catches my eye across the table. "A house just fell into the ocean. Seems like peak bad to me."

I beam down at my plate.

Then there's a long conversation about college. I move my pasta around while the three of them debate the merits of dining-hall pizza versus ramen, and if you have to have a roommate, whether it's better to have one or two. Ellis has a lot of inherited opinions about these things because of all the college visits Coop's done, but I don't have much to contribute. It's hard to picture living more than a half mile away from Ellis, let alone sharing a room with a stranger.

"We should visit a couple schools in August," Mom says, more to Dad than to me.

"Is there anywhere you're interested in, sweet pea?"

They all look at me. I stab my garlic bread into my pasta sauce until it turns pink and soggy. "We're waiting to see which schools want Ellis to run for them," I say.

Ellis gives me a little half smile and then concentrates on his plate while my parents have an intense, wordless conversation across the table. I haven't told them about The Plan in detail, but they know enough to be worried. Mom wins the staring contest. They drop it, for now.

Dad shovels more salad onto my plate. Clears his throat. "So, how's Tommy doing?" he says in the same tone he'd use to ask about the weather.

Ellis had been gamely inhaling a second round of spaghetti. Now he's forgotten how to chew. Not Heimlich worthy, but it gets close.

"Not sure," he chokes out at last.

"He only gets to call home once a day," I explain, trying to scold Dad with just a look.

Our nonverbal communication is not as good as his and Mom's. "What does he do the rest of the time?"

Ellis jumps up from his chair. He holds his plate so we can all see it, empty but for a single strand of pasta.

"This is the best garlic bread of my entire life," he announces.

We all watch the lonely spaghetti slide down his plate and drop soundlessly onto his chair. He turns on his heel and disappears into the kitchen.

I round on my dad. "Tommy talks to a shrink. Does arts and crafts. Who knows?"

He nudges his glasses back up the bridge of his nose. "It seemed reasonable to think his brother might."

We don't stay for dessert.

—

Little critters like bunnies darting into the road. Outdoor cats. Ellis impatiently drums his fingers against his door, but if everyone drove like I do, there wouldn't be accidents.

"Don't forget we have Goose's vet appointment Wednesday," I remind him as we pull into his driveway. It takes at least two people to get Goose in and out of the vet's office without her asphyxiating herself on her leash or nervous-peeing.

In front of us his house is dark. I put the car in park but he doesn't get out, just stares at his phone in his lap without waking it.

"He left a note after all," he says, voice flat. "Mom and Dad got them too. I guess he scheduled them to send later so we wouldn't go looking."

He unlocks his phone and hands it to me. It's open to an email from Tommy, delivered around lunchtime today:

I hope you get everything you want. I know you will.
-T

Below that, a detailed guide to caring for Goose.

So that answers whether Tommy was planning to swim back and whether he wanted someone to find him.

No and no.

"What does that even mean?" He rubs the back of his neck in a very Tommy way.

"Writing notes is nice," I try. "I mean, at least you were thought of. I'd want a note, if it were me."

I hand his phone back and casually, so casually, pull my own phone out of my pocket and check my email. Nothing. Not even a "Screw you, Harlow." If this was somehow my fault, he would've written to me. He'd have wanted to make sure I felt guilty for his death for the rest of my life. I know because I would've done the same to him.

"Whatever. I'm done trying to figure him out."

I nod supportively as I refresh my inbox again. Just to be sure.

He peeks at me out of the corner of his eye. "So, Coop is going to that cross-country camp in Vermont again."

"Camp Hood?" Inbox empty. The relief is instant.

He tells the windshield: "I kind of want to go."

I blink. Pluck at my still-buckled seat-belt strap. "What for?"

"It's perfect. Distance runs every day, hill workouts." His voice gets loud, like he's trying to scare something off. "Coop got varsity when he came back last year and he met tons of new people."

He met girls, mainly.

"There are hills here," I point out. "I'll find you a hill. You can run it until you puke."

He presses his hands together and makes a single fist. "I already put down the deposit."

This isn't strictly part of our get-into-the-same-college Plan, but if it gets him on varsity, it's certainly Plan-adjacent. I should be proud of him for showing initiative, probably. Instead I feel myself plunge to the bottom of the Y's pool: pressure on my eardrums, the sharp pinch of chlorine up my nose. I'm meant to be retrieving something, but if I open my eyes, I'll make the ten feet of water above me real. It will crush me. I squeeze the steering wheel until I run out of air and the feeling passes, then a bit longer.

"How would you even pay for it?"

"I'll mow lawns or something. It's not that much."

I sink into the car seat. All I really know about this camp is, it's four weeks right in the middle of summer. I'll spend June dreading it and August trying to catch up on all the parts of his life I've missed. Even now I can't see him. In the dark he's just a smooth ridge of nose, a gently rounded forehead.

"Harlow?" He waves a hand in front of my face and laughs a little. I'm too busy merging with my seat's easy-clean upholstery to join him. "What's going on in there?"

The darkness shifts as he lets his hand come to rest on the crown of my head, heavy and warm.

"I'll help you with erosion stuff before I go." He pets my hair gently. "I just want to do my own thing this one time, okay?"

If he can leave for a month this easily, what's to stop him from wanting that again after we graduate? This useless running camp, Olivia—they're little Band-Aids over an infected wound that needs stitches. He isn't used to feeling like he messed up something important. He doesn't know how to deal. Not like I do.

If Tommy hadn't asked Ellis to watch his dog, if he hadn't picked that exact spot on the beach to start swimming, if he didn't make it so hard to be nice to him, then Ellis would be getting ready to save our town, not run away from it.

"You didn't have to do your own thing last week. Suddenly now you do." I can hear how whiny I sound. So I freeze the fear in me, and when I speak next, my voice is ice. "I wonder what changed."

For a few seconds, he doesn't move, just lets himself go under too. The deep end. Ten feet. Then he takes his hand off my head.

"Nice, Harlow." He fumbles with his seat belt. I want him to yell at me, but we don't get into those kinds of fights, no matter how much I sometimes deserve it. Like now.

"Is there a universe where you stay?"

A queasy hush falls over the car. Ellis is sitting still for once instead of tapping his fingers, jiggling a foot, forever throwing his hair out of his eyes.

"I'm a little tired of West Finch right now," he says.

"Tired of West Finch" meaning his family, the diner, the erosion? Or me?

Yes, there's a universe where he spends the summer with me. No, that's not the one he wants.

"What am I supposed to do without you?"

I can only ask because we're in the dark of his driveway and I have the steering wheel to hold on to. My fingers wrap all the way around and then some, my nails sharp half-moons in my palms. He looks at me and I look at him, but neither of us can see each other.

"You'll figure something out." He hits the button to unlock the doors and touches my elbow. A tiny pinch. "You always do."

Five

HARLOW

Thursday, March 30

Goose's appointment Wednesday goes about as badly as it can. Bad like, instead of *You're all set!* they say *Let's run a few more tests.* Then, feeling her stomach: *How long has this lump been here?* The annual checkup turns into blood drawn from a fat pinch of her thigh, an MRI, and a pamphlet about letting your dog die with dignity.

The vet glances at me three times as she delivers the news. She must know what I do: that Goose's cancer came from eating a hefty portion of the chocolate chips I spilled on the MacQueen + Bell kitchen floor three months ago. I mean, I cleaned up most of them but she's fast for an old dog, and I'm not allowed to touch Goose because I make bad luck like other people make white blood cells.

Supposedly.

Tommy's rule.

It's not that there's no hope. It's just that hope is a seven-thousand-dollar course of chemo and surgery, and the MacQueens are not a pet-insurance-type family.

No matter how many alternate universes Ellis imagines, we can't make our past selves yell Tommy's name on that beach. Can't take back the shitty things we've—okay, *I've*—said behind his back and to his face. We can only fix things from here on out.

My plan takes no time to come together, like it's been ready a long time, waiting for me to get brave enough to notice it.

———

The morning after the vet, Ellis finds me sitting cross-legged and picking brown, velvety scabs off the old picnic table under me.

I don't tell him to hurry up and shower or we'll be late to school. I don't scold him for the extra miles he's just run, the ones his track coach doesn't know about. I don't put my finger to his lips to make him keep his bad news to himself. This new plan of mine requires patience.

He's still panting when he says, "They're letting him out of the hospital. Tonight."

My panic: three thousand bats. Me: the bridge's underbelly where they sleep.

It hasn't even been a week. Plus no one's told Tommy that Goose is sick, and that should definitely be a consideration.

"Can they hold his room for twenty-four hours in case he needs it? Can they do late checkout?"

"It's not a hotel," Ellis says.

A flurry of wings. I know that.

"Mom said he's 'feeling better.'" He does the air quotes. "I'm pretty sure they can't make him stay."

He climbs up beside me, face shiny from his run, and together we look out at the ragged blue seawall behind the diner. Walls like it extend down the coastline, a border between sea and shore: rock and cement, wood and metal. An ever-expanding patchwork as sea levels rise. The diner's waist-high wall has been built and rebuilt probably ten times. After the fifth, Clifford Samuels and Jim MacQueen quit using concrete to bind the rocks together. The pile's only wall-shaped right now because of gravity and hope.

Beyond it, the stone jetty stretches a quarter mile into the sea like an evil black tongue. A couple of the protestors from California are squatting about halfway down its length, silhouetted against the waves.

"Let's decide how to tell him," I say.

"Let's not."

"He's going to find out."

Ellis rolls his eyes. "We can't say 'your dog's dying' as soon as he walks in the door."

There's an epidemic of people in this town incapable of looking their problems in the face. Half of West Finch won't believe in global warming until their houses get flooded and there's a starfish stuck to the refrigerator.

"Let's give him a week. He needs to readjust to the stressors of home"— rudely, Ellis gestures at me—"and we need to find seven thousand dollars. You can plan a quick fundraiser, right? This is totally your thing."

That smile: one dimpled corner slightly higher than the other and eye contact so direct it makes me squirm. A look like he believes I can do anything.

I want to hug him. Say yes. But I'm not doing a bottle drive for this dog, or anything else that takes attention away from tearing down the jetty and saving the diner. Not if there's another way.

"The vet said she shouldn't suffer," I try. "Maybe Tommy will agree."

"Sure. And maybe he'll thank us for letting her get sick on our watch."

"Your watch," I mutter before I can stop myself.

"Excuse me?"

I examine my violet fingernails. "Goose is your responsibility, not mine. For the record."

He hops off the picnic table and lands hard in the grass. "If you want to tell him his beloved dog is dying, fine. He already hates you. Just don't say anything awful."

Sea spray mists my cheeks and I wipe it away. Picture Tommy diving into a steel-gray wall of water again. Ruby Lee's eyes going wide. I've done enough damage already. He's right about that.

Then I think that's not quite fair. Tommy decided he didn't like me before we'd even met, but out of the goodness of my heart, I still make efforts. When I see dog grooming coupons in the newspaper, do I not clip them out and slip them under his bedroom door? Don't I look at the scribbly drawings he leaves around the MacQueen + Bell house with the misguided hope that Ellis will notice anything past his own belly button? Was it not me telling him said art looked like trash that pushed him to get better, until now, when he's so good his stuff knocks the words out of my mouth?

Okay, yes. Maybe I said some things I shouldn't have in the days before his latest meltdown. How was I supposed to know? Like always, he wrinkled his nose when he found himself in the same room as me. Rolled his eyes whenever I spoke. One day I scolded him for leaving a Lucky Charms box in the pantry, empty except for a few lonely frosted Xs. *You really should throw those things out instead of letting other people get their hopes up.* Without breaking eye contact, he ripped the package from my hand and threw it in the trash, cardboard box and all. And he knows how I feel about recycling.

I'm not saying all this makes up for my behavior. Only that I wouldn't tell somebody "just die already" unprovoked.

Six

TOMMY

"The no-art thing. That for safety reasons?"

The nurse, a redhead, stops halfway through my hospital room's door. No, not door. Archway that leaks light from the nurses' station all night. I point at the blank wall directly across from my bed because he looks confused.

"I get you can't frame stuff. But what about a poster and tape?"

The nurse peers at the blank wall. Me. An *is this kid in danger of hurting himself and others?* look. This would've for sure ended up on my chart if I'd said it yesterday. But I'm almost not this guy's problem anymore.

He watches my flawless performance of Boy Swallows Pills and drops off a "dinner" tray before leaving. Half a peeled orange split into frosted-glass wedges the only edible thing on it. I choose one segment and lean back against my pillow.

When I close my eyes, I can see the washed-out shitty abstract that should go on that wall. Feel the oil paint's body as I work it with my palette knife. Here's a thing Ruby and I used to do: sit beside each other with our elbows knocking, her right-handedness hitting my left, pick a thing, and go. But this time my fingers don't move with that old twitch of wanting to make shit. My hands are about as alive as two loaves of bread. Thank fucking god.

There's not much to pack. Balled-up clothes. The history textbook I haven't opened since December. Mom grabbed it at random from the tower on my desk at home. Maybe she hoped reading about the Great Depression would put things in perspective. I flip it open and there, right there, on the inside front cover. This isn't even mine. I touch my brother's name with my thumb.

He's not coming. I know it. But I remind myself so I won't forget: Ellis will not be out there when you walk through that archway.

My duffel bag zipper catches. Hands still doughy, useless. I rub them on my jeans. Think of how the waves tossed Cliff's boat like it weighed nothing. No, don't. Yank the zipper again. Piece of shit. But god, how small we were. How hard Cliff must've searched, as if there was a damn thing special about me. Just one more creature treading water. The linoleum under my feet now cold under my hand. The coffee I forced down this morning in my mouth. Antidepressants don't do much for seasickness. Fun fact.

Why now? the doctors wanted to know when I got here.

Why *not* now? Would I be any less a burden on my parents when I was eighteen? Twenty? Would there be something worth giving a shit about? Because from what I've seen, things get small or they get empty. If you think your best days are behind you then they probably are.

Why now? Some things have stories behind them and some things don't.

"Ready?" It's the redheaded nurse again. I abandon my half-zipped bag and follow him before the tide comes back for me.

Just Mom. That's my final answer. It's close to dinnertime (see: suspicious-looking tray) so Dad will want to stay behind and keep at least his half of their restaurant slash bakery open.

Some parents can be two places at once. I've seen it. They're on the sidelines at Ellis's meets, talking on phones out of one side of their mouth and cheering for their kids out of the other. Dad's not one of them, but he's managed to hit visiting hours a few times. Once with Mom. It was weird seeing them sit in the same room without arguing. Clinical Depression: Bringing Families Together.

I scan the common area. Beige couch, tan armchair, plastic fern, no Ellis. Like ripping off a Band-Aid.

Mom pulls me into a hug, then holds me at arm's length. "How are you?"

My face a mask. I don't want Mom thinking I'm disappointed to see her. I expected this. But part of me still hoped he'd show. I shrug one shoulder. *Good* won't cut it anymore. Even if I were good who'd believe me? "Fine."

Getting discharged takes a long time. I have my new prescription. A typed list of therapist referrals. I don't have to see the names to know I won't feel comfortable spilling my guts to any of them. While Mom finishes up I go back to my room to grab my bag. If they put up something on that wall across from the bed, I hope I'm never back here to see it.

"Still packing?"

Nurse back for the third time, Mom asking me to hustle, the next sad kid who needs this bed for a few days. Wrong guesses all.

My brother's leaning in the doorway. Hair washed and quite possibly blow-dried, white stripes running down the sides of his track pants.

I want to shove him back into the common room with its fake plants and lifeless couches. Away from these rooms with no doors, bathrooms without locks. Why did I want him to see me here?

"When'd you get here?" I twist my plastic hospital bracelet back and forth on my wrist. He wasn't out there just now. Sure of it.

"I was making sure Goose is comfortable. She's in the car." He cracks his knuckles and considers my duffel bag. "Need help?" I say nothing as he brute-forces the zipper closed. He's glad to have a job. I get that. He throws the strap over his shoulder and looks around again. Nods. "Cheery."

When we were little, we'd trade places for no reason except to prove we could. Like when we wore matching polos on picture day because he was better at smiling even then. Now I couldn't pay him to swap with me.

Tell him they're not allowed to have even the worst of paintings, I think. Tell him Cliff tried to send Mom with a whole jar of sea glass for decoration and it wasn't allowed. But I shouldn't have to tell him anything. Shame is a wet blanket across my shoulders so heavy he must feel it too. Why can't he feel it? I suck in a quick gasp of air through my teeth. I've twisted my bracelet too tight. Fingers turning pink. I shove my hands in my pockets. "How's Goose?"

"Great!" Voice loud, smile gobbling up the rest of his face. He should see someone about that. "She's in the car. Like I said. With the windows cracked, don't worry."

When I was at my lowest, Goose curled up in bed beside me and it was like, as long as you're breathing, I'm breathing. I need to get out there. Now. She's got half a crayon box in her coat alone and I want to remember colors other than beiges and grays.

Mom makes the nurses talk her through all my discharge paperwork one last time. Then we wave goodbye and walk outside. The sky showing off. Brilliant, embarrassing blue.

Mom uses the walk to the car to catch me up on all the requirements for my return to society. I must sleep normal hours. I must take my medication. I agree because I want those things too. Also because what else can I do? She hands me my phone and I immediately stash it in my back pocket without checking it. The most important part of being healthy is for other people to think I'm healthy. As long as I'm managing my depression, and managing other people's opinions of my depression, they can't put me back here.

"We have an appointment with your guidance counselor next week," Mom says. "No one expects you to go back this semester, but summer school is an option."

Then the conversation stops because Goose sees me through Mom's car window. She's barking in this way that makes my bones ache: a half-howl, half-crying sound because even though I abandoned her, somehow she still loves me. I throw open the back door and lower my forehead to meet hers. Hold her against me as long as she'll stand it.

Ellis takes shotgun and Mom turns the key in the ignition. I climb into the back seat next to Goose and buckle up. Reach over to do the same for her. But she's just wearing her basic harness, not the one that hooks into the seat belt.

"We couldn't find it," Mom says when I point this out. Then she backs out of the parking spot anyway. I throw a protective arm around Goose's body.

"It was on my desk." I'm looking at the front seat as if through binoculars, the wrong end. Fingers lost in fur. "It was in the emails."

Mom glances at Ellis. He stares determinedly out the window.

I spent weeks getting rid of junk. Divvying up old artwork. Writing and rewriting those damn emails. I'd already been checked into the hospital and had my phone taken away before I remembered, and I stayed up all that first night thinking of a fix. I could try getting permission to use the nurses' station computer. Beg Mom to never read her email again. But when she called the next morning I said I was feeling better and that was too big a lie to add on to.

"Did you read them?" I ask now. I want the emails to be sitting in a spam folder somewhere. But I also want my family to have memorized every word.

Mom glances at Ellis again. A look I can't decipher. About me, not to me.

"We read them, honey," she says.

"Sorry," Ellis adds, voice raw. Maybe he's been taking this harder than it looks. Maybe they both have.

Or they just don't give a shit about Goose. At least now I know. And then I hate myself for thinking that because isn't Mom taking time from work to come get me? I shouldn't have put any of them through this in the first place.

Mom's eyes appear briefly in the rearview mirror but I don't have anything else to say. Goose sniffs my armpit. Stretches to lick my cheek, stumbles, lands with her head in my lap. I use the bottom of my shirt to wipe the brown stains under her eyes (also in the note). She doesn't squirm like normal. Just sighs happily and, too fast, falls asleep.

"Is something wrong with her?" Not letting my voice go sharp. Touching my finger to her ear as I say it and she doesn't paw my hand away or move or blink.

Ellis's nose almost touches the window. Must be something good out there. Ten-car pileup at least. "I took her to the vet Wednesday. Like your email said. They sent us home with some pills."

"For what?" I demand.

"She wasn't really eating," he admits.

I press my hand to the coarse fur on her side. The shallow swell-fall of her breath. But she was fine when I left. I wouldn't have gone if she wasn't. Whatever junk he's giving her, I'm throwing it out as soon as we get home.

Mom looks at Ellis a third time with raised eyebrows.

He sighs. "So, listen. There's a party waiting for you at the diner. Real low-key. But, um, like, be prepared. It's possible Harlow went overboard with the decorations."

"You don't have to go," Mom adds quickly.

No time ago I would've taken her up on that. Spent the night at the Samuelses' and pretended trading in your family is a thing you can do. But I can't make myself give a shit. Harlow's been dead to me for months, anyway. Since whatever day I landed beside Ruby at lunch, flipped open my sketchbook, and she said, "Don't." Looked at me like I'd killed her cat. I remember the trees had already flamed out, leaves sweetly rotting, brown as dirt. Must've been October.

But the leaves weren't all that was rotten.

During my shift at the diner that afternoon, I felt everyone's eyes on me. Not everyone's. Harlow's. She bolted and I tore after her. I caught her in the entryway, my hands flat against the wall on either side of her head. "What did you say to her?" Jaw clenched so hard I had to talk through my teeth. Careful not to let my fingertips brush even her hair. Everything she touches combusts. Brothers lose legs, pet fish find their way to the toilet, girls who once dragged their easels next to yours at the start of every class stop.

Harlow's earlobe dangled dangerously close to my thumb. "So sorry." She smiled a smile stolen from my brother. "Can't remember."

I wanted to squish her skull between my bare hands. Would have without Cliff's hand on my shoulder yanking me away.

In the painting studio after school the next day: "It was Harlow, wasn't it? That bitch. What did she say to you?"

Ruby: "It really doesn't matter. I don't want any part of . . . this." She gestured at me.

Copy of a copy of a *Where are* you *in this work, Tommy?* brainfogged colordrained me.

So what if a dead girl throws me a party. So what if West Finch wants to gawk. I'm fine. I'll get good at saying that. Maybe I'll even feel it.

Sand hisses under the tires as we pull into the too-full MacQueen's parking lot. I ignore the rising tide of dread that comes with walking Goose to the signpost out front and attaching her harness to the chain coiled in the grass. She whines. "I know," I say. We both can't believe I'm leaving her so soon. Or it's just me. Only a dozen steps toward the diner and she's already curled into a comma blinking back sleep. I wind her leash around my fist. Promise I'll be back.

The dining room's half-assedly decorated for a child's birthday. Confetti and balloons. Homemade WELCOME HOME sign along the back wall. To be fair, I don't think they make "You survived!" party sets. Harlow's corpse smiles and says something nice, which means it's fake, and anyway, I can't see or hear dead girls. Dad, all eight feet of him and none of it tears, comes out of his kitchen. He says, "Feeling better?" or something like it. Good that he didn't come to the hospital. Bullet dodged.

But then his arms wrap around me once and again. Three times total. Realizing how hard I was working to hold myself upright when I let myself lean into him. The kind of tree they make state parks for.

He doesn't always show up but when he does here's how it looks. All the times he insisted I bring Goose to his place even though he's allergic to dogs. Vacuum roaring to life as soon as Mom collected us Sunday mornings. Why should I get to ask him to say the right thing when I've spent the last year glad he didn't try? No *You okay, son?* or even *What's really going on?* when I picked up another shift at the diner because it was a clock-in, clock-out, bury my feelings by helping someone else bury theirs in a basket of fried clams type gig, better than therapy. I wanted him to leave me alone and he did.

Now—palm hot on my scalp, eyes squinting like he's really trying to see me—he says, "Hang in there. Can you do that for me?" Not sure I can, not sure I want to, but I nod. The least I can do.

He lets me go and Harlow's right behind him. All clouds of brown, frizzy hair. Dark eyelashes and darker brows. All white face with freckles, palms smooth, knees unscraped, unscarred, both feet present and accounted for.

She hugs me too.

Sweat and orange blossom. Cold hands and conviction. It ends before I think of a nice way to say back the hell off. My parents are close enough to hear and I don't want them thinking I have rage issues or something. Though when it comes to Harlow maybe I do.

Even after she retreats to the other side of the room it's like I'm in an orange grove. My nose must be more sensitive after the hospital, where the only smells were cleaning products and whatever body fluid they were mopping up. But I'm fine. I'm hanging in here.

There's bad music. There's pie. More people. Pat and Jeanie Albertson. They manage the bed-and-breakfast where Ellis and I used to spend every other weekend with Dad. The Caskills, who run the nearby marina. Yes, I'm happy I'm home too. I'm doing just fine. The Turners with their five kids. Chuck Halstead. Fine, fine. Harlow by the counter watching me. I remember the semester Ms. Russeau took away the black and white paint. There's purple in the crook of her arm. Auburn in the curl by her right ear. The hospital's beiges and grays weren't so bad after all.

Fine.

Bea and Yvette. Wendy Michaels.

The Samuelses. They got one of my goodbye emails too. Theirs was longer than any of my family's. There was more I had to thank them for. Kindnesses they didn't owe me and I didn't really earn. I didn't think I'd have to see them so soon.

Mrs. Samuels kisses my cheek. Cliff squeezes my shoulder.

"I found this yesterday." He drops a tiny, perfect shell into my palm. No bigger than my smallest fingernail. "Thought of you."

A wave swells. I'm ten years old balancing a warm slip of water in a mussel's shell asking does he know we only get the sparkle of shells on our beaches because the mollusks inside have died.

Only this time I can't speak. Softly Cliff says the same thing he did back then: "Ain't that something to look at? Something good from something bad."

I can never do this to him again.

The seasick feeling washes through me. I clench my fist around the shell. Five seconds. Ten. I'm about to go overboard, but inside my nose it's like a goddamn orange juice commercial. Fuck Harlow and her party. I drop to one knee and yank my sneaker untied so I can re-knot it. Make an exit plan. When the feeling passes, I manage a thanks and talk loudly about getting some water.

I escape through the restaurant kitchen—Dad's half of MacQueen's diner and bakery—then out the back door. It opens onto a patch of dead grass with a dumpster and the old seawall past that.

I unlock my phone. Dismiss all the messages, missed calls, and voice mails. Then the sent folder in my email. A note to Mom. To Dad. Ellis. Cliff and Mrs. Samuels. I delete all four without reading them. Empty my trash.

Once that's done I throw Cliff's seashell as hard as I can over the wall, into the waves, knowing they'll take care of it like they take care of everything but me. They roar back hungrily but I don't have anything else I'm willing to give them. Not right now.

From behind me I hear, "You're littering? *Seriously?*"

Salt sweat orange blossom cold fingers hot tar.

"Never mind," she says. "I don't want to know."

I don't want a lot of things. To live. To die. To swim or stay dry. To know her by just her voice. But I do.

Harlow Prout.

Seven

HARLOW

How to Save the Summer, Part 1: Find something, anything, Tommy can live for. A hobby or club. Not swimming. Maybe an evening graphic design class at Southern Maine Community College. A lobstering apprenticeship with sweaty Clifford Samuels. A catastrophe of a hookup the likes of which Ellis could be jealous.

Or something—someone—more durable. Find him a girlfriend on the internet. I'm sure a tolerable photo exists of Tommy holding Goose; he'll look halfway cute beside her mismatched eyes and grizzled coat.

But I'm not a miracle worker here. With Tommy coming home later today, the slim pickings at school will have to do.

When I'm not politely asking Ellis and Olivia to quit exchanging saliva right in front of my locker, I'm asking Bailey, Krystal, Paige—anyone who's ever had a crush on Ellis, or is too kind for their own good, or has a pulse— "Have you ever thought about Tommy?"

And they go, "MacQueen?"

Good ol' leaky-pipe feeling makes a reappearance as the no's pile up, but I persevere. I corner Bethany Lucas by her locker after last period. She's a West Fincher, born and raised, and she invited Tommy to her sweet sixteen last year, so she definitely has a soft spot for underdogs. I explain about Tommy coming home earlier than expected, Ellis not being himself. If she could just stop by the diner tonight and smile at Tommy, maybe add a flirty wink, that'd be a huge help.

"Thursdays I have trombone lessons," she says. "Anyways, isn't that a little mean?"

"Bethany, it's nearly April of our junior year and you're fourth chair," I explain patiently. "I don't think these lessons are a great use of your time."

She almost catches my arm in her locker's slamming door.

Riding high on that failure, I have to hustle to get to the math hall on the other side of the building for the after-school block. I excuse-me and elbow through knots of jocks who apparently don't have GPAs or best friends with self-destructing brothers to worry about and cut through the art wing. This is Tommy's territory, so I haven't spent much time here, but it's empty like I thought it'd be. I start a light jog. The walls are covered with student art-work. Dull acrylic on paper. An open studio door, a girl at an easel. Anemic graphite still lifes. I freeze mid-stride.

I shouldn't.

But there's something to be said for improvisation when one is out of options.

If it's not her, I'll write off this whole part of the plan and be on my way to AP Calc.

Door thrown wide. A whiff of turpentine. And sure enough, there she is, wearing headphones and a paint smock.

"Hey, Ruby."

"What's up?" Her expression is warm, like she'd been hoping for a sur-prise visit from me.

The painting she's working on looks like nothing I recognize. There are lots of yellow and blue shapes with green, mold-like splotches around the canvas edge. I check for a reference photo or something next to her easel, but this weirdness is straight out of her head. No wonder she liked Tommy.

"Not much." I pause to watch her earrings sway. She probably made them herself from pieces of a very old, very valuable chandelier. "Tommy's coming home today."

"That's great!" Like on Monday, she seems to mean it.

Promising. Very promising.

"So, this is going to sound weird. But I wondered if you might reach out and let him know people at school have been thinking of him?" On the workspace next to us, I touch a palette knife with my finger. Catch our reflections in the metal. "I know you don't talk anymore, but it'd mean a lot, coming from you."

She taps the tail end of her brush against her mouth (toxic, definitely). Her lipstick today is a warm peach. "I think I could do that."

This is going so much better than expected. Talk about signs from the universe! I'm doing it, I'm going in for the kill. "I also wondered if you might give him a second chance? Like, around five p.m. today?"

The effect is immediate and impressive.

Color drains from her face. Irises, washed out. White eyebrows and lashes. Even her lipstick goes gray.

"Are you serious?" she whispers.

I watch as she understands everything that went down last October, all because she trusted me. Big mistake. Tommy could've told her so, if she'd asked him.

But I made sure she wouldn't.

Now she could tell anyone at school that I'm the liar, not Tommy, and they'd believe her. Only Ellis knew before right now. My mouth tastes like I'm drowning. Or like blood? Same difference. I remind myself talking shit is not a very Ruby thing to do.

She whirlpools her brush in a brownish cup of water, then stabs the excess onto a paper towel and wrings the bristles dry with the hem of her smock.

"I think you should go," she says, glaring at the mangled bristles. "And I think you shouldn't make me tell you twice."

———

We always park in the same distant corner at school, on account of the 13 percent of car accidents that occur in parking lots. The walk gives me plenty of thinking time. Things like, is an idea bad just because everyone else thinks it is?

Is compassion a luxury no one can afford in this day and age?

Do I have to do everything myself?

Even I could suffer through a single kiss. Two to four seconds of mild discomfort to give Tommy a jolt of self-esteem, like a mental-illness booster shot. I wouldn't be his first choice, but it's not like people are lining up for the opportunity, and if he freaked out, I'd shrug and say, *What? Near-death experiences look good on you.*

So, yeah. Part 1 is a long shot.

How to Save the Summer, Part 2: Treat Tommy like he's a great person with a lot to offer. The Welcome-Home party was my idea. What better way to mask the shittiness of his life than with streamers and confetti?

After track practice, Ellis drives us to MacQueen's to set up. We haven't told his parents about the party, so the diner is open while we decorate, people still licking whoopie-pie filling from their fingers and sucking meat out of lobster claws. I don't let myself feel sad about using the supplies for the jetty demolition party. We can get more when the new demo date is announced, and this is a worthy cause.

When it's time to get Tommy, Helen comes out of the bakery kitchen on her half of the restaurant. (After the divorce, they had a construction crew build separate his-and-her kitchens. Totally custom.) She frowns at our child-size party hats. Under her gaze, I cut out the wonkiest *M* yet and add it to a pile of letters that will turn into a "Welcome Home" construction paper banner.

"We're going to tell him about Goose," I explain.

"Except in a way that says, 'Here's some bad news, but there are still things worth living for,'" Ellis adds.

We smile like two fat cherubs in a bad Renaissance painting.

"Absolutely not," Helen says.

She's never been much of a visionary.

She's taking off her apron, putting on her jacket, and Ellis has switched from balloons to confetti. He's really going for it with this one package of sequins, spreading them in a thick, even layer on the diner's countertop.

I go stand next to him so I can quietly remind him, "You're going, right?"

He tears open another confetti packet, avoiding my eyes. "Nah. I'll help you finish up here."

"Ellis."

"Harlow."

"If you don't show up for him right now, you'll regret it forever."

"I *am* showing up for him." He spreads his arms and sequins rain from his fingers. But he looks uncertain.

"Do you want to live in a universe where you avoided him for a week?"

He mournfully considers the bare spots on the counter. Shakes his head.

"Then get going."

He nods and moves his lips silently, hyping himself up to do this hard thing. Then he touches my shoulder and squeezes once. I focus on the feeling of it, the precise temperature and pressure, so I can imagine it into existence again whenever I want.

He and his mom leave without clarifying which thing's not allowed, the telling or the party. I string up the banner anyway and hang streamers off the lobster tank. Mr. Albertson, West Finch's traitorous mayor, fishes an errant sequin out of his afternoon coffee, glares at me, and leaves before he's finished reading the paper. Bethany's going to show up after all, I can feel it, but I chew a piece of spearmint gum just in case.

I'm almost finished setting up when this white guy I don't recognize comes in. He looks just a bit older than me, with dark, windswept hair and a warm-looking black wool coat with the collar turned up.

"Do you work here?" he says.

His eyes water, probably from the cold, but I can't help thinking he's about to burst into tears. I give him a practiced look that says *beat it*.

"Oh, sorry. I'm not from here. We're . . ." He looks over his shoulder, toward the window. From where we're standing, we can see the jetty's black rocks. "What's with the balloons? I heard someone died."

So this rock-sitting, tree-hugging, sad-boy activist thinks he can walk in here and be a part of something he knows nothing about. How on-brand.

I point to my party hat. "Do I look dressed for a funeral to you?"

"Uhh . . ."

"This is a private event. You should go. Now."

Finally he realizes what's good for him and leaves me to finish my preparations in peace.

It's all wrong, of course. The decorations. The Top 40 I pipe through my phone's speakers. The problem is, I don't figure that out until Tommy arrives.

I must be nervous because there's a half-second where I wonder why Ellis shaved his head.

Tommy's nothing like his brother. Different in a million ways. But I can't help thinking this is how Ellis would look if you kept him in a fluorescent ward with no locks on the doors for almost a week. Tommy's skin is waxy, almost transparent, and his shirt doesn't hang right on his shoulders, or maybe it's that he's slouching. He wears his body like a hand-me-down. Ellis *was* born first.

"You're back!" I cry, forcing a smile. Tommy frowns, but I detect some hope in that scowl, too, that things have changed.

Jim comes around the counter, along with his signature cologne of the hundreds of lobsters, clams, and baby shrimps he probably boiled alive today. His beard's trimmed for the first time in months (good), but he's also wearing sunglasses on his head indoors (yikes). I once heard Helen say Jim has the arms of a baseball player but the brains of a football player. Harsh but true, as is the fact that he probably should've closed the diner for an hour and gone with the rest of his family to pick up his kid. He's basically what Ellis would turn into if I weren't around to redirect him.

Jim pulls Tommy's bristly head against his shoulder and, okay, it's impressive for a deadbeat dad. Solid bear-hug territory.

Of course. This is how you greet someone you're going to be nicer to.

After Jim lets him go, I cross the dining room and wrap my arms around Tommy's middle. Hugging him isn't bad, exactly, but it's like wearing a shirt inside out. Maybe I can't do this. He's too surprised to fend me off, though he does pat my back twice in a way that roughly translates to "get the hell off me." I have to hug Ellis after to rinse away the awkward.

"Mom says don't tell him about Goose. Seriously," Ellis whispers in my ear before letting go. I give him a thumbs-up to say thanks but no thanks for your input.

Somehow word has gotten around that Tommy's back and it's like a real party. Mr. Albertson returns looking far more chipper, followed by Joe and Fran Caskill, who manage the marina. There's Mrs. Samuels and Clifford. Helen Bell pulls a couple chocolate cream pies out of the refrigerated case and cuts everyone a slice. I watch Tommy dance around the room until at last Clifford and Mrs. Samuels corner him. They love him no matter what, now more than ever, and he's swimming in it. Clifford Samuels hands him something, and oh boy, Tommy hates it. He's shaking the tiniest bit. Still the old man's smiling! Tommy squats down in a move that usually ends with him burying his face in Goose's shaggy coat, but since she's outside, he pathetically unties and reties his own shoe. If he regrets any of last weekend, I'll bet he regrets leaving Goose the most.

Which means the mangy, smelly, something-to-live-for solution has been in front of me this whole time.

I have to tell him. Soon, while there's time for him to get a job and do something about it. Forget what Helen and Ellis think. They can only guess what's best for him, whereas who knows my nemesis better than I do?

Tommy coughs theatrically, then announces he's going to get some water. A lazy lie. Water won't fix how clammy he looks. How pale. Like a raw page ripped from one of his sketchbooks. But the Samuelses let him go, and Jim and Helen bicker about when they should switch to MacQueen's summer hours this year, and Ellis takes over DJ responsibilities, and this boy who tried to kill himself five days ago has no one paying attention to him. Except me.

I slip behind the counter and follow him into his dad's kitchen. The silver sideboards are messy with pots and pans, stained dishrags, big plastic bins of soaking mussels and clams. No Tommy. I crack the door to the shared basement (dark), peek into Helen's bakery kitchen (empty), push open the diner's back door, and let it shut silently behind me right as Tommy chucks something into the waves.

"You're littering?" I blurt out. "Seriously?"

A shiver rolls down his spine. He knows it's me. Of course he does.

"Never mind. I don't want to know." I'm pretty sure whatever Clifford Samuels gave him is on its way to the Mariana Trench. Good riddance. "I have to tell you something."

"What?" His hands make fists, open wide, back to fists. He's still not turning around.

How am I supposed to do this? Pretend he's Ellis, I think. I had a crush on him in my younger and more vulnerable years, it's true, but that only makes pretending harder. That wasn't this.

"Everyone said not to tell you yet but I know you'd want to know."

A bird arcs across the sky and lands lightly on the diner's seawall. Feathers the color of sand. Black collar around its little neck. No bigger than Tommy's fist.

It's too early in the year. We don't have enough sand. And yet.

"What the—"

"*Fuck*," Tommy finishes.

I wonder if it means something that he knows a piping plover when he sees one. If everything means something, or if we're both mere victims of my dad's bird-watching lessons.

Salt clings invisibly to everything. Stings my nose. I know without thinking about it that if I take my eyes off that bird, it'll build a nest on our beach. Because I'm bad luck. Tommy's staring hard like he thinks the same. No. Like he's drawing the damn thing. His fingertips don't move but they don't have to. I already see the finished piece. Rash of black lines, misplaced wing, beady eye blinking out of the feathered chest, but unmistakably a piping plover. What do I despise more: the bird, or how badly I want to watch Tommy draw it?

I make myself notice the tender skin on the back of his neck. The creases in his T-shirt. Did he guess how long he'd be there, pack enough pajamas? I picture him shoving dirty clothes back into a duffel, wondering whether this is goodbye or the first of many hospital visits. I'm on the other side of him now, between him and the seawall. My hair blows in his face, where it tangles in his eyelashes, brushes his lower lip.

"Go back to the party, Harlow," he says, still looking at the bird. As long as one of us is.

My strategy for sharing bad news is like the game Two Truths and a Lie. I say:

1. "I'm glad you're okay."
2. "Goose has cancer."
3. And then I pull his face down to mine and kiss him.

April

Eight

ELLIS

Tuesday, April 25

Today has got to be my luckiest day alive because if you look at the road, at that sharp turn, there's no way this doesn't end badly.

You wouldn't see me and think *here's a lucky guy*. But luck is all about perspective. It could've been worse, we say. You should see the other guy.

Behind the guardrail that I missed stands a wall of sturdy oaks, and today I'm lucky enough to hit the biggest tree in the woods. I squint at its trunk through the cracked windshield and feel like I should thank it for bringing me to such a decisive stop.

It also crunched the hood of Harlow's car, accordion-style. Nobody's perfect.

I move my arms and legs one at a time. Experimentally wiggle the toes I don't have. My right foot isn't hurting exactly—not yet—but the pressure, like a tight sock, is impossible to ignore. I touch my face and my fingers come back red. My driver's ed instructor was right—the airbag really can hurt you.

When I try my door, it won't open. Neither will the passenger side. In the end I have to kick out what little glass is left in the window and climb through, left foot first. It's a brilliant plan except for the part where I underestimate the distance to the ground and promptly, gracefully fall in a heap on the grass.

If I were closer to home, not on some back road twenty miles away, half of West Finch would've stopped for me by now. But the street is empty. I ask myself like Harlow would: *What's the plan now, Ellis?*

This assumes there even was a plan when I peeled out of the school parking lot. As if I can be expected to think straight upon learning that, despite what I've been told the past four years of my running career, outdoor track is not merit based.

The closest I'd had to a plan was to drive and not stop until my phone rang. Either Coach saying it was a huge oversight not to add me to the varsity roster, or Coop giving me his place because I've been beating him at the mile since indoor track ended over a month ago.

Will Camp Hood give my spot away? Since I put down the deposit last month, I've gotten good at picturing the morning and afternoon trail runs. Girls in sports bras. Boys who sparkle like they're made of glass. That they're strangers will be the best thing about them. They won't know I have a twin I don't understand. A best friend who will never let me go.

I wake my phone. No notifications, no missed calls. Not in this universe. But maybe in another, you know? A universe where Mom hasn't spent the past month trying to hug me whenever I'm in reach. A universe where I've let her. A universe where no one will look at this wreck and wonder if getting hurt in car accidents is becoming my thing.

So what's next?

If I call Bea, the mechanic who works on my parents' cars, then the whole town will know what happened before I make it back to West Finch. But if I call a different garage, there's no way the Prouts will get a decent price. And I don't exactly have a job.

My phone vibrates in my hand.

ARE YOU OKAY?!

Like a message from God, except it's from Harlow. How does she even know to ask? Did she hear the crash-burn of The Plan from wherever she is? The skin under my nose itches where the blood's dried.

I could start walking.

I could jump in the first car that stops.

I could call my brother. It's near dinnertime so Mom and Dad'll be busy: ignoring each other until closing, then leaving in opposite directions for home and the West Finch Bed-and-Breakfast, respectively. Dad's had a room there for going on ten years because *of course your father likes someone to clean up after him.* Nice, Mom.

Tommy serving with a smile, like that'll earn him enough in tips to save his dying dog. Harlow barely let him breathe before she broke that news. Cornered him at his welcome-home party last month. Tommy's face was bright red when they came back to the dining room, and Harlow couldn't carry on a conversation the rest of the evening.

Tonight Goose is asleep outside the diner. Cured of cancer, in another universe. Tommy's depression too. Or better, in this world there's no depression to cure. He's never been unhappy a day in his life.

My family will drop everything as soon as I walk in. I'll explain about varsity—how I made it, which we all knew would happen—and Harlow will give me a standing ovation. Not one to be upstaged in any universe, she'll announce she single-handedly saved the diner from certain doom and flew the college activists back to California. I'm genuinely happy for her because I'm about to escape to Camp Hood, which in this universe goes all summer long.

And they'll tell me how lucky I am. A foot to the left and I would've caught the steel guardrail head-on. Small cars get launched in the air in an impact like that, or severed in two.

I go into the dining room and catch my reflection in the tabletops, in the silver tape winding around the counter. Dried blood cracks on my face as I smile and wave to show them I'm all right. My parents look through me. My brother looks through me. I'm light without the weight of their eyes. I could float up onto the roof and ride the diner like a snow sled down the beach, into the surf.

What can I say. I'm a lucky guy.

Nine

TOMMY

Harlow somersaults into the diner and nails her landing: a power pose with one hand on her hip, the other flat on the countertop so now it belongs to her. That's what it feels like. She can't walk into a room like a normal human being. Has to storm, skip, twirl.

"Your brother is driving me insane," she announces to the room at large—me and two families all minding our own business. She wriggles out of her navy winter coat, revealing a black long-sleeve shirt, black leggings, obnoxious mustard-yellow combat boots.

"Try living with him."

Though she practically does. In some past life they crawled inside each other's bodies and died there and now they can't live on their own. I don't have a connection that deep with anybody except maybe Goose.

I rip a napkin from the holder and grab my pen. Harlow watches as I sketch a school bus with a black stripe down the side. Line of windows. Folding door. I draw Ellis's tiny frowning face in a window. My ballpoint hovers over the bus's body.

"Where should he be going?"

"Soviet forced-labor camp," she says way too quickly. Jesus.

"What'd he do?"

"He's not responding to my texts."

It takes everything not to roll my eyes.

"How about Ohio?" I suggest. "There's nothing for him to do there."

She nods. I write OHIO in block letters down the bus's side.

We're both leaning over my drawing from opposite sides of the counter. Our heads almost touching. I look up and so does she. I study her clumped eyelashes. The crumbs of mascara stuck to her cheekbone since this morning. We hover inches apart like that for a few seconds in a truly admirable show of restraint.

"I think you're running out of coffee filters," she says.

Then I'm out of the dining room, slipping through the bakery kitchen where Mom is baking a loaf of bread. I burst through the door that opens onto a staircase down to the shared basement pantry. Harlow right behind me twirling a lock of dark hair.

"You're not supposed to be back here," I say.

I pull her into the tight space and shut the door behind her.

The darkness is pillow-over-face complete. We find each other's lips and then we have to stay that way for as long as we can because taking a breath means finding each other again.

Harlow and I have this weird thing recently where some days we make out and some days we pretend to barely notice each other. Recently as in since my homecoming party last month. I've been trying to figure out the pattern so I can set my expectations accordingly.

Only on overcast days?

Only on days Ellis does a distance run?

You don't want to wake up thinking you're getting made out with and the only kiss you get is your dog licking your face.

I don't like her. Don't think I do. But I want to trace the length of her body with my fingers as her warm hand squeezes the back of my neck.

Now I get why Ellis is a jerk. How can you think about anyone else when Harlow notices and has an opinion about *everything*? What time I wake up in the morning. My life's ambitions or lack thereof. Before, her undivided attention meant she was collecting intel to provoke me with later. Feels like something else now. She's the girl who laughs at me, not with me, but she's also the girl who gave it to me straight about Goose. No tiptoeing. I don't know which girl's real or if it's possible the answer is both.

We break apart only after what feels like a risky amount of time for me to be away from my waiter/busboy/cashier duties. I grab a handful of coffee filters, then retrace my steps through Mom's kitchen and add them to the tower next to the coffee maker. Meanwhile Harlow mirrors me through Dad's kitchen, where earlier today I husked corn and peeled potatoes. She lands back on the other side of the counter like it never happened.

It's been like this for weeks and if I say anything I'll jinx it. Obviously no one can know. How to explain to Mom that I mash Harlow's face against mine on a semi-regular basis? Can't imagine Ellis's reaction. They'll think it's a cry for help and I'll lose any tiny progress I've made convincing my family I'm okay. They'll say she's manipulating me. But if looking forward to something and feeling my own heartbeat is what manipulation is like, I don't hate it.

Harlow removes a stack of books from her backpack and spreads them across the counter. Ruffles through her giant stack of SAT flashcards. Somehow she flunked the vocab part. When she's sure I'm watching she nudges a small book across the counter. A poetry anthology curated with aqua sticky notes.

"Did you know some of David Hockney's paintings were inspired by Walt Whitman?" she asks her notebook. Then, raising an eyebrow at me, "You know who that is, right?"

Of course I know. But I don't make shit up from words. From nothing. I draw what I see.

Drew. Saw. Past tense.

"Borrow it." She nudges the book again. "Maybe something will speak to you."

I haven't made anything worth looking at since I went on antidepressants last year. Eventually I stopped taking them. Spent more time in the drawing studio. Lost my fingerprints blending charcoal into paper. My nails never not black. But no matter what I did, I couldn't go back to the way I worked before. I just kept getting worse.

"I don't do that anymore," I tell her.

"Read?"

"Art."

Right then my mom comes out of her kitchen and stands next to me behind the counter. Harlow and I can't look away from each other quick enough.

"So you never told me your SAT scores," I practically shout. "Heard you bombed."

Harlow's face a storm cloud. "Is that supposed to be funny?"

"It's what Ellis said."

Her face screws up and please let her holler whatever terrible thing she's thinking so Mom won't suspect. Like: Jesus, Tommy, what a thing to say considering you didn't take it and your mom had to find out by calling the College Board because Ellis and I got our scores but for yours the website said "not available." But Harlow's face smooths. She tucks a curl behind the pink seashell of her ear.

"Helen?" she says, pulling a monstrous three-ring binder from her backpack. "Do you know what you'll do if the erosion negatively impacts the bakery? Because I put together some contingency plans—"

"Not a good time, Harlow."

And Mom returns to the kitchen. Did she come out here just to check on us?

More likely: to check on me.

"That's what she said after the last storm," Harlow whines. "But now that you're better, she has to talk about it sometime."

Ever since my swim everyone's asking if I'm feeling better. Except Harlow never asks. She tells. Now that you're feeling better. Now that you're taking your medicine again. Like an incantation she can recite until it's true. She doesn't give a shit how I'm actually doing. It's fucking great.

She continues. "The protestors are too comfortable. Literally. The Albertsons are letting them stay at the B and B."

"Apparently they're protesting in shifts."

She chews her lower lip. "You don't think your mom wants to move away, do you?"

"Why don't you leave the binder here?" I hold out my hand, and when she hesitates, I add, "Ellis didn't say that about your SATs."

She slides me the binder—even heavier than it looks—then quickly stacks the poetry book on top. "Just in case."

Does she only kiss me when I do what she wants?

I take the book.

Harlow begins her homework for real. A few months ago, just watching her highlight history notes would've bothered me. I'd already fallen behind in school due to a number of embarrassing episodes around New Year's and this would've felt like she was mocking me. But the kissing helps. So does knowing I don't have to go back until August. School doesn't know how to handle me and I don't know how to handle school so it's a mutual decision. That's what we're all telling ourselves.

The phone rings, and when I answer, I'm ready to scribble down a takeout order.

"Don't bring Harlow," my brother says as soon as he hears it's me.

I actually write it down like it's an order. I guess it is. But I don't know where I'm supposed to not-bring her. Pretty sure I'm not going anywhere.

"I need you to pick me up." The wind blowing across his microphone makes him sound like he's inside a paper bag.

"Do you want Mom?"

"I'm asking you."

Since we started whatever this is, Harlow's been taking the bus and letting Ellis drive her car home after practice. That Volvo's in good shape. But doesn't matter what's the matter. He picked me.

Harlow's kneeling on her stool. Way more excited than when it was just her and me in this conversation. "Ellis?" she guesses.

Do we only make out on days I snooze my alarm three times?

She holds out her hand expectantly. Like she's about to kick a puppy and like it. She's itching to tell him off for whatever he's done. Can't just be ignoring her texts. The phone's ancient cord barely stretches into the bakery kitchen where Mom's kneading a ball of cinnamon raisin dough.

"Just come south down Willow. You can't miss it." He's getting bored. "Listen, is Harlow there?"

She's leaning on her elbows. In a few minutes she'll have successfully leaned her way onto the other side of the counter.

Do we only kiss when I wear blue? When she wears blue? Today we're both wearing blue.

He can tell from my silence the answer is a huge YES.

"Don't bring her. I mean it." He hangs up before I can say anything else.

He should know it's not so easy. That I can't help it. She senses something big has happened before I do, even though it's my own brother.

I put the phone back, cross into the diner kitchen, and tell Dad I'm stepping out for a few minutes. He's less likely than Mom to ask a bunch of questions but they've both been doing this just-checking-in thing since I came home. Mom popping her head into the doorway of my bedroom. Dad doing the same at the diner to make sure I haven't fallen into the fryer or shut myself in the chest freezer. I tell him I'm meeting up with Ellis and he nods way too encouragingly.

"What happened?" Harlow demands as soon as I return to the dining room.

"Stay here."

She follows me outside.

Goose lies where I left her tied to the diner's signpost. Even though she's tired from kicking cancer's ass her tail thumps against the ground as we approach. I unclip her collar and lead her to the car. Harlow trails a couple feet behind. I told her once she couldn't touch Goose and it's the only thing I've said that she's ever listened to. With the cancer she preserves an even bigger radius. Goose climbs into the back of Mom's car and, while I strap Goose in, Harlow claims the passenger seat.

The silence doesn't last. Never does. As soon as we're buckled up and navigating out of the parking lot Harlow asks again, "What happened?"

"I don't know."

"What'd he say?"

Kicking myself. The one time Ellis asks for my help and I can't follow simple instructions. "He just needs a ride. You didn't have to come."

"Was I supposed to sit and wait for you to get back?" She snorts. "I'm not *that* desperate."

Does the kissing only happen when I feel for a moment we could be friends? Or just before I go back to needing fifty, one hundred feet between us at all times?

I'm the one Ellis called. For good reason too. She's freaking out in the seat next to me. Aggressively thumb-typing on her phone. Scanning the side of the road for a kid with short shorts, an obscenely expensive prosthetic running leg, and an entitled look on his face.

A squawk escapes her as she points through the windshield. Of course she's spotted him first.

Ellis was right when he said he'd be hard to miss. He's leaning against Harlow's car like he's in a photo shoot. The car's nose is crushed against a thick tree trunk and his nose doesn't look any better.

I haven't even come to a full stop when Harlow launches herself out the passenger door. He tries hard to keep his face blank when he sees her, the way he must've practiced, but the line of his mouth goes wavy.

I crack the window for Goose and take my time crossing the glittering grass. One leg and then the other over the guardrail as in front of me the last seven years repeat themselves ad nauseum. Harlow's wrapped her arms around him and will probably never let go.

I do my best to ignore their sad little reunion. Touch the body of the Volvo where it ripples around the tree trunk. Try the door handle. It won't budge. Under the tires no grass at all, just two long smudges of soil. He's lucky he was able to get out of the car. Lucky he's not dead. Is this why he didn't wait around to see me after my swim? Thought I'd climb out of the water as easily as he can climb out of his own wrecks?

And Harlow. Has she *seen* what he did to her car? She's still holding him. His arms hang at his sides and he's saying I'm okay, I'm okay, I'm—

"Your nose is broken," I point out.

There's a shadow on his lip where the blood ran, nostrils to chin, though he tried to wipe it away before we got here. My head swims imagining it. I blink hard a couple times to get steady. Harlow peers up at him.

"Maybe you should go to the hospital," I say.

"I'm okay," he says airily. "I'm *grand*. Just drive me home so I can get cleaned up."

I shrug. "Your face."

We pile into the car, this time Ellis in back with Goose. Harlow's miles away next to me. Legs crossed, arms crossed, whole body leaning toward the passenger door.

Do we only kiss on days she's too mad to look at him?

Ellis clears his throat and announces, "There was a deer."

I find his face in the rearview mirror. He's looking at the back of Harlow's head.

"It ran out in front of me and I swerved."

There was no deer. Not a chance. Forget that they're unlikely to wander out of the woods in the middle of the afternoon, my brother hardly brakes for people at crosswalks. Harlow must be thinking the same thing. No way she'll let him get away with this one.

"You were trying to save it?" she says.

And from the back seat, eyes now fixed out the window: "That's right."

She might be crying. Can't tell. "Hey." I touch her shoulder, hoping Ellis is too wrapped up in his own story to notice. She drags her hand across her eyes and squints straight ahead.

"Is the deer okay?" she asks.

"I don't think it made it," he says gently.

So here we all are. Pretending she's crying for the blood and smear of fur that don't exist.

We make it home all in one piece and car intact. Harlow and Ellis walk to the front door together. Her arm looped in his. They don't look to see if I'm coming.

Do we only kiss when I'm certain we won't?

When someone gets hurt?

When I remind her of him?

Then there's only Goose snoring in the back seat. The distant rumble of waves. Live here long enough and you get used to that hum like it's the refrigerator running.

You get used to a lot.

Ten

HARLOW

Things I Must Not Do

1. Let Ellis fall asleep. Potential concussion. Why can't we let concussed people rest? Need to look this up for practical purposes and own curiosity.
2. Kiss Tommy again. I estimate it took Ellis ten minutes to call us after the crash. Ten long minutes to check himself over, climb out of the car, and work up the desperation to ask for help. That puts the crash at right about the time I was hooking up with Tommy. Not a coincidence.
3. Fucking cry about it.

This last a mandate from Ellis himself, said under his breath as I walked him to the front door. He saves up his curse words for so long you forget he knows them. Lands them like a gut punch.

He shuts himself in the bathroom and the white noise of water comes down like a sheet between us. I sit on his bed as a hill rises in my throat. On the floor: the baby blue hoodie he wore yesterday, a faint orange stain on the right shoulder from Olivia's foundation. At my back: pillowcases that smell like his shampoo.

How many times have I waited for him like this, or fallen asleep on this bed with the door cracked open an inch, Helen's request? We were twelve the first time she asked, and Ellis said right away, laughing, "Mom, I'll never think of Harlow like that." Now a well fills in my stomach like it did as we pulled up to the wreck in those five seconds before he was okay. Muddy stripes in wild roadside grass. Glittering-glass car seats.

We almost lost him once before. Me the only one who saw it. And this afternoon, I had to picture for the second time what my life might be like with an Ellis-shaped hole in it. I wasn't even sad for all he'd miss, like winning a race, and going to the running camp he's so excited about, and getting into college. The ruined future I saw was my own: the corkscrew of guilt I'd feel at my own Big Life Events, missing him. How selfish is that?

After he showers, he stands in the bathroom doorway in just a pair of basketball shorts. He pulls an old T-shirt over his head and I let my eyes sweep over him, counting the pink and purple bruises that ink his arms, a scratch on his chest over his heart. I also accidentally catch sight of the sharp lines of his hip bones disappearing into his waistband.

"Like what you see?" He grins as his head pops through his collar. I'd say I can't believe he's joking at a time like this, but that'd be a lie. Mostly I hope I'm not blushing.

He tosses his dirty clothes in a pile on the floor and, carrying his prosthetic leg and a liner, hops the short distance from the bathroom to the bed. I look anywhere but the scarred end of his limb, where a scabbed-over sore gleams red. Evidence he's been running too many miles. This sore is bad news, and hopping could strain his other leg (I've read all the pamphlets Dr. Diaz, his orthopedist, has sent home with him over the years—and Ellis knows better, since he has too). But I keep my mouth shut.

"Sorry about your car," he says as he stretches out beside me. "I'll pay for everything, I swear. And, hey, silver lining! You won't have to drive for a while."

He doesn't sound that sorry. He sounds like he practiced what he was going to say in the shower. I pick flakes of orange nail polish off my thumb.

"This is what happens when you abandon me and take the bus home. I need supervision." He smiles. He looks like a jack-o'-lantern turned to mush the week after Halloween.

Now there's a thoughtworm in my brain and I can't get it out: kissing Tommy again will kill Ellis. If it wasn't true before, it is now. Just because I've thought it. That thing they say about how you're responsible for someone's life after you save it? What if the opposite is also true? Like if someone almost dies because of you, there will always be some deep-down rottenness in you that wants to find a way to finish the job.

"Want me to help you study?" he asks, oblivious to my tiny crisis.

He's flat on his back now, head propped on one arm, the other holding his SAT flashcards. Even though he'll never have to take them again, could go to college anywhere he wants. I stare up at the gray ceiling, swallowing.

He glances at the topmost card. "Ha. You should know this one," he says and holds it up.

Peremptory.

We made our flashcards together one night, a box of loose markers between us, but I've never seen this word before.

"Pass."

"Just try."

I split my hair into three sections and start braiding. "Is it when you do something ahead of time?"

He shakes his head. Has that thin trickle of blood on his lip been there this whole time, or did it split open again? He shows me the next card.

Culpable.

That one I know.

"Do you think you should do something about your face?" I lean around the flashcard to get a good look. "Like take it to an emergency room?"

"You haven't studied. Don't make this about me." He uses the corner of the flashcards to poke me in the ribs.

I poke him right back. He makes a sound like a disgruntled cow. "I don't want to be responsible if something happens to you."

"Yeah, how would you live with yourself?"

I stare at him. Did he mean that like I think he did? Like, you and me have been there, done that?

He raises an eyebrow. "Sarcasm."

I choke/laugh. "I know."

Where would they bury him? And will they save the plot next to him for Tommy? That seems like the right thing to do. He should have a will so we don't feel guilty when we pull the plug. He could at least spare us that.

I peek over. His hands pillow his head while the rest of his body stretches lean and long in his baggy shorts and threadbare T-shirt from a long-ago cross-country meet. There's a spot at the hem that's unraveling, and oh god, I haven't considered the state of his internal organs. Could kissing Tommy a few times really have made this happen?

"I think you should go to the hospital."

He groans and covers his eyes, careful not to touch what I'm now positive is a broken nose. "Here's what happens if we go to the emergency room. We fill out some forms. We wait several hours next to people who are actually sick, dying, bleeding everywhere, and then they slap some Band-Aids on me and tell me I can't practice for a week."

"If you show up looking like this, your coach will send you home anyway," I point out. He winces as his hand slides down the length of his face, and dammit, I have to ask. If there's any other reason for this besides the cosmic wrongness of me and Tommy, I have to know. "What really happened?"

His face twists into an expression that's something like his signature grin—but also nothing like it at all. "I hit a tree. Thought you noticed."

"Before that. Was it something at practice?" I know I'm close because suddenly he's yawning, exhausted, so I add, "I'll ask Coop tomorrow."

His eyes narrow. He knows I'll do it.

He holds his pillow against the sides of his head so he won't hear himself say, "Coach wants to move forward with a 'mature' varsity team this year."

The comforter bunches under my hands. "Meaning?"

"He's keeping Coop. My last race of the season's in three weeks."

In the past month, Ellis has run faster than ever, each race a personal best. Getting on varsity means more practice, but if he makes it, he won't *have* to go to Camp Hood. The Plan will be back on track.

"It won't matter if I run a strong cross-country season," he continues. "By fall, recruiters will already have their rosters."

His twenty-five-thousand-dollar running leg. The nonprofit that helped pay for it, the fundraiser his parents did to cover the rest, which is pretty much the only time they've asked anyone for money, ever. Entire weeks of his life spent in practice. All for what?

"Once I start sweating, I can feel the pin pulling on my leg," he says. He means the metal pin at the end of the gel liner that goes under his running blade, and locks into the leg's socket with a series of clicks. Then, more quietly, "What if I can't get any faster?"

I can't play this game of alternate universes and what-ifs. I'll fall into hypotheticals too inane to share. If he still had two legs, would getting stuck on junior varsity be enough to crash a car over? Or would he have secured his spot already, ignorant of what it's like to have to prove himself every time he hits the track?

"You've been beating Coop for months." My voice jumps an octave, like he's a child, like that works. "You should talk to your coach. Make him explain."

"Clearly he thinks I can't keep up."

"So prove him wrong. Run another strong time, beat Coop by a lot, and he'll have no choice."

"I guess." He finally lets the pillow down, uncovering his ears. "Good thing I registered for camp. It's fully booked now."

Good thing.

He turns his head away and I slide down next to him, a careful two inches between my arm and his.

"What are you doing?" I ask suspiciously, right in his ear.

"Resting my eyes," he mumbles into the pillow.

"You can't sleep!"

"So keep me awake."

The backs of my arms prickle. I'm aware of every movement in his body: the blood lazy-river floating through the veins in his arm, which is right next to my arm. If he takes a deep breath really quickly, it might make me dizzy.

"C'mon, Harlow. Hit me."

"How bad?"

"I-crashed-your-car-into-a-tree bad."

It's a game we've played since the first day we met. We were only nine (going on ten, he would've said at the time). I followed him out the bakery kitchen's back door to where the jetty cut a narrow, jagged path through high tide. Watched him jump from rock to rock with bare feet—still two at this point—and wings spread for balance.

"Is it safe?" I called.

"Sure isn't," he shouted back. "Three people have died on it this year. Come on!"

And when that (untrue) tidbit didn't tempt me, he doubled back. Held out his hand. We nestled in a sheltered crag between some of the bigger rocks at the end of the jetty and sat facing each other, kneecaps pressed together as the wind tied knots in our hair. It was warm in this pocket we'd found. Safe.

"We're not supposed to go all the way out here," I said through a mouthful of hair. "My parents said it's dangerous."

He made a face. "Do you always do what you're supposed to?"

I had the feeling like he was sizing me up, and whatever conclusion he drew would stick. "No."

His eyes rolled toward the clouds. "I bet you've never done a bad thing in your life."

"Have so!"

"Oh yeah? Hit me with it."

I told him that while we were unpacking our new house, I'd found my dad's favorite blue-footed booby figurine and hadn't given it back. It was important because my mom had given it to him when they first met in the lab at grad school.

Ellis didn't laugh at the name like the classmates I'd left behind in Illinois would've. He knew a blue-footed booby was a bird. In fact, he'd seen plenty. Most important, he didn't ask me why I took it or tell me to give it back. He just shared a misdeed of his own.

"Sometimes," he whispered, "I wish I didn't have a brother."

He said he wanted to be treated like his own person. Not Tommy'n'Ellis. As an only child myself, I would've adopted Tommy into my family on the spot, sight unseen, had Ellis offered.

By the end of summer, the game had already grown difficult. We'd spent more time together than not, and few of our mistakes were secrets. Years later, it's hard not because there's nothing new to tell, but because we have to wade through a myriad of bad, obvious sins first. Thoughts I've had about Ellis that would hurt him. Thoughts he's probably had about me.

Telling him about Tommy would be easy. Then impossible. He'd know just what to ask. How did this happen? Who kissed who first? Tommy? *Really?* A list titled, "Questions I Don't Have Answers To."

But I can tell him I'm ending it.

"I've been kind of seeing someone for the last few weeks," I begin.

He rolls onto his side to face me, knee pressed into my thigh. Does he look a little disappointed? I could be imagining it.

"It's not official or anything." My cheeks warm. "It's just . . . something I was trying."

"For fun?" The corner of his mouth twitches.

"I guess."

The twitch turns into a full-on smirk. "You're doing something because it's fun?"

I scowl. "I am a fun-loving person."

He nods like I'm a small child who insists she be treated like a grown-up.

"I am! But I'm ending it. I should've told him already—that's the bad part."

"Wait, why?"

I shrug, touch a hand to my cheek. Still hot. I can't exactly say *because it's bad luck and you almost died.*

"Do I know him?"

I groan. "Sharing time is over, okay?"

"So that's a yes." He props himself on his elbows. At least he's awake. "Do I like this person?"

A laugh catches in my throat. "Sometimes."

"Do *you* like him?"

I think of the heat of Tommy's fingers tracing my jaw. The flushed look of him after a makeout session, when we sneak back and everything's normal except how often his gaze lands on me.

I used to find him unbearable, so anything else is an improvement. "More than I thought I would."

"Then you're going to keep doing it," he proclaims.

"We're not *doing it*." Now I'm definitely blushing.

He snorts. "Mind out of the gutter, Prout. Whatever it is. Hooking up."

I should've picked a different misdeed. Made something up. "It's definitely over."

"Okay," he says cheerfully, and gives me a knowing look I don't like one bit.

Eleven

TOMMY

Arguing with myself the whole drive back about telling Mom before she finds out from someone else. My parents almost lost one kid already this year. A trend I started. Don't I owe them this info and a hell of a lot more? But on the other hand, Ellis called *me*. How can I betray that?

In the end it doesn't matter. Mom isn't even at the diner.

"She went on a walk with Chloe," Dad says. "I told her you'd be right back with the car."

There's a cream-colored shell balanced just so on top of the clock on the wall. Could've appeared while I was saving Ellis's ass or been there for weeks. Dad follows my gaze. Whistles. "How'd the old bastard get up there?"

I try not to picture Cliff up on a chair, arm outstretched. If he'd fallen. My fault. I drag a stool from Dad's kitchen and when I retrieve it the shell's light in my palm.

I guess I'm supposed to look at this and think about how a mollusk spent years making it and then a snail moved in, and maybe a crab's lived in there too, and now it's in my hand. He'd want me to admire the perfect spiral. The eggshell ridges. Like the perfectly round rock I found next to the register, the piece of mint-green sea glass on the roof of Mom's car, and all his other gifts, I can feel Cliff in its warmth. Its weight. His forgiveness like an anvil on my chest. Enough treasure to bury me, X marks the spot.

I'll toss this out first chance I get.

"Everything okay?" Dad says, because he thinks depression could make me pass out at any moment.

But I don't drown like that anymore. The waves are calm and I'm wearing my life vest. "Fine."

If I can't decide about telling Mom where I was then I'm sure as hell not telling Dad. Not like he can't handle it, just don't know how he would. Black boxes both of us. We have a lot to say but not to each other. I used to think it was because we've always lived with Mom, that he and Ellis only got by because they had sports in common. But the month I lived with him at the B and B last year disproved that theory. This back when Cliff told my parents he was worried about me and Dad said I just needed a change of scenery. *Get some sun, put down the pencil, and talk to someone, why don't you. Just look at your brother.*

Dad's Dadisms only stopped when the Sox were on. He'd make us root beer floats with chocolate ice cream and yell like the umpire was in that double-queen suite with us while I sketched by the TV's blue light. Contour drawings, the kind where your eyes can't leave the subject and the pencil can't leave the page until it's finished. But Dad was going through a family pack of tissues a week with Goose there. And see how much good the change of scenery did me.

"Any plover sightings?" Dad asks as I grab an apron from the hook on the wall.

I suspect Harlow and I were the first to spot the bird last month, but lately it's been seen on the beach at all hours of the day. "Not today."

"Caleb Prout thinks there are two. Look damn near identical to me."

I drop my apron over my head. This is what he wants to talk about? I'll tell him every bird fact I know if it convinces him I'm getting better. Then I spy something in his hand. I point. "What's that?"

The envelope in Dad's hand now in mine. It's my paycheck. Also not my paycheck. I hold up the wad of bills stashed inside the envelope. Maybe two hundred bucks extra. "Lose this?"

"That?" He catches the back of his neck in his hand. "You know our payroll system's a piece of crap. It was trying to stiff you and I couldn't figure out how to fix it so I just made up the difference."

"Uh-huh." Another kindness I don't deserve, won't be able to pay back. "Nothing to do with Mom telling you Goose is starting chemo."

"She didn't say a thing." He shakes his head. Hand on heart. "That's definitely all yours. But if you want any help with that chemo business, a loan, even." He thumps his chest. "You know who to ask."

Already my parents paid for my five days in the hospital. Weeks of therapy sessions that didn't work. Meds that might've, if I'd let them. No, I'd never ask.

The evening's slow enough that I start cleaning up before dinner's over. I erase and rewrite the specials on the whiteboard, the same ones, because the marker's a bit faded. Scrub the countertop. Contemplate ways to get out of therapy tomorrow morning. If I don't go, then I won't have to decide if I like this one. Tell Mom it's not the right fit. Again. I'm so bored I even pull out Harlow's poetry book. It's thick with sticky notes, and she's made a graphite list on the inside back cover. A poem of poems:

I believe in a heaven I'll never enter.
the jingle, the periwinkle, the scallop
full of moonlight.
"The sea is salt"
"And so am I"

This is coming from a guy who walked out of the SATs, didn't study, but how's someone who reads poetry for fun screw up the vocab so bad? Almost my level of self-sabotage.

I should find a way to put the cash back in Dad's wallet. But if he wants me to have it. If keeping it makes him worry less. I pack up most of the pastries but leave a couple of each in the case. Paper-bag a few coconut macaroons for Dad to take home. They're his favorite, but he won't ask when Mom's around.

Maybe he did this for her, not me. He's still a little bit in love with her. Everyone in town says so. But Mom says he should've thought of that before he had a drunken one-night stand with one of their former high school classmates. All this back before he got sober. Ellis and I were six.

Personally I learned a lot from it. People think being in love with someone means you can't hurt them, but if anything, it makes it more likely.

I'm scooping a cup of dog food from the bag in Dad's kitchen when I see Cliff pull up in his truck. A Dodge Ram older than I am, but a fair share of its miles are mine. A weekend last fall: Cliff pulling bright orange cones off the truck bed, teaching me to parallel park between them. Another: one of countless trips to the Portland Museum of Art. We were there so often Cliff knew the security guards by name. He didn't rush me when I perched on a bench for an hour, replicating the same pieces in my sketchbook as last time. Never complained when, more and more frequently, I stared at a Winslow Homer seascape for ten minutes, then asked to leave.

Cliff eases himself out of the cab, tops of his ears tucked into his red cap. Moving slow ever since his heart attack. That was the worst week of my last twelve months, recent events included. I was taking my meds back then, every day at the same time, like a good depressive. But that doesn't stop shitty things from happening.

Hands shaking, I roll up the dog food bag and grab the poetry book while Cliff disappears around the corner. Approaches the front door. That's when I slip out the back with my apron still on. Goose licks my hand as I get her buckled again in the back seat of Mom's car and guilt makes a quick fist around my stomach. How'd I ever convince myself it was okay to leave her behind? To leave him?

Besides bringing me half the beach, Cliff's made some obvious attempts to corner me for a talk since he fished me out of the ocean last month. He wants a chance to say all the things he didn't on our silent ride back to shore. After I heard his boat's motor and pretended not to, because then this would be just another thing I'd screwed up. After he killed the motor and called my name. Five minutes he waited, but it felt like twenty: starting the boat again to keep up with me, shutting it off, waiting some more. How he lied and told my parents I was already swimming back when he found me.

I've imagined the talk a thousand times. Cliff looking at me like he used to. Like I'm enough. But it's impossible. That email I sent him, the longest and most rambling of them all, and he wrote back anyway. The only one who did. Telling me point-by-point in the most loving way possible that I was wrong. Yes, I was enough. No, my now wouldn't be my forever. After everything, how can I tell him I still don't buy it? I toss Harlow's book in the passenger seat and think maybe poets are onto something. Saying so much with hardly any words.

I start Mom's car and pull out into the new darkness, not realizing until I'm halfway there that my headlights are off.

The crash looks worse the second time.

I try the Volvo's driver's side door before remembering it's jammed shut. Grabbing hold of the roof for support, I ease each leg through the window frame, imagining Ellis doing the same in reverse. I settle in and wrap my fingers around the dimpled steering wheel. My right foot rests on the brake pedal. The seat is the perfect height and distance from the dashboard, like it was me behind the wheel.

I'd told myself I was only going for a swim but of course that wasn't true. There were those emails I'd written. The boxes under my bed. The planning had calmed me. Realizing my forever didn't have to be as long as everyone else's was the happiest I'd felt in a long time. I can't think further without cringing about Goose, who must've already been sick from the tumor I didn't catch, now grown to the size of a grape. Mom, who sobbed even after she ran out of tears. Cliff, kind and patient at the end of all those museum trips I ended early, eyes crinkling as he promised there'd always be a next time.

I've been sitting in that damn car for twenty minutes when a deer and her two fawns emerge from between a pair of nearby trees. They pick their way across the grass. The little ones have backs speckled white like a dusting of powdered sugar. They rake the tips of their hooves through the mud tire tracks, poke out their pink tongues, and taste the broken air.

Twelve

HARLOW

I promised Tommy I wouldn't let Ellis sleep, but as we talk about our American lit quiz later this week, his eyelids flutter and finally close. I try asking him questions, poking his face. He's actually snoring when Tommy texts:

OK?

Does he mean Ellis or me?
All good, I reply.

My plan was to kiss Tommy just once. I figured I'd power through à la my first kiss with Coop in seventh grade. I didn't even let myself consider the most dangerous possibility of all.

What if I liked it?

The sandpaper of his scalp against my palm as I pull him toward me. The basement stairs sharp against my back. Secret smiles. Pins and needles in my lips whole minutes after we break apart.

Three weeks and five days of no self-control later, here's my punishment: Ellis so black and blue that if I hadn't just talked to him, I'd think he was dead.

I slide his phone off his belly and unlock it. He's got a bunch of unread notifications, including the texts I sent while Tommy and I were en route to pick him up. Rude. Olivia texted that she bought tickets for a movie we already saw last week. *It's a date!* her message says. I type *It's not!*, then erase it. I've caused enough damage for one day.

Downstairs, the front door opens and slams shut. I listen for Helen's keys hitting the bowl by the shoe closet. Instead there's the slow rumble of Goose climbing the carpeted stairs and Tommy's steady encouragements behind her. Across the hall, his bedroom door closes and locks. *We're done, Tommy. It was weird and now it's over.* Can I say that? Not, like, is it conscionable, but can I physically say those words out loud with my mouth? I hope he doesn't cry.

I gently replace Ellis's phone and switch to mine.

Are you home?

The timing's not right, probably. If he says no, I'll leave him alone and take care of it another day.

A bubble pops up on my screen. He's typing. After twenty-six seconds (not that I'm counting): *I'm here*

Before I can chicken out, I slip into the bathroom that connects the boys' bedrooms—a formerly-unfortunate, now-convenient architectural quirk someone must've thought was cute—and shut Ellis's door behind me. The door to Tommy's bedroom is closed and Ellis's wet towel is bunched on the rack. I straighten it out so it will dry properly. In my head I practice: *We're bad luck. You hate me, remember?*

I lean over the counter so its edge bites into my hips. My face so close to the mirror that I can see my pores and also all the gunk in my pores, the fine colorless baby hairs and a couple not-so-colorless ones on my upper lip. I rummage in the drawer on Ellis's side of the counter. No tweezers, but there's a sticky, poison-apple-red lip gloss I stashed here sometime in middle school. Definitely expired. I apply a gloopy layer and—great, I look worse. The red gloss only highlights how plain the rest of me is. The question is, did baby Harlow have the sense to stash an eyeliner in here too . . .

Ellis lets loose an extra-loud snore and my hand freezes. I double back to check the door to his room, unlocking and then relocking it to be sure. What am I putting on makeup for, anyway? Without breaking eye contact with myself, I grab a tissue and rub until my lips are chapped and pink. Then I march across the bathroom, knock, and wait to break Tommy's heart. At least, I wait to break the tiny part I accidentally acquired. The lower left ventricle, perhaps. Hopefully he doesn't need it.

He wasn't supposed to be in his freaking pajamas. That was the first thing.

Faded flannel pants and a soft gray tee. The kind of shirt you had to find a way to touch, so thin you'd feel his skin through it, and it'd be warm, and you wouldn't hate that one bit.

He wasn't supposed to open the door mid-yawn, scratching his belly with the side of his fist. He was supposed to ask what I was doing there so I could say *ending this*. Instead his eyes balloon and his shirt hem drops as he smiles. Nervous, sheepish, excited. It's the most feelings I've seen on his face maybe ever, but especially since he got home from the hospital, when he's been about as expressive as a refrigerator door.

Maybe it's only bad luck if I'm the one who initiates the kiss?

"I let him go to sleep," I blurt out before I embarrass myself.

"Uh. Okay," he says. Like, *of course*. I feel myself flush because as far as he's concerned I'll forever be maiming his brother.

I put a finger to my lips and cross the threshold into his room (*Tommy's room!*) so I can close the door behind me. I push the lock hard, until it clicks, then launch into a careful self-defense, an attempt to recover my dignity, "I tried to keep him awake but he didn't . . ." Trailing off in shock because his bedroom looks like it belongs in a hotel. So completely different from the last time I was here, when I raided the art supplies under his bed for a history project and found those labeled boxes. There are clothes draped over sparse furniture, and some oversize cardboard leaning against the wall by the desk, but gone are the postcards and prints, the art books that used to take up two full shelves. I look for anything sentimental—a doodled-on sticky note, a foggy piece of that sea glass Clifford Samuels leaves him like a weird obsession. But there's nothing of Tommy in here.

That thing we do, breathing? Not happening. My ribs are a too-small cage for my lungs. It's not that I didn't think he was still depressed. I just didn't consider what it meant that he tried to erase himself. He wanted the waves to close over him, and if all had gone to plan, he wouldn't have come back up.

Standing in the middle of his room, rolling his shirt hem between his fingers, Tommy clears his throat. "He didn't what?"

I can't remember what I was talking about, whether it was important or just something to say. Goose lies in a tangle of sheets at the foot of his unmade bed. She lifts her head and watches us. Can't he train her to mind her own business? After a couple seconds she wrongly concludes I'm not a threat and lowers her head onto her paws. I can't even blame her because his bed looks comfortable. Probably smells like him. I imagine towing him by the front of his shirt and pulling him down on top of me so I can't breathe again. It wouldn't be as bad as it sounds. It wouldn't be bad at all.

But that's my hormones talking. Pheromones and mitochondria and whatever. I spy a line of pill bottles running along the back edge of his desk and walk over, pretending to look at the textbooks. His and Goose's names appear on various bottles. Beside those, small stacks of cash.

"Bea was on her way to the diner as I was leaving," he babbles, still playing with his shirt hem, a slice of white skin showing above his boxers. "Mom will deal with him."

If he kisses me right now—if his skin touches mine, if he looks at me funny—I'm done for. I need something to look at that's not the spot where his waistband meets his hip.

"He's gonna be fine. This is just what he does."

My gaze trails up his body and finally lands on his face. Everything in the room stills. His fingers, my thoughts, all of it.

"No," I say. The silence in the room fills my ears. I swallow. Doesn't help. "It's not."

He gives me a look like *yeah right.* As if Ellis has some dark death wish just like his and it's not my fault at all, which, after two hours of careful consideration, I've concluded is plain untrue.

"How can you say he's fine when you can't even take care of yourself?" I spread my arms wide, gathering his whole room, him and what little crap he has left. "You're not staying long, I guess. Have another swim planned?"

His breath catches and he goes a shade whiter and it's possible I've gone too far. Could be everyone in town is right to approach only on tiptoe. But also he can't say shit like that, making it sound like Ellis could do this again, no big deal.

"I've been busy," he says, eyes glittering with something that's probably hate.

I tap a stack of bills on the desk next to me. "I'll bet. You've made, what, six hundred bucks?"

His expression doesn't change, but his shoulders rise several inches toward his ears.

I almost ask when Goose's surgery is. I'll do the math for him, write up a schedule on a calendar so he can draw in little smiley faces as his savings grow. But that counts as getting involved. Which I'm actually here to stop doing.

If I'm not capable of ending things with him, he'll have to end them with me.

So I scoff and add, "Tell Cliff if he wants to help, he should bring you cash instead of rocks."

The glitter in his eyes goes out.

I wait for the eruption, when he snaps and sends everything crashing off his desk with the swipe of an arm or calls me a terrible name. Many names.

"Shut up," he says without anger or malice. The way he might tell some-one *It's Tuesday*.

I turn on my heel and let my fingers dance along the surface of his desk, piled with textbooks I could return to school for him, then over the card-board leaning against the wall. "Don't—" he says as I wiggle my nail under a piece of masking tape and pry open one of the largest pieces. There's an acrylic painting on paper inside, and in clear, legible black Sharpie in the cardboard's top right corner: *Mrs. Samuels.*

This is private. But I can't stop now.

It's like I'm watching someone else's hand as I flip through the oth-ers. Acrylics and oils. Spirally drawings, more ink than paper. Oil pastels imprinted on the cardboard facing them. My mouth's gone dry. Even though I've seen his artwork over the years and watched him improve, I can't believe this stuff came out of this boy.

I know I won't find one with my name on it but I keep looking anyway, until I've checked them all. He stands behind me while I do this, not moving, not speaking. I want him to put a hand on my waist and pull me away, or tell me it doesn't matter there's not one for me and kiss me on the forehead. But also I don't want those things. Can't. So my hand keeps going, and to fill the horrible silence, I just straight up ask, "Did you quit art because of Ruby?"

I think I hear Ellis snore during the silence, which lasts for about one month.

"I quit because I was bad." Tommy's behind me, so I can't see his face, but I can hear—it's made of granite now.

"Says who?"

"Ms. Russeau."

I drag the fleshiest part of my thumb along the corner of some card-board. "Really? Your art teacher said, 'Tommy, you suck'?"

"'Everything you make looks oddly the same.' That's what she said." He sucks in a breath. I press harder into the cardboard's sharp edge. "Some reverse-psychology bullshit. Guess it didn't work."

I tuck my sufficiently punished thumb inside my fist. "Well, I like your stuff."

"Lucky me."

But I mean it. His art makes me feel things. Too much sometimes. Little details in a drawing, a scuff mark on a shoe or a faded letter on a charcoal street sign, that make me remember there's at least one person paying as much attention as me.

I check my thumb. Still indented, still purple. "Seriously. Why quit something you're so good at?"

"Why flunk the SATs?"

I spin around and he's already produced the poetry anthology I lent him. He holds it out to me with raised eyebrows.

I ruffle through the book. A blue sticky note whirls to the carpet. "You can read poetry and still suck at standardized tests." Another thoughtworm, though. Did I maybe rush through the vocab section? Leave too many answer bubbles blank? "If I messed up on purpose, I wouldn't be retaking it, would I?" I say triumphantly, slapping the anthology facedown on his desk.

He shrugs a shoulder. "I'm not judging. World's ending. Do whatever the fuck you want."

It sounds almost like a joke. But there's his refrigerator-door face. Room full of nobody and nothing. He believes it.

"Yeah? That why you went for your swim?" I say, surprising myself, but apparently I cannot. Leave it. Alone.

I'm even more surprised when Tommy answers in the same flat tone, "No, that was because I didn't want to be alive anymore."

Questions form an orderly line: Is that the same as wanting to die? Does he want to right now? Surely if he wanted to die he would've done it.

"But you were swimming back when Clifford Samuels found you."

He swallows. "Not exactly."

"Well that's what he told people."

Tommy doesn't say anything.

"So that's why you're avoiding him." His brows draw together and I feel the truth of it in my bones. The kind of cold you never warm up from. "He's the only one who really knows what happened."

"Him and you."

I feel a shiver on the back of my neck. The dog is watching us with her ears perked, her face still on her paws. Tommy glances over too. Smiles a little. When he turns back to me, his expression is still soft.

I pretend to search for a particular piece of art in the pile, my fingers scraping against the thick paper. "Well, how do you feel now?"

He looks at me dubiously.

"Like, *right now*."

"I don't want to die, but I don't want to live, either." He bites the insides of his cheeks. "Everything feels a little . . . pointless? It's hard to explain." Then he lets out a big sigh and—strangely—a smile. "This is way better than therapy. I guess the trick is talking to someone who doesn't give a shit."

I think maybe I do give a shit, though, because I've gone back and forth through this stack of artwork maybe ten times now and I'm sure. There isn't one piece with my name on it. Must be something for everyone in West Finch but me. Even the one for my parents is labeled "Mira and Caleb," not "The Prouts." There's a colored pencil self-portrait that's freaking intended for Goose.

"So what's with the shells ?" I ask.

He stiffens. "What?"

"From Clifford Samuels. They mean something, right?"

He gazes at the ceiling. Clears his throat. "Something good from something bad," he recites, then looks back at me, sheepish. "I used to find shit on the beach and bring it to him when I was little. He has this big jar at his house. It's like a reminder that there's beauty in everything. Reasons to live. Whatever."

I'm trying to rationalize what he's said with the Clifford Samuels I know. Because that guy is utterly careless. Can't see more than a foot in front of his own face, better yet all the way down to his boots in the sand. Has never made anything beautiful. But then I think of all the times I've seen Tommy draw a study of a shell. A watercolor pane of robin's egg sea glass. A bounty of sand dollars, stones, and glass, enough to spread in an even layer, tile this floor, a private beach that will never wash away—was it all from Cliff?

I cross my arms, more to hold myself together than anything. If I did something nice for Tommy and found out he was flushing it down the toilet, I'd be so pissed he'd never be able to make it up to me.

"You shouldn't throw them away, then. That's just rude."

"Okay," he says. I hear him move closer and then there's his fingers barely grazing my lower back. He smells like cooking oil and burnt sugar. I breathe through my mouth.

"Even if you can't talk to him right now. Just, like, put them in a nice jar so you'll have them later."

Grip on my arm careful but firm, he turns me around and tilts my face up.

Ellis says that sometimes, from the outside, it looks like I break things just so I can fix them. And here's Ellis's face—same faint dimples, strong nose—but with hollow cheeks, and eyes bruised by lack of sleep. I could count his eyelashes. Trace his humid sigh on my cheek.

"Are you going to let me kiss you?" he asks softly.

My mouth tastes like I am going to regret everything. Bad luck I take with me everywhere I go. But I must have answered because his face splits into a ghost of Ellis's grin. And when his lips meet mine, I breathe him in.

Thirteen

ELLIS

I wake up with an invisible knife in my right foot, a second in my neck, and a vow not to tell Harlow. She'll say my neck's broken, or how the last time my phantom pain was this bad, I'd had strep for a week and didn't know it. But really, we just can't fit in the same twin-size bed anymore. A sad fact of growing up.

I roll onto my back and stretch out, expecting a halo of hair in my face, the small of her back under my fingers. But her side of the bed's empty. The sheets aren't even warm.

The bathroom door creaks, I keep my eyes closed, and a moment later, she slips under the covers, our bodies parallel lines.

"Where'd you go?" I mumble, pretending I'm still half-asleep.

"Bathroom."

"But the bed's cold."

She gives the blankets a yank, which isn't what I meant. They parachute over me. Then she unwedges her phone from between the mattress and the headboard.

"Did your boyfriend call?"

Her eyebrows pinch. "He's not my boyfriend."

"But did he?"

"Let's pretend I never told you that, okay?"

I pick a wiry piece of Goose's black fur off her sleeve and try to picture someone Harlow would hook up with, but my mind goes blank. We don't have the same taste in guys. When I point out someone I think is cute, she usually frowns and changes the subject. And there's only a sample size of two to compare to: Coop in seventh grade, and then this guy from a two-week oceanography day camp she did a few summers ago. I met him on their last day. He seemed okay. Boring, I think I said out loud. They officially broke up a week later.

That's not counting the year she had a not-so-secret crush on me. She got over it, thank god, but it was flattering. No one's immune if I don't want them to be.

Still, none of this is fair. I tell her all—kisses and crushes and everything beyond—and she won't drop even a hint.

"My parents called. Twice," she says, grimacing at her phone.

My stomach sinks. The car. "I bet Tommy ratted me out."

"He wouldn't."

But of course he would. Telling on me would make him look like a saint in comparison. He'd get to be the good kid for five whole minutes.

Her phone lights up and dances in her hand. HOME.

"I'll tell them it was me," she offers. Then, hopefully, "Maybe they'll confiscate my license."

I'm tempted, but I don't actually want Harlow to take the fall for me. It's more about knowing she will if I ask. Instead I say, "They won't buy it. You don't have a scratch on you."

She smooths out the comforter between us. "Are we sticking with the deer story?"

I imagine saying that out loud to my mom. Shake my head.

Harlow presses her phone to her ear. "I was going to tell you. He feels fine. Well, Bea hasn't even seen him. I don't know why she's saying that. Yeah, I'm putting my shoes on now."

She slides off the bed as she talks, readjusting the blankets behind her like she was never there. I sit up too and start rolling on the liner that goes with my prosthesis. I'm starving, and I'll wear my leg downstairs to raid the fridge. I don't want to check my own phone for at least a few more minutes.

After she hangs up, she asks, "How are you feeling?"

"Like a bird with a french fry."

My headache hasn't gotten worse but it hasn't gotten better either. My shoulder blades are basically pinned to my spine, too stiff to move, and there's a rusty stain on my pillowcase from a cracked scab. I flip the pillow before she mentions it. She looks around to gather her things.

"Shoot. I left my backpack at the diner."

"I'll drive you," I offer, already going to my closet and grabbing a hoodie.

She looks like she wants to lock me in an attic. "You're not driving me anywhere."

"It's five minutes down the road."

She holds out her hand. Keeps giving me the look.

I hand over the hoodie. "Make Tommy take you. He's a very safe driver."

She grimaces.

"Be nice. Remember you agreed you'd be nice?"

"Yes and I've given it up."

My brother used to have so many feelings they'd seep out from under his bedroom door. I'd step into our bathroom and get hit with exhaustion and dread, sunshine and stomachaches. I'm not sure if it stopped or if I just got better at keeping my door shut.

I cross through the bathroom now and knock on his door. He opens up right away, dressed for bed in old plaid pj pants. Even though it's obvious he has no plans for the rest of the night—or let's be real, the rest of time—he's still alarmed when I ask him to take Harlow.

"I'd rather walk," she adds unhelpfully, squeezing into the bathroom behind me.

He shrugs. "I'll do it."

"You don't have to." She catches my eye and adds, "But I appreciate the offer."

For two people who hate each other, they're being quite good. It must be taking Tommy some effort to see Harlow and not think about that time she had a sinus infection and made it a point to throw away her tissues in his room. And I know it takes Harlow's everything not to think about the time in fourth grade—and again last year—when Tommy told the school I was lucky to only have my leg amputated, considering she almost killed me.

I've imagined countless universes, and Harlow's a given in all of them, no matter what. Who am I without her? Just like I don't imagine myself with two legs. Erase my accident, my amputation, and I wouldn't be *me*. But most people believed Tommy, and deep down, I think Harlow does too.

Tommy asks, "Are we going or not?"

"I'd rather be by myself right now," she says.

I roll my eyes. "Is this practice for your breakup? Because your boyfriend will *love* that line."

She gives me a look of drama-club-level disbelief.

"What? Who's he going to tell?" I jerk my thumb in Tommy's direction. He pales and clenches his hands around nothing.

Then no one says anything. Harlow stabs me with her eyes and Tommy glares at Harlow. I look between them both. How am I the bad guy here?

She breathes loudly through her nose. "I'm going now."

"You'll need someone to let you in the diner," I call after her. "And I better get that hoodie back!"

Mom appears at the top of the staircase just as Harlow reaches my door. We didn't even hear her come home. Hair falling out of its bun, bottom of her shirt wrinkled from being tucked in, she puts a hand on her hip and the other on my door frame. "Good night, Harlow," she says firmly.

Harlow says some jumble of words—sorry and goodbye and something else I don't catch—then she's gone.

Mom comes into my room and gives me a once-over. She doesn't flinch at my face, which is starting to throb now that I'm standing.

"Ready to go?" she says.

"Where?" But I know.

"After you've been in a serious car accident, it's customary to call your parents and go to the hospital," she says, voice louder with each syllable.

"But the insurance—"

"Ellis Griffin MacQueen, don't tell me about my health insurance."

I glance through the bathroom doorway. Tommy's still frozen. "Snitch," I spit.

Looking dazed, he takes his phone out of his pocket, rubs the screen on his pant leg, and stares at it.

"He didn't tell me anything. Bea came into the diner going on about 'we should preserve that car as a lesson for kids everywhere.' Were you drinking?" Mom says sharply.

I don't dignify that with a response.

"Let's go. You too." Mom's tone softens when she speaks to him. Subtle, but it's there.

His knuckles whiten around his phone. "I'm not part of this."

"It might be a couple hours," Mom says.

He stands in the bathroom in strangled-looking silence. Something about the yellow light brings me straight back to the day we picked him up from the hospital. I stayed in the car with Goose for five minutes, no plans to take a single step closer, until I thought about what Harlow'd say if she saw me chickening out. He looked genuinely surprised to see me when I came in. Kind of like he looks now.

He glances at his phone again like it will give him a hint about what to do. The screen's still black. "I really don't want to go back there. But I'll come if you want me to."

This makes Mom all kinds of flustered. She's got everything figured out in the rest of her life, so it's weird to see her this way. Ultimately, she just kisses his head and tells him to call if he needs anything, and he stands like a plank of wood in her arms waiting for her to let go.

Mom starts in on me as soon as we back out of the driveway. This is less about my health, more about trapping me in a car for a twenty-minute lecture.

I rake my fingers through my hair and let my hand land on the back of her headrest. "I know you're disappointed."

"I'm *furious*. Bea showed me Harlow's car. She said you had to be going at least twenty over the speed limit."

Try closer to thirty.

"I've already let the Prouts know you'll pay for the repairs in full."

I was going to propose that on my own. How does she expect me to be an adult when she doesn't give me a chance to actually do it? "How much?"

"Bea didn't say. A lot."

"Are you going to tell me I can't go to camp?" Camp Hood doesn't cost much because it's literally just food and cabins, and running is free. But that's not the point.

"I haven't decided."

"You could make me stay home. But then you'd have to put up with me."

She rolls the prospect over in her mouth like an old piece of chewing gum. It's moments like these I wish for a universe where I lived with Dad. He wouldn't hold camp over my head like this. He'd make me pick up some shifts at the diner, and after a few weeks, he'd forget. He'd also forget to buy toothpaste, pick me up from doctor appointments, and show up for parent-teacher conferences, if history's anything to judge by. Mainly I've never lobbied for it because the room at the B and B would be too small to have Harlow sleep over.

"You had your brother pick you up, didn't you?" Her voice is a cliff, and one wrong move will send me over it.

Now that I know he didn't tell, I can't rat him out, either. But Mom knows.

"Did you stop and think about how he'd feel seeing you like this?"

"Like what? Alive?"

Her expression darkens. "He'll do anything you ask. *Anything*. That means you have to look out for him. Seriously, Ellis, do you care about him at all?"

He was happy I called. I did the guy a solid! That's what I thought, anyway. But I also thought we'd automatically get closer after he got back from the hospital, the way people do when they've been through something terrible together. Instead, the rivers and forests that have sprung up between us over the years have grown wild. And if I wanted to tame that wilderness, it's not like he's ever around. Even when he's working he's always just disappeared around a corner, down the basement stairs.

"Well?" she says.

I trace a snow-capped mountain in the fogged window. "Just thinking how if I lived with Dad I wouldn't have to have this conversation."

At the hospital, we wait a couple hours for a cute young doctor to shine a light in my eyes. I let him reset and tape my nose, which feels worse than the original break, even after the numbing spray he mists up there beforehand.

"It's so much easier when they just cut it off," I joke, swinging my right leg a little so the aluminum pylon winks under the fluorescents. The doctor gives me an awkward smile.

"He runs track. Should he take a break from that?" Mom asks, raising her eyebrows significantly.

He agrees that even though I'm not concussed, I should take it easy for a few days, and she makes him write up a note so I can get out of practice. I slip it into my pocket. It'll disintegrate in the wash by the end of the week. He also says I can take over-the-counter pain medicine, ice my face, and best of all, sleep, which means I won't be lying when I tell Harlow she doesn't have to call every three minutes to keep me awake. Tomorrow morning I'll go for a run before school. If the doctor really didn't want me to run, he would've sounded sterner. There's hope for The Plan yet.

I fill a baggie with ice when we get home. Upstairs, Mom's in Tommy's room talking to him in this soothing, measured voice she never uses on me.

The hospital was the safest place for him, but it didn't feel safe. It felt like failure. Somehow, we'd handled my brother so poorly he had to be sent away and reassembled by more skilled hands. But suppose this death wish can't be fixed, only distracted for a while? Maybe this thing will ricochet between us for years, bikes hitting cars hitting trees, underwater, back and forth, until one of us doesn't make it.

I brush my teeth in front of his closed bathroom door, imagining the infinite universes of small talk if I knocked: about Goose and the diner. Track and school. All these things to talk about and nothing to say. He's the one who keeps his hair cut short, walks around the track in gym class when he's supposed to run, but he's not the one who let the bone-deep connection between us fray and disappear. Because Mom's right that I don't know how to look out for him. I don't *know* him. And as I face the closed door between us, I wonder if anything has really changed at all.

Fourteen
TOMMY

Therapists love it when you recognize the things you're good at, so let me say: I am very good at weeding out therapists.

Like this guy across from me. T-shirt-and-jeans, leather-bound note-book, Mr. Let's Talk About Why You're Here. How goddamn original.

I paint in broad strokes. Once there was a boy who felt himself rotting from the inside out. The kind of decay that takes months. Smile so fake his lips cracked and bled and people noticed. A doctor prescribed antidepressants that made him feel more himself—then less. The shrink said high school's hard for everyone and told him to give himself a break. So he took a break from homework. That made people worry. So he took a break from people. They fell away from him like dry pine needles, the ones that burn first when a forest fire blooms.

"Being dead seemed less exhausting," I finish. That's five minutes gone already. Another forty-five and I'll be back in the car with Mom.

Cool Therapist raises an eyebrow. "Has anyone actually bought that?"

They have. Or maybe they just didn't call me on my shit. I'm shrugging on the outside and on the inside wondering is a therapist supposed to talk to me like this.

I don't even need this guy. I'm okay. After Harlow left last night what'd I do? Popped my antidepressant and vitamin D. Drained a goddamn water bottle. Picked up a pencil, first time in weeks, and drew the spooled gray storm cloud that followed me all March. Thinking if I couldn't give Cliff my words, maybe this could be a substitute. And I hung on to that cream-colored shell from him after all. Not because of Harlow but because of me.

This guy crosses his legs at the knee. Closes his bougie-ass notebook. He thinks he can wait me out? Cool Therapist is also Fifth Therapist in Four Weeks. My stamina's off the charts. He's looking at me but I'm not even here. I'm standing in a pool of yellow light, learning Harlow's been fucking with me. Five enormous fluorescent orbs above the bathroom sink, too bright to look at, and she's dumping me through my brother. Because of course. Figuring out why I swam when I did and why I can't talk to Cliff is secondary to figuring out what I'm going to do about her.

A part of me thinks it doesn't matter she's been playing me because when we make out it's hot. This road leads to questions like have I always been attracted to her and didn't know it? And her to me? The answers solid no's. I'm the worse version of Ellis, as she likes to remind me. I see the way she looks at him. He's either oblivious or cruel to not notice. Or both.

"You have to decide to put in the work. I can't do that for you."

I've seen this office before. Four others just like it within a thirty-mile radius. Same soothing off-white walls. Same soft lighting.

An echo, to quote Ms. Russeau. *A copy of the real thing. It's not a bad painting. I just don't see you anywhere in it.*

Cool Therapist leans forward. Elbows on knees. "Want to try that again, or should we call it?"

I imagine leaving early and telling Mom not this one. *These things take time,* she'll say. But she's called the hospital to get another list of referrals once already.

Is Harlow right and nothing's changed? Don't I at least have to try?

"I guess I'm here because of gym class," I say.

Tell him about swimming. Every winter we spend a month of PE doing laps in the indoor pool. It wasn't half bad. If you could pretend not to see the rainbow of hair product at the water's surface, if you didn't mind smelling like chlorine the rest of the day. When I dropped underwater the world got quiet and so did I.

Mom thought I wanted to join the swim team. I thought maybe I did too. I had that long wingspan. Lungs that wouldn't quit even if I sometimes wished they would. Made it all the way through tryouts before Harlow helpfully reminded me I'd never be my brother no matter how hard I tried.

I'll never tell, but she was right in the end. I didn't want an assigned number of laps. I wanted sun on my back and salt stinging my tongue. My eyes shut inside my goggles. Diving down until my eardrums throbbed. Letting my own buoyancy drag me back to the surface.

"What else?"

The wet suit. Ghostly white prunes for fingertips. Hair sun-bleached if I ever let it grow out. Always cold, not that I felt it. I felt nothing. Finally my outsides matched my insides.

"That's not why you're here."

I used to be able to disappear inside my sketchbook for hours at a time and figure anyone out. The trick is to look past their shiny exterior selves and draw two layers under that.

I'm not drawing Harlow ever, but if I did I'd use a hole punch after to evict her from the sketchbook. Then I'd draw us lost in each other like a Klimt couple on the very next page. Block her number but also wear all blue socks and boxer briefs and everything.

I touch my hand to my chest. The old brag of my heart. I am nothing. I am no one. I am not sure what I want.

"I'm here because I want to feel better." And it has nothing to do with Harlow.

Fifteen

HARLOW

"So much for global warming," Chuck Halstead says, stomping his boots in the MacQueen's diner entryway.

West Finch woke to a light dusting of snow. It promptly dissolved into gray slush, but the climate change doubters and deniers aren't missing this opportunity. Snow! At the end of April! It's the fourth time Mom and I have heard that joke this morning, and we haven't even had breakfast yet.

While we wait, we're doing a final review for the town hall tonight, quizzing each other on the latest projections for sand loss volume, moving text around on slides. I have notes of my own spread out on the table too: the start of a petition I want to send Mr. Albertson opposing his decision to halt the jetty destruction. A rather short list of West Finchers most likely to show enthusiasm about the task force Ellis and I are starting. Everyone else on the second, much larger list. Mom and I aren't making much progress, though, because every few minutes someone slides into our table's open seat and wants to know how bad the car is, and am I mad at Ellis, and to my mom: *how mad are YOU?*

"Pretty mad," Mom answers each time with an increasingly strained laugh.

Also because I'm trying to figure out what I'll say to Tommy. Through the window I see Goose rolling around on her back, so he's definitely around.

But I haven't seen him yet. Don't know if he's mad or what he's going to do about it. Stand on the countertop and tell everyone I kissed him without asking? Cry in the basement pantry? It could go either way.

After last night, I almost called off my standing biweekly breakfast with Ellis. But the pancakes Helen makes twice a week are worth suffering for: deeply browned and buttery, the same circumference as the plate beneath them. You can only get them on Wednesdays and Sundays, which is a rule, just like it's a rule MacQueen's has pies but no cakes, except birthday cakes, and you have to pay for dinner and dessert at separate cash registers on opposite ends of the counter because Helen and Jim don't need a joint checking account in their lives, thank you very much.

I should've called Tommy as soon as I fled their house. First thing this morning, even. I know he wakes up early. But how to explain? I *was* planning to break up with him. At least, I was before we started kissing. And then I thought about the artwork for everyone in town. Those shells. How relieved he looked when he said he doesn't want to die or not die and he was glad he could tell me.

And this: a hunk of driftwood the size of a tissue box by his dad's register. It's gotta be from Clifford Samuels, and if Tommy is here and the driftwood is too, that means Tommy hasn't thrown it out yet. Makes no difference to me if he keeps it, but the sight makes my pulse hum.

The bell above the door announces Ellis's arrival. He's flushed and sweat-shiny, looking like he's been beat up. The bruises have spread and changed colors in the last twelve hours, and there's a gooey scab forming under his eyebrow. Somehow his dimples were spared. I let my eyes sweep down the diner's counter once in case Ellis's appearance triggers his brother's, but still no Tommy.

The bubble of conversation bursts, and for a moment, the dining room's all whispers and stares. Then Ellis doffs an imaginary hat and takes a little bow for the crowd.

"Hello, Prouts." He flings himself into the empty chair at our table.

"Oh please. I'm not going to peek," he adds as I throw my elbow over the color-coded map of the town.

It's not so outrageous. People ask me for intel starting two weeks before our town hall, and while anyone can figure out what will happen just by walking the beach, we preserve an air of mystery so people will show up. I'm still amazed how much stock people place in an official pronouncement, considering how skeptical they were of my parents' work when they were first assigned to West Finch. Now most people at least believe the erosion is getting worse. Even if they're not committed to *doing* something about it.

I check my phone for new messages proclaiming forgiveness or hatred or anything at all, while across the table, Mom and Ellis are making some intense eye contact.

"Harlow's told us she gave you permission to drive her car, but I speak for both Caleb and myself when I say we're extremely disappointed," Mom begins.

Then a condensed version of the lecture I got last night, all *We gave Harlow that car to improve her confidence behind the wheel* and *This was a betrayal of our trust.*

"I hadn't thought about it like that," Ellis says, surprisingly somber.

He launches into a perfect apology. He admits he was wrong. He acknowledges that his actions hurt everyone. He offers to pay for the repairs, or work for my parents when school's out, organizing the mountain of files in our dining room, maybe. I'd be impressed if I weren't having an epiphany about how he's never actually apologized to me like he meant it.

Helen comes by a couple minutes later and, a plate of pancakes in hand, glowers at Ellis and says, "You might have a concussion and you went for a run?"

My mom purses her lips like this is what she's been thinking too. It gets me a little panicky because of course they're right. There's reckless and then there's whatever this is. Ellis squints down at the menu as if he won't just eat half of what's on my plate like always. "Dad said running was okay as long as I didn't feel like throwing up."

Jim was the catcher for our high school's championship-winning baseball team twenty years ago when, according to Bea's wife, Yvette, he was known to risk a swing to the head if it meant catching a foul ball. Truly something for Ellis to aspire to.

Helen doesn't look thrilled he's taking his dad's advice over hers, so before either says something they'll regret, I speak up. "Helen, have you had a chance to look over the binder I left you?"

My question makes her look even more unhappy, if that's possible. "Not yet."

"What binder?" Mom's finger pauses above the laptop's backspace key.

"I researched options for saving this place." Then I say to Helen, who's still holding our pancakes hostage, "You can read the first thirty pages for now. I ranked the solutions from most to least effective, then by time required and cost."

"The first thirty pages," Mom repeats.

"A *binder*?" Ellis says.

"There are diagrams," I admit.

Helen doesn't look impressed. Mom totally agrees with me, but she taps the corner of the map I'm still covering with my elbow and says, "Let's worry about the rest of West Finch first."

Finally Helen puts my plate down. It's late April and the pancakes have wild blueberries, tiny and intense. Could Tommy have cooked these for me? I scan the dining room again, half-kneeling on my chair to find a sight line into the bakery kitchen, as Wendy Michaels, West Finch's best and only dentist, informs us from her seat at the counter that these berries are the first harvest of the season.

"Your face looks like a rainbow fish," she adds to Ellis. Then she gets him to smile at her and prove all his teeth are present and accounted for before she lets him dig in.

"Today's the big day, huh?" Ellis says when he's done being examined, tipping his chair back on two legs. "Any shocking revelations?"

"Nothing you don't expect." Mom sips her coffee. "Erosion rate's going up year-on-year. Property damage will soar accordingly. More of the same, unfortunately."

Ellis shakes his head with what only I recognize as mock sadness. "Not what you want to hear." A glint in his eye. "You know, there's a rumor about the Caskills' old house. Some people say it'll be in the flood zone this year. What do you think?"

"Don't answer that!" I interject.

Ellis pretends to be offended. "I'm merely an inquisitive citizen."

"Are not. You've got a bet with someone and you want to find out if you should go double or nothing before the town hall."

He blinks twice. "If that were true, wouldn't you want me to win said bet so I can spoil my friends and loved ones rotten?"

"It's gross. Like betting on when global warming will make the polar bears go extinct."

"That's 2041, right?" He raises his eyebrows expectantly. I'm not laughing. "Speaking of bets, you still owe me ten dollars for the Ocean Drive house."

"There *was* no bet," I say hotly.

He pats my arm, nodding with fake pity. Then speaking to my mother only: "I'll see you tonight, Mrs. P."

"And me! I'll meet you in thirty minutes."

Once he and my mom leave, and I don't have to play town-hall-plans defense, I can properly survey the dining room for potential task force members. Helen hates joining things. Chuck doesn't trust even local government. I spot Mr. Albertson, the mayor, waiting for his coffee near the bakery register. He's kept the town email list under lock and key ever since a few years ago, when Girl Scout troop 3324 blasted out a link to their cookie site and it turned into the reply-all chain from hell. I have a good chunk in my own contact list, but I don't want to get on Mr. Albertson's bad side this early in the task force's life—traitor though he may be for letting the protestors stay at his bed-and-breakfast.

I've got the empty petition on a clipboard in one hand, a fresh pen in the other, and I'm halfway to the counter when I hear Wendy ask, "How *are* you?" in a too-sweet tone.

Tommy's emerged from one of the kitchens wearing his navy-blue apron and a gray MacQueen's T-shirt so old it's gone soft and velvety. I know because I've felt it. Considered sneaking into his bedroom to borrow it. Wearing it to bed. I wouldn't, of course, but that's how nice it is. And— gosh. The skin under his eyes is definitely puffier than usual.

Could be allergies, I suppose. Sudden seasonal allergies.

He hasn't seen me yet. I could make a hasty retreat. But I won't get another chance to speak to Mr. Albertson before the town hall, so I make myself step forward. Can't let a little awkwardness stop me from doing real good for West Finch.

"Happy Wednesday, Mr. Albertson," I say with all the cheer I can muster.

Out of the corner of my eye I see Tommy pause.

Mr. Albertson doesn't so much turn to face me as look down the length of his nose. With a glance at his wristwatch, he asks, "Miss Prout, is school attendance no longer mandatory?"

My smile hangs on for dear life. "They pushed class start times back so students would get more sleep. CDC recommended."

He brushes his closely trimmed gray goatee with the back of his hand, unimpressed.

"I was hoping you could email this out to the town this morning." I thrust the petition at him. "I want to collect as many signatures as possible before tonight."

I wait an eternity while he retrieves a pair of reading glasses, perches them on the tip of his nose, and scrutinizes the mostly blank page. "And this is?"

"A petition," I explain, though it's pretty obvious. "As our mayor, you should listen to us just as closely as you listen to some college kids, don't you think? Plus sending it out would be a good way to reestablish your loyalty to West Finch."

"Excuse me?" Like he doesn't know what I'm talking about.

"Considering your clientele." I raise my eyebrows. "Your *new* clientele."

"Are you referring to the students from California? Because if I didn't put them up, we'd have the blight of camping tents along our shoreline."

If they had to sleep in tents, they'd have left by now, I want to say. But we're veering off course. Tommy brings Mr. Albertson's coffee, not looking at me at all. I suddenly feel small, like a raisin.

Mr. Albertson shakes his head. "College admissions may like this sort of thing, but it won't get you far with me."

Next to us, Wendy taps an empty sugar packet over her cup of coffee, and several seats down, Tommy repeats Chuck Halstead's order back to him three times before Chuck confirms it's right. I blink. A lot. "You think I'm doing this to get into college?"

"Soup on a Scooter. Litterbug Busters. No Sea Turtle Left Behind." He's ticking them off on his fingers. "Not exactly successes."

I shut my mouth. Open it. My teeth feel cold. "I was thirteen when I founded Litterbug Busters."

"And you were thirteen when it stopped."

That stings. Especially because, at the time, he mentioned me during a town hall. *How admirable when youths get involved in their community.*

"You know, I made a donation to the piping plover foundation in your name some years ago. Or is that another thing you've given up?" He frowns at the clipboard. "I can't help you. The West Finch email list is not for promotions of any sort."

I shrivel. He turns to his steaming coffee and I take stock of who heard our exchange. Is he just saying what everyone thinks? Someone touches my arm and I jump.

"Oh, hand it over, Pat. I'll sign," Wendy says, reaching past me toward Mr. Albertson.

I could hug her. Wendy Michaels, dentist and goddess!

My clipboard makes its way around the counter. Mr. Albertson's gaze doesn't leave his newspaper, but every time the petition changes hands, his grip tightens on his mug. I follow the petition to Chuck, who's sitting near Jim's register and the well-populated lobster tank. His signature seems to involve a lot of loop-de-loops. Before I can intercept it, he delivers the clipboard into Tommy's outstretched hand.

This feels just like a misty morning several years ago, when Ellis and I turned a corner and saw a moose on Main Street. My instinct then feels applicable now. Hold very still. Speak softly. Hope the wild animal doesn't do something terrible, like rip up your petition.

"I didn't know you were here," I say.

He raises his eyebrows, unamused. "Where else would I be?"

I don't know. Sleeping for twelve hours because I blabbed to Ellis and broke your heart and pushed you down a big twisty slide of a major depressive episode?

He's staring at me the way he did before we started hooking up, like I'm something stuck to the bottom of his shoe. My stomach knots up a little. So we're going the pretend-we-never-kissed route. Fine. Good.

"Goose looks"—I search for a word that's both kind and true—"*alert* this morning."

"She starts chemo next week."

"Congratulations?"

His knuckles go perilously white against my petition, matching the paper, and okay, he hasn't forgiven me. In fact, he's seconds away from throwing the entire clipboard into the lobster tank.

"That came out wrong. I meant, I know that must be expensive. I'm glad you can afford to do this for her."

He squints like he's trying to work something out about me. It's the look Ellis gets when I'm telling him about a big, complicated problem I'm trying to fix, and he's almost figured out what I should do to solve everything. Except in this case, the problem Tommy's working on is me. He holds my gaze so long the back of my neck starts to itch. Finally I nod at the petition.

"Can I have that back?"

"What's the magic word?"

Either he's screwing with me or this is a test. Something he told me, once, when I was supposed to be paying attention? Talking has never been our thing, though. Especially not these last few weeks. My face flushes at the thought of the dark basement stairwell. Coffee filters. Focus.

What's the one thing he'd most want to hear? Ellis's off-hand remark echoing off the bathroom tiles. Tommy's shock multiplied in the mirror above the sink. I've got it.

"It's sorry, isn't it?" I keep my voice low. "For last night, I'm—"

"Please."

"Okay. But I shouldn't have said anything to Ellis. That was wrong."

His expression flickers. Was that all the explanation he needed? Are we good? Then his gaze drops from mine, down to the form in his hand. He clicks the pen twice. Scrawls his name on the next blank line. Slaps the whole thing onto the counter and slides it toward me.

"*Please*," he says again. "That's the magic word."

I grab for the board but his hand's still weighing it down. Electricity hums across the inches between our fingertips. Static electricity, must be. I did thoroughly wipe my shoes at the front door. One side of his mouth pulls back into a lopsided smile. Then he disappears into the kitchen. I hug the clipboard to my chest.

I survived. There are eight names in ink at the top of my petition. And I have no idea what just happened.

Sixteen

ELLIS

I'LL LEAVE WITHOUT YOU, Harlow's text says when I climb out of the shower. Like it's been two hours since I left her at the diner, when it's been thirty minutes max.

Plus it's an empty threat. The worst she could do is quit banging on the front door, use the key she knows is hidden in the flowerpot, and discover me on day one of a new ritual: searching my brother's bedroom for I don't know what exactly. All I know is Mom was right that I don't know him. And that has to change.

I peer into his closet. Between his mattress and the box spring. Inside shoeboxes under his bed, sides scribbled over with Sharpie, and paintings leaning against the wall, shimmering with some meaning that never, ever reveals itself to me. A gun or misplaced razor blade would be obvious, but a few quick internet searches have taught me almost anything can mess a person up. Tommy's orange bottle of pills—antidepressants, I guess?—sits on his nightstand. I count four left for the month, as there should be, though he could be hiding them or flushing them down the toilet.

How did we get here? The millions of ways my path split from his and his from mine have led to this: two guys, one running as fast as he can and the other not moving.

We were Tommy'n'Ellis even when our parents tried to coax us apart. Especially then. My current bedroom was a guest room for the first six years of our lives, then a place where Dad crashed while he looked for a new house he never found.

The divorce sucked the oxygen out of whatever space my parents occupied. It sent us running for cover under our beds, or into the dry bathtub with pillows and blankets, gasping for air.

If your brother joined the circus, would you? said Mom when we gleefully recounted how our third-grade teachers had accidentally swapped us after recess that day. *Yes!* we both shouted.

Until I met Harlow. Pure luck that I was there and Tommy wasn't. Would everything have turned out the same but different if I'd been home that day and he was in my place?

Harlow and I were magic. We walked on water and landed in an effortless tangle between the jetty's rocks. My ankles were hers. Her wrists were mine. The wind stole hairs from each of our scalps, confessions from the backs of our throats, but unlike with Tommy, I couldn't predict anything that came out of her mouth. She sighed and sent the tide out. She blinked and scattered the clouds.

If your brother moved into a cave
shaved his head
jumped off a cliff
would you? Mom asked that night.

Yes, yes, yes, we answered in near unison. I was only a half-beat late.

Tommy came to the beach with us the next day. It was June, and instead of diving into the water we let it numb us, proceeding farther only once we'd lost feeling in our feet, ankles, legs.

Tommy sensed something coming between him and me. We both laughed when a wave finally wiped Harlow out, but Tommy laughed the loudest. He told her the salt water she'd swallowed would make her go crazy. One of those lies with just enough truth in it to make her go nuts trying to find out how screwed she was.

I moved to the bedroom across the hall within the month.

Tommy stayed behind in the room with the slanted ceiling and the sunrises and our names carved into the baseboard inside the closet where Mom will never find them.

Harlow laughed and I grew three inches taller.

She believed I could fly, so I learned to run.

In some universe, unraveling this cord that binds Harlow to me, me to her, would change everything.

In this universe, it's not that simple. I don't want to hold her at arm's length. I want to explain about checking Tommy's room and ask will she do it while I'm at Camp Hood. But I can't mention camp. I want to tell her she was right about how quickly Olivia has gotten on my nerves, but can't admit she knows my patterns better than I do. Not when she won't trust me enough to say who she's hooking up with.

She's on the front porch. As soon as I lock the door behind me she grabs my arm and hauls me down the steps, scolding, "Ruth Ann is always on time."

"We're taking the bus?" I yelp.

"Don't be dramatic." This because I've planted myself in the middle of the driveway. "Taking the bus will keep us humble."

"It will make us look like sixth graders." Also, West Finch's only bus stop is a mile away. I ran four miles this morning and have practice this afternoon. My right leg's ghost is doing this awesome thing where it cramps whenever I least expect it. My nose hurts. Not that I'll admit any of that.

But Harlow does have her town hall speech tonight, and if we're fighting, I can't cheer loud enough to embarrass her.

And I did wreck her car.

"If we're walking all this way, let's at least talk about something interesting." We're hardly past the driveway and already my leg feels hot.

Harlow's all smiles. She even skips past the Caskills' house in those yellow combat boots. "Okay."

"Topic is, the identity of your secret boyfriend. Discuss."

She flails. "He isn't—Don't you—I *will not* discuss!" Her face a tomato.

"I'm a junior with a driver's license, and I'm taking the bus with you," I remind her. "You have to give me something."

"We're being environmentally friendly. That's your reward." She pokes me in the biceps.

"I'll be sure to let our friends from California know." I poke her back. Then I say, "Oh. OH. Is it a protestor? Is it that goth guy?"

We stop walking so she can pretend to puke in some bushes on the side of the road.

"Sorry, not goth," I say over the retching. "Aspiring-sad-indie dad. He listens to songs about slowly growing apart from the love of his life and finding solace in a bottle of bourbon."

"Sounds like you've given him some serious consideration." She waggles her eyebrows.

"I'm not the one who gave my tenth birthday money to an endangered—"

"Nearly threatened!"

"—bird. You two are obviously meant to be."

She and her boots stomp ahead and won't say anything else on the subject.

But once we're on the bus, I eye every dude who gets on after us. I'll be supportive, whoever he is. Within reason. The first one has pretty blue eyes . . . and a thin mustache that unflatteringly accentuates his upper lip. Ugh. The next guy carries his lacrosse stick down the aisle like it's an important part of his anatomy. Harlow doesn't react to either of them, thank god, just pulls out her vocab flashcards.

"This weekend let's make a list of all the schools you like and just start emailing the coaches," she says, expertly shuffling the cards. "I know you wanted to let them email first, but in chem I heard Coop say he got invited to an overnight at UConn."

Even though I'm faster right now, Coop's been on varsity since freshman year, so he's getting invited everywhere. I don't like that she knows, don't know what to say. "Go Huskies."

"Calm down. I refuse to go to school in Connecticut." A clump of wavy hair escapes her ear. "You should be doing overnight visits by now too."

Oh? I should be running practices with college teams and eating pasta in dining halls and getting coffees with coaches who are excited about my potential? I didn't know.

She taps the flashcards on her lap to straighten them out. Raises an eyebrow. *Truculent* stares up at me in my own handwriting. "Do you disagree?"

I slouch down, pick at a hole in the vinyl seat in front of us. "No."

"Then stick to The Plan."

Meaning Harlow's grades, my mile times, the same college. The Plan has been The Plan since the middle school guidance counselor passed out high school course books. Pages of electives that could make you into anyone you wanted to be. By the end of the week, Harlow and I had the next four years planned out.

Most dreams fade over time, but The Plan only gets more specific. Whenever we miss a milestone, we add a shiny new detail like a fresh coat of paint.

Harlow gets a B+ in bio? Announce one should never aim for Providence when one could go to Princeton.

I get stuck on JV all sophomore year? Decide not only do I want to get recruited, but that The Plan also requires an athletic scholarship.

Getting a free ride to college will be a thank-you to my parents, who raised money for my running blade when we found out insurance doesn't consider anything medically necessary but a walking foot. Then I won't owe them anything or be responsible for anyone but myself. I won't have to come home if I don't want to. There might not even be a West Finch to come back to.

"Did you sign up for the May SATs?"

She makes a show of squinting at the card in front of her—*germinate*—and turning it over to examine the definition. "I'll wait until June."

I suppose secret boyfriends are distracting.

Her math was near perfect. Her math's always damn near perfect. She likes the rules: tackle a problem the right way, everything works out. Happy ending always. But I don't get how she crashed and burned so hard on a little vocab. According to The Plan, she should've beat me. Instead she halved my verbal score.

I think we may need a new plan. But I'm not ready to be the one who says it.

"I thought of a name for the task force," I say instead.

She doesn't look up from her flashcards, but she turns her head slightly. I get a nose full of hair. No one scent I can pick out. Just her.

"Bring Back Our Beach."

As she mouths the words silently, a smile breaks out over her entire face.

She breathes and all the windows fog.

She hums and the sky spits snow.

She hooks her ankle around mine and my pulse lands on a brand-new rhythm.

Then I go, "So, about tomorrow morning. Does your boyfriend have a car?"

———

While Olivia squeals and sandwiches my bruised face between her palms, and Coop calls me a turnip, I follow Harlow with my eagle eyes as she opens her locker.

Didn't she tell me the combination once? Should I search it for clues?

Watching for her in the halls between classes, and the one time I see her she's alone, no boy toy in sight.

I sit with the track team at lunch. Harlow isn't around, but that's normal. She says she eats in the computer lab or sometimes the library. It always makes me feel a twinge of guilt, but never enough to invite her to sit with us. Knowing her secret now, maybe it's not as sad as it sounds.

Coop squeezes little packets of hot sauce over his usual spread of string cheese, shredded chicken, and several hard-boiled eggs. That finished, he delicately picks up an egg with two fingers. A sudden, heinous intuition punches me in the throat.

"I have a real question that needs a real answer," I say, resisting the urge to gag. "Are you and Harlow hooking up?"

The hard-boiled egg slips between Coop's fingers and goes flying past two tables, sliding to rest under the third. He stares after it, stunned.

"She's seeing someone but I don't know who," I explain. He's still looking wistfully after his lost egg. "So I was thinking, who wouldn't she want to tell me about?"

He turns to me with an incredulous look. "Come *on*."

"It's not you?" I'm so relieved it's embarrassing.

"It's no one! She's trying to make you jealous."

He's convinced there's something between Harlow and me, but my love for her isn't the romantic kind. I have plenty of options nowhere near as messy as that would be.

I think back to last night, how flustered she got when I mentioned her breakup in front of Tommy. "This guy's real. I know it."

Coop loads chicken onto his fork and lets out a happy sigh. "You and your wife are delusional. It's friggin' adorable."

I talk about West Finch as little as possible at school, so of course he doesn't understand. That's kind of the point.

I scarf down what's left of my sandwich and sling my backpack over my shoulder so I can test my next theory: all these lunch periods in the computer lab aren't just because Harlow's a nerd. Her mystery man must be a nerd too.

———

I think at first I must be in the wrong place, though there's only one computer lab. Twenty-nine dark desktop screens and her, glowing, alone in the farthest corner with her peanut butter sandwich.

"I thought there'd be other people here." I slide into the plastic chair beside her.

"Nope," she says, sounding pleased. "I get a lot of work done."

She swears me to secrecy, then shows me part of her town hall slideshow. The photos are a mix of the ones she takes after most big storms—shattered roads; homes spilling into the surf—and several black-and-white images from a version of West Finch we've never seen.

"There used to be a set of train tracks there." The screen fuzzes around her finger. "And a pier, like at Old Orchard Beach."

There are pictures of recent happy times too. The annual clambake. Mrs. Samuels reading a chapter book aloud to her fourth-grade class. Two kids building a sandcastle, backs to the sun, faces so underexposed they could be anyone. They make me nostalgic for the small-town life I've pretty much grown out of.

"This is really good," I tell her. "It'll remind people why they've stayed in West Finch."

Besides the normal reasons, like the nonexistent property market that makes it impossible to sell a house. The people who stay in West Finch never leave, and the ones who leave never come back. Hardly a choice. If you want to set a national record or just visit another country, only place to be is in that latter group.

"The Army Corps of Engineers still supports tearing the jetty down. We only have to convince Mr. Albertson. They'll complete the demo, we'll reinforce the diner's foundation . . ." She's beaming, and it's not just the computer's blue light. "Go eat your lunch. I'll have official Bring Back Our Beach work for you later."

———

Later looks like this: Harlow's indomitable march down the hallway as she cajoles, intimidates, and threatens all in her path. Some kids are trying to catch buses and she throws herself in front of them, backs them into lockers. Each confrontation ends with them signing whatever's on her clipboard. She's effective. Can't deny that.

Coop, Olivia, and I are sprawled at the end of the junior hallway killing time before practice. Coop leans against our pile of gym bags and backpacks while Olivia and I sit with our backs against the blue metal lockers. She keeps kissing the side of my face, asking does it hurt. Three times Coop silently mimes barfing without Olivia noticing. He's more like Harlow than he'll ever know.

When Harlow gets close enough for me to see the second clipboard tucked under her arm, I groan. The sheet's printed with dozens of blank lines for names and email addresses. The heading: PETITION TO IGNORE PRO-TESTORS AND DEMOLISH WEST FINCH JETTY, AS PREVIOUSLY AGREED.

"I'm not signing." Coop pouts as she waves the clipboard under his nose. "I trusted you. How could you let this happen to his beautiful face?"

"It's not that bad," I say at the same time Harlow says, "It's not my fault."

She holds out the second clipboard to me.

I think of single-serve applesauce, ruled paper covered in shaky cursive. When we were nine, Harlow organized the fourth grade in a peaceful sit-in to demand recess be extended by ten minutes.

Maybe sit-out is more accurate: picture forty runty kids scattered around the playground, sitting with our legs crossed, unmovable. We had a quiet, heads-on-desks recess as punishment the next day, and it was ten minutes longer than usual, which even now strikes me as cruel. Must not have been Mrs. Samuels's idea.

In the junior hallway, Olivia winds her fingers through my hair and sticks out her lower lip. "Can't you do it tomorrow?"

"Coastal erosion won't wait," Harlow reminds us, tapping her pen on the clipboard.

Olivia frowns. "Coastal what?"

I pick up the second clipboard for old times' sake. Coop snickers.

I'm delusional. I'm whipped. Whatever. Harlow and I know each other's worst parts and still like each other. Coop and Olivia will go their whole lives without experiencing anything close to what we've got. I feel sorry for them. That's what I'm telling myself.

I chase down teachers and custodial staff, the tennis and softball teams, the entire boys' locker room in all its degrees of undress. Dad picks me up after practice and I accost every last person at the diner before the town hall, even three-year-old Garrett Turner who can't spell his own name yet. When there are no more blank lines, I draw some. I channel Harlow, I don't take no for an answer, all in the hopes it will be enough to lock down my place in her good graces until Camp Hood in July.

No promises after that.

Seventeen

HARLOW

A red fish pings me between the eyes and falls to the floor. Ten rows of folding chairs back, Ellis grins and sinks his arm again into the two-pound bag of gummies on his lap.

It says a lot about how things are going that I barely flinch.

So does the fact that Tommy's not here. Not standing in the back with his parents or even sulking by the water fountains. My parents' annual presentation is the most important of all of West Finch's monthly town halls. Everyone should be here, even those of us with dying dogs and puzzling not-relationships that may or may not be over.

The more I think about how he acted this morning, the less sense it makes. Didn't he hear what Ellis said last night? His stunned expression in their bathroom sure made me think so. Or maybe he wants to let things go back to how they were before. Kissing. Fun. Except there's no way I'm that lucky.

But not even Tommy can dampen my mood tonight because the town hall is the best ninety minutes of every month. For starters, it's held in the gymnasium at Black Bear Elementary, which always makes me think of freeze tag and chocolate milk cartons. Ellis and I go no matter what, even when it's just the local lobstermen griping about permits. We sit in the back, pick from one of those two-pound bags of red gummy fish, and make wagers: how long until someone storms out; when Mr. Albertson will let his first *godammit* fly. Either can be as early as the first ten minutes if the topic's a juicy one.

Tonight it's standing room only. Three seats are occupied by the protestors, which shouldn't be allowed. Ellis is in our usual spot near the back. The skin on his nose has turned purple and yellow, and he's wearing what I'm pretty sure is my blue bandana around his neck. He could go straight from a Boy Scouts meeting to robbing a bank. When he sees me looking, he launches another red fish over the heads of ten rows of people. It soars past me and hits the bottom of the wooden podium. Mom gives us a disapproving look, but Mr. Albertson's too busy shushing everyone to notice.

"Good evening," he begins, 8:00 p.m. on the dot. "Before we dive into the undoubtedly fascinating content the Prout family has planned for us, a brief reminder to lock your homes and cars. In April we saw a hundred fifty percent increase in reported thefts, and the Seaborough police force has advised me most break-ins can be prevented by such small precautions as turning the deadbolt, especially as we head into the summer, when there will be anonymous tourists roaming about."

There's some murmuring. More than a few people are trying to puzzle out how much a 150 percent increase is. And what a roaming, anonymous tourist looks like.

"Whose window got smashed?"

"No one's window was broken, Chuck," says Mr. Albertson. "This is merely a cautionary tale."

"I bet it was that one time Fran forgot where she put her wallet."

"And a half!" Ellis calls out. "One and a half!"

"Remember that, Fran?" Fran's husband, Joe, nudges her.

"It was under Norma the whole time," Fran says.

Norma is their well-fed cat.

"This is neither the time nor place to go into detail," Mr. Albertson says as half the room gawks at Fran, who's waving gleefully, just happy to be mentioned. "You all have newspaper subscriptions. Feel free to peruse the crime section on your own time."

The only crimes attributed to West Finch in the *Portland Press Herald* are things like twelve-year-old Stevie Turner calling 9-1-1 because a seagull came down their chimney.

While Artie reads out the password for his *Herald* digital subscription, and Wendy Michaels searches her purse for a pen, Tommy slips into the back and stands next to his parents, a well-loved Red Sox cap pulled low over his eyes.

"I also received a request that all dogs stay leashed on the beach in consideration of the piping plovers. We're fortunate these birds have chosen our proud, historic town as their home for the next three months, so let's do our part to ensure they don't become puppy chow." The joke elicits a few groans, which makes Mr. Albertson visibly pleased.

If those birds are really building a nest they're being awfully slow about it. This is why they're endangered. Nearly threatened. Whatever. Reluctantly I turn my attention to the protestors in their three stolen seats. That sad indie guy I kicked out of Tommy's homecoming party. Next to him, a tall-ish white woman with long auburn hair, and on her other side, a similarly pale-yet-sunkissed woman with a bright blue ponytail.

Mr. Albertson continues. "In the interest of time, I suggest we move on to the topic at hand. Caleb?"

Dad takes a deep breath. In his sneakers with the good arch support and a short-sleeve button-up, he sticks out like a guppy in a gumball machine. He goes to the podium and Mr. Albertson takes his vacated seat beside me, the only one available. I reach into my backpack and pass him the petition Ellis and I worked on today.

"You're lucky it's not an election year," I whisper.

He looks up at me from under his bristly gray eyebrows and clucks his tongue in warning, but takes the pages and tucks them into his jacket pocket.

"Thank you for coming out, everyone," Dad says into the podium's mic, and promptly drops his notes.

Between me, him, and the four Turner kids in the next row over, we manage to pile the notecards back together in an unordered mess. But both Dad and I know he doesn't need them.

"Right," he says at last. "West Finch lost nearly five and a half feet of beach over the last twelve months, three times greater than the typical average."

He outlines potential solutions: continue to replenish the beach with hauled sand twice a year; make the jetty larger or smaller (you can argue it either way, that's how little data is available); build a second breakwater; demolish the jetty altogether. Of course, that last one should've already happened by now. I twist in my seat to see if the protestors have any reaction to this (remorse, preferably), but the two women are listening quietly with their hands folded in their laps, and the guy is lost in his phone. Behind them, Helen puts an arm around Tommy's shoulders. Is he as upset as he looks, and she's comforting him? Did he tell her what Ellis said last night?

Dad explains that, although one solution may be more effective than the others, we can't know for sure how the ocean currents and surrounding ecosystem will react. Each option has its own slide with images I picked out. When it's over, there's some anemic applause. Dad offers to take a few questions as I hurry to the podium to prepare our second set of slides.

"Yeah, I don't believe in global warming," Chuck says when my dad calls on him, which isn't exactly a question and is in fact news to no one.

While Mom and Chuck bicker about the believability of cold, hard, scientific facts, the other attendees chat with neighbors, swap folding chairs with people a few rows ahead and behind, and treat this like the monthly town party it is. Except Tommy. Now that I'm behind the podium I can watch him easily. He's still leaning against the wall by the door, hands in his pockets, and I just *know* he is not okay. Recovered people don't leave goodbye boxes and paintings unmoved for a month. I picture myself walking back there in front of everyone, wrapping my arms around him myself.

Something red flies perilously close to my face. Tearing my eyes from Tommy, I pick up the gummy fish that landed on the podium. Ellis mimes like he's going to throw another. Mr. Albertson gestures to his watch's face. How long was I staring? Feeling hot, I press a key on the laptop so that a color-coded bird's-eye view of West Finch fills most of the wall behind me. A hush falls over the room and right away I feel better, or at least like I know what to do next. This is the part everyone came for. Some of the senior citizens get up and approach the projection to get a closer look, until the shadows of their heads pop into frame and others shout at them to sit down. A few people seated in the very last rows actually stand on their chairs to see properly.

"Although it's difficult to hear, this update shouldn't be too much of a shock," I begin. That's one of the things I like to do: remind people this isn't new information. "The dark red section—the area likely to see the most severe property damage and beach loss in the next twelve months—has expanded since last year to include Bayside Road, Birch Street, Shell Street, Pine Drive—"

"Aw, man," Ellis says from the back. He turns, still standing on his chair, and hands Artie a twenty-dollar bill. I glare and wait for him to face forward before continuing.

"Long Shore, Schooner Way . . . and all of Shoreline." The diner's street. I try to catch Tommy's eye, but he's burning a hole in the map behind me, arms crossed. Heat blooms in my face again. *Get it together, Prout.* I continue. "Hurricane season officially starts June first. We probably won't get the worst of it, though, until closer to peak—" I hit the clicker, and 128 DAYS floats in huge text on the screen behind me. "Powerful storm surges, seventy-five-mile-an-hour wind. It's all coming and we have a hundred days to do something about it."

I use the little remote to dim the gym lights and everyone ooohs. Behind me, a slideshow of collapsing homes and businesses over the years.

"Two years ago, Congress ordered the Army Corps of Engineers to assess the jetty and take care of it once and for all. They were on track to see that plan through until just last month."

Here I look pointedly at the protestors. The one with the blue ponytail—their ringleader—arches a brow.

"Although I'm sure he had good intentions, Mayor Albertson caved to the opinions of people who don't even live here when he put the jetty demolition on hold. He thought there'd be more blowback online than in his own backyard. But he was wrong." I hold up a copy of the petition. Mom puts her hand over her eyes, and beside her, Mr. Albertson's ears are turning red. "Three hundred people have called for action today alone. The state and federal government owe us this aid. They built the jetty in the first place! But there are steps we can take too. Fundraising from the tourists who enjoy our beach. Demanding the attention of local and national media.

"Which is why we're putting together a task force of like-minded people who want to help. It's called Bring Back Our Beach. The first meeting will be a letter-writing campaign next week. Look for the flyer in your mailbox. I'll see you there!"

I'm out of breath when I finish, but that's nothing compared to Mr. Albertson, who's a few shades from purple. People clap politely, except for Ellis, who augments his applause with several whoops. Then the blue-haired protestor's hand shoots up.

"I have a question," she says without waiting for me to call on her. "Why is this so urgent?"

An easy one. I smile and find the button for the laser pointer.

"There are nine buildings—that's potentially millions in property damage—sitting in the high-risk zone today. As you can see, this includes part of Main Street, which is the lifeblood of this community. If we don't take action now, we'll lose these structures within the decade. Destroying the jetty is the fastest, cheapest path to changing that reality."

The gym hums with appreciative murmuring. I nod at Minister Dickens, whose hand went up next, but the protestor with long, red-brown hair is talking now.

"Demolition on that scale will disturb the ecosystem and impact the fishing industry. That's the most important part of your economy, right?"

"The research on that is inconclusive." My smile's still pleasant, but my hands are fists at my sides. "We don't have much time to act, so it's a risk worth taking. Minister Dickens?"

"Are you familiar with Newtok, Alaska?" the blue-haired woman cuts in.

In the front row, Mom's eyebrows try to send me a silent cease-and-desist order. I ignore them. "Is that where you spent last spring break?" I retort.

The protestor smirks. "They were being displaced by rising sea levels too. They voted to relocate their town. The government's going to buy everyone's homes, and the residents are moving to another town a few miles away."

"Is that true?" Bea Hirsch asks from the second row.

Dad tilts his head, absently shuffles his speaking notes. "A few smaller towns have tried that. It's an interesting idea."

Interesting, sure. Practical, not even a little. The houses in West Finch aren't anything special, but funding like that still takes years to approve. Nowhere near fast enough to save the diner.

"It's not an option," I say. "People's homes and businesses are at risk *today*."

"So that means you don't have to do the right thing?" the third protestor calls out. He's hunched awkwardly in his aisle seat. Clutching his phone, I realize. Recording this whole exchange.

"The right thing is to help people," I say through my teeth. "After we tear down the jetty—"

"Once the jetty's gone, the Army Corps of Engineers won't help you anymore," the long-haired woman says. "They'll tell you you're on your own."

The residents of West Finch look back and forth from the protestors to me like they're following the Ping-Pong match of the century. Where are the budding revolutionaries who signed my petition only hours ago?

Mr. Albertson keeps jumping to his feet like, okay, *now* he's going to restore order, then dropping back into his chair. Mom mouths at me to *sit down*. Near the back, Ellis's mouth is catching flies. The protestor with the phone holds it higher and says in a booming voice, "Why are you pushing a solution that will make things worse?"

I search the crowd for Tommy. He must be loving this. He's still against the far wall, but the messy public argument has pulled him out of his slouch. He looks on edge, like he's waiting for something, and I have a wild thought that somehow he knew the protestors were going to do this to me. Is this karma because I didn't actually break up with him like I was supposed to?

"Let's all ground ourselves," the blue-haired woman says, like we're in yoga class, like she didn't start this. "The point is, an easy solution in the short term becomes a bigger problem in the long term. You're simply not painting a full picture."

"Fuck the full picture," I spit. "*And* your sancti-fucking-monious attitude."

How's that for vocabulary! I expect cheers. Yvette doing that thing where she whistles with her fingers. Instead, a collective gasp goes up around the gymnasium.

"Hey! Mr. Albertson!" someone calls out from the back. Tommy's waving his arm over his head. "It's one question per person max, right? Can we wrap this up?"

There's no such rule. In fact, one town hall, Mr. Albertson and Bea argued for twenty minutes straight about whether riding her motorcycle home after 10:00 p.m. violated West Finch's noise ordinances. They only stopped because Mr. Albertson had to use the restroom.

Mr. Albertson had almost landed in his chair again, but at Tommy's prompt, he springs to his feet and puffs out his chest. "Rules are rules," he agrees, looking relieved. "One question each. Exactly right. We'll have to ask our visitors to listen for the remainder of the meeting."

Since we can't handle more Q & A, Mr. Albertson locates the minutes from the town board meeting and reads them aloud until nine. I sit beside Mom, her hand heavy on my shoulder like a warning. Especially useful when Bea leans forward from the row behind to whisper in my ear, "You better tell that boy thank you," and I almost jump out of my seat and land in the rafters.

She's right. I should. And I can picture it too: I'd excuse myself to go to the water fountain, pass him on my way, and give him a look full of Meaning that he'd immediately understand. A few seconds later he'd follow me out. I'd be looking at the kindergarteners' art on the bulletin board and he'd come up behind me, spin me around, stroke my cheek with his thumb.

In the town hall's front row, I flush and smile at my lap. But by the time I twist around in my seat, the boy with the buzz cut and newfound chivalrous streak is already gone.

Eighteen
TOMMY

Through my bedroom door like a flash flood. Hair three times its normal size. Lips parted to explain but I know why she's here, like Ellis knows, like maybe everyone knows and me last.

I touch her skin and see everything that's led to this.

———

It's six days ago and everything in MacQueen's makes me think of her.

Fresh coffee so hot I can trace its path through me. Lemonade, the powdered kind that comes in cans. A drawing I did once: the earth black and the waves black through the seawall's cracks and the wall itself a ghost. Concrete paver rough with handprints out back, hers and his and mine.

People say lobsters can't feel but if trees can communicate through their leaves and roots maybe we don't understand everything yet. When I first started working I'd wrap them in damp newspaper and chill them in the fridge beforehand. But that's not fast enough.

Now I make deals with myself. If I kill a hundred lobsters this week, Goose's tumor will shrink. If I earn a hundred bucks in tips every day, I can move her first chemo appointment one week earlier. So for Goose I pluck the lobsters from their glass tank at the end of the counter. Slow swim through the air. No screams when I toss them in the boiling water because they can't.

"When my dad cooks lobsters, he kills them first by sticking his knife right here. It's more humane," Harlow told me once. I picture it again now: her tapping the tender, freckled center of her forehead, a spot I'm never going to kiss now, should've when I had the chance. Unbearably earnest. The way she gets about even the smallest things if she cares for them.

I try. The tip of the knife splits the lobster's skull with a crack. Its legs and antennae shiver straight, go limp.

———

It's five weeks ago and I've planned for all of it.

Goose: bathed, nails trimmed, dog food bin in my closet full. A note with the date of her next vet appointment. My possessions: donated to strangers or labeled for family and friends. My art—only the decent stuff—pressed between cardboard, tied off with string. Life's a campground and I've reached the end of my stay. Leave no trace.

The only loose end is Harlow. If she jumped off a bridge, my brother would follow. No. Jump first. With me out of the picture, he'll probably let her feed Goose treats and take her on walks. I don't know what to do about that. Can't make myself care.

I don't feel anything through all of this. At the hospital, my doctor will explain this was my depression talking. Then why am I still numb when I'm on my meds? It's a different flavor of nothing, a more bearable variation, but nothing all the same. They don't have a good answer for that.

———

It's seven weeks ago and I'm backing away from the check-in table. Half the junior class gripping number two pencils like this is the first day of the rest of their whatever. I wasn't going to register but even art schools want to brag about their students' standardized test scores.

Not that my future's anything but fucked. Ms. Russeau showed me old portfolios from students who got into RISD and SCAD. Their warm-up sketches alone could drown a person. My work next to theirs like a rat beside a puppy. But my brother and Harlow are leaving West Finch with or without me. Either I get out or get left behind.

Alphabetical seat assignments posted on the lobby bulletin board next to where my brother's standing. He cracks a joke and then it's him and Coop laughing, me smiling like I get it. Imagine sitting side by side for three hours taking a test that will prove just how different we are. Smile harder so maybe then it will reach my eyes.

The thing about the SATs is no one makes you study. You sign up and guidance counselors stop worrying about you. If for some reason you just leave on test day they figure you'll sign up for the next one. And if you accidentally catch Harlow's eye, and she opens her mouth, flip her off on your way out the double doors.

———

It's four months ago. Christmas lights and electric menorahs wink down the hallways of the cardiac unit. In the space between Cliff's jaw and the collar of his gown I see bones through skin. Not even doctors can fully mend a broken heart.

"What have you got for me?" he says, eyes twinkling, looking almost like himself now that they let him wear his red cap.

The sound like a wind chime being born as the treasures cascade into his lap. Sea glass in perfect triangles and squares. Shells intact, no holes, no chips, sturdy enough to drop from a height. The best I could find.

Cliff levels me with his skyscraper gaze. He can see everything from there, even lying in bed looking up at me. "Anything else?"

Third time in two days I've been here but I still can't make myself show him the page in my back pocket. A contour drawing of his house made without lifting my pencil. Supposed to be. But I kept losing my place, leaving and dipping back in, until I ruined it.

"What more do you want?"

He doesn't say anything. I sound angry. It's just that art happens in my head and my head is no longer a safe place to be.

I flip the dusty baggie over a second time and shake crumbs onto his white hospital blanket.

———

It's six months ago and Ruby's dragging her easel as far away from mine as she can. We're three days into the still life arranged in the center of the room—unblemished plastic oranges and grapes scattered among cups, saucers, and a pleated blue cloth I've been trying to get just right. When Ms. Russeau tries to talk her out of moving, I think of joining in. It will ruin her painting. I'm not worth that.

Ruby layers more black on her lips and paint on her canvas. Alters the light bouncing off the cups. The shading on each grape.

One day we're the only ones there after school. She's working on my cloth. Her palette a swimming pool.

"Don't talk to me," she says after Ms. Russeau leaves us to check on the sculpture students next door.

Twice Ruby goes back to the paint table. While she shakes a container of phthalo blue acrylic, I tell her what Harlow's done, why she's not trustworthy. Ruby says nothing. I tell her again, adding more details: the Lucases' mailbox that went flying off the post and landed at the pedestal of their birdbath. My brother's face, drained of blood, like a new coloring book.

Ruby drags her brush in a spiral and lets the phthalo blue run into the black white red on her palette. "Maybe your problem is that you think Harlow Prout is always the problem."

At the end of the week we hang all our still lifes in a single row down the hallway. Everyone agrees she captured the blue cloth the best. So real you could tie it around your neck.

———

I'm fourteen and my brother and I haven't had a real conversation in five years.

We talk weather, sports, rights to first shower in the morning while the water's hot, forgotten house keys, the location of missing English-class novels. These exchanges run up to but no more than five sentences. They naturally die out beyond that.

We're fourteen and Harlow moved here when we were nine. Anyone can do that math.

———

I'm twelve, asking which dog's been in the shelter the longest. The volunteer leads me to a pit bull mix with behavioral problems and a stubborn case of worms. Goose is the second-most tenured resident.

She comes when I call. Sits when I ask. Sleeps in my bed. Without talking we sense when the other is sad or sick, like we're the same collection of thoughts and feelings in different bodies. It's familiar and dangerous. I've had something like it before. I ask the internet: Do dogs get tired of their people?

———

I'm eleven. I wave my finger over the countertop candle's flame and stare at the back of my brother's head. Waiting for a shiver. A twitch. Anything that shows he can feel me through the force field of Harlow sitting across from him, kicking his chair and humming.

My fingerprint tight. Ellis bows low over his math homework, tackling the problems one by one in tidy rows. Mom walks into the room and I stand with my hands clasped behind my back, finger pulsing. "What's that smell?" she says. I spin the candle so she can see. Sea salt vanilla.

———

I'm nine and now that Ellis is hurt my parents are getting back together. I'm certain. Dad sleeps on the couch and Mom never looks at his face when they're talking but that's not as important as how bad they want us to be a family again.

I'm hastily enrolled in a free summer art program in Portland. Mrs. Samuels gave Mom the flyer. The counselors let us squirt our own paint onto ridged paper plates, as much as we want. There are stacked prints of classics. I try to replicate Monet's *Impression, Sunrise* for days on end. Each copy better but still wrong. I bring these attempts home and explain all the ways they fall short. Finger brushing the dried chalky acrylic that won't let me build up any texture.

I'm not home for my parents' fights. Don't see the way they're short with each other even when they're not arguing. How they keep something between them at all times. The breakfast table. Me.

These first paintings still exist. The Samuelses' house, a refuge from the storms at ours, filled to its eaves with my scraps and failures. They insist when I'm famous they'll sell their collection and retire to the Florida Keys.

———

Nine. Just a couple weeks earlier. I don't know yet that my brother's right ankle has been crushed under the front tire of an SUV, but Harlow does.

I come out of the garage to find her puking in my mom's flower bed.

"What's wrong?" I ask. "Where's Ellis?"

She wipes her mouth and looks up. Breathing hard. Cheeks wet. "I haven't seen Ellis all day."

How much more blood does a boy lose when the ambulance takes five minutes longer? A leg's worth? A life's?

I scream into the backyard where Dad's secretly mowing the lawn to get Mom to love him again. He loads us both into his car. As he drives, he asks if anything looks familiar. Her fingernails make ten red half-moons on her cheeks. She won't speak.

Something with claws climbs out of me using my ribs as a ladder.

———

I'm sixteen and everything leads to now: the town hall an hour ago and Harlow rushing through my bedroom door.

"You were sleeping." Sounding like she might faint or laugh or show me a winning lottery ticket. Like she pictured this whole scene way worse.

She peels off her coat and underneath is the same flowy, too-cold-for-April tank I stared at from across the gym all night. It'd destroy me but still I want to cup that shoulder, slip a finger under the tank top strap. No, I wasn't sleeping.

She presses a hand to either side of my neck. A chill jolts through me. *Ruined! Dead!* I think as I peel her fingers off. Like she hasn't touched more of me before. I want to kiss her. I want to hurt her. Her to hurt me.

She peeks around me to get a look at Goose dozing on my bed. Leans farther and points at my desk. Cheerios for eyes, that's how round they get. "You did it."

Cliff's treasures. I found a large, clear jar with a hinged lid. The massive piece of driftwood he left me this morning won't fit, but on break I scoured the beach and found a pebble of a shell that looks kind of like the one he gave me when I came home from the hospital. The only thing in there so far. But it's good to have room to grow.

I allow myself a microscopic smile, then shrug to balance it out. "It's just a jar."

She gets up close to it. Turning it a full revolution with a gentle touch, admiring how the shell's shape curves and distends from different angles. My left hand twitches wanting to draw her like that.

Then, straightening and hugging herself: "I guess you know why I'm here."

If only a dusty jar could be enough to stop this conversation in its tracks.

I turn my muscles to stone so she can deliver the gut punch that killed Houdini. Instead she reaches past the jar, over my desk, and unpins a pay stub from my bulletin board. On its back she makes quick strokes with a pencil, then holds up the finished product. It's a school bus, kind of. Like the one I drew her only yesterday that sent my brother to Ohio as punishment for ignoring her texts. Except in Harlow's drawing the stick-figure passenger is herself.

"Where to?" she asks breathlessly, moonbeams on her shoulders, shoving the sketch closer to my face when I don't have a quick answer. "Bottom of the ocean? Outer space?"

I rub a palm across my scalp. Fake or not, I don't want to let her and her shoulders travel any farther than New Hampshire. Even that's pushing it.

"What Ellis said in the bathroom last night." She enunciates each word as carefully as she prints *Newtok, Alaska* down the side of the bus. I picture her there. Bundled in a coat with faux fur trim. A village a lot like ours at her back, only this one's falling into the Pacific. "We have this game, right, where if someone does something bad, the other person tells them something equally bad or worse."

I've heard them play this. Harlow never spills anything real. So that I don't have to look at her, I take the pay stub and pencil, hunch over the desk, fix her bus. Round out the flat tires. Add a steering wheel. A roof.

"He crashed into a tree, so I told him I've been secretly kissing someone." Her voice drops to a whisper and I glance up. Her eyes now a pair of violet storms. Pleading. "I didn't want him to play detective. You know how he is. So I just said it was over."

My first outrageous thought is wondering what Ellis felt when she told him. Was he jealous, and did it count as being jealous of me if he didn't know I was part of it.

Getting it—that she thinks I'm so mad that *I'll* break up with *her*—comes after.

The all of me bracing for a hit is still too scared to let go completely. Like I'm a crumpled ball of tinfoil, sturdier the more it collapses in on itself. But under all that a balloon inflates in my chest.

She covers our drawing with her palm. Touches her frigid hand to my neck. "I don't want to go to Alaska."

Like I'm gonna make her.

There's my lips on the curve of her jaw. The automatic way her back arches under my hands.

"I still don't like you," she says with her lips on my ear, her hands under my shirt. "Just to be clear."

"Me either," I gasp.

Because sooner or later she'll get tired of me. Blow up this thing between us. Never speak to me again. I'm sixteen years old and I know better. But for now I trim the wick. Strike a match. Candles are made to burn.

May

Nineteen

HARLOW

Thursday, May 4

If I don't get axe murdered here in the basement of First Congregational, I'm killing Ellis.

And it'll be for four very good reasons. First because he's the one who said no way the diner would be big enough for Bring Back Our Beach's kickoff event. Second because it was his idea to ask Minister Dickens if we could use the church. Third because this task force *was also his idea*. Fourth because he promised.

Now I'm alone in this church basement and it's plain spooky. Think massive, low-ceilinged room with a glossy concrete floor and pillars throughout to support the weight of all that stained glass upstairs. There's a small kitchen, too, with only pickle relish in the refrigerator. I've checked all the closets and corners big enough for a person to hide in to make sure I'm not in the opening credits of a horror movie. I'm not opposed to a tragic death but the timing isn't right.

The three pizzas I ordered arrive. The West Finchers do not.

Twenty-four slices of failure.

Actually, the only person who mentioned my letter-writing campaign with any sort of enthusiasm was Tommy, this morning. Helen had already forced me to take down the flyer I'd hung in the window, so I was scouring the diner for less obvious real estate.

"Maybe I'll stop by?" he said, intensely focused on wiping down a menu sleeve.

"Probably shouldn't."

I liked that he wanted to come, but it was a bad idea. I knew because I wanted it too much. It was that dusty jar in his room with the lid popped open, waiting to be filled with Clifford Samuels's beach debris, that's what got me. It was telling him I don't like him and, by saying it, giving myself permission to pretend otherwise.

I could call him now. There are plenty of shadowy corners to hide in if an axe murderer does show, or worse, a nosy West Finch resident. I picture us toppling into the coat closet and sliding the door shut just in time, his breath hot on my ear, fingers counting ribs.

But it's Ellis who's supposed to be here. Ellis who promised, whose name I listed on our BBOB stationery as a founding member, and whose phone is now off.

Maybe it's going straight to voicemail because it's dead. Because *he's* dead. Teenagers die tragically all the time. Always at this time of year, too, and then there are features in the newspaper with quotes from their friends and family, talking about the big plans they had for the future and how they never went to prom.

The worst part is, this plan? It's a good one. Writing your representatives is Activism 101, and we all know Mr. Albertson is highly susceptible to public pressure. At the very least, it's a small act of defiance against the protestors. Jeanie Albertson heard from Yvette who heard from Bea that the college kids do in fact have names—Skye, blue hair; Hunter, sad-dad-boy; Zoe, red-brown hair and lots of earrings—and friends. Apparently Skye's brother just graduated high school and is flying out to join them.

With the knowledge that the protestors are multiplying, I write two letters: one print, one cursive so it looks like they're from different people. I leave Ellis an irate voicemail. I eat four slices of pizza. Then I lie on my back on the long folding table where the reception snacks get laid out on

Sundays. I dig out my SAT flashcards and place them on my belly, still rubber-banded, and pretend they're one of those kettlebells my mom sometimes swings around at the gym. I feel my body hollow out beneath it, my breath coming in little shallow gasps.

Taking the SATs. Going on a roadtrip where I'm the only driver. Items on a list titled "Horrible Things I'd Rather Do."

Another: watching West Finch's piping-plover power couple build up and tear down yet another nest. They've done this twice already, hours gathering shell fragments and pebbles to adorn the divot in the sand they've selected, only to give up when the tide comes too close. Each morning I think they're gone, but no, they're just evaluating a new nest location, as if all this sand won't be washed away as soon as the next storm hits.

Tommy and I have both checked on them whenever we walked by this week. Not together, of course. He gets up before me and messages me that the birds are north of the jetty, or to the south in the dune grass. His texts the first thing I see when I wake up. It's sweet.

And by sweet I mean alarming. What if he falls in love with me? I suppose I could make myself love him back, if I had to. Self-hypnosis, or something more Pavlovian. I could eat a piece of chocolate every time I think nice things about him. The kissing part is already good.

But what if I break his heart?

I ask my phone, *do piping plovers mate for life?* (They do.)

I check the forecast for hail, acid rain, the kind of wind gusts that can blow birds into a whole different state.

I call Ellis back for round two: "I ordered a pizza with pineapple for you. It's the grossest thing I've ever tasted. So I'll be throwing the whole thing in the garbage. Which is also where you belong."

The church's basement door creaks open, slams shut.

"Hang on. I'm about to be murdered," I tell my phone as I hoist myself up to await my fate. I'm not hanging up. Let my grisly death be recorded in Ellis's voicemail for eternity. It's what he deserves.

A shaved head and an ugly dog peer around the corner. I flop back down on the table, but my stomach lurches hopefully.

"Please confirm you're alive." I end the call.

Goose comes over first, tail waving politely. I'm not allowed to pet her, of course, but if I really am bad luck, and she's already dying, then that rule feels obsolete. I scooch so my body lines up with the edge of the table and peer down at her. She looks back up at me with both eyes: mud-puddle brown and toothpaste blue. Her nose is a bit runny. I wonder if he'd yell at me for touching her through a napkin, just to dab it.

Tommy's carrying a brown paper bag, looking around the empty room. "My dad thought you could use some food to fuel your civic unrest." His eyes land on the stack of pizzas and he deflates a little.

His dad didn't send him. I mean, clearly no one but Tommy thought of me at all. But with him and Goose here the basement already feels less creepy. I'll let him stay temporarily.

He sets his bag on the table near my head and removes cookies in wax paper, a stack of foil-wrapped burgers. "Vegetarian," he adds.

"I'm not that hungry."

Paper cartons overflowing with greasy french fries, onion rings, a tiny side salad with two cherry tomatoes and a single black olive. My throat hurts. It's so nice.

"What if Ellis had been here?"

He unpacks cardboard clamshells, ketchup in foil packets, tiny salts and peppers.

"You knew he wasn't coming?" I guess.

He studies the pipes on the ceiling. "Not for sure."

I've long suspected the twin connection thing is healthier than either of them will admit, and this confirms it. Or else everyone but me knew Ellis would flake. Maybe deep down I knew too. I reach over my head and come back with a pale, limp potato wedge.

"I don't even like takeout fries," I tell him as I squish one of the soggy ends between my fingers.

"Oh, I know. Those are for me. But I did bring a little something extra for you." A small plastic sandwich bag passes from his hand to mine. "So, we writing letters or what?"

It's a whoopie pie. My chest tightens and, see, this is how I know I don't like Tommy that way. He's nice to me and I feel like my skin might peel off. I gently set the treat on top of the two letters I've already written.

He cracks open the two-liter bottle of orange soda I got at the General Store. While he's preoccupied, I casually let the limp french fry hit the floor. Goose disappears it in seconds, but then she smacks her lips, flinging little globules of slobber onto Tommy's arm. He scowls down at me.

"I was testing her reflexes." One of his sleeves is rolled up. I want to smooth it down to match the other. I trap my hands under my butt. "Did you see how fast she moved? She still seems really healthy."

"Don't."

I forgot Tommy is superstitious too. Of the three of us, only Ellis would willingly walk under a ladder. I knock on the table for good measure, though I'm pretty sure the wood grain is just a sticker.

The orange soda glugs into two cups. With a rare glint in his eye he slides one toward me. "If my brother does make an appearance, we could just tell him about us."

Orange soda everywhere. Waterfalling off the table and soaking the ends of my hair. Goose laps up most of what dribbles onto the floor before Tommy can clean up my mess.

"We can't tell him." My voice is definitely not doing that weird shaking thing it does when I'm scared. I grab a wad of napkins and wipe my hands, but they're already sticky. "He has a race to worry about. It'll be too distracting."

He smiles like a shark. Rows and rows of teeth. "Then don't feed my dog."

I'm sorely tempted to pour the remaining cup of soda over his buzzed head. Sensing this, he wisely retreats, plopping down on the concrete a couple feet away and unwrapping a veggie burger . . . and proceeds to give Goose people food! Chunks of his burger bun, right in front of me! So it's okay to make out with me in a stairwell that smells like shrimp, to let me sit on the desk in his bedroom and wrap my legs around him as he traces my jaw with his lips, but I'm not good enough to pet his dog?

Fine. If he wants to sit there with his ankles and his arm muscles in that baby-blue MacQueen's shirt and try to distract me, let him. I grab a fresh piece of stationery and roll over onto my stomach.

"Bea said your car parts came in yesterday," Mr. Double Standard says as he combs Goose's coat with his fingers.

I focus on the letterhead in front of me. So far I've written "Dear Mr. Albertson" with my left hand. It may or may not be legible.

"It's a nice car. You shouldn't be afraid to drive it."

"I'm not."

His fingers slow, still lost somewhere in Goose's fur. She paws at his knee and he immediately resumes petting her. "Right. I'm just saying we could go for a ride together when you get it back, or, I don't know . . ."

"How about you do what you're supposed to, and I do what I am?" I gesture to Goose and my task force stationery, respectively.

He and Goose both tilt their heads sideways in the same direction. And, like, of course this is what happens when your best friend is a dog.

He wipes his hands on his jeans. Stands up so that my favorite inch of his ankle disappears, thank god, and now I can *really* get back to these letters. Crumpling the foil from his demolished burger in one hand, waving Goose to follow him with the other, he reaches over my head for another veggie burger. Then he's sitting on the table at my side, bumping my hip with his. I don't want to move and break this contact between us, but also I want to see what he's doing, so I scramble to sit cross-legged beside him.

He peels the foil back on the new burger. "Fries have too much sodium.

They're bad for her kidneys." He flips it over and peels off the bottom bun. "No sesame seeds. No onions." He scrapes off the mayo with a knife. Holds the pinkish, soggy bread out to me. "Trade you?"

"I'm not . . ." Safe? Ready? I take the bun and cup it gingerly in my palm.

Tommy wipes his hands again, then picks up a fresh piece of stationery off the stack. "Just whatever I feel?"

"Yeah," I breathe, but I've got a new project now.

I break the no-sesame bun into small, even pieces. Goose eats them right out of my hand, no teeth, smiling with her whole body. Tail wagging, body wiggling, trying her best to stay like Tommy asked her too. It's pretty cute. I'm smiling too, totally not in control of my face anymore. My heart's not growing three sizes or anything, but maybe by 50 percent or so.

Next to me Tommy chews his pen cap. Fills the front page and most of the back. I want to read it. I can always just tear open the envelope when I get home tonight and reseal it again. I guess I could also ask.

"Why are you helping?" I ask instead.

He picks the corner of his paper until it begins to curl. "The diner's the only reason my parents still talk to each other. Plus they let me work way more hours than they're supposed to." He looks up. "Can't I just do something nice for you?"

I consider the question seriously. "No."

He stands, swoops in, kisses me deep in one smooth motion. For a moment I watch us overhead, thinking, who are these silly-happy people? He pulls away too soon.

"There. I brought you food and handwrote a letter so I could do that. Better?"

Worse. Now that I've made that happen once, I want to see if I can do it again.

He moves toward Goose (who's watching a little judgmentally, I have to say), but before he can get away I grab a handful of his baby-blue T-shirt. He lets himself be pulled backward until his leg bumps the table. He touches a finger to my collarbone, the crook of my arm. Then he taps the sticky, blank stationery page near my hand.

"How many letters have you written?"

"Two."

He kisses me again. Only a peck. "Don't talk to me until you finish two more."

And then he sits back down on the floor facing away from me, pats Goose's butt, and hunches over his own letter, flipping to a new page.

If he weren't Tommy MacQueen, I'd probably find a way to make myself love him just for that.

Twenty

ELLIS

Saturday, May 6

Saturday morning run: shorts and long-sleeve, old-school digital watch, sneaker on my left foot and running blade below my right knee. I pop into Tommy's room and do a quick check, thinking maybe this time I'll leave him a note, though the only uplifting words I have for him are running related. *Pain is weakness leaving the body. Tough times don't last but tough people do.* The kind of nothing anyone could say.

Harlow straddles her bike at the corner of Schooner and Maple, and when I reach her, she kicks off hard and keeps pace beside me. Biking is one of her many dislikes, for obvious reasons. But besides races, weekends are her only chance to watch me run, and she's a decent pace car when she doesn't get too freaked out.

So here she is, wearing a dorky white helmet for safety, brown hair poking out in two stubby braids. The hot-pink rubber bands at the ends match her nail polish, which matches the stripes down the sides of her leggings—all color coordinated with the raspberry pink mark on her neck.

I stumble over nothing when I see it. Nothing, except that I'm right and Coop's wrong. Her mystery boyfriend's real after all. But I'm not wiping out. Not here, not now.

She doesn't say hi or even really look at me, though I catch her eye as she takes a quick inventory of my ten-day-old bruises and scabs. Her head snaps forward and she pedals faster.

My race Tuesday is my last chance to continue postseason and get noticed by college recruiters. I don't want to waste my energy on this deserted street.

"You're supposed to set the pace," I remind her, surging to keep up.

"I am."

This is about me skipping erosion club the other night. She knows about my race, has my schedule on her fridge at home, but she doesn't slow down, and I don't ask again. Instead I visualize a red track behind a chain-link fence. The tingling feeling that spreads down my arms after a couple laps at top speed. Mouth gummy, throat hot. I'm flying.

We turn onto Birch. The street is pitched in the middle: good for water drainage, terrible for knees. She stays on the road's edge while I run straight down the middle. No cars are coming but it makes her nervous like I knew it would. She keeps looking over at me, lips twisting as she nibbles the inside of her cheek. Almost runs into a mailbox.

"Is that a hickey?" she says.

This is how she chooses to break her silence.

"You're one to talk."

Her fingers touch the bruise on her neck self-consciously, then grip the handlebars twice as hard as she pedals even faster. I have to pump my arms to keep up.

"It's over," I pant. "Olivia and me. That's why I missed it."

Olivia has not totally accepted this fact yet. But it's for her own good. She'd be kissing me and my brain would go back to something serious, like the puppy chow smell of Tommy's bedroom, or the impulse to check my inbox to see if any college coaches reached out offering to change my life, especially because Coop sends me a screenshot of each one he gets.

"Meanwhile I was alone for *hours*," Harlow complains. "What if the protestors showed up and ambushed me?"

"Like stole your pizza?"

There's a universe in which I went to the First Congregational basement and spent two hours writing letters and eating pizza with Harlow. There's no universe where anyone else showed up.

Hit me, I think of saying, a little because I should've told her I wouldn't make it Thursday night, a little because I'm over this routine where I piss her off, let her down, dream too big, beg for forgiveness. If she wants to be mad at someone, it should be her secret boyfriend. The guy must be a real tool to maul her neck like that and then not show up. What I did is nothing.

Electricity shoots down my right leg, a twinge, hardly anything, as I find a burst of speed and finally catch up.

"Are you taking the June SATs?" I ask. She's no saint either, let's not forget.

"Don't change the subject."

I want to believe she's been studying and The Plan's still in reach. But then why hasn't she signed up already?

I check my watch and signal that it's time to loop back and let the world slowly grow familiar again. I hate this part.

"You better register," I say. She stops pedaling and coasts down the road. I'm flying alongside her. "If we don't get into Middlebury-Institute-of-Wesleyan because you forget what *chimerical* means, I'm never letting you forget it. I'll slip it into our conversations every day for the rest of our lives."

She eyes me narrowly, but a smirk plays at the corner of her lip.

And then we're tearing down the street.

We pass still-brown lawns and fire hydrants with red flags sprouting from their lids. Winter was long this year, and I trained through all of it. Endless laps around school's tiny indoor track. The squeak of hardpacked snow on distance runs down these very roads. When I run is when I feel most a part of this place. Salt air in my lungs. The coastline snagging and knuckling, sweeping low along the surf and soaring to cliffsides. But it's also when I'm most certain I'm getting out of here—and that she's coming with me.

Let her be furious with me. Let her bike chain wear out. Let my legs give way under me. Let us lie together, laughing and magnificent in the dead grass on the side of the road.

—

Back in town we swing by the jetty to do some quick reconnaissance on the plover situation—birds: present, watchful; plover patrol: the same—then continue toward the diner. Goose rolls over in greeting. I scratch the fur on her chest and avoid the golf ball tumor on her belly while Harlow keeps a safe distance. Our table by the window is occupied, so we take a pair of counter seats.

Tommy comes over straightaway, a little bounce in his step. He looks happy, but maybe that's just what I want to see.

"Hey," I say, all friendly.

He blows right by me to deliver Harlow two rubber-banded stacks of envelopes. I make a grab for them but she twists away.

"No one went to her thing the other night," Tommy explains as she flips through a stack with her thumb like she's about to divvy up the loot from a bank robbery.

"Yeah, I know that. How do *you* know that?"

"I brought her dinner." Then, like that's the most normal thing in the world, he points at the envelopes and tells her: "I guilted the early crowd into writing them."

She scowls, but only at half wattage. "If they care so much, they should've come."

"They're very sorry."

This is bizarre. As far as I know, Tommy and Harlow have said all of three sentences to each other since he came home. Now he bites his lip and stands there, waiting for her to acknowledge him or toss him a smile or something. And she looks like she just might—until her gaze flickers to me.

She places the two stacks of letters on the counter in front of her. Smiles with teeth.

"Thank you, Tommy. This is *so* thoughtful. But we just burned a lot of calories . . . maybe you could put in our order? Sometime today?"

His brow furrows and his entire face falls into its shadow.

"Two french toasts with—"

"—real maple syrup. Yeah. Got it." He turns on his heel and disappears into the bakery kitchen.

"Harsh," I scold, spinning on my stool to face her. "And you lied."

"Did I?"

"You told me no one showed up!"

She shrugs. "He's no one."

I shush her and glance toward the kitchen's entrance.

"You agreed you'd be nice to him," I whisper.

"Oh, are we back to keeping our promises to each other?" She rolls her eyes. "No, wait, let me guess: Technically, you never promised to write any letters. Is that what you're going to say?"

"C'mon. Spill."

She launches into this story about Tommy showing up at the church. How she generously let him stay, but it pained her to spend that much time with him, like physically. Pained. Her. Later she kept sneezing.

"I might be allergic," she concludes.

"To Goose?"

"To depression."

I kick the bottom of her stool and shush her again. She tries to kick me back. Her toe connects with my running leg and she gasps. Karma is real.

The letters disappeared to I don't know where during her speech. She pulls out her phone but I can see she's just opening and closing random apps. She asks me to get us coffee. Neither of us drinks coffee.

"Don't do this."

"What?"

I gesture at her seated next to me, all helmet hair and self-righteous and *her*.

"He can't handle it right now."

"For your information, he told me he's feeling better." She crosses her arms like that settles it.

"Then he's a liar too."

"How do you know? You never talk to him."

I grip the bottom of my stool, as much to feel the sharp metal lip against my palms as to make sure I don't fall off. "We talk."

"Right. I'm sure you have thrilling conversations about who gets to shower first in the morning."

The worst things we say to each other are also the truest.

"He's off-limits," I say flatly. "I shouldn't have to tell you that."

She pockets her phone and slides off her seat. "If he offers to help, I'm not saying no."

With that, she flounces to the opposite end of the counter, where she claims an empty stool.

When Tommy emerges from the kitchen, he does a double take at me before he spots Harlow. She beckons and he trudges over, scowling at first, still wounded, until she perches her chin on her hands and smiles up at him. Her mouth runs nonstop, but what's amazing is Tommy's talking too, and nobody's yelling. He must say something funny because her smile gets huge and she reaches over the counter to swat his arm. She's trying to annoy me and she's damn good at it.

I don't want to watch. I can't look away.

He delivers her french toast. I pull up the map I saved to my phone of Camp Hood's running trails and try to memorize it, building myself a schedule of seven- and nine-mile loops, wishing for July. But I can't help noticing when Harlow looks at me pointedly as she drenches her plate with maple syrup.

I wait another fifteen breakfastless minutes before waving Tommy over. He glances down the counter and rubs the back of his neck.

"She told me you wanted to cancel your order. And—well, I just sent out the last of the brioche. I can make you plain toast?"

The toast he brings me is whole wheat, not even the kind with seeds, and there's only smooth peanut butter.

"Triangles make everything taste better?" he tries as I examine the plate.

I could ask him what really happened that night. I open my mouth to say you can tell me, I'll talk to her. But he takes my struggle to speak to mean something else. "Sorry about your toast," he mumbles, and hurries away. I spend the rest of breakfast practicing for next time, when I'll tell him the sorry one is me.

Twenty-One
TOMMY

Tuesday, May 9

Bea's garage is a squat building on Main Street, a few lots down from the diner. The paint's a few different colors, all of it peeling, and one of the doors yawns open to reveal the tail end of the Volvo. Bea waits next to it with her hands on her hips.

She's been on Harlow's case to pick up her car for a week now, and even if I'm not sure why I'm here—the way Harlow treated me at breakfast the other day is proof I might be letting things go too far—it's a public service to everyone if I help get this done. Plus it feels good to take care of someone instead of always being the one who's taken care of.

Or, okay, fine. I'm here because she asked me. Because it's Harlow. Because I want to.

"Look what the tide dragged in!" Bea crows as we approach.

"Aren't you worried she'll talk?" I ask Harlow under my breath.

"Just follow my lead," she whispers back. Then to Bea, playfully: "No one says that, but yes."

Bea waggles her eyebrows at me, so I wave. Harlow glances over her shoulder.

"Ellis sent him to help me." Rolls her eyes so aggressively it has to hurt. "He's trying to crawl back into my good graces."

I know she doesn't mean it, but it's like I've missed a stair. She could've warned me this was the plan.

I cross my arms. "Let's get this over with."

"Two rays of sunshine, both of you," Bea says.

But she seems to buy it. She disappears into the back to find the Volvo's keys and leaves us trapped dangerously close in the small garage. A long, narrow space with bays for three cars and the barest wiggle room between them. Everything smells of gasoline except for Harlow, who also smells like oranges and school and the perfect slice of blueberry pie I served her not ten minutes ago. I could get used to this.

But she's going to his track meet today. I'm not.

When I warned her not to ask, she said, "Wouldn't dream of it." And somehow that was it. No snide comments about how I don't have anything better to do. No giving me shit for missing every race since the first. I only know he's good now because other people tell me.

She wouldn't want me there anyway. My memories standing next to her on the sidelines during that first race are anything but rosy: waiting twenty minutes for him to emerge from the woods, inevitably last, inevitably cheered for the loudest. That's what made him get faster. More than Harlow's training regimen, more than the growth spurt, more than anything.

Harlow picks up a cordless drill and passes it from hand to hand. Then she holds it close to her face, like she's a secret agent sneaking around a corner, squeezes, and jumps when the drill bit spins a couple inches from her nose. She sets it back down in a hurry and keeps moving. I follow behind her, wondering again. *Why am I here?*

Because I knew it would mean something to her. Like when I brought her dinner and collected the letters. Or maybe it's guilt for the message I got at 10:32 a.m. this morning, right before second period started.

Tommy, it's ruby. I hope you're doing ok. Let's get coffee?

If I were still in school, I'd have been in the Painting II studio scraping curls of dried-up paint off my palette.

There was a time last fall when we texted pretty much every day, so it feels weird that Ruby thinks I deleted her number. Considering she asked me not to speak to her again, maybe I should have.

Coffee is just coffee. I don't even know if I'll write back. But as I test the point of a screwdriver with my finger, I think of saying Ruby's name aloud just to try and make Harlow jealous.

"We should drop off those letters with Mr. Albertson tomorrow," I tell her instead. Wipe my hand on my jeans.

She beams. Too surprised to pretend not to be. "Okay. And we can pick up Goose after, if you want." She doesn't say chemo out loud but it hangs in the late-afternoon dust motes. She remembered.

I should be excited Ruby even thinks of me, better yet wants to meet. I should give myself the buzz I'm long overdue for. See if I can draw anything worth looking at. I practice now: on my jeans, my index finger traces the quick planes of Harlow's face, the shape of her cloud-hair, and, oh, the tentative smile she's just sent over her shoulder as her fingers trail along the yellow, fuzzy body of an old pickup Bea's been restoring for the better part of my life.

The last time there were leaves on the trees Ruby was everything. Now her message leaves me empty. Did I only like her attention? Or is this the fog of antidepressants, the storm of Harlow? The kinds of questions I could ask Cool Therapist, though if I told him our messy history, he might consider this self-harm.

Or ask Cliff. He'd palm his crimson-red hat off his head and listen without speaking until finally I'd ramble my way to my own answer. Then he'd grip my shoulder. Tell me I'd be just fine.

But that'd require talking to him. And last time he came by I hid in the bathroom. Imagined what I'd tell him about my life right now if I weren't so afraid, then sketched it on a blank page in my order pad: a glass of lemonade I later colored in pink.

Harlow looks down at her nails. They're painted the color of new grass. "Will you come get me if the car breaks down?"

"Bea wouldn't let you take it if it wasn't ready," I reassure her. "It's probably better than before."

"Better than new!" Bea calls as she comes out of her office. Sidestepping toward us between the better-than-new Volvo and the ancient pickup, jerking her thumb at me. "This one's got sense."

Harlow grimaces and makes the five-feet buffer between us six.

Bea tosses me the keys. I catch them without deciding to, then immediately lob them at Harlow, whose hands are in her armpits. All three of us watch as they arc toward her and drop to the concrete at her feet.

She stoops down. Grips them in her fist for a magic trick. Opens her palm like she's expecting *poof*, gone. Of course they're still there.

But no, that was the misdirection. The trick is that she's suddenly right in front of me. Did she forget Bea's still here? My palm faces the ceiling. Somehow the keys are in it. "Help me back out?" she asks quietly.

I slide into the driver's seat. Bea gives me a look through the windshield. It translates to something like *you poor asshole*.

The engine purrs to life. If I had a car like this, I'd take Goose for long drives along the shore. Let her sit in the front seat with the window down. I ease the Volvo out of the garage, careful of the mirrors, careful to keep the wheel straight, careful not to feel anything about Harlow looking a tiny bit more at ease as she watches.

I'm thinking of the Ohio school bus, the empty church basement, french toast, the deer lie. Even though I know better than to think any of it could split them apart. Not an asteroid. Not nuclear fallout. Not me. If he's running she's there.

I'm thinking of yesterday. Harlow drank her pink lemonade. Ate a whoopie pie so slowly the filling oozed onto her SAT workbook. Made out with me on the basement stairs while Dad and Cliff smoked a secret cigarette out back. There was a fan-shaped seashell the size of my palm on the counter when we got back. Guilt wringing my stomach like a dirty washcloth. But Harlow was excited. "For your collection," she said, hands flapping like she might take flight.

Not plague. Not hurricane. Not me.

Probably not me.

But maybe.

I turn the car off before she can reprimand me for suffocating the environment. Swing the keys around my finger as I climb out. Harlow's asking Bea, "Was that your phone ringing?"

Bea hustles back to her office while Harlow draws close. Squeezes my arm. "Come with me," she says like she promised she wouldn't.

In case the car gets worse.

We had fun that time we hung out at his meet.

Remember?

I remember freezing my ass off on a playground padded with wood chips. Goose at the end of a leash knotted around my fist. Harlow's gaze trained on the starting line as she paced figure eights in the grass. I remember predicting he'd come in last when Mom was out of earshot.

Harlow's eyebrows arched in response. "You didn't have to come to this."

"Oh yes I did. Ellis needs me."

She stopped her figure-eighting to snort.

"When his blade makes him trip and face-plant into a rock, they'll have to take him to the emergency room to reconstruct his face," I explained. "I want to give the plastic surgeon something to work with."

"Better if they used Goose as the model," she retorted with a scowl.

Then the race. The runners a wash of arms and legs. Ellis's silver shin flashing in the sun like bicycle spokes. I'd only ever seen him train on empty, cracked streets. Never with or against anyone else. It cemented me to the spot. Not even Goose straining against her leash could move me.

He finished last. Wobbled to a halt on the other side of the line. Smiled weakly at Harlow. Vomited into the nearest trash can.

The gasoline stings my nose as Harlow insists, "It'll be like old times." But the old times are shit and I don't want them.

I imprint her car key on the length of my thumb, then hold out the key and say, "I'll go if you drive."

It's only a hunch, but it's the right one. Her eyes get a little rounder. Her height a little shorter—except for her hair, which rises another electric inch in pure alarm at what I'm suggesting.

Bea comes back and opens the Volvo's driver-side door. She's had enough of us, I think. But we don't move. The car dings and dings and Harlow blinks a few times. Not a single lie at the ready.

I guess she expected I'd roll over and do it. Maybe I would have, if it was anything but his race. Heat rises in my cheeks. I already offered to go with her to deliver her letters to Mr. Albertson. Isn't that good enough?

"That's what I thought." I shake my head. Take a step toward her. "I came here out of the goodness of my heart—"

"A living saint," she snarls.

"—and I'm supposed to, what?" I step forward again. "Be honored you treat me like your—your—"

"Friend?" Her eyes spark, ready to eat through me like kindling if I get too close. But I'm not afraid.

"*Chauffeur*," I finish. Right up in her face now. "I'm not your personal waiter or delivery boy, and I'm definitely not your goddamn driver."

I'm shaking. A rumble of smoke coming from my chest. Inches from her pale, chapped lips and if I stand here much longer I don't know what I'll do.

Bea rolls her eyes toward the sky and keeps them there. "Christ on a cracker. Make out already, why don't you?"

That shuts us up. Harlow looks as warm as I feel. I don't know if we're that obvious or if Bea's being Bea. I don't think I care.

I stuff my hands in my pockets and say to Harlow as coolly as I can muster with a volcano in my chest, "If you end up dead in a ditch, don't call me."

"That doesn't make any sense!"

I've already stomped too far across the parking lot to argue.

During the walk to the diner, my thoughts wander back to Ellis's first race. The car on the way home. Harlow begged him to recount the parts of his race we couldn't see, so he did, foot bouncing against the back of my seat. I watched the black road through the windshield, its edges lined with mile markers.

"Cliff said he would've taken you," Mom said to me, her eyes on the road too. "I can't be two places at once. We'll do your thing next time."

There won't be a next time, I thought. But I said, "I already won. I don't need to go for them to tell me that."

"Won what?" Harlow butted in.

"Second place in a state art show." I should've been proud. Mostly I felt embarrassed, like I was showing off just by talking about it.

"What for?" Ellis scratched Goose's ears, only halfway interested.

"A painting," Mom said.

"The one you did in art class last year?" Harlow asked.

I shut my eyes. "No."

But she was right. If there's one thing I was good at, it was painting something and making it look like nothing. Two careful swipes of black, limbless, tossing in waves of cerulean. Sun sprinkled like gems on each crest. I'd signed the back instead of the front so not even I could tell if the figures were sinking or floating.

When I get back to the diner, I scrub a smudge of grease off my knuckles, slip my apron around my neck, and make juice out of all the oranges we've got. Until orange peel's all I can smell. Until finally I'm sick of it.

Twenty-Two

HARLOW

As I watch Tommy storm away from the garage, I don't know what's worse: that he saw right through me or that I have to drive myself to Ellis's meet.

I climb into the driver's seat and, okay, I do know. The driving, that's the worst part. I have to check all my mirrors, make sure the daytime running lights are on so I'm visible to others, scoot the seat forward so I can reach the pedals, but not so close the airbag will kill me on impact, like Ellis's nose but worse because Tommy wouldn't pick me up if I called, he doesn't owe me anything, wants me dead in a ditch. But I can't not go. Can't not breathe. In my rearview mirror, he shrinks to the size of a gumball, a peanut, a grain of sand.

"Eyes on the road," Bea says, smiling faintly.

"I don't appreciate your tone." I slam the car door shut. Open it. "Thank you." I shut it again.

I manage to stay focused on the drive. Mostly. I also manage to mentally draft about seven possible apologies I might send Tommy, and to battle myself over whether he even deserves an apology. I asked him for a ride. So what? How he feels about that is his business.

A bubble of guilt gurgles and pops in my belly, but who's Not Bothered? Me.

And why does it have to be that I wanted a ride *or* I wanted his company? I can want both.

If he doesn't come with me to my showdown with Mr. Albertson tomorrow I'll be so pissed at myself.

The stands behind the school are full of people encamped on silver bleachers or around the chain-link fence. Indoor track had barely started when Tommy took a break from school the first time, in January, so Jim and Helen haven't been to a race yet this year. I'll be the only one in Ellis's corner today. I join the moms and dads of other runners from Seaborough High. They greet me by name, and I smile back, but ultimately I stand by myself against the fence, facing the track. It's the way they talk about him. Claim him. *Our charming, inspirational Ellis.* Like he's someone they feel good knowing but not real competition. At least there's this: He's been gaining on their sons for the last four years.

Ellis and a couple of his teammates are warming up around the track's grassy inner perimeter. Their thin blue shorts fly up their legs with every stride. Ben, a sophomore with platinum-blond hair, keeps trying to make the fabric cover more leg. He ends up jogging around the whole track with his hands pressed flat against his thighs. I don't even try to get Ellis's attention when they pass. He won't talk to me right now.

Across the track, a skinny, leggy thing tries to vault over a bar and misses, landing hard. Olivia, I hope. Then I remember Ellis broke up with her so I should give the girl a break.

Ellis jogs over ten minutes before the boys' mile is scheduled to start, cheeks pink, grin easy and wide. Even with the faint bruises staining his nose and forehead, it's hard to believe anything has ever or will ever go wrong. Bad stuff happens to other people, not him.

"Guess what," he says. "Coop has mono!"

"Coop has mono?" I repeat so enthusiastically I know the universe will find a way to punish me for it. "You don't recover from that for a minimum of six weeks. And since he was anchoring the four-by-mile—"

"Coach is running me and Ben in the 1600." He scrubs a hand across his forehead. "Whoever finishes first gets his spot."

"And your best time is five seconds faster than Ben's."

"Well, anything can happen," he says humbly.

I loop my fingers through the chain links. The next several weeks unfold before us: Ellis anchoring the four-by-mile at sectionals and handily winning it for the team. A college recruiter coming up after and shaking his hand, saying, "Let's keep in touch." After that, states, regionals, Camp Hood (though I can still talk him out of that). Fear pulls my smile taut, but there's relief in it too. We're out of time for new schemes. The Plan will work or it won't, and it'll happen in the next ten minutes.

Ellis's hands are everywhere: unsticking his wet singlet from his chest, worrying his prosthetic leg's socket, pushing back his hair. A sweaty strand falls into his eyes. My fingertips ache to brush it away, to pull him into a hug too quick for anyone to see.

"You've got this," I tell him. "You've put in the work and you have the times to show for it."

He's nodding. "I'm gonna go out fast. If I puke, I puke."

He always pukes.

Ben moves toward the starting line and waves Ellis over. My hand reaches for his shoulder. I don't mean to. It's just telling someone you'll love them no matter what happens doesn't really explain it right. He steps sideways and slides right out from under my fingers. My skin damp now too.

He jogs to the starting line and joins Ben. Coop's there in regular clothes, presumably to cheer them on but also, it seems, to distract them. He shakes Ben's hand to wish him luck, then pretends to go in for a kiss, which elicits much protesting from Ben. Rebuffed, Coop looks both ways before crossing the track. He comes right over to where Ellis was standing, way too close for someone infected with something called the kissing disease, and grins.

"Hey, Princess," he says.

My narrowed eyes should say it all, but for good measure, I add, "You know that's an extremely condescending way to greet a woman, right?"

"Yup. Aren't you going to tell me 'get well soon'?"

Ellis seems to have calmed down. He's staring at a spot on the ground in front of him, shaking his legs out one at a time.

"Get well soon," I say as unenthusiastically as I can.

He shakes his head. "Just what I suspected."

The only way to get rid of Coop is to talk to him. "What?"

"You don't have time for me anymore. Your boy's about to be on varsity track."

My mouth twists. "He's not 'my boy.'"

"Okay. Just checking."

This is the fastest heat, and Ellis is assigned one of the middle lanes because his times are not the best, not the worst in this group. Today we don't care about anyone but Ben, and Ben's in a lane even farther out.

"If you and your fake boyfriend break up, maybe I'll find a way to spend time in West Finch this summer. I know you'd like to see more of me," Coop teases.

I'm not going to look at him. I don't want to see the smug look on his face, or reveal the thoughts probably flashing across mine (Ellis spilled my secrets *again*? And is "fake" a Coop embellishment, or an Ellis one?).

On your mark.

The runners freeze as if in mid-stride. My heart in my throat again.

"Oops. Am I not supposed to know about that?"

"Coop!" I shoo him. "Get out of here!"

The gun goes off and it's mayhem, a jumble of limbs and singlets as the runners vie for position. Coop is off too: running despite the mono, alternately screaming Ellis's and Ben's names. A couple years ago that would've been me, but it's weird to cheer so fiercely when you're not even on the team. Or so I was told.

I used to stand in the grassy middle section of the football field, where the runners hang out, so I could see him pass twice each lap. Then some of the boys started imitating my cheers. I knew because they'd yell, "What are you waiting for?" in high-pitched voices, the exact thing I'd find myself yelling even though it obviously wasn't helpful. I knew Ellis must have been secretly making fun of me too, or at the very least letting them. Otherwise it wouldn't have happened. I don't care about that stuff but I finally had to cut it out when he got embarrassed enough to tell me I shouldn't come to his races anymore. Now I stay behind the fence and I don't cheer.

Finally I spot Ellis near the front as they go around the first turn. Someone who hasn't watched him run hundreds of times could hardly pick him out of the group, that's how smooth his form is. Sometimes when he gets tired it's sloppy, but this afternoon, there are no wasted movements.

The two guys in the lead surge at the second straightaway. It's aggressive; they still have over three laps to go. Ellis stays with them. They put five, ten feet between themselves and the rest of the runners. When they cross the line (one lap down) he's in the very front, his strides textbook perfect. Ben's a hundred meters back but he doesn't matter anymore. Who cares about Ben when Ellis could win?

Establishing a tenuous lead of a meter. Now two.

The parents near me are cheering for him. Coop's screaming himself hoarse from the side of the track. Ellis's coach yells instructions. *Keep your knees up! Use your arms!*

There's over half a mile to go but you wouldn't know it the way he runs. He pumps his arms harder like Coach says. I follow him like keeping track of a moth, how if you look away once you've lost it for good. Without moving my lips or making a sound I scream, *What are you waiting for?!*

As if on cue, the worst happens.

One moment he's running too fast. The next he's not catching himself. There's no one close enough to have tripped him. No hurdle, no pit where his right leg collapses under him and he bounces (chin, shoulder, hand last) on the rough red track. A collective groan from the bleachers. But not me.

Falls happen, I know, and any second he'll get up and disappear into the pack again, clawing back his lead.

The runners who were on his heels manage to avoid him, or in one case, leap over, their spikes barely missing his splayed fingers. Still on the ground, he momentarily fumbles with his socket before pulling his prosthetic leg off and dropping it next to him on the track.

This is how I know it's bad.

The runner in seventh with no chance of placing stops and kneels down to help. Someone with the first aid kit and Coop and a bunch of the other Seaborough guys run over too. The fence presses into my knees and the chain links have grooved my palms so now they fit together perfectly, the lines on my hands shiny and colored like the inside of my mouth. The runner who stopped tries to help Ellis up, but Ellis wrenches himself out of the other boy's grip, his face neck ears a blotchy scarlet.

The wet-towel heaviness over me is old, familiar. Swallows me so that I keep not moving. I'm nine again, and the longer I go without running to him, the less it seems like I should. It would embarrass him if I go over there now. Provide material for the next year of jokes. Best if I leave.

I sidestep the length of fence in the opposite direction of the few Seaborough parents who haven't dashed to Ellis's side. A little boy leaps up and down the three lowest bleacher rungs. Somewhere a dog barks. Coach turns his attention to Ben, his remaining runner, and says, "Knees up! Pump your arms!"

Harlow!

It's not Ellis's coach calling me, who still never remembers my name, but Coop. I shrink back but he calls again and this time he's looking right at the round blue trash can I'm half-hiding behind. I go around to the inside of the fence, staying close so the metal brushes my back.

The gun goes off to signal the lead runner's reached his last lap. Ellis has been moved out of the way but not his leg, which lies in lane one some ten feet behind where he now half-sits, half-sprawls. I inch closer, grab the curved end of the blade, pull it toward me. It's the first time I've touched it without it being attached to Ellis and it's lighter than I expect. I hug it safely against my chest with both arms.

"I'm fine," Ellis says when the woman with the first aid kit tries to pry his fingers away from his right thigh.

"I'm fine," he says again when someone suggests they see if the school nurse is still around.

I wish he'd stop talking. They can all hear the effort in his voice. His face crumples in a wave of pain he hides against the back of his arm. Ellis, who doesn't cry as a rule. Coop crouches on the ground with his ear close to Ellis's bowed head. Even this asshole is a better friend than I am.

"Harlow has it." He jerks his head in my direction.

Ellis has never been so happy to see me in his life. He stretches his hands toward me and my stomach turns but I can't not with so many people watching so I take one of his hands while holding his prosthesis securely in the other.

"Give me that," he says in a gravelly, to-me-only voice that makes me hug the limb tighter. It presses against my sternum, warm through the fabric of my top.

"I'll hang on to it for you." It's no stretch to imagine him wiping the sweat off his liner, clicking his leg back into place, and insisting he finish his last two laps.

A gaggle of track girls appear, including (unimpaled) Olivia, who claps her hands over her mouth and soap-opera gasps. Ellis's grip on my hand tightens but I can't think of what to do, a way things still work out like they're supposed to. We need The Plan. Any plan.

"Let's go," Ellis says. I can't feel my hand anymore. "*Now.*"

So I straighten up. "He's fine," I pronounce. "I'll call his doctor when we get home."

The parents and runners stare at me. I look to Ellis.

"Right? Dr. Diaz will know what to do."

"I don't need a hospital," he says, which wasn't really the question.

Just like that, everyone's happy to let me whisk him away. Crutches are retrieved from a supply closet in the snack shack; Ellis only takes them when Coop asks if he wants to be carried instead. We get him into the car and tilt the seat back so he's kind of lounging. He returns the crutches to Coop and looks at me expectantly. I'm still holding his running blade hostage.

"Buckle up," I order.

Sweat beads at my temples, and not just because the car's warm in the sun. Ellis obeys and at last I hand over his running leg. He doesn't try to put it on, thank god, but holds it like a shield across his body. He settles back with his eyes screwed shut.

Coop still hasn't closed the door. "Want me to ride back with you?" he asks.

"We're good," Ellis answers through gritted teeth.

Coop looks at me. I swallow and echo, "Yeah. Good."

After Coop goes, I let myself sit with the seat belt unbuckled, my forehead on the dimpled ring of the steering wheel. Ellis leans out his door. I think he's going to make a break for it but he just dry-heaves a couple times before sitting back and closing the door hard.

I chance a look at him. I tried not to see anything when he was on the ground but I think the back of his leg's beginning to bruise. And with his face barely healed.

"We should call Dr. Diaz."

"Just take me home."

"But if it's bad—"

He shuts his eyes and slams his head back against his headrest with enough force to make me jump. "This is why I told Tommy not to let you come that night. You don't listen."

My lungs aren't quite working. "You said you didn't want to upset me. Because of the crash."

"Yeah, I made that up."

Isn't it weird how it only takes a second for that pressure to creep up behind your face, as if your body knows what's in store before you do?

"I'm better than Ben *and* Coop, you know," he mutters, bowing his head now so that his seat belt bites into his neck.

"Coop's probably been sick all season, and Ben finished the race," I snap. "And I'm the only one who comes to your meets, *you know*. I tried to get Tommy to come with me today. He doesn't care about you so he didn't."

He scoffs. "He didn't want to watch you hyperventilate."

I could hit him across his ugly, perfect face.

"I should've left you back there," I tell him.

"Wouldn't be the first time."

The leaky-pipe feeling in me again. Chest, behind-the-eyes, all of it.

Is that a throwaway line he saved up because he knew it'd hurt me? Or is his mind transported, too, back to pavement so hot it shimmered, and colored plastic beads raining down spinning spokes? Yes I'm over it, because Ellis is the one who lost a leg, and if he's over it then obviously I am too. But that doesn't mean I forget.

I get out of the car and lean against the door, breathing for a minute. I try in through my nose and out through my mouth, but my lungs are tight and that isn't enough air, so I do both at once. My phone connects.

"Hey," Tommy answers. "You're not dead in a ditch."

He must've had his reasons for not coming. Maybe Ellis is right and I'm one of them. But I can't keep being someone who runs because it's easier than staying. I can't stand that girl.

I don't know how to say it, so I just say it. "Ellis fell during his race. It seems bad. I thought someone else should know."

He's silent. I know he's still there, though, because dishware clatters into a sink in the background.

"Are you okay?" he asks.

The question stuns me. That it's the first he asks. That he sounds like he wants the real answer. I press my knuckles into the side of the car.

"Do you feel like you can drive back?" he tries again. His voice is soft but solid, and I'm certain if I asked, he'd come get me after all.

"Uh-huh." I clear my throat. "Yes."

"I'll tell my mom to call his doctor. Just take your time, okay? Pull off at a rest stop and take a break if you have to."

"Okay."

On the drive home, the car fills with the smells of sweat and metal. Ellis wakes up ten minutes from home and runs a hand through his hair.

"I'll call Dr. Diaz tomorrow. Promise."

This is as close to an apology as I'll get. I let it hang between us. He knows too well what to say to people to make them love him again.

"Burgers?" he says. "I'll shower first."

I park in the driveway and make him wait in the car while I let myself into his house using the flowerpot key. His forearm crutches are leaning next to his bed. I hurry back with them, expecting he'll have already hopped up the walkway and made his injury worse, but thankfully he's still in the passenger seat.

Fifteen minutes later, he emerges from his shower less surly, more boyish. It's a superpower to be able to wash off embarrassment and shame as easily as dirt. He yanks a clean shirt over his head (not that I'm watching) and digs around his track bag for his regular prosthesis and matching left sneaker.

"Maybe you should use your crutches," I suggest. A longshot. As is, he'd literally rather slip and fall hopping to the bathroom at night than use them.

Instead of answering, he swipes deodorant under his arms, then sits next to me to click his leg into the socket of his prosthesis. He rubs his quad with the heel of his hand—the only clue anything out of the ordinary happened today. I've sucked my lips back against my teeth to keep from saying anything. But when he pushes off the bed, I blurt out, "Do you think—?"

I don't have to finish. Everywhere on him tenses when he puts weight on his right leg. He's forced to sit back down.

"I'm not that hungry."

"We're going," he pants, face drained of blood.

Finally we're back in the car. He brings his crutches after all, and although the stretchy shrinker sleeve he rolled up his shin is meant to reduce the swelling, it has the added benefit of hiding the bruises purpling around his scars. He must've banged his limb on the inside of the socket when he fell.

And speaking of falling, he has a lot of ideas about what might've happened. The likeliest explanation (overuse injury) is obviously not up for discussion.

"Maybe one of the spikes popped out of my shoe and I rolled my ankle," he says.

His left ankle isn't hurt at all, but it's not like that matters in this thought exercise. Most compelling to him are theories of foul play: that he was tripped by a competitor (how, when he had such a big lead?), or sabotaged by a jealous teammate (who . . . what, spiked his Gatorade?).

One thing he doesn't mention: The Plan.

One thing he doesn't say: *We can still fix this.*

I want to throw myself into the game. Can't. I rewind, replay as I drive—tangy fresh-cut grass, crowd groaning in unison—watching until I see a version where, with everything I've done, I didn't as good as trip him myself.

Twenty-Three

"Why do I feel like she's gonna egg my car?" Coop says when I climb into his passenger seat five hours after the worst race of my life. His chin rests on the steering wheel as he peers up at my bedroom's second-story window.

I shut the car door as quietly as possible. "She's not here."

"But you knew exactly who I was talking about." His eyes widen. "Maybe you should think on that."

Harlow's the last person I want to think about. I was a dick to her after my race. Couldn't stop myself, like those birds by the jetty can't help but build their nests in the worst possible place. I looked across the car at her and saw my own disappointment reflected back at me. Same as the times I've tripped during a cross-country race and fallen hard. The worst part never the precious seconds I spent in the dirt or the guys who passed me while I got up, but the mud smeared down my leg. Knowing that'd be the first thing Harlow would see.

But there were roots and rocks for me to trip on in the woods. It's never happened on a track in front of so many people. Never that I couldn't get up.

I kept expecting Harlow to swoop in with her magic wand and a backup plan. A way to make everyone forget everything but the half lap I led. And when she didn't—because that's impossible—I screamed at her.

So I don't want to think about Harlow. We're headed to a party, or more specifically, closing down Friendly's. The closest thing to a party a bunch of sober track nerds can get. That's all I want to think about.

"This better be the best movie we've ever seen," Coop grumbles as he backs out of the driveway.

Coop doesn't know we're going to Friendly's, but that's where we'll end up. He didn't want to go out at all tonight—apparently mono's exhausting—so I reminded him he ran around the track all afternoon and seemed fine. And when that didn't work, I texted him, *This is my hour of need!!!*, the three exclamation points to show I'm mostly joking. Harlow'd freak seeing me sit this close to someone contagious, but it's not like I'm going to kiss him. And she's not here.

He waits until we're halfway down the street to turn on his headlights. There's nothing sinister about ice cream at 9:00 p.m., and I've never had an official curfew, but Mom's policy may have changed since I wrecked Harlow's car.

"Sooo," Coop says to fill my silence. "How's Tommy?"

"Dunno."

I think of what I found when I checked his room this morning: beach garbage in a jar on his desk, a thousand dollars cash, a crumpled pay stub with a terrible drawing of a stick-figure girl on a school bus headed to "Newtok," whatever the hell that is.

"Well then, how's your leg?"

My grip tightens around the crutches propped between my knees. "It's a pulled muscle. Could've happened to anyone."

He raises his eyebrows. "Okaay. I didn't mean—"

"Yeah, well." Jesus. I'm being a dick again. "I just don't want people to think I'm out for the season."

"Oh, they don't think that. They know it," he says lightly. "Seriously though. Everyone could see it was your hammy. Even if it wasn't, no one'd make fun of you if you fucked up your, uh . . ." He gestures vaguely in my direction. "Residual limb."

I burst out laughing. "Did you have to look that word up?"

"Maybe I did." Coop grins back.

"Hey," I say as we approach a blinking four-way stop. I'm a good actor and make it sound like I just thought of it. "Ben just texted me. What if, instead of this movie, we meet up with everyone else for sundaes?" He rolls his neck pensively, so I add, "I'll buy you mozz sticks."

"Will you let me dip them in my ice cream, though?" he says, serious as a heart attack.

"I won't stop you."

Coop turns the wheel hard at the last minute. I wave in thanks at the oncoming traffic flipping us off.

—

The track team has the biggest table in the carpeted dining room. They cheer and hoot and blow paper straw wrappers at us when Coop and I come in. Normally I'd make a big show with a bow or a curtsy.

But this was a mistake. I'm going to have to walk over there on my crutches and answer questions about how I'm feeling when I just want to be treated like normal. I *am* normal. If I rest for the next few days and stay off my leg, I'll be running by Sunday or Monday. Maybe I can still challenge Ben for his varsity spot.

There's an open seat next to Olivia, but that's a bad idea if I've ever seen one, so I squeeze into the space between Coop and a sprinter named Sheila, whose hair is still in two long race-day braids. I carefully lean my forearm crutches against the wall next to me, and do it again when they fall over with a clatter so loud it interrupts conversations at the far end of the table.

I order a chocolate shake, then perch on the edge of my chair and try not to move. I've decided a guy from Falmouth tripped me and everyone saw it. That version's better than the alternatives: that I tripped over myself;

that I overtrained; that my body isn't capable of doing everything I thought it was.

Tripped is the story I stick with when my teammates ask how I'm feeling. Ben believes me because he was running too. Doesn't know better. Coop gives me a look but goes with it, like, whatever you have to tell yourself. And when Sheila asks, "But weren't you out in front?" Coop tells her to shut up. Normally I wouldn't approve of talking to anyone like that but it's true. Shut up, Sheila.

This feels like the closest I have to peering into a potential future. A universe of track practice and dinners, surrounded by people for whom the worst thing in the world would be boredom, who know their hometowns will be there when they go back for Thanksgiving. The Plan isn't dead, can't be, but I also can't picture inviting Harlow to a gathering like this. Can't picture her letting me look away from her for even a minute.

Harlow wouldn't like that we're the loudest ones here, either. There are a couple people in Friendly's uniforms lounging in a booth by the back who probably want us out so they can go home on time. A young, tanned white guy with black hair and glasses, looking doleful as the waitress fills his coffee cup. And then our group in the middle of the restaurant at a row of several tables pushed together.

Olivia's seat is empty. There's a plate in front of it with all the salad eaten around the croutons. This feels like the one lucky break I've gotten all day. Must be safe to escape to the bathroom, at least until my shake comes, and then I can drink whenever I don't know what to say. I grab my crutches and stand, clenching my teeth through the pain that shoots down my hamstring and missing calf. As I go, Coop jingles his car keys at me and I take them. I'm not leaving, but maybe I look ready to. Maybe I look like crap.

I make eye contact with the coffee-drinking guy as I pass his table. Oversize glasses. Dark and, honestly, kind of bushy eyebrows. Cute. There's a duffel bag on the seat across from him, and if I were in the mood, maybe that'd be an opening. *You on a road trip?* But when our eyes meet, he quickly looks down at his menu.

The bathroom light's unflattering. Yellow, my worst color, and I'm pale under the last of my bruises. The faucet gushes and splashes my front. I pat myself dry with gobs of paper towels. My hair's deflated. I would feel sorry for me. How could Harlow not feel sorry for me?

"Don't worry about The Plan, okay?" she said when we got back to my house after dinner.

I stared at her. "I wasn't."

She blinked and the floorboards cracked. I splintered, too, and fell into the spaces.

Now I realize she's been distancing herself for a while now. Secret hook-ups? That moony look like she's dreaming of something she shouldn't? Those freaking flashcards? I'd bet money that she'll get the score she was supposed to all along and The Plan won't be called off. I just won't be part of it.

When I come out of the bathroom, there's a flash of blond. Olivia has materialized in front of me, all three calories of salad raging through her. The car keys in my pocket and the wink that came with them make a lot more sense now. Dammit, Coop. Olivia's almost my height, but I look over her head and give him a dirty look. He shoots a double thumbs-up back.

"I saw you sneak away," she says, like an apology but not. Then, more hopefully, "You looked good out there today."

I shrug. I know I did. I move toward the voices of our teammates at the table, trying to ignore the pain jolting through my everything.

She jogs—actually jogs—around me and plants herself directly in my path and I don't want to do this right now. Can't have this conversation, again, and explain, again, that I broke up with her. So I try patting her arm. My crutches almost fall, *again*, and I catch them, but then she pats *my* arm and says *"Ellis."* If my name were a question mark, that's what it'd sound like. "You can talk to me. How are you feeling?"

I feel nothing. Is this what it's like for Tommy all the time? How can he stand it?

Her hand's still on my arm. I should move. But somehow it makes me think of Harlow, and *that* makes me feel something: too guilty and self-righteous to think. She reaches and cups my face in her hand, and that feels like something too. She's flushed and pretty. Somebody's dream but not mine. I lean back first and she looks up at me all eager.

"That's never gonna happen," I say.

She stares at me openmouthed. I wish she'd yell.

"Sorry, I actually know that guy." I point vaguely past her ear. "I have to go say hi."

I hardly believe I'm doing it but I walk past the track table, ignoring the catcalls that follow me, and make for the guy with the coffee and the glasses. He watches my progress with some interest. Even more when I give his duffel bag a gentle shove and slide into the booth opposite him.

"We're old friends, okay?" I say, quickly grabbing a menu from behind the napkin holder and ducking my head.

The guy immediately mirrors me, head bowed, peeking up at me through dark lashes. "Where did we meet?" he whispers.

"Summering on the Vineyard, of course," I say, because it sounds like the thing a me in a vastly different universe might say, and I'm trying to get as far away from mine as possible.

"Oh yeah." He gently smacks his forehead, then points an accusatory finger at me. "You were the guy with the dimples."

Is he flirting?

I hadn't been aware my dimples were on display. I smile a little wider. "And you were in those hideous salmon shorts."

He snorts. It's incredibly endearing. "Don't forget the boat shoes."

Now that I'm closer, I notice what I didn't before: dark hair shaved close on one side and long on the other, plus an angular, bristly jawline that makes him look older than he is. Round, wire-frame glasses. No one under seventy years old should be able to pull them off, but he does. He's probably a couple inches shorter than me and stockier too, built more like a rower than a runner. Cute, confirmed.

"You really should put those things away," he says, tapping his own cheeks. "You look miserable."

I'm temporarily stunned that he can see right through me. I thought I was hiding it.

I eye his duffel bag. "Well, you look lost."

He puts a hand to his chest, like, *Moi?!* Good he has a sense of humor about me using him to dig myself out of the grave Olivia's probably making me.

"Bay Area. You got me," he says. "But I'm only temporarily lost. My phone's dead, and I was promised this coffee would eventually come with a charger. Was that your girlfriend?"

If he saw, the whole track team definitely saw. Fantastic. I force myself not to look over.

"We broke up." And then, a stroke of genius: "She thinks I'm still in love with my ex, but I was only with that guy for two weeks, so how's that work?" He smiles again and licks his lips. Did he really just lick his lips? "We had a track meet today." I gesture toward my table.

"I ran a mile without stopping in eighth grade," he tries.

Everyone I've ever so much as flirted with has known me by my accomplishments. First amputee runner ever on the school cross-country team. Straight-A student. The supposed better half of Harlow-and-Ellis. To this guy, I'm a different version of myself, one he could only be meeting through this particular alignment of universes. God, I'm practically a different person. He doesn't know Sheila or Coop, hasn't talked to anyone else at my table, so he'll believe me when I tell him about being tripped. He won't even know to ask about my brother or my hamstring. And did I mention his face?

In the back seat of Coop's car I kiss the boy with the glasses like I'm dehydrated and it will replenish my own electrolytes. I forget the pain in my leg, my teammates' disbelief, the way I treated Harlow. At least for a little while.

After, we sort out whose shirt is whose, button buttons, zip flies. I wipe my mouth on the back of my hand and look across the back seat at this beautiful boy who appeared from far away and, of all the suburbs and culs-de-sac, ended up in the same one as me. Coincidence? Fate? Do I look like I care?

"I have to call a ride," he says through my goodbye kiss, which, granted, is turning into more than a goodbye kiss. "I'm putting my number in your phone."

"Where you headed?" I move my lips to his neck. He groans a little and I smile.

"Tiny town a few miles away. You've never heard of it," he says. "No one has."

"Mm-hmm." He's reaching not-so-subtly for the back pocket of my jeans and no way am I stopping him.

"I mean it. Not the person next to me on my flight. Not the waitress in there." He pulls back and holds up my phone triumphantly, which he stole right off me. Then he adds his number to my phone and I text him mine back.

"Try me."

He sighs. "I'm staying with my sister in a place that's falling into the ocean."

Of course he is.

I look down at this new contact in my phone. Back up at him.

"Congratulations, Jules Mercer. You're not lost after all."

Twenty-Four

HARLOW

Wednesday, May 10

At first I think the plovers are dead, gone, both. Because when I wake up the next morning there's no text from Tommy telling me they're making a new nest under the rickety wooden steps that lead to the beach, or scouting out a clump of seaweed.

Then I remember yesterday. The garage. Bea. Me saying I wouldn't ask him to drive me to the meet, and then, well, I kind of tried to guilt him into driving me to the meet.

Since wallowing's not a cute look on anyone, I take it upon myself to fulfill our little morning ritual. I switch up my usual route, walking along the coast with my eyes peeled for flapping wings, a flash of blue hair, anything. But I can't find the plovers or their nest. There's not even a protestor on the jetty's rocks.

About damn time!

. . . is how I *should* feel. I'm uneasy, though. Like, if I was looking for signs, the disappearance of birds that have been around since the exact moment of our first kiss isn't a good one.

But I'm not looking for signs. Not wallowing. I walk into the diner, like normal, and wave to Ellis at our table, like normal, and then hop into the bakery line, pretending to be highly interested in the pastries on display instead of the guy with the fresh buzz cut behind them. When I get to the front, I dazzle Tommy with a smile. He returns it with a rather curt "What do you want?"

"Have you seen the plovers today?" I blink rapidly because I think that's how you flutter your eyelashes. He doesn't react. "Feathers? Yea big?" I cradle an imaginary lemon in my hands. "I think they're gone."

His face still doesn't move. He folds his arms over his chest and this close I can see the tiny freckles on them. "Good."

I swallow. "Well. Yeah."

"So, what can I get you? Zucchini muffin? Carrot cake?" He points out each with the end of his pen (as if I'd ever order a vegetable-based dessert). "A ride somewhere?" And then his face does move: a tightening of the skin near his eyes.

Okay, it wasn't *that* big a deal. If it was, why was he so nice when I called him from Ellis's meet? My mouth tastes bad even though I brushed my teeth.

"Very funny," I say without laughing.

Tommy stares at a spot over my head and I back away, until I almost bump into our table.

Ellis's hair is molded into the most perfect, desperate sculpture, all volume and waves. He's wearing his favorite outfit, and he's already enjoying his half of our breakfast.

"What was it?" he asks, cutting the chocolate chip pancake with the side of his fork.

"Huh?"

He nods at the counter. "Why'd you get in line?"

Hell if I know.

I lower myself into the chair across from him. If I don't answer, it's like the question doesn't exist. He chews and raises an eyebrow at me. I raise both of mine back, then let my gaze travel to his forearm crutches leaning against the wall beside him—barely a glance—and he yelps, "Only temporary!"

I nod. Believe him. Now that he's distracted from his earlier line of questioning and I can think, I even feel a little sorry for him. Because unlike *some* people, I don't hold grudges longer than I need to. When it really matters, Ellis and I can move past anything.

I pick up the second fork lying on the table and dig in.

———

Ellis misses lunch for an appointment with his orthopedist, but otherwise, school drags on in the usual monotonous blur. I don't even think to make Ellis tell me what it means that he's staying after school for practice until I'm on the bus home.

But I didn't tell him where I'm going, who I'm hoping to go with, either.

It's not lying if he doesn't ask.

At home, I pick up the letters for Mr. Albertson, then drive my car to the diner so that if by some miracle Tommy still wants me to go with him to pick up Goose, we'll have a ride. There's a lot to pay attention to behind the wheel, so there's no room to worry about what Ellis's doctor told him (though it's obviously bad; if it weren't, he would've texted me already). Or fret about the plovers' disappearance. Or wonder if Tommy will be outside waiting for me when I get there.

Spoiler alert: He's not.

I park where I know he can see me through the big picture window. Sit for a minute. Two. The sky is the gleaming blue of a gas-fed flame.

If he won't forgive me, there's no point apologizing.

I leave my car in the diner parking lot, though. Mr. Albertson's office at the bed-and-breakfast is practically next door, and this way, I'll be back just as Tommy goes to pick up Goose. Not that he still wants me to come. But just in case.

———

Mr. Albertson's office is messier than I've ever seen it, with paperwork fanned out across his desktop, and drained cups of MacQueen's coffee abandoned on the bookshelf and even in a potted plant. The shades are half-drawn, bathing the whole scene in harsh stripes of sunlight. Mr. Albertson himself stands behind his desk in his L.L. Bean quarter-zip, the ends of his mustache pointing in wildly different directions, a walkie-talkie broadcasting static into his ear.

He gives me a look like I personally chased away the plovers by beating a pan with a wooden spoon. Then, bringing the walkie-talkie to his mouth, he holds down a button on the side and says, "Artie, I missed that. I kindly request you repeat yourself."

More static. Mr. Albertson hits the side of the device with the palm of his hand.

"Aren't you supposed to say 'over'?" I suggest helpfully.

Then his walkie-talkie pops to life with Artie's voice. "We've got eyes on the birds. Over."

Any other time I'd give a little *ahem* to really drive home my point about walkie-talkie etiquette, but I'm too busy bouncing on the balls of my feet and saying, "Where?! *Ask him where!*"

Mr. Albertson does, fumbling with the buttons, forgetting to release so we miss Artie's message again and have to wait an excruciating thirty seconds before we hear, "Back where they started. Funny thing. Maybe they needed a vacation."

Those anxious little birds with their tidy black collars and orange beaks. Not just safe: safe here. I'm so ridiculously relieved.

Before I lose all my credibility, I slap my letters down on the cluttered desk between us. "Now that's solved, let's talk."

Mr. Albertson sighs.

"I'll put this as plainly as I can," he begins, massaging his temples. "Stop. Please."

I open my mouth to retort. He holds up his hand.

"You and I want the same thing, I promise you. However, the piping plovers are a protected species"—*nearly threatened*—"and removing demonstrators is . . . unpopular. So you can understand we're in a bit of a bind."

"Is that why you're being so nice to the protestors?"

"It's a little something called tact, Miss Prout. Perhaps you should try it."

Perhaps. But it's not like they're nice to me, either, barging into the town hall where they don't belong, asking too many questions.

"If you can't manage that, I'm simply asking you to wait them out."

I give him a doubtful look. "And then?"

"Once the protestors and birds leave, the jetty gets taken down as planned."

Altogether it rings true. Like me, Mr. Albertson was a vocal proponent for tearing down the jetty, at least until the plover fiasco began earlier this year. But it still feels like a trap. After everything the past few weeks, is it really that easy?

"You have my word," he adds solemnly.

I'm not positive I should believe him. But I want to. And he shakes on it.

I practically skip back to the diner. Already I'm thinking about how I'll tell Tommy. He got people to write those letters, and here it is, proof him being alive makes a difference. I want him to be the first to know. With news like this, he *has to* talk to me.

But when I get there, I stumble to a halt.

Tommy. Leaning against my car's driver-side door with a hip bone here, a shoulder blade there, head tipped back, eyes closed. The end-of-day sun-beams hit his forehead and cheekbones and linger on the parts of him his shirt doesn't cover. The place where his shoulder curves into his neck. Where his hand turns into his wrist turns into his arm. I stay a moment and just watch him. His chest fills and grows. When he exhales, the wind stirs dead leaves into a dust devil at his feet.

Somehow this moment's too perfect to shatter, even with good news. But he opens his eyes on his own and sees me. I brace myself for a scowl. His expression stays soft, though, and he holds up his hand for me to toss him my keys.

Thinking of Ellis, and how the only reason we met for pancakes this morning was routine. We just did the same thing we'd normally do. As if nothing's changed.

Thinking of the plovers. Ruffled and agitated, picking apart another start of a nest that looks fine to me but must not feel right. How damn afraid they are.

Or brave. Because doesn't it take nerve to see things aren't working and try again anyway?

Since he's standing in the way, I circle around the car and let myself into the passenger door. Climb over the console, fasten my seat belt, insert the key.

With the window rolled down I say, "Get in, loser."

He tilts his head at the sight. Me. Driver's seat. I think again of that thing about dogs and their owners looking alike, how Tommy and Goose look more similar than he and Ellis do.

Bemused. That's the word the College Board would use.

"For the real experience, I'd suggest sitting in back." Another joke. Also, the back seat is the safest place in the car, and *also* also that makes him less likely to talk to me or look at me or god forbid touch me, turning me into a distracted driver with just a hand on my knee.

"Is this because of yesterday in Bea's garage?" He peers through the open window as I start the car. I'm careful to keep my foot on the brake, my hands at 8 and 4 (10 and 2 will break your thumbs), so he'll know I know what I'm doing.

"What do you think?" It's really not as romantic when I have to spell it out. Not that this was supposed to be romantic. All I want is to erase yesterday and go back to how things were.

"You can just say sorry like a normal person."

But he wouldn't believe me. It'd only be words, like saying I don't like him when I think I might.

He realizes I'm not gonna budge and climbs in. He chooses the passenger seat instead of the back, which pleases me despite the aforementioned safety concerns. I suppose it never hurts to have an extra set of eyes on the road. I release the parking brake and shift into reverse. Under me, the car shudders slowly out of the lot.

He takes up so much of the car. The cooking smells of MacQueen's but also the stick of mint gum between his teeth, his long limbs, his sighs. Again there's no room to worry (1) whether Goose's chemo went well, or (2) how I'll explain myself if Ellis gets back before we do. No room for bad things at all. From in here, I can make believe Ellis already knows about us and is fine with it. Happy even. I never said a word to Ruby. I've never spoken to her in my life. In here, I'm not bad luck. I fix everything I touch. I'm never too much.

"What are you doing?" he asks when I find the courage to take my hands off the wheel and let down my ponytail at a red light. I even allow my hand to linger next to his on the console for a couple seconds. There's a small smile playing at the corner of his lips that, with a bit more time, I think I could coax into something more.

My smile back isn't small at all. "Pretending."

When we finally reach the vet's parking lot and I tell him the good news about the plovers, the jetty, he grabs my face and kisses me. I remind myself to slow down. I'm always too much. Sooner or later, the Tommy who can't forgive, can't forget will be back. But today is not that day, and every slice of my bare skin that touches him grows warm, like I'm burning in the sun.

Twenty-Five

TOMMY

Pretending, she says. And I'm too afraid of rupturing this perfect bubble we're in to ask *pretending what*. Watching her watch the road. Not lifting her eyes from the yellow and white lines. Until one stoplight when she holds her breath and yanks out her hair elastic. Waves fall down her back, and that orange smell. The split-second sight of our hands on the same armrest, almost touching.

She oversteers. She white-knuckles. But I compliment her driving and she sends it back to me. Tells me I'm a much better driver than Ellis. Already knew that. Still makes me unreasonably happy. I almost tell her Cliff taught me but then keep that to myself. Anything to protect this from all the bullshit outside.

But that's impossible.

Because when we walk through the vet's double doors I can't control what happens next. If it will be good or bad or—I guess it won't be good. Goose sick and even if I had the money no guarantee I could save her. The air in here's warm and thick with pet hair and my skin's a too-small container for my body but Harlow doesn't feel a thing. That cloud she's on too high to notice the air's changed down here.

"Goose MacQueen," she says as she floats up to the guy at the front desk. I stand beside her, feeling the bubble around us expand until it bursts. "I like your scrubs," she adds.

I dig my nails into the desk edge so I won't elbow her in the face and I think she can finally sense the danger she's in. That something's shifted. She takes a single step outside my radius and goes right back to humming a jingle from a pest control commercial.

The guy at the desk plucks at his pawprint scrubs. Consults his computer. "They're finishing up now. She'll be out soon."

He slides me the bill. One thousand dollars.

"I called last week and they said I could just pay half today," I tell him quietly. Harlow's having a mini heart attack next to me wondering how I let this happen. I know it.

"No problem, man. Let me update that for you."

I write a check for what still feels like way too much money to have poison pumped through Goose's veins. The vet's warning echoes back at me that chemo doesn't even help cure cancer in dogs. Just halts its progress. Goose needs surgery to beat this.

Harlow finds us spots directly across from the door where they'll bring Goose out. I land in the seat next to her. Not thinking how she can save our whole town and I can't save one dog. Or how I'd thought dog chemo would be like people chemo. Goose would get a comfy chair and I'd hold her paw. Harlow had been the one to tell me. She'd said it like I was hopeless. No. She'd said it like how had I not done the research on this? I wrap my fingers around my armrests. She mirrors me. Our hands are pale spiders. Her nails tiny robin's eggs.

"It shouldn't be long," I say, looking at the dead TV in the corner, not her.

"How many times does she have to get chemo?" She's about to do it. That thing where I let her in and she tries to fix my life whether I asked for it or not.

I don't want to talk about this with her. Goose has always been just mine. The one thing Harlow can't reach. Nothing between us changes that.

"Five times? Six?" She chews on her lip. Drums her fingers. Our chairs are on top of each other and I can feel the vibrations in mine. "Or will you keep bringing her until you run out of money? Because I could—"

"If I want your help, you'll be the first to know," I say as her hand lunges off her armrest, toward mine. It dive-bombs to brush imaginary lint off her sleeve at the last second. I press the heels of my hands against my eyes.

Now she's back at the front desk. Jesus. Is she asking for Goose's treatment plan? No. She's raiding the jar of dog treats on the counter with the delight of a kid in a cookie jar. Her palms full when she turns to me.

"Can I give her a treat?" she asks in a whisper louder than her regular voice.

"One."

She gives me the "most traditionally beautiful" of dog biscuits for safekeeping. The rest she bundles in the crook of her arm and delivers to every other dog in the waiting room. She chats with their owners. Gets down on her knees. Even breaks the treats into tiny pieces for the little black pug. This whole production's as adorable as it is annoying.

"Can you just sit down?" I plead once she completes her loop.

"That pug's name is Pickles. Can you believe it?" She tucks a chunk of hair behind her ear. It pops right back out again. I scrape a hand across my own bristly scalp to stop from pushing that strand of her hair back in place.

"Sounds like a typical dog name. So, yes."

"It's just *so perfect* for that specific dog. How did you pick Goose's name?"

"It's the one she came with."

She almost rolls her eyes. Catches herself just in time. I swallow a laugh because, damn, at least she's trying. Even if she can't help but be herself.

"I really like it when dogs have people names. Imagine if you'd called her Barbara."

There's something desperate about her smile. The kind you have to return or you're an asshole.

"She should be out by now," I, an asshole, grumble at my fingernails.

Maybe it's a not wanting to be indebted to her thing. Maybe it's a not trusting her with more than a foot of leash thing. She can dip in, dip out of this whenever she wants and if I smile at her now I'll never pull myself out. I can't do it.

She slowly leans into my periphery until she's right in my face, impossible to ignore. "Can we play a game?"

Can I stop her? I wait expectantly as she takes inventory of everything around us: chairs, my radioactive hand, more dog biscuits, something hissing in a dark pet carrier, fur tumbleweeds. She grabs two pens from the check-in desk and a pamphlet advertising dog tags in every shape and color.

"Okay," she says as she hands me a pen. "Whoever's pen runs out of ink first wins." And she starts scribbling.

"Stop, stop." My fingers brush hers as I snatch the pen, and she goes quiet. Amazing. "Maybe something less destructive."

It's a cheap ballpoint. Still warm from her hand. I draw a single spiral and pass her the pamphlet.

She turns it sideways. Upside down. "This is certainly abstract."

"Now you add a line or shape. We pass it back and forth until we make something."

"But you don't do art anymore," she says with a sly look.

"It's not art if you're participating."

She's too delighted with this proof of her positive influence to let that sting.

We take turns adding to our drawing. Her additions are tiny—a dot here, a line there—and I do my best to connect them back to the bigger picture. And it's easy. Whether it's these new meds or what. Nothing like last winter when I second- and triple-guessed every line. I relax into my chair for the first time since we sat down.

"But that was supposed to be an arm!" she complains when I make one of her squiggly lines into a flowering vine. She taps her pen cap against her nose and scowls at me over it, failing miserably to hide a smile. "You're taking a lot of artistic license."

I look at her sideways. Cover my mouth with my hand to hide what's happening there. Back down to the game. "Just trying to elevate this from the ditch you keep dragging us into."

We end up with one drawing of a house choked with vines and five drawings of what can only be categorized as monsters. The kind in kid's cartoons, with googly eyes and polka dots.

"Cute monsters," Harlow pronounces as she examines our handiwork. "Actually, this one could be called Barbara too. Just like Goose."

She rubs her arm with her hand and I see it again. Glitching. Like she's about to reach out and—

"Tommy MacQueen?" calls the guy at the front desk.

I blink. While I wasn't looking, the whole waiting room has filled with new owners and pets. Pickles the Pug nowhere in sight. Has it been that long already? Beside me Harlow folds our drawings into careful quarters. We stand just as the door across from us swings open. The familiar click of Goose's nails on the tile floor and next thing I know she's barreling around the corner. So happy to see me her whole body wags.

"Goose handled the treatment like a champ," the vet says. "We'll see you in two weeks."

That's when I find my hand interlocked with Harlow's. I quickly let go in case I did that. Maybe those tries earlier weren't what I thought they were.

Without looking, she grabs mine again and squeezes tight.

Twenty-Six

ELLIS

If you look at this seawall, at those waves, there's no way this ends well. And that's good. Because all day I did everything right and still ended up here.

Checked Tommy's room like every morning. Goose's first round of chemo was today, so high alert or whatever, but there was nothing pointy or stabby or leave this world-y. Just a sheet of stationery from Harlow's beach club covered in crosshatched lines.

I worried Harlow didn't exactly internalize my warning to not involve him in this stuff. I worried checking his room wasn't helping. But these weren't the type of worries I had to do anything about.

I packed my regular prosthesis in my track bag—and my running blade, just in case. Used my crutches, though. Ate breakfast with Harlow at our usual table and gave her the pancake half with more chocolate chips and didn't say a harsh word to her, the whole day, not one.

But none of that mattered.

Because at my lunchtime appointment, Dr. Diaz said: *Keep weight off that leg for a month and you might be able to run by August.*

No, Ellis, I don't care about recruiters. Someone talented as you can be a walk-on, no problem.

Well, that's your choice. If you run on a hamstring tear as bad as this one, you might never run again.

The logical part of my brain knew he was right. I had good grades. I could get financial aid and academic scholarships like everyone else and still get my pick of decent schools. But the other part said there was no point going to college at all if I didn't stick to The Plan, this golden future Harlow planned down to every detail.

Still I stayed optimistic. After Mom dropped me back at school and classes ended, I called Camp Hood. I could cross-train, right? Coop said they have aqua-jogging belts, and Vermont has at least one lake.

"If you're injured, hon, you'll have to talk to your coach," the woman on the phone said. "There's a long waitlist."

It wasn't a conversation. When I showed up at practice not wearing my running blade, Coach shook his head.

"Just don't let camp give away my spot," I begged while, on the track beside us, the team ran a brutal speed workout I itched to join. Muscles tight, lungs burning, I'd take some of that.

"Sorry, MacQueen. Someone else on the team could use the training." Coach clapped me on the shoulder. Even with the tips of my crutches planted in the ground, my whole body swayed.

Now in front of the seawall I sway again, shifting my weight and shivering as an icy breeze blasts through my hoodie. I'm wearing my prosthetic leg against Dr. Diaz's orders and already regretting it. But I need my hands free.

Even at the lowest, smelliest tide this time of night, the diner's beachfront is nothing to write home about. Between the water and rocks there's ten feet at most, and the seawall's loosely stacked stones could cave in any minute. The kind of thing no one realizes they need until it's gone.

It's easy enough to shove off the rock near the top. There's the satisfying thud as it hits the earth. The even better smash of a second falling on the first. I use my shoulder, excavating my way straight through until there's a me-shaped hole. It doesn't take long.

Still ten feet to the ocean, though.

The rocks are so heavy I can only carry one at a time. My leg pangs with each step, a hot, steady thrum in the back of my thigh like the thickest string on a guitar plucked over and over. My shirt's plastered to my body after just a couple trips.

A flashlight's beam finds me. I'm panting, my fingertips raw around another stone, but I force myself to take another step. The beam drifts away. It's coming from the jetty. Maybe Jules. He knows I live in West Finch but not that this is my parents' restaurant. He has no reason to think I'm out here doing whatever I'm doing right now.

I pull out my phone and type:

hey
heard they found those birds
how's the b&b?

Nope. No way those boring words came from my brain. I hold down the backspace.

this weekend?

I hit send.

I dare the sea to take it: the barely-there beach and the wooden walkway through the dune grass. The damn picnic table where I couldn't sit and wait for my brother long enough. The dumpster rotten and sweet from baking in the mid-May sun. The kitchens and the countertop, the lobster tank, the diner's checkered floor. In my head, I've dismantled every last stone, brick, plank of wood. It's easier to leave something that doesn't exist. The Atlantic can swallow them all.

Twenty-Seven

HARLOW

Saturday, May 13

Figures it takes Ellis tunneling straight through the diner's sea-wall to make Helen talk to me. Tommy's on break, afternoon sun making his hair glint gold as he sits beside Goose in the grass outside. Three days post-chemo and she seems the same, which I've finally convinced him is a good sign. Another good sign: The piping plovers have built their nest, near where Tommy and I first saw them. Dad says they'll lay their eggs any day now.

Helen's supposed to be covering for Tommy. Instead she drops the binder on my table and almost spills my lemonade.

"Where should we start?" she says. There's a big streak of flour under her left eye. "How about we can't afford any of this."

"What I'm hearing is, you don't want to leave West Finch if you can help it." With my foot I nudge the chair across from me and push it out from the table.

"What do you think? Our whole lives are here. I grew up down the road." She yanks the chair back and sits. Her legs crossed and her arms too. "But how many people will still be living here ten, fifteen years from now?"

"I discussed it with Mr. Albertson, and we're seeing eye to eye about the jetty now. Ten years out is pretty much settled."

She laughs. "I've seen at least five of these grants, ballot measures, whatever they've decided to call it that year. They all fall through."

Ellis tries to slink into the diner without attracting a ton of attention but of course the bell rings, and there's the fact he's on crutches, and also he dug straight through the seawall Wednesday night like an overgrown mole. Helen and I glower at him.

"The grant is a long-term play," I agree, turning back to her. "How much will your flood insurance cover if something happens?"

"I'll read up on it." She flips back through the diagrams in my binder and continues more loudly. "Of course, my eldest son will probably tear this place down first."

Ellis (older by four minutes) freezes behind the counter, arm halfway to a block of rocky road fudge in the bakery case.

He straightens empty-handed. "Why do you think it was me?"

"Jeanie Albertson saw you," she says.

"Everyone knows," I add.

The seawall wasn't in good shape, but still. It must've taken him hours that evening—hours I spent in Tommy's bed after we got home from the vet. Watching cute dog videos and feeling the rise and fall of his chest under my cheek. Goose's side was pressed against my foot the whole time and she isn't any worse for it. Through my sock, but still. All while Ellis was destroying family property. And he says I'm bad luck!

When Helen returns to work, Ellis slides into her empty seat, leaning his crutches against the wall behind him. They promptly clatter to the checkered floor and he leaves them there. Total safety hazard.

"Way to have my back," he snaps, giving me a withering look.

I can't spend more than ten minutes at a time with Ellis these days. The seawall was shocking, but it's not just that. He's been relentlessly unpleasant since the track meet. Sitting in his anger too long makes me want to throw up and, frankly, I have other options now. One looks at me like I'm the eighth wonder of the world whenever I feed her a treat, and the other looks at me that way if I so much as smile at him.

"What's the matter?" I ask as I hit start on my mental timer.

"You have time to gossip with my mom, but you can't bother telling me about your talk with Mr. Albertson?"

"I told you." Pretty sure I told him. I've replied to every message he's sent me in the last few days. The bare minimum, but I've responded.

"Did not. I heard from Tommy. In fact, he knows a lot about what you've been doing."

I don't know when he got so observant, but I certainly don't like it.

"He helped with the letters," I say slowly.

"Yeah, I still don't get how that happened."

I sip my lemonade. I won't let him make me feel bad about his brother too. I'm tackling Tommy's life like a fixer-upper: Sometimes you have to knock down walls before you can put up new ones. Sometimes you discover there are parts of the old house you kind of like, and you don't want to demolish them. It's a little messy and confusing right now. The last thing I need is Ellis poking around while I renovate.

I look for Tommy without really thinking about it. He's back from break, working the bakery-side register for the end of Saturday breakfast. Mrs. Samuels crinkles at the front of the line in her lilac windbreaker. When it's her turn, she leans to point at the cheese danish on the countertop, and he looks past her and finds my eyes immediately, like he's been keeping track of me too. The smile he flashes me is almost too quick to see, but it's enough to fill my chest with something that feels an awful lot like bees. The fuzzy, noisy kind, lovers not stingers.

"Did he go with you to pick up your car?"

Ellis is staring at me over steepled fingers.

I make my voice light. "Of course not."

He smiles like *that's what I thought.* "He told me he did."

Dammit, Tommy.

"If you knew, why'd you ask?" I mutter, then chug my cold lemonade, which makes the bees settle down.

Ellis fingers the drawstrings on his oversize black hoodie. Up close, there's faint stubble along his jaw, and his hair's a deeper brown than usual. I wonder when he last showered.

I'm no fashionista, but in my red plaid button-down over a faded Sea Dogs tee and cut-offs, oh-so-subtle lip gloss, and clean hair woven into two fishtail braids, I'm actually making him look shabby for once. I wonder if Tommy will notice, sit up straighter, and hate myself, in that order.

"I'm not on my deathbed, you know," Ellis says.

"What?"

"Just because I'm on crutches doesn't mean I can't help with your erosion club. Task force. Whatever."

"I didn't think you couldn't help. I thought you wouldn't."

"Fine, don't believe me." He waves a hand dismissively. "I'm getting a second opinion next week. I'll be walking and running in no time."

Now he just sounds delusional. What about Dr. Diaz, his doctor of seven years?

The bell above the door rings and I hear her before I see her: Skye, the blue-haired college student slash activist slash nightmare, greeting Tommy by name.

Me and my bees hold our breath as she walks to the counter like she's been here a hundred times, ponytail rippling in slow motion. Which is ridiculous, because there's no way Tommy would serve her, no matter how singsongy she makes his name sound. He's on my side. He's made that clear.

"I don't think you're supposed to get second opinions just because you don't like what you hear," I say to Ellis as, to my horror, Tommy returns Skye's smile. The bees migrate from my chest to my stomach.

"Fascinating. What else do you know about going to an orthopedist? Please, tell me everything."

"I just meant . . ."

He moodily turns to his phone. Discussion over.

At the counter, Tommy's getting Skye coffee. Isn't there coffee at the Albertsons'? Isn't that the point of a B and B? Tommy's a traitor with the backbone of a chocolate éclair. Otherwise why's she still talking to him and why's he letting her?

"I'll be right back," I breathe.

Ellis makes a sound of disbelief but I get up anyway and hustle to the counter.

"Hey, Harlow," Skye says. Her tone's pleasant enough, but not as melodious as when she said Tommy's name.

Tommy whips around, pitcher of iced coffee in hand, and gives me a look that says . . . well, I'm not sure exactly. It's all raised brows and dinnerplate eyes. Perhaps she threatened him into getting her coffee, and he's relieved I've come to his rescue.

"I was giving Tommy an update from the mayor so he could pass it along to you."

"You could've told me yourself," I say lightly. "I was right there."

"You looked busy." Her gaze lingers over Ellis a beat too long and my stomach buzzes again. Good thing he's absorbed in his phone. This is the type of nonsense he can't resist.

"Well, Skye, you can save your breath. I was at the B and B three days ago and Mr. Albertson said he looks forward to the end of your time in West Finch as much as we do."

Skye raises her eyebrows, which are blue like her hair. People can do what they want with their own bodies and all that, but if you're dyeing your eyebrows, you're trying too hard.

"There was an article in the paper this morning. Hang on. I'll send the link," she says.

A few seconds later, Tommy's phone chimes.

That thing would be a puddle of melted plastic in his hand, if only I had heat vision.

"Skye kept an eye on Goose for a couple minutes yesterday," he explains as Skye smirks to herself.

As if they'd need to exchange numbers for that!

He sends me a link to the article. I quickly find the paragraph Skye's so eager to share:

> In a statement Friday, West Finch Mayor Patrick Albertson said, "We'll continue to take the plover concerns very seriously, even if that means preserving the jetty indefinitely. We won't settle on a solution unless it strikes the right balance between addressing the environmental and economic concerns of my constituents."

"But you're not even constituents!"

"A lot of the town agrees with us," Skye says. She pays for her iced coffee with cash and reminds Tommy not to give her a straw. "They're bad for the sea turtles," she adds, looking at me.

Like I'm not familiar with the plight of the freaking sea turtles.

Take Tommy, for example. If he were a sea turtle, we might say he's cold-stunned. That's what happens when the temperature gets so low that sea turtles can't move, can't digest food, get beached on Cape Cod, die.

Once she's gone, he tries to offer me coffee too. But I have principles. Also, I don't like it. I stomp back to my table and shove my phone in Ellis's face. He scans the article for maybe three seconds. "What am I supposed to be looking for?"

"The part where Mr. Albertson goes back on everything he promised."

"Did you see where they mention you? 'The most recent town hall ended in a heated argument between the activists and young West Finch residents.'"

I snatch my phone back. It's there, along with a link to the video that guy, Hunter, took of me. Fantastic.

"If she cares so much about the sea turtles, she should bring a reusable mug," I mutter.

"Have you met the new kid who joined up?"

I've glimpsed Skye's brother from afar, with his glasses and puffy coat. "No, and I don't plan to."

Ellis goes on and on about how he doesn't know what the summer holds for him, but he'll help deal with West Finch's intruders however he can, and also prep me for the SATs, which I'm taking again next month. But the SATs are the last thing on my mind. Tommy is a hypothermic sea turtle and Mr. Albertson is a liar.

"Why don't you go check and see if the birds have hatched yet," I suggest.

He pulls up his hood and takes a swig of my pink lemonade without asking. "They haven't even laid the eggs."

"Well, why don't you go check?"

"Maybe I'll ask them to start a live feed," he says, wiping his mouth on the back of his hand.

I start rereading the article from the top. "That would be very convenient."

"Maybe I'll just stay out there with them."

"Whatever you want." I'm still thinking about how Skye took a plastic to-go cup. I should buy her the tackiest travel mug, stick a note on it, and leave it for her by the jetty. *FOR THE SEA TURTLES.* ☺ ☺ ☺ Passive-aggressive smiley faces required. Three minimum.

"Let's do something Memorial Day. Just you and me." His hood's still up, and one tuft of brown hair sticks out above his forehead. "It can be erosion club-related, I don't care."

"Task force," I correct him automatically. "Monday's fine."

I'd forgotten Memorial Day weekend is coming up. Tommy's already talked about taking a day off, and I want to go to the beach with him and hand out Bring Back Our Beach flyers. The boy could use some sunshine. I can hang out with Ellis afterward; it's not like he'll wake up before noon anyway.

Ellis reaches across the table and covers my phone with his hand. "C'mon, Harlow." He's a little pitiful staring out at me from under his hoodie. "Hit me, if you're mad about the wall."

It's not just the wall. It's that we have no plans and I don't know whether I want to kill it on the SATs or go down in flames, don't know if it matters, anyway, because Tommy will still be in West Finch the year after next and what if I want to stay?

My gaze sweeps over Tommy, Helen, the video of me playing silently on my phone in my lap. "I saw Tommy leaving the SATs last time but I didn't say anything."

He gives his sweatshirt drawstrings a yank and the tuft of silky brown hair disappears. "Good one," he croaks.

I want to reach across the table and push his greasy hair off his forehead, or at least pass him a tissue so he can rub the sleep from his eyes. But who's to say my skin on his won't tell him everything about the kind of person I am, as clearly as if I'd said it?

"You okay?"

He's asking because I'm standing, and my chair has toppled backward.

"Sorry. I forgot I have to . . ."

But I don't have time to finish that sentence. I walk out of the diner, then run. It's been ten minutes.

Twenty-Eight
ELLIS

Monday, May 29

If I didn't Know Harlow and I are good, I'd ask if she's trying to punish me.

She *should* be applauding me. I walked into Tommy's room this morning, and when I found him wearing swim trunks, deciding between three boring T-shirts, I didn't let on I was about to go through his stuff without his permission.

"Plans?" I asked instead.

"Mom made me take off to pretend I'm still in school and everything's normal." He plucked at the waistband of his trunks. "Might go to the beach."

Way more detail than I was expecting, but also my perfect in.

"Us too. You should come." My good deed of the month. "Harlow's handing out flyers but it won't be a big deal."

Actually, it was a huge deal. Crutches on the beach suck even when it isn't crowded, as Harlow's well aware. But imagining how many brownie points I was about to get from her almost made my forthcoming pain and misery worth it. Add inviting Tommy and I'm Brother of the Year over here.

His face did a funny thing where it went totally blank for a second. Just when I thought he would say *Eff that* he said, "Sure."

But does applause ring out anywhere on Pine Point Beach? No it does not.

Memorial Day brings beer cans in foam koozies, music playing from tinny speakers, and sunbathers in varying degrees of undress all acting like this is the first and only time they'll see an amputee on crutches. Their lips part slightly as they peek through mirrored sunglasses, over the tops of pulp fiction novels they'll toss in the garbage on their way to the car. I want to shout that I have my follow-up with Dr. Diaz tomorrow, so they can bet I'll be off these things and running in no time. With how slow I'm going, I'd have time to tell each and every one of them.

Harlow and Tommy are walking at a snail's pace, but even that's too fast. Each time I move my crutches, the tips sink into the sand, and it's that much harder to pull them out again. I take five steps—place my crutches, sink, left foot forward, again—and they've gone ten. Even Goose outpaces me. She's thrilled to be at the beach, or anywhere besides tied up outside the diner. She barks at other dogs, tramples abandoned sandcastles, and pauses to sniff every unattended tote bag of snacks.

When we reach a section of beach where the crowd thins, Harlow makes an executive decision that it's time to double back. We still have over half the flyers left, so she's getting more aggressive, saying things like:

"I'm Harlow Prout and did you know your beverage is resting in sand that costs a hundred thousand annually to dump ten miles south?"

"I'm Harlow Prout and did you know the worst storm systems in Maine's history will be upon us in ninety-five short days—or as soon as next weekend?"

Swing forward—the sexy tan lines I'm going to get from these forearm clasps.

Again—the tantrum I'll throw if Dr. Diaz doesn't let me off these things tomorrow.

Tommy follows a step behind Harlow and passes each victim a flyer. Carrying a palmful of something in his other hand. And then, impossibly, he passes her Goose's leash and a stack of flyers, and lets them go ahead as he falls into step beside me.

I have no evidence he feels anything but his usual quiet loathing for

Harlow. No proof anything's changed except I still don't get why he's happily participating in an outing even I no longer want a part of. Why he'd let her lay a finger on Goose's leash. But I'm a terrible person when I can't run, so I find myself saying:

"I said come to the beach with us, not kiss her ass."

About twenty pebbles and seashells fall from his hand as pink ripples up his neck, across his forehead. A few feet ahead, Harlow comes to an abrupt stop. She might've heard me. So what. She straightens her pile of flyers, dropping Goose's leash in the process, and Tommy and I watch as, for a moment, she and Goose lock eyes. Then Goose capitalizes on her good fortune and Harlow takes off after her.

I shouldn't be like this. When I go to the diner with my sports-meditation dream-it-believe-it-achieve-it workbooks, Tommy lets me keep working at the big table even when it's busy. I'm sure he heard me sneak out the night Jules and I met, and he didn't snitch. In another universe, I'd be happy to get through this afternoon without one of them strangling the other. But now that it's happening, I'd allow some strangling in exchange for one of them treating me like I'm not the third wheel.

Whenever I need Harlow she's somewhere else. I go to her house and, oh, she's at the diner. I go to the diner and she's back home. When I finally find her, she acts happy to see me for like five minutes, then assigns me a new task. Get "the enemy" to set up a livestream so she can spy on them ("Great idea!" Jules agrees. When I tell Harlow it's in progress, she says, "Oh my god, Ellis, that was a *joke*."). Tail Mr. Albertson and report back, in detail, about how he spends his Saturday (diner coffee; paperwork; plover check-in; B and B board-game night).

It's easier to go on these errands than to explain no one cares. Most West Finchers would rather get the insurance payout and buy a little plot of land up the coast, order one of those prefab houses that have to be delivered by the trucks with the lights and the oversize-load signs.

I return to her like I'm reporting back to a boss in a video game.

"That was fast!" she says, the compliment feeling like off-brand Oreos taste. Then she sends me away again.

Tommy's still a mystery. Even if I'd been able to secretly search his room this morning, I wouldn't have found much. He brings his bottle of antidepressants to work now, so I can't count his pills, and in my month of daily breaking-and-entering, I've searched his closet, bed, bookshelf some thirty times. No signs of a downward spiral. Not even a frowny face doodled on a sticky note. The only out-of-place thing I've found is that hoodie Harlow borrowed after I wrecked her car. Mom must've missorted when she gave back our laundry.

Tommy chases Harlow and Goose down the beach. He catches them— Goose immediately takes a seat in the sand and pants—and he whispers something in Harlow's ear. For some reason, this secret communication he knows I can see but can't hear makes me white-hot mad, but at least it makes Harlow turn around and actually look at me.

"You and Goose should go for a walk," she says when I catch up for the umpteenth time. Tommy holds out the leash.

I don't want to.

I take it anyway.

"People like a man with a dog," she says, which is true.

So now it's me and this butt-ugly dog. I have to coax her along by saying enticing words ("treat," "snack," "dinner") every few feet. And, yeah, let's give the dog to the guy on crutches. Though, after that sprint? This particular dog's not going anywhere fast.

I should've invited Jules instead of my brother. That would've really pissed Harlow off. I'm not seeing Jules *because* he's Skye's brother—I swear I liked him before I knew that—but it's a bonus.

Yesterday we went to a diner thirty minutes away, for a breakfast the internet promised would be "the mouthful of a lifetime." Jules is dedicated to their four-person protest—he already knows he wants to major in environmental studies when he starts at University of Montana this fall—but he doesn't want West Finch to be the only part of Maine he sees. No offense, he added. Like that didn't make him just that much cooler.

The dining room was bigger than MacQueen's, but there weren't as many windows, and the pancakes were hard to slice with the side of my fork, which means they were old. He raised a gloriously bushy eyebrow as I doused them with syrup.

"You have a sweet tooth," he observed as he nudged his glasses back up the bridge of his nose.

"Syrup is the first line of defense against bad breakfast food."

"It's bad?" He sawed off a bite and experienced it for himself. His face fell into beautiful ruin, an amber slick of syrup smeared across his lower lip. "Oh my god. My mouth is so sad now."

His mouth looked perfectly good to me.

I'd planned to tell him nothing about my life. That was kind of the point of dating a guy who's from the other side of the country. I mean, besides obvious reasons like his illegal cheekbones and the way everything he wears makes you want to see him take it off. I'd told him the night we met that I have a twin brother, a common courtesy in case he runs into Tommy. And I knew he'd hear stuff while staying in the Albertsons' B and B. But he wasn't going to get anything else from me.

Turns out when I look at Jules I can't shut up. I told him about getting tripped at my race, and how I'm supposed to go to camp but my coach is being a dick. I told him how easy it usually is between Harlow and me, but that something's changed, and neither of us will say what. I'd probably tell him about Tommy, too, but I haven't figured out how to recount those details to myself yet. I talked until I was laid bare: not the almost-varsity boy wonder, not Harlow's partner in crime. For once I was no one but the reluctant heir to a crumbling empire of pancakes.

"But yours are hella better than these." Jules poked his pancakes with his fork. "So you have that going for you."

I hooked my ankle behind his under the table. "I can't believe you unironically said 'hella.'"

"I can't believe I get to look at those dimples all summer." He leaned toward me and his glasses slid down his nose again.

"I can't believe you only like me for my looks."

"I can't believe this isn't the mouthful of a lifetime!"

Both of us lost it. Laughing into our fists. Crying by the time the waiter checked in to make sure all was okay.

Even Jules has obligations, though. I wonder if he's sitting by the bird nest in his little green fold-out camp chair right now. I wish I were there too, pulling up my own little chair beside him.

I text him: *goose + i banished from flyer handout. sentenced to walk beach for rest of time. some say when the sun reaches its highest point, you can see our ghosts.*

He writes back right away:

HOT
Spooky
Wear sunscreen, boo
(Get it??)

Goose and I walk near the water. The packed sand's easier on us both, although today's exertions have already pushed this dog beyond her cardiovascular limit, and the tips of my crutches still sink in. I dodge kids digging holes in the sand until they hit warm water underneath. They gape as I swing past, eyes round beads in their fat-cheeked faces. We stop and Goose looks up at me curiously, her pink tongue lolling.

"Stay," I command, pointing like Tommy does, though there's no way she'd mistake me for him.

I lay my crutches in the dry sand behind her so they won't get washed away. Sit and unlace my sneaker. Peel off my soaked tank. Feel Harlow's judgment from a half mile away as I break Dr. Diaz's no-hopping rule, let out a single whimper at the fire that lights in my hamstring, and wade in.

We never felt the cold when we were kids. Today it numbs my toes and ankle and holds my crotch in a tight grip, my basketball shorts clinging to my thighs. I get to waist-deep and dive, breaking into a front crawl. Goose barks. I hope she didn't come in after me, but I don't look back to see.

A wave smacks me when I come up for a breath and for a few seconds I'm drowning. That's what your brain thinks when there's water where air should be. It was drilled into us as kids that if somebody's drowning you don't be a hero and try to save them yourself. Boy Wonder or not, a drowning person basically turns into a monster. They'll use your body as leverage to push their own nose above the waterline, just to steal a couple extra seconds of life. I can't remember what you're supposed to do instead. They never reached that part of the lesson.

Salt burns my mouth. It's not far enough. I look toward the horizon and still see long slivers of land. I keep treading water and breathing. Tommy's more fit than I thought, to swim as long as he did. Or more desperate.

In one of my parallel universes I'm running. My arms pump. Sweat stings my face. I'm so fast that people stare for the right reasons. And I've done so many good deeds Harlow's and Tommy's hands hurt from clapping.

Twenty-Nine
TOMMY

Ellis gets his ass out of the water only after Goose jumps in a second time. I haul her out again. Hug all fifty wriggling pounds of her against my chest. The tumor on her belly is somewhere in this armful of fur and bones, and I swear if we go for chemo next week and they say she's worse that's on him.

To think I started off the day believing it meant something that he'd invited me. Of course, I already had an invitation—Harlow and I were supposed to hand out flyers today, that's why I took the day off—but apparently she made him the same promise and he actually remembered.

Ellis stops, up to his waist in the waves, wobbling a little as he balances on his left foot and looks expectantly at us. His crutches at Harlow's feet. She's clutching a thick stack of her remaining task force flyers. Working the inside of her bottom lip with her teeth as waves hiss and dissolve into the sand. She looks down at the crutches. Up at him. Doesn't move. When the history books write about how Harlow and Ellis imploded, they'll start with that look.

I set Goose down, kick off my shoes, and walk his crutches out to him like the sucker I am.

"I told her to stay," he insists as he pats Goose's side with a wet slap.

Like hell he did. I dig the Volvo's keys out of my pocket. "Let's just go home."

We brush sand off our feet in the parking lot before getting in the car.

I buckle Goose beside Harlow. She's careful to keep the middle seat buffer zone between them. One that Goose immediately breaks by starting a careful cleaning job of Harlow's sweaty arm with her tongue. Harlow spares me a guilty glance, but I pretend not to see and shut the door, letting Goose continue her task.

I can almost pretend the car-wide silence is voluntary between the rolled-down windows and the radio. I peek in the rearview mirror. Harlow's turning her fingers pink against the edge of the stack of flyers. Either she's in lockdown or about to explode.

"I really did tell her to stay," Ellis says to me. "The vet didn't say she can't swim, though, right?"

"It's fine."

"Doctors are pretty conservative about these things. I'm not supposed to swim, either, but I felt pretty good out there."

A little *hm* comes from the back seat. Ellis's fingers fly to turn down the radio.

"What's that?" he says eagerly. "Speak up, Harlow. We can't hear you."

Nothing comes from the back except the sound of Goose panting.

"C'mon. I'm sure you have thoughts to share." He twists sideways in his seat. "I'll get you started. How about, 'Ellis, you're not supposed to swim.' Or, 'Ellis, the seat belt won't protect you if you sit like that.' 'Ellis, look at all these flyers I have left. You've thrown off my entire schedule.'" He rolls his eyes. "I get tripped and this is how you treat me."

"No one tripped you," Harlow says.

"She speaks!" He faces forward with a smug smile. Mission accomplished.

When we get home she calls the first shower, then practically runs to the front door.

"'Course she's first. She's the only one who's not wet," Ellis grumbles. He jerks his head to the side to dislodge some stubborn water from his ear.

Goose is covered in sand. I squeeze between the bushes in front of the house and start unraveling the hose.

"Did you see that new seawall Artie put up?" he says. "It's massive. Really sturdy-looking."

When did he get so into seawalls? "I'll have to check it out."

He sits on the front steps. Scratching behind Goose's ear and making her back leg thump. Staring at nothing.

"What are you two even fighting about?" I ask.

It used to be our feelings could jump between us with just a look. A storm of anger in him could scale the dinner table and curl my fingers into my palms. But that line got clipped around the time my brother moved into his own bedroom. Now I have to give myself a pep talk to even ask.

"I ruined all her big plans for us."

"She said that?"

He shrugs, frowning. "Doesn't have to. She's been like this since my race. But it's not like I wanted to tear a hamstring, you know?"

I guess it's fair to expect your best friend to be there for you. Even if you're both kind of assholes. I twist the spigot and test the temperature against my palm. Goose trots over. Water runs off her in gritty streams. She's had chemo twice now—I just paid the first one off last week—and she's handling it. But still moving more slowly. Eating less.

Ellis brushes some sand off his sneakers. "I don't need her to entertain me or anything. I just wish she wasn't so . . ."

"Herself?" I chance a look up and intercept a brief smile.

"I told Jules about her and he's rightly terrified."

"Who?"

"The new protestor. Skye's brother." He blushes. Adds defensively, "We met before I knew who he was."

If I concentrate, I can almost feel the prickle of his happiness in my own chest. He must like this guy quite a bit. Harlow will flip if she finds out. Maybe that's part of the appeal.

I kill the water and Goose shakes off just as Harlow comes outside. Her hair's wet. Almost straight. Ends of her stretched curls disappearing into the collar of a T-shirt that has something to do with running. The short shorts his too, though they're a normal length on her. The whole effect gives me a feeling like I've inhaled a swamp.

"I want to go home." Hands on her hips. She's looking at me.

Ellis scoffs and gets up. "Swear to god, if you used all the hot water . . . ," he says as he pushes past her.

I drop Goose off in my room so she can rest and then Harlow and I are off again. It's a short drive. Three streets, two turns. So much easier than the ride home from the beach.

"I can't wait for him to get over this," she says.

Get over what exactly? But I nod. Ignore the part of me that feels like it's betraying him. I don't want to say if we're not careful he's going to notice. I don't want to say I don't care if he does.

"Did you pick classes for the fall?"

"Yeah." My guidance counselor sent Mom and me an email with suggested courses slotted in. Remedial math, US History (again), a study hall where studio art should be.

"What period do you have lunch?" she says, tone light, like this is normal.

"Fifth?" My voice weirdly high. Normal normal normal.

"Oh, good. We can sit together."

I picture the noisy, low-ceilinged cafeteria. Remember the smell of square pizza with too much sauce, the bullshit of trying to do math problems I should've finished last night, none of them coming out like they're supposed to. Sitting next to Ruby and her asking do I have my sketch pad and I always do, even the times I lie and say I don't.

The thoughts of bringing us—*this*—into that space is a little scary. Like it'll be exposed to too much sunlight. That thing that happens when you stick an inside plant outside and it withers, dies. But I can already feel us outgrowing the nothing spaces we have. Just the diner's basement staircase and this car. We have to step outdoors at some point.

"Prom's next weekend," I say. Thrilling start. "You going?"

She digs at a bug bite on her ankle. The back of the shirt she's wearing yells MACQUEEN. "No."

God, what am I doing? For all I know she asked him to prom and he said no. I smell our bodywash on her. Grapefruit and mint.

"I didn't want to," she clarifies, gnawing at a hangnail on her thumb.

"Oh."

"The storm," she adds. Which makes no sense because the storm next weekend has only been in the forecast a few days now, and prom's been planned for months. And she's going to the SATs. But no way I'm calling her out. She continues. "I guess you'll go to the Samuelses'?"

Because they have a generator. Because that's where my family always ends up when our power goes out.

"Could be a good thing. You never know." We're almost at her house now. "Maybe you'll see him and just . . ." She shrugs. She doesn't know what I'm supposed to say to Cliff, either. "Want to come in?" she asks her orange fingernails.

I want so many things. To pick her up from school in the afternoons so we have more time together. To share a look across the dining room when something bizarre happens, the way she and Ellis do, no fear of getting caught. Take her on a date and pretend we know how to function in front of other people. No passive-aggressive arguments about who has whose number and which blue-haired girl is watching Goose. I wonder what that'd be like.

I turn onto her street and we both see her parents' car in their driveway at the same time. Her face falls and my chest pangs once in response.

"Don't worry." I'm already executing a flawless three-point turn. "I think I know a place."

It's obvious Mom's the one who decorated our house because the only decor in Dad's room at the B and B is Red Sox–related. A signed baseball enclosed in clear plastic on the dresser. A poster of Fenway. There are two full beds, the one closest to the door unmade, the other covered in a woven Sox 2004 curse-breaking championship throw. Clothes tower in an impressive mountain on the armchair.

Harlow locks the door after us. Deadbolt and chain. I drop my keys on the table next to the door.

"Bedroom. Kitchen. David Ortiz jersey." I point to each.

"I've been here before."

Oh. Right.

She's eyeing the sketchbooks on the shelf under the TV. Wanting to give her something new, something she hasn't seen, I say, "You can look. I don't care."

I use the bathroom and try to make the best of a damp and sandy situation with Dad's deodorant. By the time I'm back she's sitting cross-legged on the second bed with the entire stack of sketchbooks fanned out around her.

I sit next to her as she turns each page like it's tissue paper. It's excruciating to watch her look at my old stuff. I have to resist asking what she thinks every other page. All those times she told me I was shit, did she mean it? Or was that just to screw with me?

"When are these from?"

"This time last year. When I lived here."

Her forehead wrinkles. "Interesting."

"What?" I check the page open before her. It's the same line work as all the pages before, views of this room from every angle, warm-ups, boring stuff.

"You were taking antidepressants then, weren't you?" She sucks in her cheeks a little. "I know some people think mental illness and creativity are, like, a thing. But this is one of your better scribbly drawings."

She has a point. Without seeing the dates, even I couldn't tell these drawings apart from the ones that came before my meds.

"Contour drawings," I correct her. "Not scribbles. They help you practice drawing things the way they actually look, not just the way you think they do."

She looks skeptical. So I gently turn her shoulders until she's facing away from me. Point out the coffeepot across the room.

"Let your eyes slowly follow its outline," I say in her ear. She laughs nervously. Her breath catches when I touch my finger to the center of her back. "Start at the spout. Don't look away."

I slowly trace the pot's shape on her skin. Over the letters of my last name on her shirt, the lines of her sports bra. My finger never leaves the warmth of her back but my eyes stay on the pot as I outline its button lid, curved spout.

I think of the pictures I've seen online of Parisian museums I'll never go to. The Musée d'Orsay, built in an old railway station. The Musée Marmottan, with its largest Monet collection in the world. If I could take her there, I bet she'd be the person who has to go in every gallery and give each piece its due. She could look at the art and I could look at her.

"I have a present for you," she says, disconnecting from my fingertip. "Don't freak out."

She rummages in her backpack and digs under the stack of printed flyers. At last she dumps seven bottles of acrylic paint onto my lap.

"For glass," she says, pointing to the label. "I thought you could paint the diner window."

MacQueen's isn't that kind of place. The big sign near the road is faded to hell, and our specials are on a whiteboard. There are a few old buoys strung on the wall but that's it. No net draped artfully from a corner. No fake-ass polished ship's wheel. I rub the plastic bristles of a cheap paintbrush against my thumb. Nudge one of the tiny tubes. Want to say yes.

"I don't do art anymore," I remind her.

She crosses her arms. "Yeah, and why's that?"

If I look at a blank page, a canvas, it will swallow me up. Too many places my brain could go. I need takeout orders to memorize. Long shifts shucking clams until my brain's too exhausted to play its usual games.

"It's not because of your meds." She counts on one hand. "It's not Ms. Russeau because who gives a shit what she says."

Just two minutes ago I drew the most devastatingly precise coffeepot in lines on her spine and she's right. I was fine. She's cross-legged in front of me and I touch my fingertip to her knee, outline the heart shape of her face. Just to see. Making art with a sketchbook or canvas still feels like driving down the highway in a car without brakes, but if this counts too? I let my finger trail a couple inches higher to the smooth skin on her thigh, tracing the wavy shape of her hair now. She grabs my wrist and covers my hand in hers on her hip. That moment before our mouths touch.

Then we're pressed together and making molasses-like progress toward being horizontal on this bed. Sketchbooks and paint tubes hit the floor without a sound. She smells like bodywash, *my* bodywash, and I smell like wet dog. I want her out of my brother's clothes, so I pull the shirt over her head and she yanks off mine. Sand coming from somewhere, from me, and as she reaches between us to brush it off her bare stomach, her hand nudges me through my swim trunks.

A sound escapes me I didn't know I could make. Low and kind of . . . catlike? Her hand springs back like she touched a hot pan, and she goes, "Sorry, sorry, I'm sorry."

This is the part where a normal person would say it's okay. I'm aching to let her touch me again. But I also really, really don't want to embarrass myself.

"I'm just not ready," I tell the ceiling. "I mean, not like I'll never be ready. But with my meds, I don't know if I can—"

"I'm not ready either," she says.

Great. Good talk. I want to pull the covers over my head and also go take a shower because nothing's worse than continuing to lie here. I roll onto my back with my arm over my face.

She tucks herself against the side of my body and gently peels my fingers off my face one at a time.

Lays them down one by one until the top of her rib cage is in my palm.

I feel the tender skin like paper over her collarbones, her heartbeat in her throat. Kiss her again. So slow we might be going backward. Then there's the click of a key in the door. Her sports bra under my fingers. The door. "*The door,*" she chokes and we spring apart because *someone's trying to get in the fucking door.*

"I'll get it, I'll get it," I say from inside my shirt. The chain lock the only thing saving us, thank god for that. A glimpse of Harlow through my collar. How'd she get hers on so fast? She reaches over and roughly yanks my arm through the correct sleeve before crossing the room and opening the door herself.

Dad stands like a stranger on his own doorstep. Shirt splattered with what smells like vinegar. His mouth a perfect O of surprise in his beard.

"Hey, Jim," Harlow says brightly. A definite quiver in her voice. "What's up?"

Dad looks between us, trying to make sense of what he's seeing. Harlow's curls wild. Lips swollen pink. Me surrounded by relics of a hobby I've given up. Bed looking distinctly rumpled.

Me. Harlow.

"I was just coming by to clean up." He unsticks his damp shirt from his chest. "Is everything okay?"

"Everything's . . ." I trail off. I've got nothing.

"I'm trying to convince Tommy to paint a mural on the diner's window," Harlow says smoothly. "We were looking for inspiration." Points to the sketchbooks and glass paint. "It was supposed to be a surprise. But now he's not sure it's a good idea. What do you think?"

What does Dad think? Why, it's the best idea he's ever heard. Mom will *love* that. Of course he won't say anything. Does he look like someone who ruins surprises?

"Sorry for breaking in." I scratch my shoulder. My shirt's inside out.

"Come over anytime!" Dad says. "You too, Harlow. Keep him busy! Ha!"

I don't move until he leaves, then leaves a second time after he forgets to grab his clean shirt. Harlow relocks everything behind him and leans with her back against the door.

"Oh my god. His face." Body shaking. *Laughing.* "You'd think he walked in on us naked."

I crack a smile as I cross the room to her. "Worse. We were talking about art."

"Ohmygod." Her hand to her chest. "I thought I was going into cardiac arrest."

The muscles in my face are stuck. "I don't think someone finding out we're hooking up would *kill you*." I chuckle. It sounds hollow, which makes sense, because somehow I feel emptier than before. So I press my lips to her jaw. "My dad would be thrilled I'm undressing a girl instead of drawing one."

I feel her smile. "Yeahhh. But he'd tell people."

"Maybe not."

She pushes me back a little so she can look me in the eye. "He showed people pictures of the lady he cheated on your mom with."

"Well, she hadn't been back in West Finch for like ten years. No one could remember what she looked like." But she's right. It's pretty damn weird.

She crosses her arms, stalks over to the window, tries to move the curtain on its rail. It won't budge. She paces back. Eyebrows raised like she's heard all she needs to. It's not the same though. Dad's dying for me to be cured. If I tell him my health relies on his secrecy he'll get that. Anyway, he seemed to buy our story.

"We'll tell people someday, right?" Out of my mouth before I can think but it suddenly feels like the most important thing. "We should tell people before it gets out some other way. We can start with my dad and see how it goes. Or the Samuelses."

Her lips press together. She touches her face and shakes her head. "Tommy, no."

Like she feels sorry for me. Except she's the one still trying to deep-breathe her own pulse away.

"What are you so afraid of?" I ask. But I know. "He won't care. He won't give a shit."

"It's not Ellis I'm worried about." Pink circles growing on her cheeks. "West Finch loves you. But it's not like that for me. They'll say so many things."

She goes quiet imagining possibilities. Deciding that, whatever they are, I'm not worth it. I think of explaining about the inside plant that goes outside, how we can't go from hiding straight to the cafeteria.

"We shouldn't do this again for a few days," she says. "Just to be safe."

I look around Dad's room and remember how small I felt when I lived here. The sketchbooks and paint my shields. Now my skin's see-through. Bones glass. Shirt inside out.

"You don't have to be mean to me. But no more of *this* for a little bit." She points back and forth: my body, her body. "No more risks. No secret trips to the vet. No sneaking off every day like the world's going to end. But think of it this way."

She puts something in my hand. A tube of blue glass paint.

"If you want to change my mind, you know how."

June

Thirty

ELLIS

Thursday, June 8

After school Coop and I hit the weight room. We have the place to ourselves, so while I roll out a slightly sticky mat and start Dr. Diaz's hamstring exercises, Coop messes with the stereo system until it blasts his "workout beats." After he's selected the perfect warm-up song, he stalks up to the pull-up bar, heaves his chin over it once, then flips upside down so he's hanging by his knees.

"Show-off," I mutter.

He crosses his arms over his chest and starts doing crunches.

"Dick."

I've been off my crutches and back on my prosthesis for almost ten days—luckily that endless beach trek last week didn't hurt anything but my arm muscles and ego—but it's still slow going. School's out next Thursday. By now I wanted to be packing for camp, not giving Coop a glute bridge demonstration. I take a quick break to pose for a mirror selfie to send to Jules. Scroll through my social media, skipping anything about track post-season, cross-country preseason, endangered birds, the big storm that's supposed to hit tomorrow. Nothing else to see.

"Will you go if I find you a date?" Coop says from across the room, voice squished because he's still upside down.

I groan. Prom is all the juniors and seniors can talk about. That and the

SATs happening the same morning, which only matter in that they'll leave the people taking them less time to pregame.

"It's our last weekend together!" Coop's eyes are bulging a little but he's fine, probably. "My sister leaves for New York in two weeks, so I have to hang out with her or get my ass kicked."

Pretty sure the bar association frowns on ass-kicking. But Ash Cooper isn't a lawyer yet, and maybe Columbia Law doesn't mind.

"Then July first I'm going to Vermont."

My phone silently slips out of my sweaty hand. "You're not."

He flips right side up on the bar and lands on his feet. "My doctor gave me a clean bill of health. So warm up that arm"—he makes a gesture Harlow would not approve of—"and get ready for some old-fashioned letter writing. Reception sucks up there."

My phone ended up facedown on the smelly mat. I flop down beside it, turning my head to the side so I don't suffocate, and wonder who will get my bunk under Coop's. Probably Ben. The complete varsity team.

Feeling sorry for myself, I roll onto my back. Watch upside down as Coop picks up his water—a gallon jug with the labels ripped off—and chugs. Then he splashes some down his shirt and his face lights up, so eager he is to ask: "Will you go if *I'm* your date?"

Standing now. Ignoring him. I jump and grab the pull-up bar with an underhand grip, pull myself up so that my chin is just above it, and hang there, weightless. Nothing for Dr. Diaz to disapprove about this. Somewhere below my phone vibrates. "What's it say?"

He stands under me and holds up my phone so I can see. Jules. A picture of him on the West Finch beach. They've set up a small wire enclosure over the piping plover nest to keep predators out, though the holes in the fence are big enough for the birds to come and go. Around the perimeter, on the seaward side, a few cinder blocks to act as bird-size seawalls. Photo-Jules crouches over these and flashes the camera a double thumbs-up.

Coop whistles at Jules. "How's your wife feel about him?"

I aim a half-hearted kick at his stomach.

"Ooooh, she doesn't know?!" He dances out of range of a second kick.

Jules isn't a secret but he's not *not* a secret. I thought she'd figure it out. Hear something. I've never had to tell her what's going on in my life before. Sure there's been some weirdness between us lately, but we don't need to have a long, drawn-out conversation about it. After Memorial Day she stopped disappearing, and I stopped doing her erosion club errands, and she complains and I make her laugh and once again we're back where we started. Harlow and I can't stay apart for long. It's as easy and hard as that.

I tighten my grip. My arms are shaking but it's the good kind of burn. I could stay up here all day.

"Shit, man. You know I don't want to abandon you," Coop says, cradling his gallon jug like a baby. "But you've got arm candy and tasty pancakes and these little tiny birds to look at on your little tiny beach. Relax."

I've got Harlow studying for the SATs this Saturday. Tommy willingly handing out her flyers and bringing her pink lemonade without asking. And I'm wasting away doing basic leg exercises when I should be in the best shape of my life.

Coop's playlist cross-fades into a bass-heavy song that makes the bar shiver under my hands. He taps his finger in time on his jug.

"Or don't relax. Burn shit to the ground. Consummate your marriage. Spend time with your brother. How's he doing?"

I breathe out through my teeth. "How should I know?"

You could ask. The voice of reason in my head always sounds like Harlow. I shouldn't have to ask, though. I should just *know*.

Even as I think it, I know I'm wrong. Believing-global-warming's-caused-by-hairspray-level wrong. Flat-earther level even.

"Go on. Call me on my bullshit," I pant.

Coop grinds the toe of his sneaker into the floor.

"Nah, man." He levels a steady gaze at me, so I can see he doesn't mean it when he says, "It was a shitty question."

I realize I'm waiting for Coop to tell me what to do. A new plan. Better options than the ones he gave me. But eventually I'm going to have to make better options for myself.

Thirty-One

TOMMY

Friday, June 9

I know how to leave a room before I'm in it. How to say nothing, and if I must speak, say nothing again in a different way. Being brave— not letting the paint tubes roll around my backpack for a third week, not piling shells in jars—doesn't come natural. But I better figure it out pretty damn fast.

It's trash day when the storm hits. Tipped garbage cans leave apple core trails and dental floss tangled in long grass like a game of cat's cradle. I help Dad fit boards over the diner's windows and unplug the ovens before locking up.

When the lights at home flicker, then go out, we pack our things. Ellis stops halfway down the driveway. Tips his head back. Lets the rain pelt his face. As Mom backs out he says, "You can just drop me off at Dad's."

"He doesn't have room for you," Mom snaps. Lying and we all know it.

Meanwhile I try to summon courage from somewhere. Anywhere. The folder in my backpack full of drawings I'm too cowardly to share. Goose's quiet calm next to me. My daily ration of text messages from Harlow.

Her: This is your chance!
Me: What am I supposed to say
Harlow: . . . Thank you??

I can't. Guessing this, she writes back:

Or don't say anything. Just sit with him.
Don't you DARE tell me you can't do it.

Mrs. Samuels is already at the front door when we pull up. She tiptoes to us in bare feet, past Cliff's lobster traps in a pyramid on the lawn, to deliver an umbrella. Of all the things for Harlow to be wrong about why's it have to be this?

Goose trots ahead as I let raindrops travel the length of my spine. They're already exchanging hugs. Through the open door I see him, and I know if I let him, Cliff will start a conversation I won't be able to get out of. So I push past. Making excuses as I head straight to the kitchen for a damp paper towel to wipe Goose's muddy paws. Cliff's eyes follow me, but he keeps his distance, and I feel guilty for how grateful that tiny act makes me.

One thing I forgot about the Samuelses' house is how much of me is in it. Every piece of art I was ready to throw away they'd take if I gave them the chance. And on the fridge one of the last pieces I ever gifted them. A colored pencil drawing of Cliff's boat that has so many claustrophobic lines it brings me to the edge of a trench. But I don't let myself fall in.

I'm mindful like Cool Therapist taught me. I notice: an itch on the back of my arm where a bug bite swelled up. The closed bathroom on the second floor Cliff warns us is "experiencing technical difficulties." The Samuelses being the Samuelses. Acting like married couples do in TV commercials. Stolen kisses in the hall, love notes scribbled on napkins. Even the way they move around each other in the kitchen an unchoreographed ballet. You're not supposed to see this kind of thing in real life I think. It creates unrealistic expectations, like maybe I won't become my parents with their separate kitchens and broken promises.

The bad weather means it's one of Cliff's few days off. He loses his breath taking out the trash, then catches it again at the kitchen table. Worse, Mrs.

Samuels acts like it's nothing new, just brews him tea and makes him take a nap.

I notice: guilt like a hot ball of wax in my gut.

Has he been like this long? Not like I would know. I haven't seen him from anything but a distance since I came home from the hospital. Before even then. Sometime after his heart attack. After I ditched my meds. Like we were both magnets and I silently reversed my poles.

I notice: how unfair that a person's heart can be so full in ways we can't measure but broken in all the ways we can.

—

To survive this weekend all I have to do is keep Goose comfortable and avoid Cliff Samuels. He looks at me? I look at my hands. He walks into a room? I walk out. I catch him pausing for a break after climbing the stairs? I retreat into the room with twin beds Ellis and I will share and hang my hands off my shirt collar like it's a life jacket until he's okay and I'm okay and we each go on alone. Courage is overrated. Self-respect can bite me.

That afternoon Ellis sits at the kitchen table with a box of crayons. The kind with a built-in sharpener. Feels like we've switched places. I should be throwing a baseball onto the roof and letting it bounce back down for me to catch, over and over, while he hunches over a sketch pad and ignores me.

He rolls the crayons across the table and I sharpen them until all sixty-four have the finest points I can get. Wet leaves slap the back door. He slides me some scrap paper.

"Jules out there?" I ask.

"Nah, fire department made them move."

Two sentences of our allotted five.

I find the orange Harlow's nails were last week and slowly fill a page with it. Think of what it'd feel like to coat the diner's big picture window in those paints. Above the table where they always sit. It would have to look as good facing in as it does looking out. The sun shining through the panes and making stained glass of her face.

He draws a storm cloud. A mountain.

Even if what I'm doing isn't technically drawing, it feels a tiny bit like bravery to hold something pencil-like in my hand. I think wildly I could do it. I could talk to Cliff right now. I set the crayon down until I get my head on straight again.

Ellis draws a shoe with wings. Pushes back his chair. Circles the kitchen and comes back with his phone pressed to his ear.

"He's fine. He's here. Say hi, man." I stare at him. "He says hi. He's drawing. Well, first he sharpened all the crayons. But now he just colored an entire piece of paper—what's that one?" I hold up my crayon. My eyes flutter closed. "It's called Wild Blue Yonder. Hey, Harlow says you should draw me."

Once upon a time we made self-portraits in elementary school and the only way to tell us apart was by who was more careful at coloring. I grind my crayon into the paper so that the wax builds up on the page.

"Harlow should study for her test," I say.

He relays my message, then listens to his phone. Nods. "Never mind. She says she wouldn't want to see your art even if you paid her. Not even if it's of me. She'd only look if she had to, like if you painted the goddamn diner or something."

———

The next afternoon I message Harlow to ask how her test went, knowing she probably won't reply. My daily ration of texts didn't come this morning—maybe the SATs' fault; maybe because she meant it about the painting—but I won't let that stop me from trying. There's sun coming through the window. It hits my face and I stop in the upstairs hallway while Goose finds her own patch of sunlight and curls up on the carpet. The storm isn't supposed to end until tomorrow, but if there's already sunshine, maybe we can go home. I can show Cliff my shitty sketches tomorrow. The next day. After that. I shut my eyes, too distracted by the warmth on my face to notice I have company.

Cliff's eyes are kind but his grip's firm when he catches my arm and says, "I've got to show you something. My best find yet."

Goose trots over and begins to paw at his leg, and even though I'm standing in the sun, I freeze solid.

"Can it wait?" I say like the piece of shit I am. But it's fight or flight, and all my body wants to do is bolt in the other direction. I wonder what's worse: letting him down again now or later. I've already done it once. Can't promise I won't do it again. And he doesn't deserve to be treated like that.

He pats my arm. "Really can't."

It isn't supposed to happen like this. *I'm* supposed to approach *him*. Drawings in hand, not stashed in my backpack down the hall. If I could go get them, show instead of tell him—

"I know how hard it is."

I search his blue eyes. Clear like a pool of water. A sheet of ice. "What is?"

"Letting someone help." His lips press together and his well-lined face crinkles even more deeply. "But it's a lot to go through on your own. Isn't it?"

Salt brine hangs heavy in the air, like someone dredged the bottom of the ocean and discarded it all right in this hallway. Like last storm. The smell of Cliff's boat. Of my own skin in the hospital, still pruny.

His misty eyes catch all the stormy light coming through the window and he looks how he did when he pulled me out of the water. Just like it. Face chiseled and wise, so used to hauling things from the waves that talking about this must be as easy as discussing the last lobster he caught. But if I let myself go under, who's to say he can save me a second time?

He squeezes my arm. "Take all the time you need, son. I'll be right here. Just want you to remember that."

His words snap me back to this moment, this hallway. The cross-stitched family tree on the wall. Dried flowers in a vase. Waves roaring in my ears though we're so far from the coast. And Cliff standing in front of me so fragile and gentle I want to break him in half.

"That was months ago," I say, my voice flat.

A stream of terrible things fills my mouth. I already had therapy this week. If I wanted to talk to you, you'd know. Why can't you just forget about it like everyone else? I don't know which things I say out loud. If it's all of them. Except the last thing, which I say for certain.

"And one more idea: Quit trying to help people who don't need it."

———

Harlow lifts the ban on us with a call after midnight.

"Are you in bed? Is he there? Cough or something for yes."

I glance at my brother sprawled on the bed across the room. Clear my throat.

"I canceled my score," she admits. "I didn't finish."

She explains yes, this is a real thing the SATs let you do. No, she's not proud. I'd say something comforting if I could speak. At least I'm not the only one who screwed up today.

"So." She stretches out the word. "Cliff."

I press my hands against my closed eyes until stars burst across their lids. Through the scattered light I see him: small without his cap, back in a hospital bed as the doctors crowd around. The man with the twice-broken heart.

"Can you tell me something about the plovers?" I whisper, hands still covering my eyes.

I hear something creak on her end. A bed maybe. The rustling of sheets.

"Plovers?" she echoes. But I don't have to ask twice.

As she talks I pretend moonbeams on the windowsill instead of lightning. Gentle rain patter instead of Ellis snoring in the bed opposite mine. Picture her cocooned in bed. The pastels of her childhood room, the only one I know, while she tells me all the ways those birds could pull through this storm. But I hear all the ways that she and I might. And after we hang up, I quietly reach for the paper and crayons on the nightstand between the twin beds and begin filling the pages one at a time, each a darker color than the last.

——

We drive to the diner the minute the cloud cover breaks Sunday morning. I can paint the next scene a thousand ways but won't know the truth until I see it. Maybe nothing has changed. Maybe everything. I'll bet Ellis has all his fingers and toes crossed that it's gone. On the off chance MacQueen's survives all this, he's made it clear I'm to inherit the place and leave him the hell out of it.

"Did you say goodbye?" Mom asks as I get in the car, but I haven't seen Cliff since our collision yesterday. Last thing he needs is me opening my mouth again.

The sky that same dusty ochre I remember from the last storm. When I got tired and floated on my back and—not drowning. Not today. We pull up and the diner doesn't look good but also no worse than anything else. Lights work when Dad flips them on. Ceilings and floors dry. Then Ellis and I circle around the building.

The back steps are soaked. Dumpster full of foam, air mostly mist, the sea all we taste. My eyes can't make sense of it. I search for something to break the plane but the seawall's strewn at our feet. The portion Ellis dismantled blends in with the rest.

I pick up one of the rocks and stack it. Another. A haphazard pile because I don't know how to still my hands. I want Harlow here to tell us what to do next.

Me: If someone was painting a window as a big gesture or whatever what would he paint?

My phone vibrates as soon as it's back in my pocket.

Harlow: If he wanted to do it right, he'd surprise me.

Thirty-Two

HARLOW

Saturday, June 10

The only good thing about taking the SATs in the middle of a storm is that Mom takes pity on me and doesn't make me drive myself.

During the ride I crane my neck and stare up at the gray velvet sky, willing it to open, even if that means we have to (gasp!) turn and go home. But the storm system has already quieted some in West Finch, and the weather only gets tamer the farther inland we drive.

When she drops me off, I'm not thinking about last time I was here. How I checked this bulletin board for my name and turned in time to see Tommy exit these same doors, the thoughts that drove him to swim two weeks later no doubt already swirling.

I'm also not thinking about how the other kids in this lobby probably haven't flunked yet. They're more worried about having time to pick up their corsages before prom tonight than about mistaking *decent* for *descent*.

Not thinking about the diner (*robust*) or the piping plovers (*fatuous*).

Not thinking as I squint at the multiple choice bubbles that language is inherently subjective, and if I can communicate effectively, what's it matter if I'm a bad test taker?

Here's something that would be worse than failing again: if I get a good score, beat Ellis even, and in the end, he finally admits he doesn't want to go to the same school as me. Or, worse than that: we go to the same place and he still forgets me. The possibilities build up in my chest and suddenly I'm out the door.

Mom's car is waiting in the parking lot. It's pouring, and the wipers are going as fast as they can, but we still can't see anything through the windshield. I buckle up. A lukewarm raindrop slips down my back.

"Don't be mad," I say. "But I may have canceled my score. And by 'may have' I mean I did." Then I explain the option exists for a reason and if I'd waited until we got home, we'd have to pay fifteen dollars, so really I was being frugal.

Mom turns off the wipers and the car is silent. The world outside disappears in a curtain of rain.

"You don't have to go far for college, sweet pea." She tilts her head thoughtfully. A strand of wavy gray hair sweeps across her forehead. "You don't have to go at all. You could take a year or two to figure out what you want."

"I know what I want." Wanting has never been the issue for me. It's getting what I want and not screwing everything up in the process.

By the time we get home, I already have a message from Tommy asking about the test. I can't walk down certain streets in West Finch because they bring back bad memories, but here he is, first big storm since his swim, and he's asking how my thing went. Maybe he's silently freaking out. It's normal to feel weird when you're back where something bad happened, I could tell him. Sucks that he can avoid swimming forever if he wants but not the weather.

I probably shouldn't let him get away with not talking about his swim last storm, or what's going on with Cliff. Clearly Ellis isn't asking. But what was it he said to me in his room, that he could only tell me shit because I don't care about him? So I don't respond. What choice do I have?

I brainstorm new fundraising ideas for Bring Back Our Beach (cakewalk, movie night, auction off a date with Ellis). I send Mr. Albertson a "friendly" email for the second week in a row asking for updates on the jetty situation.

Of course I don't want the piping plovers to die in this storm, but if they do, what's the plan?

It's been hours since the test when Ellis texts, *1600?*

I'm thinking about how bored he sounded on the phone yesterday. I'm thinking Tommy was right that maybe Ellis wouldn't care—wouldn't even notice!—if we were a couple in public. I'm thinking how he didn't ask until now because he forgot.

I type the words before I can think twice. **Want to hear something bad?**

He replies immediately. **how bad?**

I canceled my SAT score.

His next messages hit in quick succession:

**HARLOW
WHAT
RIP The Plan** ☹

I feel a twinge of guilt before I remember The Plan was already on its last legs. I write back: **Who needs college anyway?** I mean, *we* do, clearly. Despite what Mom said, college is what's supposed to happen next.

Three dots appear, then vanish. His name on my screen. Calling me.

"You're brilliant," he says. "That's what they'd say about you in the UK, which is where I think we should go first."

I move to a spot closer to the window. It's midafternoon, but the storm has picked up again, so the sun's hidden under a veil of orange and purple clouds. "I think you cut out."

"Why are we so set on plunging ourselves into debt and being apart? Have you *met* other people?"

"I try to forget," I agree. My pulse beats in my ears because no matter what he says next, I know I'm in.

"So screw it. Let's not go to college. Not right away."

He talks fast as he explains. I can practically hear his hands as he gestures. But I've seen my share of Ellis's fantastic ideas crash and burn, or more often, get abandoned partway through.

"What about track?"

He scoffs. I picture him batting my worry right out of the air. "I can run in Miami Beach."

"And eat croissants in Paris?" I try.

"Drink wine in Paris!"

"Sleep in the Arctic Circle."

"Climb Machu Picchu."

These places mean nothing to us. Neither of us has ever left the country. Ellis hasn't even been on a plane. But it's the idea of doing these things together. That no matter what it looks like around us, rain forest or marshland, waterfalls or cobblestones, we'll be us. Ellis, Harlow, dream team.

Who wouldn't want that?

———

It's after midnight when I call Tommy.

"Are you in bed? Is he there? Cough or something for yes."

He clears his throat.

"I canceled my score. I didn't finish." I pause a moment. "I know you can't say anything, which I guess is why I wanted to tell you now." I twist the end of my braid around my finger. "Don't worry, I can imagine what you'd say. Probably that this whole canceling a score thing sounds fake, which it's not, or that I'm stealing your moves, or how you're a bad influence."

He chuckles softly. It makes my stomach swoop.

I pull my blankets up around my face. I've been researching and we could travel all over Europe without getting in a car once. I don't want to talk about that with Tommy, though I'm wondering if I could get Ellis to wait so his brother can come with us. I'd have a year to convince him. To *tell him.*

"So," I say with several extra syllables, hoping he'll interrupt me. "Cliff."

His silence is a world of its own. One I can't fully understand, except for the shame, which I know well. It's the last thing I'd wish upon anyone.

"Can you tell me something about the plovers?" he whispers.

I switch my phone to my other hand. "Plovers?" I repeat.

He coughs several times.

So I tell him about the other research I did today. How when Hurricane Sandy hit New York, the piping plovers came back stronger than ever because the wind and floods gave them new areas to nest in. Or the plover couple on Martha's Vineyard that, when their nest was overwashed during a springtime storm, rolled the egg back to safety with their little beaks.

"They're gonna make it," he says, already half-asleep, almost too soft to hear. "Us too."

Despite my better judgment, I believe him.

Thirty-Three

ELLIS

Sunday, June 11

I don't care which universe you're in: You can't help but be optimistic after a storm.

There's damage, sure. Downed power lines and trees stripped of limbs. Floodwater pooled around the pile of Cliff's lobster traps when we left this morning. An annihilation of the diner's seawall so thorough it makes my earlier attempt look like nothing but a toddler knocking over a tower of blocks.

But there are also more pictures from an adorable, bespectacled boy that show a chicken-wire pen in the sand, and in it, a pair of black-collared birds and their nest. Their two eggs washed up maybe a hundred feet away and they used their tiny beaks to roll them back. It's pretty amazing, even I'll admit that.

Better still: flying down the damp streets on my bike with Harlow next to me. She hasn't had power all weekend, but I've done plenty of research for the two of us.

"We can ride an elephant in India for only a couple dollars each," I say as we coast side by side down Birch Street.

She wrinkles her nose. "That doesn't sound humane."

"Fine. You can watch me ride an elephant." She scratches her chin under her helmet's strap. I continue more loudly. "And we'll be of age in lots of countries. We can have a pint in Glasgow. Or drink one of those beers brewed by Belgian monks."

"Sounds like a lot of things you'll be doing by yourself."

My ears feels hot. "Well, yeah. I'm describing the stops that are tailor-made for me." *Nice save, MacQueen.* "Want to hear what I have planned for you?"

"For me?" she echoes. A damp strand has unraveled from her braid and plastered itself to her neck. She tightens her grip on the handlebars and chances a quick glance my way.

I tell her about the ruins as we pedal down the empty street. Chichén Itzá. The Acropolis. Pompeii. Places that saw disease, war, famine, bad luck, yet still exist. Where you can touch stones carved thousands of years ago and see that most things can be saved, if not always in the ways you expect.

Smashed flowerpots, swamped lawns, and a post with a missing mailbox fly past us. We're going fast now but keeping pace with each other, and all over again I'm grateful to be off my crutches, the only logistics to worry about the usual, as simple as hopping on my bike and securing my right shoe in the pedal's toe clip.

"You'll go to all of those with me?" she says, a little wonder in her voice. Water arcs from her back tire as she rides through a puddle.

I give her a winning smile. "I'll go wherever you want."

———

We're headed back to the diner when I spot the coast guard boat with the bright orange stripe down the side docked near the marina, a couple streets north of the diner. I steer in that direction and Harlow follows. What kind of West Finchers would we be if we let someone keep their business all to themselves?

Inside the life-jacket-cushioned walls of the marina store, I find Mom on the phone behind the counter; Fran and Joe Caskill, the marina's owners; and four members of the coast guard. The whole store smells of them, sweating in their navy-blue uniforms.

It's only after scanning the room twice that I notice Tommy. He's sitting on a small stack of overturned buckets next to a display of fishing poles, his face pinched. Harlow goes to interrogate him while I float to the counter like a fly to a porch light. Half-drained paper coffee cups from the diner polka dot a surface otherwise littered with artifacts: stainless-steel thermos. A pair of silver keys on a neon-plastic key chain designed to float if they fall in the water. A Swiss Army knife. A cigarette carton, the same brand my dad and Cliff sometimes smoke.

"What is this stuff?" I ask.

Harlow comes up beside me as I run my fingers over a pilled fleece blanket. There's a rotating display of kitschy key chains on my other side, so there's not much room, but she presses in close, her hair tickling my ear. I nudge her back with my elbow. She catches my wrist. I'm still trying to place the blanket. It's old and probably cheap, but, god, it's familiar.

"You family?" says the nearest member of the coast guard, a twenty-something baby-faced blond, as Harlow says in my ear urgently, "Ellis, it's Clifford Samuels."

I look back and forth between them, not sure what either means. And then Harlow and I see the last two items at the same time:

The jagged pieces of a crushed sand dollar strewn across the counter.

A red knit cap.

What my parents know: Cliff went out on his boat right after we left their house this morning. Mrs. Samuels tried calling him because he was late for dinner. Then she called the coast guard. They found his boat within an hour, but he'd already been gone awhile. Heart attack. Second time.

Harlow evaporates into thin air, and knowing how she feels about him, I'm not sorry to see her go.

My eyes land on Tommy again. His elbows are propped on his knees, his chin on his hands, hands clenched together in a single fist. Cliff's been looking out for him for so long. Even though it's impossible, he's who needs to talk Tommy through this. The only one who can.

But he's stuck with me.

I narrow my eyes and squint hard at my brother. We lost the connection thing a long time ago and, like my leg, I know it's not growing back. But maybe if I sit near him for a few minutes I'll feel a twinge of what used to be, like the pins and needles I feel in all ten toes. Just a prickle to tell me how bad it is in there.

I stop short in front of him, rocking on the balls of my feet. "Want to go for a walk?"

He looks up at me darkly. "Sunlight cure? Really?"

I don't know why what I said is bad. I don't know what else to say. This is why I don't try to help. We have maybe a quarter of what he and Cliff did. An eighth. I take a small step back.

He sighs through his nose. "Just—don't try to cheer me up. That's all."

I can manage that.

I stack a few of the big plastic buckets together and drag them behind him so that we're sitting back-to-back, then interlace my fingers behind my neck and let my head hang. I don't think I believe it about Cliff yet. Won't until I go to the diner on a Sunday and don't find him there for supper, or see someone else's catch fill the lobster tank.

I tell myself if Tommy gets up, I won't go after him. If he says he has to be somewhere, I'll pretend to believe him.

But he sits. So I sit.

Long enough for the coast guard to leave, and Mom and Dad to go back to work, because literally come hell or high water, MacQueen's doesn't close.

"I can't stop thinking about that fucking seawall," Tommy says behind me.

I knit my hands together in a single tight fist. Steel myself.

"We should rebuild it for real," I say. "Like Cliff and Dad used to."

"So you can take it apart again?"

Ouch. Moving right past that one. "We'll have to get supplies. Rocks, I guess? Concrete? I'll ask Dad for a list."

He rubs the back of his neck with two hands, then freezes like that, a statue with its head bowed toward its knees. The nape of my own neck warms.

"You really want to?" he says.

Neck still hot, I'm not ready for the dizziness when it hits: a sickening, heady wave like I stood up too fast, or like my head's between my knees.

Something of my brother's. Moments late. But *something*.

"We have to."

Thirty-Four

TOMMY

Monday, June 12

The first morning after he's gone I'm up at dawn for an early shift. I put Goose in the back seat and wait for Mom in the driveway, where I'm bathed in a sunrise so blue and gold it makes my teeth ache just thinking I'm the one alive to see it. Could've died but haven't yet. Me and Goose and the birds with their eggs on the beach.

We get to the diner and somehow I do all my usual tasks in the same order as always, right down to checking near the register for a new piece of treasure from Cliff. Like today is any sort of normal.

There's no guarantee he would've left me anything after what I said last weekend. What I didn't. Except knowing Cliff, he would've. Because it was important. Even our final conversation started with him trying to show me what he'd found. Just for a second.

Now I'll never see what he wanted me to.

As I peel potatoes over Dad's sink, they keep coming. A flood of finalities. Never get to apologize. Never try asking about his life with the same interest he showed asking about mine. No making good on our agreement to go back to the South Solon Meeting House, this middle-of-nowhere church with art on every wall that we visited in March but neither of us saw properly. No thanking him for saving me the storm before last, and all the times before that. And after. By the time I'm through my hands are gritty with potato starch and I've hit the bottom of their tall paper bag.

Voicing my worst thoughts first thing—even silently, in my own head—quiets them for a few hours. Makes the rest of the day feel like a dream. For once everyone is more miserable than I am. Dad forgets to flip the sign on the window from closed to open, and Mom burns everything she tries to bake. Several hours of failure later she sends me on a secret trip to Hannaford and I buy any baked goods that look like she could've made them.

The biggest difference in a world without him isn't how I feel. It's how other people treat me. Questions about how I'm doing dry up now that there's an obvious reason to ask them. Either they're all tongue-tied at the thought of saying the wrong thing—or they never wanted a real answer in the first place.

If they did ask, my answer would be the same. Fine. And that'd be true. Everyone so expects me to fall apart that I just *can't*. How can I let myself go when others feel it more? Mrs. Samuels. My mom, who knew him more than twice as long as I did. Last night after we got home from the marina I found her standing over a kitchen sink full of soapy water and dishes. The water gone cold when I dipped my finger. I drained the suds and sent her to bed.

I don't have to think about Cliff. He's there when Chuck brings in his lobster haul at six instead of Cliff's clockwork quarter-to. The roar of the ocean when Goose and I walk home is all Cliff, as is the sound of a boat motor cutting out, and the way Dad rushes over to help when I distractedly let a five-quart pot boil over. Mrs. Samuels wanders in around midday and never finds her way out, so Mom puts an apron over her head and flours her hands.

I spray down the diner's picture window and see Goose tied up in her usual spot when it hits me that I forgot to give her her medicine last night. A scramble to call the vet. Dropping my phone. They tell me to skip it and just give them to her tonight, like it's no big deal.

But it is. Because if I didn't give Goose hers, it means I accidentally skipped my meds too. And I don't feel any different at all. Like maybe I'm just as okay as I told Cliff I was. Maybe I don't even need them.

I've been down this road before. I know better. I'll take them again tomorrow, back on schedule, but if we're just *noting things* like Cool Therapist says to, then it's interesting I didn't miss them. A temporary experiment.

Another temporary experiment: digging the tubes of paint Harlow gave me out of the bottom of my bag. Before I can think too much I rip the protective plastic off the caps.

And then I paint. Choppy waves, navy blue layered on smoked indigo spires, smudged white foam. When I go outside to check how it's coming along, I can see my reflection in the window too, the feathered waves halfway up my chest. I may look like I'm drowning but I'm not.

I add the number 81 in orange to the upper left corner: the countdown to September first, peak hurricane season. Harlow's doomsday. She has the sense to stay clear of the diner today, but whenever she's back, I hope it'll make her smile.

The first time Mom sees it she walks up to it, reaches over the empty table where Harlow and Ellis have spent half their lives. Touches the dry brush-strokes, then my arm with the same motion, checking if I'm real.

"Awesome work!" Dad says later, doffing his Sox cap in admiration. His smile so eager, I think his face will shatter into a million pieces.

⸻

My family treats me like I just got out of the hospital again. Watching me, pretending not to. The only time I'm alone is when I sleep and I'm not getting enough sleep because Ellis comes into my room at eleven at night and just starts *talking*. Seven years of silence and now I couldn't shut him up if I tried.

Sitting on my floor as he does a complicated series of leg exercises with a stretchy band, he talks about how in another universe he'd be getting ready for running camp, and should we put the seawall plan on hold out of respect for Cliff and start after the funeral?

About the protestor he's seeing, Jules: "You know what he said when he heard about Cliff? 'He seemed like a special guy. I'm sorry I didn't get a chance to know him.'"

"That's really kind," I say, trying not that hard to stifle a yawn.

"*I know*. And I could tell he wasn't saying it just to say something. He actually meant it, you know? It was very mature. I think I can only date older people now."

"What about when he goes home?" I draw a spiral in the carpet.

"Months away." Ellis swats an invisible fly. "Speaking of nice people, you still talk to Ruby?"

My phone in my butt pocket burns with her unanswered text from last month.

"I have her number, if you want it."

Anger pricks my insides. Of course he thinks I don't have her number. The real question is, why does *he* have it?

"She messaged me, actually," I say. He sits up perfectly straight. There. I'm not quite as pathetic as he thinks. "Before your race."

His hand automatically touches the back of his thigh. "What'd she say?"

"I don't know. Just, like, I'm thinking of you or whatever."

"Show me."

And because this is the longest conversation we've had in years, I do it. I carefully tap into Ruby's message before handing over the phone so that he won't see anything from Harlow. He reads it fast.

"You didn't say anything."

I shrug. "She just feels sorry for me."

"So? When she sees you, she'll realize how great you're doing. Tell her you've been working. Wait, no. Just say, 'Sorry, been super busy. When can you get coffee?'"

"That's . . . I don't . . ." I can't form sentences. Specifically ones with "no" in them.

"I'm texting her."

Two seconds later he flashes the final message for my approval. Hits send. Grins at me and for a half-second the corners of my own mouth feel tight even though I'm not smiling.

Okay. I didn't feel this on my meds.

For the thousandth time I picture telling my family about Harlow and me. How relieved my parents will be that Goose isn't the only one keeping me going. Surely Ellis wants me happy. But could he ever be this enthusiastic about helping me write a message to Harlow? Or is she off-limits, a toy that belongs only to him?

He'd be able to tell me what's going on in her head right now. Whether this "break" is the trademark Harlow move where if she can't figure out how to solve a problem she ignores it completely. Or worse, removes herself from my life little by little until it's like we never happened.

What about when summer is over and I'm a grade behind? Maybe by September we'll smile at each other in public. Or maybe she'll apply for colleges and make numbered lists about her future and forget me. It's not the worst that could happen. The worst would be if she's only been pretending to like me this whole time—and of all the possibilities, this seems the most like her.

———

Here's a problem with the whole "I'm better" claim: My room looks exactly like it did in March. I've been telling myself there's no time to clean up between all my shifts at the diner. Been telling Mom that too. She swallows a new bead of worry each time she comes into my room, wondering does it only look this way because I don't plan to stick around. But it's not like that. More just, what if looking through that stuff makes me feel like I did back then?

My desk. That seems doable.

I stack the notebooks and folders, the math textbook I never returned, and pile them in a desk drawer. I'll need them come fall. Use my shirt to dust off the jar of treasures from Cliff until it shines. Leave the radioactive sketchbooks where they are, but order them on the shelf from oldest to newest. I hide the drawings I showed Cliff between the pages of the sketchbook I would've filled this spring and summer but never opened. Forget they exist as soon as I close the cover.

Next to the desk I pick up clothes off the floor. Can't tell if they're clean or dirty so I dump them all into the hamper. Better already. When it feels too quiet, pull up the piping plover livestream on my phone and let the speckled eggs keep me company. Caleb Prout says they'll hatch soon.

The artwork in all shapes and sizes looms between my bookshelf and the door. If anything is going to put my temporary experiment to the test—no meds for two days now, the first day a mistake, the second a bigger one—it's this.

I don't want to look. Better to throw every single piece into the trash. But considering that the last time Cliff and I spoke I yelled at him about how okay I am, avoiding these doesn't feel like an option.

I drag the canvases and paper pressed between cardboard to the middle of my room. The boxes under my bed too. They used to be labeled with names I've since scribbled out but I know who was getting what. Goose hops off my bed, paces over to me, and sniffs each item I pull out of the pile. In the box for Mom, a grimy stuffed-animal puppy from when I was a kid. In Dad's, all the Sox memorabilia he's gifted me over the years. I find the box with Ellis's name on it and the single piece of art marked for him: the small canvas with the cerulean waves that won that award the night of his first race. Can't even remember the name of it.

My clock says it's already after ten. There's more junk than carpet now. I'm tempted to shove everything into my closet and say look! Clean! But if I don't start moving this stuff tonight I never will. I pick up just the canvas for Ellis. Cross the bathroom. Knock.

My brother and Harlow sit cross-legged on his bed, faces arctic blue from the laptop screen between them. Three different notebooks and a rainbow of pens. Orange peel ribbons on the carpet. The smell of nail polish. Her extra hair band on his wrist, his T-shirt on her chest, his basketball shorts her pj's. *Ellis and Harlow*, the still life.

He jumps off his bed and waves me through the doorway. "Come on in. We're contingency planning."

Abort mission. Drop the painting and go.

"Higher education would squander our limitless potential," he explains as he takes the canvas from me and lays it on his desk. "We're building our own curriculum."

My fingers flex at the idea of stealing my painting back and retreating. "What's that involve?"

"Tell him."

Harlow stops squinting down at the laptop and peeks up at me. Her hair in two braids. Sewn up tight.

"Travel," she says in a small voice.

"But not some cliché European tour. Ruins only. Athens and Rome, Stonehenge, the Mayan pyramids, Jaipur. I'll fly back when Harlow meets a hot foreign guy and they run away together."

"He's making that part up," she says quickly.

His smile's all teeth. "The plan's wonderfully flexible."

I force myself to look away so I don't have to watch him inspect the canvas. It's wrapped in wax paper. He starts on the masking tape at the back, and a moment later, lets the wrappings fall to the desk, flips the canvas over.

"I'm throwing it out," I say. "But it's yours if you want it. Thought I'd check."

He picks up the canvas. Crosses the room. Lands next to her on the bed.

"I like the colors." He holds it between them so she can see.

"It's old," she says.

She leans closer to the painting until there's no seam of light between his knee and her thigh, and they're still sitting like that when I go back to my room.

———

When Harlow knocks on my door at 2:00 a.m., she's holding my blue painting.

"What is *this*?" she whispers as she and the canvas storm past me. Goose's ears perk up and she lets out a single, happy bark. I think she's started to associate Harlow with treats.

Canvas held over her head, Harlow steps over the drawing and boxes and squats down in the middle of the trash of my life. Part of me's embarrassed that all my weird childhood memorabilia's on display. Part of me thinks if anyone's going to see the contents of all those boxes I'd want it to be her.

"You're giving away your stuff."

I cross my arms. "Cleaning."

"You can't do this." She touches the stuffed puppy's belly. Her nails electric yellow.

"I can't make anything new with this old shit lying around. I'm trying to move on." More quietly, I say, "I'm okay, Harlow."

She looks up. Surprised. I wonder if she can see I'm not on my meds, even if she doesn't have those words for it. The night-day difference is obvious to me. Like the numb fog has burned off and I finally remember what I want.

"No, I mean you can't give away all this. It's not a good look." She stands and pats my arm twice. Double electric shock. She props the painting I tried to give away on top of my bureau. "Besides, if you give that second-place Congressional Art Award winner to anyone, it better be me. I've always liked it." She looks over her shoulder at me with a little smile. "Your painting at the diner reminds me of it."

Now that she's said it it's obvious. Of course I can't give my childhood keepsakes back to my parents or hand deliver a painting and say no matter how things went, this was meant for you. How is it she can go two weeks barely talking to me but still always know exactly what I should do?

But she doesn't always know. No she doesn't.

"Have it," I say, bland as can be. "Put in your checked luggage. Give it to your hot foreign boyfriend."

"Oh please." She rolls her eyes.

"Were you going to tell me you're leaving before you board the plane or after?"

I sound childish but also everything I feared about her ditching me is true and I want to hear her say it.

"I want you to come too." She pinches her bottom lip. Nods. "We'll wait for you."

"He agreed to that?"

She turns a little pink. "He will. I'll tell him I won't go without you."

My chest tight. *Like I need you to convince him.* Quick, savage, not helpful. I take a steadying breath. "And how are you going to do that if he doesn't know about us?"

She puts her hands on her hips. Stumped. "There's time," she says.

Maybe. But I've seen what happens when you bank on someday. You end up with a list of lasts and nevers. A half-empty treasure jar and a shelf of abandoned sketchbooks.

If I can't be brave enough for everything, I can at least start with this.

"I know you're not ready to tell anyone about us. Maybe you'll never be." I close my hands over nothing. Palms sweaty. "But I want to take you out. On a date. I mean, the vet waiting room's great, but we have other options."

I know I should be patient. But I don't want to find out through my brother about her future plans. I want to eat lunch with her at school. Look as healthy outside as I feel inside. Talk on the phone and actually speak. Only I'm too chicken to say any of it out loud.

So here I am: heart beating like it's desperate to be heard while Harlow scrunches her face as small as she can get it. Ages fifty years while I'm looking right at her. Then nods once.

It's enough.

She reaches into the pocket of her basketball shorts and pulls out a bone-shaped dog treat. "Can I?" she asks. She must've nabbed it from the box downstairs. No wonder Goose was happy to see her.

I agree and she clambers onto my bed beside Goose, who watches the treat's progress with interest. I climb up next to them and slip my arm around Harlow's middle. I wait for her to nudge me off, and when she doesn't, lower my chin onto her shoulder. Inhale.

When I got Goose, I told Harlow she wasn't allowed to touch her. Something about thinking she's bad luck. The human equivalent of walking under an open ladder. The only rule she's obeyed after all this time.

But I don't believe she's bad luck anymore. Now I know she causes her own trouble. I'm familiar with the impulse myself.

"Want to pet her?"

Harlow freezes. Treat dangling and poor Goose waiting with her mouth hanging open.

We give Goose her treat and then I show Harlow the right amount of pressure to use when scratching behind her ear. How to rub her belly in circles to make her fall asleep.

Harlow strokes Goose's head with its thick, fluffy fur. Scratches her velvet ears. Pats her belly. Holds her paw. Smiles like I've gifted her the moon.

Thirty-Five

HARLOW

Thursday, June 15

At least everyone in West Finch is home watching the piping plovers hatch. That's what I tell myself when Tommy and I are sitting twenty minutes in traffic, headed somewhere that's sure to break me out in hives.

I told him yes to the date the other day because he lost Cliff and I wanted to be there for him. Then one of the plover eggs started wiggling and I thought, hey, maybe this is that lucky break thing people talk about. Date night could be spent cuddled up in his bed, watching on the livestream as those impossible fluffballs are born.

And if we couldn't stay home—well, someone says date, you expect a movie. That's what Ellis does. From what I've gathered, you sit in the last row, find the other person's hand in a tub of buttered popcorn, and see where things go from there.

We're not driving in the direction of any movie theaters I know.

"Is it mini golf?" I guess. "I get very competitive. Fair warning."

Somehow I can picture it without really trying: me keeping careful score with the miniature pencil, looking cute with my bouncy date-ponytail and the blue date-bandana tied around it. Tommy getting a hole in one as I lose my ball in the unnaturally blue water, him retrieving it for me, smile, dimples, hands smelling like chlorine in my hair by the windmill on the final hole . . .

Tommy shakes his head. He's in a plain white T-shirt, no MacQueen's logo or anything. He's layered some sort of spicy cologne over his signature scent of frying oil, and he's humming along to the radio, which, rather self-lessly, I haven't even asked him to turn off. I gently itch the back of my arm. A hive, definitely. I should ask him to take me straight back home for the sake of my health. He keeps driving, though, and I keep letting him. The school year ended as of 2:39 p.m. today and finally we're the same. Just two people on summer break.

"Is it bowling?" Bowling isn't quite as dark as the movies, and I don't want his bowling-ball grease hands touching my face, but at least we won't see anyone we know.

Tommy puts on his blinker. We turn left, though I can see the ocean through his window, and there's nothing that way but the beach, a pier, and the seasonal seaside carnival with an ancient wooden roller coaster. He rolls down his window, passes an attendant in a yellow vest ten dollars, then pulls into a narrow parking space inches from a car with a Pennsylvania license plate.

I know he doesn't like leaving Goose alone for more than an hour. I know this is supposed to be sweet. But the Palace Playland amusement park is the opposite of a movie theater. It's people everywhere, all the time. Mostly tourists, but people from school come here too.

"Surprised?"

I stare up at the sun-bleached Ferris wheel. "You told me this place was trash."

Tommy smiles and tucks a flyaway behind my ear. "Doesn't sound like me."

"You said the only people who go to Palace Playland have no self-respect."

He unbuckles his seat belt, then mine. "I like the people watching."

No, that's an Ellis thing. He and I used to come to opening weekend every summer to eat funnel cake. This year, neither of us brought it up.

"I thought we'd go somewhere *you* like," I say, hoping I sound affection-ate, not apprehensive, as we pass under a huge archway of marquee letters that spell out PALACE PLAYLAND.

He gives me an amused glance, still looking pleased with himself. "When you plan our next date, feel free to choose something that's all about me."

In that case, I'm reserving the right to plan our next several dates. We'll paint pottery, wander an art museum in Boston, take Goose on a hike after autumn sets the trees alight, drive along Route 1 with the windows rolled down and his jacket like a blanket over me, all the while displaying impressive self-control, not falling for him, never that.

I pull him toward the ticket booth so we can get this over with. Hopefully we can just go on the swings a couple times and no one we know will see us.

I buy the smallest ticket bundle they'll allow and pass Tommy half. "Want to go on a ride? Or should we get dinner out of the way?" Pizza would be the fastest option (handheld; individual slices so no squabbling about who gets the last french fry). Or maybe we can subsist on milkshakes?

"Let's take a lap," he suggests.

Yes, let's parade around the entire park to increase our chances of seeing someone from school. By all means.

I lead him through the alleyways of brightly lit stands with striped awnings. Tommy takes in the horrible sights and smells with unabashed zeal. He says "ooooh" at every food stall, even when it's the same offering of fried dough, greasy pizza slices, and overpriced futuristic ice cream as the last one. Meanwhile I'm double-checking faces for anyone I might know. Once I think I see someone familiar out of the corner of my eye. A way of walking that looks an awful lot like how Ellis walks. I release Tommy's hand and venture off in the look-alike's direction, around a corner, past the kiddie bumper cars. But all I find is a couple sad foil chip bags trapped under the extension cables.

We arrive at the entrance again, completing our loop, then double back to the pier, where we lean over the wooden railing and watch people footprint the sand below. A group of teenagers around our age passes a handle of amber liquid around their circle, its label hidden by a wrinkled paper bag.

"The mix of booze and open water seems irresponsible," I say in Tommy's ear so he'll hear over the carnival music and the waves and the people.

He whips his phone out of his butt pocket. Doesn't say anything, which must mean he agrees. Or just isn't paying attention. I peek over his shoulder and see he's watching the piping plover feed. Okay. A bit rude. One fluffy gray chick is already cleaning its feathers with its beak; the second egg remains intact but wobbles slightly. "Cute little fuckers," Tommy mutters. Before I can knock his phone into the wet sand below, it's back in his pocket.

He squints at the patchwork of towels and coolers stretching at least a mile down the beach. His eyes have more sand and sky in them than anything else, and he's wearing his shoulders like a hermit crab's shell, and oh my god, he's having a bad time. He hates this. That old leaky pipe in my chest creaks to life and the drops from its spout are lukewarm, gray. He wanted cute, carefree fun, like we're in a rom-com and the history between us is nothing but quirky backstory. He wanted to be distracted from thinking about Clifford Samuels for a few hours. Of course he'd rather watch birds hatch via livestream than watch me sulk!

I put my hand on his arm, not like it fell there by accident but like I meant for it to. It may be too late to salvage a rom-com date out of this, but at the very least I can make him smile. He squints at me the way he looked at the beach, trying to figure me out.

"This is way better than mini golf," I say.

"But what about bowling?" he says with mock seriousness.

"Let's not get ahead of ourselves."

I lead him down a set of rickety stairs and I guess this is okay that we're holding hands, given the level of inebriation of our fellow beachgoers. The tide's coming in and there's still fifty yards of squishy sand. There's room to breathe like there isn't in West Finch, to sit and let our legs tangle in the sand while Tommy collects every shell and stone in arm's reach and piles them for me as if they are pearls. Kisses my peeling, sunburnt shoulder. The sunset turns the water pink and gold.

On this cold beach, surrounded by people we don't know, he's a different version of himself. We wait in a long line for pier fries and he talks to the women holding hands in front of us, telling them his name and hesitating at me. Settles for "This is my Harlow." It's a little like having the wind knocked out of me. As in, I know I'm okay, but I also might suffocate and like it.

Maybe I could love him.

We're almost to the takeout window but I grab his arm, pull him out of line toward a flower bed with a rock wall we can sit on, and tilt my face toward his. I don't want to share him with anyone else. He tastes like the kind of wave that will drag me out to sea and bring me back in pieces. Sand behind his left ear. We both come up for air at the same time and share a smile only we can see. I feel a dangerous rush of warmth for him, like I haven't completely chewed a piece of food. He starts to say, "Harlow, I think I—" and I sense a confession that will change the world in two seconds so I press my lips against his again until his mouth lets go of the shape of his feelings and matches mine. I slide my hands into the back pockets of his jeans, press him to me.

"Oh my god. Tommy?"

My head, his nose.

The crowd dissolves and leaves behind a familiar-looking boy with a sweet smile, dark hair, and retro glasses.

"Uh, hi?" Tommy says as I try to unstick his fingers from my waist.

The boy turns his handsome, toothy face in my direction. "And you're Harlow, aren't you? I mean, look at you. Of course you are."

"Did we meet in SAT class last year?" I ask, squinting.

His answer gets lost in the first notes of "The Entertainer" blaring from the bottle-toss game next to us. It doesn't matter, though, because Ellis is behind him.

My Ellis.

Thirty-Six

ELLIS

A universe so different from my own, I couldn't have imagined it except in my sleep.

The details, though—the bandana in her ponytail, the highlighter-yellow nails. I watched her paint them just two days ago. In my bedroom.

I'm walking down a row of carnival stalls. Rigged, every one of them. Limping even though I'm wearing my leg. Don't care.

Maybe someone bumped into them and then they bumped into each other. With their faces. But there's no one near them.

And I know Harlow.

The window-shade way she recoiled means she knows it's wrong. How completely they were tangled, the mystery of whose limbs were whose, means she knows and did it anyway. This isn't the first time.

And she knows me. So when I slap on a smile and finally catch up to Jules, sling my arm around his shoulders, and say, "So . . . you two, huh?" she narrows her eyes at my arm and correctly guesses this is revenge, part one of five million. And when I say, "Well, I think it's great," Tommy visibly melts but she grows still, eyeing the ugly vein I'm sure has appeared above my left eyebrow, until she's turned to stone.

"You do?" Relief floods Tommy's face. Does he really know me so little? "Absolutely."

The bruise on her neck, the french toast, the stack of letters, that time in the bathroom when I said she was breaking up with her secret boyfriend and they looked at me like I'd shot a piping plover.

I failed to save him. Again.

How much damage has she done? Will I know just by looking at him? I'm afraid to try and feel for our connection, sure I'll find it dead when I need it most. So I look at Harlow instead. My favorite and least favorite person, tangled hair and glitter on her eyelids, freckles like smudged dirt. Wanting to hold her hand—no, *Tommy* wanting to, because if I do I'll be electrocuted. I look at my brother, at Harlow, feel a surge of warmth in my chest, and there's my answer. Love. Beyond bad. The worst of all.

"Let's go on the Ferris wheel," Jules suggests, clapping his hands once.

Jules, who should be back with his sister and their friends, but sensed I didn't want to celebrate the end of junior year by watching a few eggs crack open. He throws his arm around Tommy's shoulders like they've known each other for years. "Tommy, you can go in my car."

Harlow's eyes widen. She's wondering why Jules is such a terrible person that he would sentence her to her death on a freaking Ferris wheel. She's wondering how she might slip away. But I know her too well. I make her walk in front of me so the one thing she can't do behind my back is disappear.

"I have to go to the bathroom," she tries.

"Hold it," I say.

When she stops to tie her shoe—her *flip-flop*—I wait. Pulled hamstring or not, I could chase her down if I had to.

Tommy volunteers his tickets and we're at the front of the line, waiting for the next rounded pod, seats around the edges and metal bars over the windows. The speakers play "If You're Happy and You Know It" on a loop.

"We could all fit in one together," Harlow points out as my brother, then Jules clamber into a blue pod.

"Bye!" Jules calls, slamming their door shut.

Loud breathing. It's coming from me. Like the swell, crash of the waves visible beyond the Ferris wheel's steel beams. Inhale-exhaling through it the way I've done during races, leg cramps and stitched sides. But the more I focus on my breath the more tightly it spools.

They lock us in.

"We were going to tell you," she begins. Blushing can't describe what her face is doing.

"When?"

"Soon." She grips the lip of the white plastic seat. "Really soon."

"When you get bored ?" My voice hoarse. "When he tries to hurt himself again?"

The day at the beach when I felt like a third wheel. The sweatshirt I lent her on his floor. If I'd been paying attention.

She looks me square in the eye. Eyes bright. "I'd never let that happen."

I was in his room every day looking for all the wrong things.

"I know it's weird," she says in a rush, tripping over words coming too fast. "But I swear it's good too. He talks to me about how he feels and he's handling this Clifford Samuels thing really well, like, *really* well, and he's making plans for the fall—I think he might pick up art again, it's not a definite, but we're getting there—so honestly, you don't have to worry at all."

"He's in love with you," I say.

We're headed over the highest part of the wheel. The bottom of Tommy and Jules's pod lowers into view. We draw level and for exactly one-point-five seconds I can see into their pod. Nobody has betrayed anybody so it looks pretty great in there. Harlow and I wave and smile until they disappear.

"No, he's not." A chuckle, forced. "It's not serious. We're just . . . just . . . enjoying each other's company!"

I know what I felt. Even now I look at her and my stomach swirls like an unplugged drain. "Then it won't be a big deal when you end it."

She pales just in time for the sun to flash through the bars on the window and paint her face gold.

"You don't even care about him," she says. "You've barely looked at him since they dragged him out of the water that day when you—ran off to do what? Homework?"

My jaw clicks. "I'd seen enough."

She gestures at me, like, *there*. "So you get it. He was sad and you were sad—"

"Don't make this about me." I lean forward and let our gondola rock. She clings to the bars behind her.

"You're the one making it about you! You're surprised so you think it must be bad. But once you get past the shock of it, it's not bad. Just complicated."

"Why? Because you're manipulating him *and* sleeping with him?"

Her face darkens. "I'm not."

"Which one?" I retort.

Her face a hurricane. Her own microclimate full of rain and wind over there. She could stir up a blizzard, summon a typhoon. The ride slows. Two pods ahead of us, Jules and Tommy climb off and disappear into the crowd.

"How long has *that* been going on?" She's turned her storm cloud gaze on Jules.

"Since you stopped hanging out with me after my race. Yeah, I noticed," I add when her face puckers.

"Well, I'm happy for you," she says through pursed lips.

I cross my arms. "I don't think you have the emotional range for that."

She shrugs. "Jules seems great. So great. Almost as obsessed with you as he'd need to be to put up with your ego."

"Maybe you can give him lessons," I spit.

She gives me a once-over, eyes narrowed. "Maybe I'll be too busy with your brother."

She breathes and my lungs collapse.

She blinks and my bones break.

I don't know how I walk down the metal steps without falling. Not waiting for her, I elbow through the bodies until I find Jules in line for ice cream. Tommy's at the stall next door shooting a pellet gun at a stack of milk bottles and missing every time. As Harlow floats to him, feet not touching the ground and hair crackling with her storm, I'm thinking of all her big plans over the years. The one for our future especially, with her half-hearted SAT attempts, and the way she never got that excited to travel the world. All this time I've been afraid of losing her and I already had. And the thing she told me back then too? Not to worry.

I nudge Jules and nod in their direction. "He looks miserable."

A breeze rolls off the water. Jules holds the collar of his bomber jacket closed around his chin and quakes with a little chill. "I don't know him that well. But, maybe?"

He buys us soft serve. Vanilla for him. Chocolate for me. Harlow and Tommy are still near the shooting game, whispering, about me, about what lies they'll tell me next, silhouetted against the lights of a carousel and not one bulb showing between them. I have to know what they're saying, like a thirst, but that well is full of poison and won't make me feel better. So when they're walking back over and I know she's looking I hold out my ice cream to Jules and move it just a little so that it bumps his nose. I use my thumb to wipe off the smudge and then pop my finger in my mouth.

"I should go home," Harlow says, addressing the dirt at our feet.

Tommy looks around at her. "After one ride?"

His mood's taken a nice little nosedive. I feel it in the way my own anger bubbles, a pot set to simmer. I wonder if he can feel me too, and if yes, why bother holding myself back. Why not let every betrayal big and small fill my head until I despise her and he does too.

The four of us traipse to the beach near the old wooden pier. The police usually patrol around here on dune buggies but they must not have come by yet because there are coolers and cardboard boxes half in the sand, half in the dune grass, which Harlow informs Jules is actually a federal offense, like he cares. I shush her and, after making sure the coast is clear, reach into one of the torn-open cartons. I pull out four sweating, unopened beer cans and offer one to each of them. Even her. I'm just that nice.

"You can't," she says in a panicked whisper. Counting on her fingers: "We're not twenty-one, they're not yours, and one of you has to drive."

"You don't have your license?" Jules asks, trying to make conversation.

"She does," I say flatly. "She's afraid of running someone over."

Jules's hand slips off my back as he looks away. Shakes his head when I offer a can. Tommy gives me a withering look the likes of which he's never turned on me. *What's wrong with you*, it says. He takes one of the beers and efficiently pops the tab with his thumb. Harlow holds herself together with crossed arms. Watches Tommy sip the beer that's flooded the top of his can. I feel a little pang of regret at what I started and catch her eye. I guess now we're both looking out for him like that.

She raises her eyebrows at me. "He's not supposed to drink on his medicine."

"I can hear you," Tommy snaps. Then chugs his beer without waiting for me. We all stare. "What? It's light beer. It has like no alcohol in it."

He crushes the can and tosses it on an overflowing garbage bin. It bounces off and foam drains in the sand. Against my better judgment I pass him one of the cans the others didn't want. I don't know how much drinking Tommy's ever really done (*How do I not know?*), no clue how booze interacts with his medication, but I'm guessing not much and not well.

"I don't drink either," Jules tells Harlow.

"Congratulations."

I can hardly look at her. I can hardly stop looking at her.

I tap my first can against Tommy's second. "I'm toasting the continued success of the West Finch erosion club. Sorry, *task force*. And since it turns out no one follows the rules anyway—"

Harlow's eyes narrow. "What rules? That we tell each other everything?"

Tommy takes another long drink.

"You've been with him longer," I point out. "You should've said something first."

"Yeah, but you didn't know that," she shoots back. "So you should've said something too."

"Can we not stand under the pier?" Jules asks loudly as a mystery liquid drips onto his shoulder from the planks twenty feet above.

I only drink one beer but I can feel—and see—Tommy get drunk at an impressive pace. He's quick to make new friends on the beach. A group with a Frisbee. They shotgun more beers. Would a happy person do this? I search "antidepressants and alcohol" on my phone. Definitely not supposed to mix.

At last he's the drunkest guy at the party. Three times he almost pukes, and Harlow's more worried about aiming him away from the dune grass than making sure he doesn't get sick on himself. But she'd never let anything happen to him. Don't worry. I'm the one who gets him into the car, the only one he'll listen to. Together in the back seat as Harlow convinces Jules to drive us all home in her car so she doesn't have to. Tommy spends the ride pulling her hair teasingly, begging Jules to turn up the volume because every song that comes on the radio is his favorite. My head swims, everything Tommy drank and my one beer, and he looks around and smiles at me.

"We should do this again," he slurs, patting my arm happily.

I'd be happy to never see Palace Playland again. But I won't give this up: the not talking, not needing to.

If I can't find my way to the right universe I'll create my own. Keep Tommy so busy he can't think. Make him eat fruits and vegetables, drag him on runs if I have to, make sure that damn dog doesn't die on him, and get rid of Harlow most important of all.

Mixed concrete. Granite blocks from a quarry in New Hampshire. A blueprint. Here's where things change. I'm dreaming of a seawall so solid you can't hear someone on the other side. Too smooth to scale and too thick to drill through. No flood will destroy it. No neon nail polish or fluttering eyelashes.

Jules drops us at home and leaves the car in the driveway, then walks the rest of the way to the B and B. That leaves Harlow and me to get Tommy inside without waking Mom. There's a moment when he misses a step and we think we're done for, but I catch him around the middle, and we make halting progress up the stairs until at last we reach his room. Goose greets us at the door, headbutting our knees until Harlow pats her on the head, simple as that. Because she's obviously done it before. More than the kiss this says something colossal has changed and I wasn't a part of it. I wish I hadn't seen it. I lower him onto his bed.

"Harlow?" Tommy slurs, hanging heavily from an arm around my neck.

"Hi," she says beside me. I peel his fingers off my skin one by one.

"I have to tell you something. S'important—" He catches her hand in his, and she squeezes back automatically. They've done this so many times before.

"You can tell me tomorrow."

"No, *now.* You don't have to say it back but Iloveyousomuch."

I'm feeling the lined palm of her hand on my lips and I'm watching him kiss it. Feeling a stutter; watching her hand shake. My head the kind of fog that takes high noon to burn off.

"Thank you," she chokes out.

I let my hand close over her wrist for real—warmer than I expected, burning—and pull her across the room. Tommy immediately begins to snore.

"End it," I whisper.

"He's happy!" She wrenches out of my grip. Straightaway my hand is freezing.

"He doesn't know better." I jerk my head toward the bed. "Go on. Do it."

"*Now?*" She swallows as she searches for an excuse. "But . . . he won't remember in the morning."

Easy for her to stand here and say it's all just for fun, but she doesn't know what it was like there. When I walked into the psych ward and my eyes skipped right over him, he blended in so well with the chairs and the linens. The longer this goes on between them, the worse it will be when it ends. And it will end. He'll get depressed again, he'll go off his meds, he'll love her too much. It won't last. Can't.

"If you won't do it, I will." I go around her. Make it halfway across the room before she throws herself between me and Tommy, who's still snoring. Her hands stop signs on my chest.

"I'm helping him," she pleads.

I feel my lip curl. "And what happens when you help, Harlow? Oh right. Things get worse. But tell yourself whatever you need to. Nothing's broken and nothing's your fault."

Her face half full of moonlight from the window and half in shadow. My chest heaving under her hands. I feel each finger. Every knuckle and joint.

"The only thing you've done this summer is show Tommy what it's like to be wrapped up in your fantasy world. And shown me why he hated you in the first place."

I want to pull her into my arms and feel her heart beat against me. I want to rip it out with my fingers and keep it in a box under my bed.

"I'd storm out, but this is my house, and I need to make sure my brother wakes up in the morning. So you need to be the one to leave."

And she does. Pulls her hands back and watches my chest cave in, making no sound until she's on the other side of his door. A single, carefully smothered sob.

My brother's feelings crawl across the carpet, invisible tendrils around both my ankles but tightest on my right, mist in my nose. I can't leave him but I can't stand it here.

I find an old blanket in his closet that smells like our childhood got trapped inside. I hold it over my mouth and nose, wrap the rest around me, and curl up on the floor by his bed.

Tomorrow I'll be there for him completely. Lower the dams and let it all in. The headache he'll have. The thirst. Embarrassment and hope and desperation and yes, even love. But until then, I let a whole new mountain range erupt between us.

Thirty-Seven

HARLOW

I give myself a solid eight minutes to just sit before I turn the key in the ignition. He loves me. He's drunk. I will always be in this car choking down stale and humid air, telling myself not to cry because that's a good way to end up dead in a ditch. All true.

Of course Ellis found out. We were never careful enough, not even at the beginning. That door to the diner's basement? No lock. And I could've made Tommy turn around when I saw we were at Old Orchard Beach, if I'd wanted to. Half the school's there any given night.

I drive home because if I don't then Ellis really does know me and I have to do something to not be the horrible person he just described. Also because if I focus on only what's in the narrow cones of light in front of me, then I can't see anything outside them. Like Ellis's face.

My brain automatically wants to start making plans. I'll force him to hang out with Tommy and me until he sees how much better his brother's doing. Carve out time just for him so he doesn't feel left out. But nowhere on the list of what I'll do to earn Ellis's forgiveness is making Tommy say he doesn't love me. Nowhere is break up.

Mom and Dad are still up when I get home. I find them on the living room couch, a bowl of popcorn kernels—and their own loosely held hands—between them. What's left of Dad's hair is sticking up in the back, like he might've taken a quick nap, and the lines near Mom's eyes look soft in the lamplight.

Dad points to the laptop on the coffee table, open to the plover live-stream. Gleefully: "They hatched."

The thought of my parents cuddled up with their popcorn, in their pj's, watching the piping plover chicks take their first steps—it's so cute I almost tear up again. Mom moves the popcorn bowl to the floor and pats the cushion between them, but I'm afraid they'll feel everything in me if I get too close.

"We thought you were staying with Ellis," she says.

"I said I might." The words come out as a whisper.

What I'd wanted to leave open: the possibility that the date with Tommy would go so well we'd want to keep hanging out. What I'd thought might happen when we got back to his bedroom: no comment.

In the shower, sand pools around my feet and I think: He loves me.

Then I memorize every true thing Ellis said about me. I file these facts away in a place where my mind can turn them over until their dirty, jagged faces are polished. I whisper everything else toward the shower drain and never think of it again.

—

The sky goes from inky black to purple as Mom drives us to the diner in the morning. We pass the plover nest, where a group of spectators is gathered at a respectful distance, and Skye's sitting in one of their little fold-out chairs near the chicken wire. A bubble of anger rises in me when I realize if she hadn't come here, her brother wouldn't have either, and Ellis wouldn't have found out about Tommy and me.

But he did find out. Now he gets to decide what he wants to do about it.

Just like I've made some decisions of my own.

Goose isn't outside the diner. I thought Tommy had an early shift today, but maybe he changed it. We walk in and find the dining room lively for 8:00 a.m. West Finch locals know to come early to avoid the summer tourists, and of course there's the plover hatching to dissect in excruciating detail and, this weekend, Clifford Samuels's funeral. Stacks of disposable dinnerware already line the shelf behind the counter. I won't be attending, obviously, but I'm glad to see they've chosen compostable cups.

Helen's behind the bakery register, burgundy hair a careful mess, arms crossed while, at the nearest counter stools, Steph Lucas and Jeanie Albertson unsuccessfully try to pull her into conversation. There's no line so I march right up. On the stool closest to the register, Jeanie gives me a knowing smile.

"He's not here yet," she says.

I don't think she's talking to me until a few faces at nearby tables turn in my direction, like a field of sunflowers toward the sun. It's not any of Jeanie's business, but to be nice, I clarify, "I'm not meeting Ellis. We're just getting breakfast." I gesture to my parents right behind me. Then I rattle off our muffin order: double chocolate chip for me and morning glory for Mom and Dad. Only Helen doesn't pick up one of those wax paper sheets to grab our baked goods.

"Is it true?" she says quietly.

Not quietly enough. Everyone on this half of the dining room falls silent. Or maybe that's an effect of the blood pounding in my ears.

That's when Ellis emerges from the bakery kitchen in a never-before-worn MacQueen's T-shirt. He knocks a hand back through his hair, which is long and silly and also perfect, and definitely not sanitary in a professional kitchen environment.

"Hello, Prouts," he says, looking only at me.

I break into a million lightning-bolt-shaped pieces and everyone sees.

If I were speaking to him, I'd say, "What did you do?" in this voice so soft it's dangerous. But I am not speaking to him. Because I know exactly what he did.

"Small town." Somehow he says this without moving his mouth. "Things have a way of getting out."

Mom's hand presses on my shoulder. Standing beside me now, she looks between Ellis and me. "What's going on?"

"Harlow and Tommy," Helen says.

"Harlow and Tommy what?"

Because of course there's no logical end to that sentence. Their faces all swivel my way.

"I didn't want to be the first to say anything," Steph Lucas says, leaning around Jeanie to do just that, "but it doesn't seem like that boy is in the right place for something casual. You know, *mentally*."

"You can't let him get too attached to you," Jeanie adds. "He's very sensitive."

The flood. I feel it in me right now and it's the worst time for it. I can't cry in front of all these people. I'll look like I did something wrong. The bell above the door jingles and, yes, I'll just get out of here, pack my bags and move away. If I can get Mom's cement-block hand off my shoulder. Before I can flee, though, Tommy barrels past me and lands with his palms on the counter.

The shirt he picked out is already stained. I'm close enough to see a bit of dried drool at the corner of his mouth and the fine stubble on his jaw, blue-white in the sun streaming through his mural.

God. He probably doesn't even remember what he told me last night.

"Slept through my alarm," he says because he sees only his mom, this apology. "I'll make up the hours. I'll . . ." And then the peanut gallery at the counter, hanging on every word, comes into focus. "Hi."

Then me.

"Are you okay?" he asks, not trying to keep his voice down, because my face must show I'm not. Like he's been programmed to do it, he reaches toward me, but his hand stops midair. He blinks down at it. Remembers we're surrounded by all the people we swore not to tell. I shake my head infinitesimally, but he goes for it anyway, exaggerated and unbelievable, "Because you look like shit."

Ellis lets out a small, triumphant "ha."

There's a version of this moment I built up in the dark back of my head where I never turn on the light, and in it, Tommy smells like polar mint and fresh air. He's had a good night's sleep. We've practiced what we'll say. No one's hungover.

I want to yell at him. I want to kiss him.

I grab a handful of his shirt and go for the second one.

He tastes like mouthwash. Smells like beer. But he's warm and solid, and his hands on either side of my face fit just right.

I've never kissed in front of a live studio audience. The peanut gallery clamors (I hope I've thoroughly offended their puritan sensibilities), and someone whistles from the back (Jim, mortifying). Ellis is watching the way I hate-watch speeches by politicians who don't believe in climate change. Mom and Dad exchange a look even I can interpret: *Family meeting! Tonight!!* I accidentally catch Helen's eye and she raises a brow at us. Skeptical, but no trace of a scowl.

"Well, good morning," Tommy says with a bemused smile. His eyes search mine. Hopeful, but like he's asking my permission to feel that way.

It doesn't matter if he remembers, if he meant it or says it back now. I'm feeling defiant and fierce and the most sure of anything I've felt in a long time.

"I love you too," I say.

The face of the boy in front of me lights up as his brother's behind the counter dims.

And then I stalk out of there slow as you please, braids swishing, yellow combat boots squeaking, letting them watch and commit it all to memory.

Thirty-Eight
ELLIS

Saturday, June 17

The first text:

This doesn't have to change anything.

The second:

We're still us, you know.

The third:

Fine. Let's talk.

I picture yesterday all over again. Syrup, a smattering of freckles, and out of nowhere that *I love you*. Like a wound so deep it doesn't hurt until you look at it, but once you do, you can't think of anything but the sight of your own pink-white bone. Worse still was the kiss that came first, and with it, a bizarre feeling like that should've been mine. Even though I didn't want it and knew it wasn't real. You only kiss someone like that if you're trying to prove something.

I kept working. Not knowing what I was doing, feeling only Tommy's happiness like a bubble of nausea in my own stomach.

If your brother stabbed you in the back, would you return the favor?

He couldn't see that she'd only said it to piss me off. Her *I love you too* code for *Oh yeah, Ellis, is that the best you've got?* But he seemed to get it eventually. By the end of our shift my stomach didn't hurt anymore, and he'd gone all quiet like earlier this year, one-word answers and no direct eye contact. I asked if he wanted to hang out and he mumbled something about visiting Mrs. Samuels. When I checked on him later, he and Goose were sound asleep.

All day I've agonized over what to text her back, whether to respond at all. And now here we are: ditching our bikes, shimmying over a windowsill, and witnessing the wreckage of something even Harlow can't save.

The Ocean Drive house still has an entryway, but it's full of standing salt water, and seaweed now adorns the grand staircase. The furniture's gone, but upstairs, the carpet in the master bedroom is still scarred with marks from the bedposts. I go to the window and flip the latch. The frame's swollen. I have to use my shoulder to shove it open the last couple inches. She follows me past the debris and dust bunnies quivering on the floor, avoiding where the bed would be, the way you'd courteously walk around someone's gravestone.

"Did you find this spot when you were looking for somewhere to make out?" she asks with a little forced laugh.

Bold, considering we're here so she can tell me just how wrong she was to make out with my brother, but I let it slide. Any minute now she's going to apologize for her mess and we'll go back to normal.

I clamber onto the roof. She follows and, after an uncertain look at whatever lies some twenty feet below, scooches up next to me as quickly as she can. We both look straight ahead and it's like having our eyes shut.

"Wow, it's beautiful up here," she says.

"Exquisite," I say back.

But actually we can see nothing. When I brought Jules here last Thursday afternoon, before we made the terrible decision to ride a Ferris wheel, we could see waves for miles. Storm clouds rolling along the horizon, headed somewhere else for once. Or so I thought. But right now it's so dark Harlow and I can hardly see the edge of the roof, better yet each other.

I'm ready. Let her tell me now how sorry she is. Let her say *hit me*, and although she knows it can't compare, ask for the worst I've ever done. This is just another thing that will bring us closer after a while. I didn't know she was capable of sneaking around like this. She didn't know I'd have Tommy's back. We've both learned something.

But even as I want to hear the apology, I also kind of want to skip ahead to the part where we've made up. We need to figure out The Plan for real, but more than that, I have to know things can be the same between us once this is over. Finally, I can't wait any longer.

"Let me help you get started." My voice sounds sharp up here in the wind. I feel her boots scuff the shingles next to me as she settles in, probably cross-legged. Clearing my throat, I continue. "Dearest Ellis, my most cherished friend, who I trust completely: I'm sorry. Specifically, I'm sorry for . . . This is the part where you come in."

"Um . . . I'm sorry for the way I treated Jules. He seems nice." I can almost hear her scrunch her nose. "Too nice for you, maybe, but nice."

She's got that right. The wind whips a strand of her hair against my ear. By the time I reach to brush it away, it's gone.

"I mean, he's helping to ensure our town is slowly destroyed, but he's nice."

"I didn't know who he was when we met. I didn't do it to make you mad." At least, not exactly. I add, "I do like him."

The waves pulse in, out. She shifts again and settles even closer. Near enough that I feel the warmth of her beside me. "I like Tommy too."

I wonder how attracted she is to Tommy really. Is it the kind of thing where when someone likes you, you start to appreciate them? Or is it his actual face? She did have a crush on me once, so in a messed-up way, it stands that she could think my identical twin brother's hot. The cold knife's edge of the sea breeze cuts straight through me.

"Listen," I say. "The more you pro-con this whole mess, the harder it will be to end it."

She inhales sharply. Holds it. "Ellis, we're not ending it."

"What?"

I will the roof to collapse under me, express elevator to the ground, because why am I even up here.

"I thought it was pretty obvious yesterday." She's blushing. Definitely.

I breathe out a laugh so she knows how ridiculous this whole situation is to me. "The only reason he's with you is because he's too depressed to know which way is up."

"Are you serious right now?"

"I know my own brother."

She lets that sink like a rock between us. Even to me it sounds like little more than a wish.

"Dearest, most trusted Ellis," she recites. My arm suddenly hot. Her hand on it. "Please forget everything else that's happening right now and make me a promise."

"You forgot cherished," I say sulkily. I shouldn't even listen to whatever she wants. Shouldn't let her keep touching me.

I picture her closing her eyes as she says: "Promise me you won't go to that funeral tomorrow."

A seagull cries. Nothing answers it.

Of course that's why she'll sit here and touch me and say almost-nice things about Jules. I was so ready to make up I didn't even think.

"I'm going," I say firmly, shrugging off her hand.

But she catches me again, this time with her fingers hooked in my sleeve. "After what he did?"

Our fights always come back to the same things.

"You really want to talk about what he's done?" I shake her loose. "Fine.

How about when my grandpa wasn't around, so Cliff walked my mom down the aisle? Or when he made sure my parents got the first chance to offer on the diner when his own dad passed? But you still hold an accident against him."

"He was driving the car."

Against the black ocean backdrop I see two kids on bikes racing down the empty street.

"It was nobody's fault and you know it," I say. "Let's not forget he saved your 'boyfriend's' ass too." Almost choking on that word. "If not for Cliff, then you should at least be there for Tommy. Since you're so in love."

Doing a voice, she says, *"Mow a kid down in the street, who cares? He's lived here a long time so we're okay with it."*

A full-body shiver passes through me. "Is that what you're telling yourself?"

She falls beautifully silent. So I keep going.

"I remember racing from one end of the street to the other all afternoon. How many times had we done it already? Ten?"

"Please don't." Her voice almost too small to hear.

But the words are coming fast now. Couldn't stop if I wanted to.

"I remember we got in trouble because I sent you flying over your handlebars the week before. Your dad had to pull the pebbles out of your palms with tweezers." Still shivering. I bite down so my teeth won't chatter. "You made a full recovery, of course. Not a single scar, right?"

Her breathing sounds wrong. Might be crying. But since I can't see her, I can pretend she's not.

"I remember the sound of you bumping my back tire with your front, and then—shitty timing!—that old Chevy Blazer—"

"Enough."

"I'm allowed to talk about it. It happened to *me*." I'm panting, freezing cold everywhere except the spot where she touched my arm. "So tell me something: How can I remember all that and not the part I'm supposed to blame Cliff for? If it's anyone's fault, it's yours."

Her shoes scrape against the shingles.

I reach into empty space.

And then I realize I'm alone on a roof almost too dark to see and my right hamstring's locked up. I grit my teeth and scoot toward the window, my foot sliding off the sandpaper shingles into nothing. My only consolation: If I die on this roof, at least I'll get to come back as a ghost and make her life miserable.

I retrace my steps back downstairs, then lower myself from the window where we climbed in. She's already propping my bike up for me because, finally, here it comes. My apology. I take the handlebars and she shines the flashlight right in my face.

"The good thing about you, Ellis, is every time I think I miss you, you remind me what a hopeless asshole you are."

Thirty-Nine

TOMMY

Sunday, June 18

My parents hugged each other when we were kids. Must've. But the first time I remember is the night before Cliff's funeral, after closing, in the middle of the dining room. Over so fast I could've missed it. "Let's remember him how he lived." Mom touches Dad's face with her hand and he leans into it. "Deal?"

———

Eleven years old and for my birthday I asked to spend a day at work with Cliff. For one day only, me and him.

Sixteen years old and I want just one thing: to get through the day without letting him down. The whole town will be there, but it will really just be me and him.

Playing dress-up. Long johns. Sweater. Waders.

Playing dress-up. Pants. Shirt. Tie.

Shoulder to shoulder on the boat deck learning to tie a bowline knot. Catching my reflection in the water beside a bobbing red and blue striped buoy.

Shoulder to shoulder in the pews. His coffin polished to such a shine we're all reflected back in it. An arrangement of potted plants keep it company, along with some of his red and blue striped buoys.

There are little surprises. Like the thrill of watching an emptied lobster pot shoot off the end of the boat and drop below the waves.

There are big surprises. Like that the cemetery gives me goose bumps. So does the sound when Mrs. Samuels drops the first handful of dirt on the coffin.

Our faces wet. Wind-lashed.

Everyone's eyes wet but mine.

The contents of a pot spilling across the deck. I measure for keepers and Cliff notches the tails of any lobsters bearing eggs before we toss them back overboard. I search for a more exciting stowaway than seaweed to show him.

The contents of West Finch's pantries spilling across the MacQueen's counter. I switch mac and cheese and tuna noodle casserole in and out of the oven, and Ellis walks them to the front of the house. He introduces Jules to Mom and Dad. I search for Harlow.

Cliff's watch flashing noon.

The number 75 painted in the window.

The bark of harbor seals swimming in circles like a group of giggling children.

The Black Bear Elementary choir arranging themselves in rows for a rendition of "Lean on Me."

Going up to Cliff at the portside railing. Politely looking away as he wipes a tear. "Ain't that something?" he says. Here's why he's the only person in the world who says he has the best job and means it.

Going up to Mrs. Samuels after. Politely looking away as she wipes a tear. "What's this?" she says. Here's why they say all those useless phrases to people who've lost a loved one: You can't stand beside a widow and not say anything. "Just a little something for the gallery." Knowing I was right not to go back on my meds yet. Not even Cool Therapist would have the heart to say better not to feel this.

It's something. And the loons calling across the waves. And the gulls diving for their lunch.

It's nothing. A sketch of their house—*her* house—I should've given him months ago to infuse color into the blank space above his hospital bed.

Holding up a hand to greet a fellow lobster boat on our way back to shore.

Holding Harlow against me when she arrives after all. Like she promised. Standing near the counter in the same place I saw her last. Whispering *still love you* into her hair to make sure she knows I do remember that I said it first.

Closing out the day. I hang my waders on their hook and step off the dinghy. A red cooler with a white dimpled handle ready to be filled with treasure.

Closing out the night. I hang my apron on its hook and step out from behind the counter. A red cooler with a white dimpled handle ready to be shared.

Gathering: a piece of glass that looks like sky.

Telling all of West Finch that's gathered in MacQueen's dining room: "This was one of Cliff's last finds. Mrs. Samuels and I thought he'd want you all to see it."

A shell with a hole in the middle that can be worn like a ring.

"One in a million and living right here in our waters." I flip the handle to the other side of the cooler to unlock it.

When all you know is sea and the sky, everything on land is something to look at.

From the depths of the cooler comes stunned sunshine in the shape of a lobster, glowing brighter than any stone or shell.

Forty

HARLOW

To be good, wait until after Tommy's little show to correct him. Yellow lobsters are thirty in a million, that's the statistic.

Don't watch Jules's hand slowly travel down Ellis's back as Tommy tells you the whole story. How Clifford Samuels caught this yellow lobster (more of a glow than a color) right before the storm last weekend and kept it alive in his bathtub. Tried to show Tommy when he stayed over—here, notice the way the words stick in his mouth like chewing gum—but Tommy turned him down and he never got a chance. Then Mrs. Samuels called Tommy over to see it yesterday. It smelled like if you stick your face in a lobster trap. Plus roses from this candle she had on the back of the toilet.

In the tank with the others, the lobster glows bright under the aquarium lights.

Do you wish the town could show half this level of enthusiasm for saving their homes from the relentless onslaught of coastal erosion? Yes. Do you say this out loud? Absolutely not.

The most humane thing would be a catch-and-release-type deal. Let it go free where it belongs. But Mrs. Samuels gave it to Tommy to keep. And her husband is dead. And Tommy loved him.

So do the right thing. Ask, "If he'd been able to show you himself, what do you think he would've done with it after?"

Tommy chews his thumbnail, something you've never seen him do before, adorable. "Same as always. Showed it to as many people as he could."

Start with a small suggestion. A little advertising, perhaps. *The rarest sea creature in York County*. If people care about this lobster, they'll start to care about the diner too.

Make sure Jules feels included in the conversation. "You're practically a tourist. How much would you pay to see a yellow lobster?"

"Don't encourage her," Ellis warns.

But poor Jules wants to be on your good side. "Five bucks?" he says.

Point your finger gun and shoot him in the chest. "Exactly. So we call it a golden lobster and charge ten."

———

Because you're being good, let Tommy take the lead.

Yes, you have a vision. You can imagine the yellow lobster beer koozies and bottlecap magnets, the hastily commissioned placard they'll hammer into the soaked earth declaring MacQueen's a historic landmark. But one step at a time. Don't overwhelm. Whatever you do, don't make it about you. Even if when all's said and done, you'll be the one they thank.

Spend a month doing everything right.

Go with Tommy to pick up sign-making supplies (paint and wood). Push the giant flatbed cart, run it over your toe, and don't complain about it once. This is about you being there for Tommy, not the other way around.

Wait for your poor big toe to heal and things at the diner to settle down. Give it about a week. Then invite everyone you know to see the golden lobster for themselves. When that means Coop appears at MacQueen's waving your own damn golden lobster email under your nose, try not to scream. When he asks where your better half is, pretend you know which MacQueen boy he's talking about. Or just ask if he's supposed to be out in public.

"I'm only contagious if you kiss me," he says with a wink. "For real though. Your boy is pretty mad at you."

Recite like you're supposed to, "He's not my—"

"Yeah, not anymore," Coop butts in. "You saw this, right?"

Touch his grubby phone with only the tips of your fingers. From today's paper:

> "We're not anti–West Finch. We're pro-birds," said Ellis MacQueen, 16, of West Finch. "Really, we're pro-animal. I'm not convinced keeping that lobster alive in a short-term tank is humane, either."

"If he starts wearing Birkenstocks, we're having an intervention. Deal?" Coop sticks out his pinkie for your promise.

Whatever you do, don't fly off any handles. Try your hardest not to be yourself.

Avoid Ellis, even if that means avoiding your own house where he sits at the kitchen table with Jules and organizes your parents' paperwork to repent for that time he wrecked your car, back when you were friends. If you were speaking, you'd throw his newspaper quote at his feet and thank him for the help. But you're not, so you pretend like you don't know, don't care, can't read.

Feel the incredible urge to blurt out, *I've got something for Tommy that will change his life. What have you got? A dreary seawall?* But your thing isn't about that. The real gift is Goose getting better, and Tommy quitting work and getting time back to draw or even build that damn wall, if that's really what he wants to do. Maybe a bit more time for you too. And in the fall, you'll have a new routine: Instead of spending every Tuesday and Saturday at a cross-country course, you'll take him to art shows or teach Goose new tricks just to prove that old adage wrong.

Watch Tommy and Ellis build an impossible seawall. When the first section gets too high they take one step back toward the ocean, Mother May I, and start another layer, and another, until eventually they'll be backed up against the water. With nothing else in your control, you'll be tempted to advise them. There's no way the structure will remain that tall (up to your shoulders!). It's leaning a little, if you tilt your head.

Instead, try something new: say nothing. Watch the boys from the breakwater's lip, where the sign marking its significance has already gotten shiny around the edges, the way the noses and shoes of university statues wear out from fingerprints, everyone greedy for their luck.

When Tommy builds this golden lobster into a big deal on his own, without your help, tell him Clifford Samuels would be proud.

Don't complain there's nowhere for you to sit when you come to the diner. Nowhere to stand.

Don't worry about forecasts for storms weeks out, the countdown in the diner's window dipping below sixty days. Don't tell Tommy he looks like he slept not at all, or ask him to use a precious day off to just relax with you. Let him mow lawns. Draw the golden lobster in twenty different ways for postcards and hats. You're happiest when you're busy. He must be the same. Wonder how he's holding up, but whatever you do, don't start a conversation you don't know how to finish.

Come up with projects of your own.

One. When concerned neighbors want to have a little talk about what you're doing to that poor boy, be quiet and demure. Thank them for their input, then ask for check or cash donations on Goose's behalf. Show yourself and everyone else good can come from even your most selfish ideas.

Two. Take up Clifford Samuels's old job because maybe that was working. Something good from something bad. The beach stuff. Every chance you get, you're collecting some gem for Tommy. Find lining your pockets with ordinary treasure strangely addictive. Empathize with the old man, maybe for the first time ever. You get now why he did this so long.

Get so wrapped up reconstructing West Finch in a jar that you miss the month-old plovers flying away. Open the livestream to static. You were farther up the beach, nabbing anything that sparkled. You're not sure what you want Tommy to do with these treasures, only that he has to have them. Even if he just keeps them in a shoebox, you want it to be your shoebox.

Later, when it starts to rain, stand next to Tommy and watch them roll up the chicken wire. Already Mr. Albertson's sent a From-the-Desk-of-the-Mayor email announcing the jetty will be demolished in August. You'll need a shopping list. Balloons, again, and streamers. But for now, you can pull Tommy's hand into the pocket of your raincoat and hold it in yours.

Worry about him, but never out loud. The one time you try to ask how he's doing, no, *really*, will be the worst conversation you two have ever had. Worse than when he accused you of turning Ruby against him because this time, instead of calling you a bitch, he just says, "Does it really matter?"

You don't know. Wasn't that the point, that he could tell you things?

But you're loyal to a fault.

Report back to your new boyfriend's parents to tell them how not-depressed he is. Moody, maybe, but not bad enough to mention. Answer every question they have. You're guilty of nothing but being their son's closest confidante, apart from his dog. Act like it.

When he asks you to watch Goose for a couple hours the afternoon before her surgery, say yes. With confidence. The check for the money you've raised warm and warped in your back pocket. Bad luck can't find you when you're on your best behavior.

Forty-One

TOMMY

Monday, June 19

Lobsters are eternal. So Harlow says. They get sick, eaten by predators, caught in traps, but there's no evidence they actually age. Their bodies don't decay and their cells don't metastasize. They don't die peacefully in their lobster sleep.

It's a lot of philosophy for a drive to Home Depot. I pull Cliff's Dodge Ram into an empty space and glance at her at the other end of the bench seat. "What's your point?"

She slides the elastics off the ends of both braids. Combs out her wet hair with her fingers. "Maybe it's a message about the afterlife."

I finger the stitching on the steering wheel's belly.

"Maybe Clifford Samuels left you that lobster as a beacon of hope."

"You're overthinking it. Something good from something bad, simple as that." We climb out and I meet her on the other side of the truck.

For someone who's not a Cliff fan, she was awfully excited about yesterday's reveal. When Mrs. Samuels showed me the lobster, I thought it was just a little something special, same as everything he used to bring me. But Harlow saw right away it could be bigger than that.

First on the list: make signs. We'll put them every half mile leading to our front door like a trail of bread crumbs for the people Harlow says will come from far and wide. Like we think Cliff wanted.

Damn, I hope it's what he wanted.

We have to walk through the whole store to get to the wood. The way milk lives in the back of grocery stores. Our hands find each other. Automatic. Interlaced. Feels like everyone must be staring. Of course no one cares, but it's hard to shake that old paranoia.

"Anything else you need while we're here?" She squints at a can of vinyl epoxy.

I could check if they have stones Ellis and I could use for our seawall. But I've been given explicit instructions to leave Harlow out of it. "Can't you give me this one thing?" Ellis asked. Hands a prayer. Puppy-dog eyes. It was enough he wanted me to build it with him. He didn't need to beg. I find an abandoned flatbed cart and roll it down the aisle.

"What about storm-proofing the diner windows?" She jogs after me. "Reinforcing the foundation?"

"Are you some sort of carpenter?"

She sticks out her tongue.

We reach the wood aisle and I pace down and back once, not sure how Cliff would do this. Hardwood or particleboard? Plywood, I decide. But poplar? Birch? Finally I reach for whatever's closest. I slide a couple planks off their shelf and maneuver them toward the flatbed. Harlow crosses her arms and steps out of my way.

"This lobster isn't going to stop the erosion," she starts. "You know that, right? We have to make a plan for any money it brings in."

The cart moves out from under me. "Hold it still," I pant.

She sticks a sandaled foot behind the back wheel and leans her hip into the handle. She's wearing one of those outfits with the bottoms attached to the top. Shorts hitting way up on her not-yet-tan thighs. I think I should probably find this pretty hot. Any other dude sees his girlfriend in that and that's what he'd think.

Harlow's still a good thing. Maybe the one good thing. It's just all the other stuff that gets in the way. Trying not to let every aisle in the damn store remind me of Cliff. Trying not to forget him, either.

Used to be when I felt like this the only way to shake it was go for a swim or look at someone else's art. Cliff and I hit the Portland Museum of Art once a week last winter. I curled up with my sketchbook on the bench at the center of each gallery and Cliff did slow laps around the perimeter. Getting his steps in. Occasionally pausing to gaze at a piece or talk to the security guard. Both of us happy for hours at a time. Or trying to be, in my case.

Not the kind of stuff I can lay on Harlow. I'm already a lot. So for her sake I keep smiling.

She watches me load everything into the truck, though she does help push the flatbed to the return carousel. When we pull up to the diner (*74!* shouts the countdown in the window) Goose's tail beats against the ground. I scratch behind her ears and let her lick my face while Harlow hangs back.

"You pet her once and you're over it?" I ask over my shoulder.

"I thought that was a one-time offer," she says breathlessly. Sinks to her knees in the gravel and touches Goose's ear between two fingers.

"When has that stopped you before?" I tease.

She doesn't answer. Just keeps stroking Goose's head, her touch so light Goose presses her tearstained, drooly face into Harlow's hand to increase the pressure. I wait for her to tell me my dog looks like reanimated roadkill, a very dirty mop, some brand-new quip designed to lessen what I love. Even just wrinkle her nose. Instead she turns to me and beams.

My organs go liquid. Totally standard reaction.

I should do something normal. Kiss her? Yes. I lean in, cup her neck in my hand. But her mouth doesn't move under mine.

"What's wrong?" Touch my hand to my face. My lips aren't chapped and I just chewed a piece of gum.

"Someone might see."

There's no one else in the parking lot. No one in sight unless you're counting whoever's out there sitting with the piping plovers and who gives a shit about them? Not her. But I know whose opinion she cares about.

"If you don't want to kiss me, just say that," I snap. She and Ellis can have years of sleepovers and walk like there are magnets in their hips but she can't be seen kissing me. Right.

"I want to!" she cries. "I just don't want people to hate me."

Telling people was supposed to make this simpler. But she and my brother can't make anything easy.

I drag my hand down my face. "Fuck's sake. No one hates you."

Sounds meaner than it did in my head but suddenly I'm pissed. This is the same bullshit she always comes up with. And of course now she doesn't say anything, doesn't look at me. Making me the asshole. She lowers herself to sit cross-legged and lays her cheek on Goose's head like a pillow.

Them like that. My girls.

The fight leaves me fast as it came. I'm empty without it. Exhausted. Point to a patch of gravel and I could sleep there.

"Are people really giving you a hard time?" It takes some effort to get my voice to sound calm, but I think I do it.

Her mouth falls open. "Are people *not* giving you a hard time?"

"I've gotten some congratulations," I admit.

"I told you this would happen." She groans, sitting up just so she can dramatically flop over onto Goose again. "But, you know, Mr. Albertson's actually supportive of us because he told Chuck maybe you'd be a 'calming influence' on me."

"That's so . . . so . . . sexist!" I finish awkwardly. And I'm the jerk who didn't believe her.

She hits me with a whiteout smile. "And not even a little accurate."

———

It's not until they're almost out of sight that I realize how normal it felt to leave Harlow and Goose together, just like I know she'll be in my driveway tomorrow morning, nails freshly painted yet another new shade, so we can take Goose to chemo. A small whine in the back of my head asks if I'm leaning on her too much, is it too good to be true, but I let the sting of salt fill my lungs and drop-kick that bad thought to the bottom of a fucking sinkhole.

On the diner's back steps Ellis hunches over one of my order pads on his lap. He tears out a slip and shows me a mess of lines that suggest interlocking blocks and steel support beams. No scale. Could be as high as our knees or midway up our chests or anything in between.

First we have to get rid of everything that was here before. We clear away the old wall, which involves lugging weathered boulders into a pile on the side and slamming the stubborn ones loose with a heavy rubber mallet. I expect Ellis to find some excuse to get away. At best stand to the side and supervise. But he's out there with me, wearing a path in the dirt back and forth to the pile of rocks, right leg looking stiff.

"Should you be doing this?" I ask uncertainly.

He grimaces as he picks up one of the larger rocks. "Did *she* tell you to say that?"

Open my mouth. Shut it. Tell myself be better, dammit. "You could lay off, you know." My voice sounds wobbly. Pathetic. "People are treating her like shit."

"I can't help it if they agree with me."

The wind changes, blowing from inland, the smell of the too-full dumpster. I hold my breath until it shifts again. Wondering if there's a way to fit them back together without pushing myself out. Feels safer not to try.

The layers start in the center of the wall and unfurl toward the edges, each of us working in opposite directions, talking or not. Sometimes we're measured and careful. Other times it's an unspoken race to see who can get down their side of the wall and back the fastest. But I can't help thinking it should be Dad and Cliff out here. Not us.

We order more rock, more concrete.

The countdown in the window says 67 days. We're putting down a new layer when Ellis says, "Sorry, man, but I gotta ask." Wipes sweat from his forehead with the back of his arm. Sighs. "What's the endgame?"

"Endgame?" I echo.

"Is she staying here another year while you finish school?"

Facing each other on opposite sides of the wall, we inch apart: place a rock, side step, place another. The sun's high overhead.

"Like, I want to get out of here as fast as possible. But maybe she doesn't mind giving up her dream school for you. Or you could do long distance." He raises his eyebrows so I'll know what he thinks of *that* idea.

My eyes hurt. I squint at my fingernails. "We haven't talked about any of that," I admit.

"So what do you want?"

A prickle of annoyance at the third degree here but he's right. I should know. Even a fuzzy idea. But I can't think that far. The most distant I get is walking her from homeroom to her first class. Meeting her at the same table in the cafeteria every day at noon.

"Um. I'll be happy just sitting next to her at lunch," I mumble.

He nods. Stacks another rock and steps away from me.

"What?" I ask, not moving.

Another rock. "I don't want to, like, ruin your happiness," he says.

The sea breeze chills the sweat on my body. "Go ahead."

He gives me a long look. "She told you she'd eat lunch with you? That's nice, except she always eats lunch in the computer lab. By herself."

Ten feet between us now. He wipes his hands on his shorts and leans against the wall to take some of the weight off his right leg. His shirt sweaty in a U around his neck. Mine too.

"I know things ended weird with Ruby. But you can't go back to school with Harlow as your only friend."

The mention of Ruby almost tips me over. I always suspected something happened between them last fall. That he knew more than he was letting on. At this point I'd rather not know.

But otherwise I just feel sorry for him. If he wants to scare me off, he has to try harder than this.

"What's the endgame for you?" I ask.

His forehead wrinkles. "Me and Jules?"

"You and Harlow."

He tosses his trowel aside. Looks down the wall and meets my eye.

"Harlow will always be part of my future," he says. "Don't you worry about that."

———

As for the yellow lobster—or as it's known, thanks to Harlow, the *golden lobster*—you could say it becomes sort of a big deal, but that wouldn't be explaining it quite right.

It's waves of people. First the families who had planned trips to Maine already, then people who've traveled to Maine *because* they read about the lobster. We set up a queue complete with those silly velvet ropes you see at old theaters. At any moment there's a crowd three-deep gathered around the tank.

Another week slips by and it's impossible to tell the difference between the regular summer uptick in visitors and the swell of lobster pilgrims until suddenly we're consistently full, and I have to tell someone there's a wait and I don't know how long. I've never had to do that math. I don't know the formula they use at a place like Olive Garden.

Gently suggesting "nearly threatened" when customers say the piping plovers are endangered.

Not flipping out when a man offers two thousand in cash for the privilege of cracking open the golden lobster's shell and sucking out its insides.

We don't drown here. See: life jacket. Swimmies. Cliff would laugh if he heard this guy. I can too.

Postponing therapy until next week. Sketching new T-shirt designs for Mom and Dad when they each ask. Yellow lobster souvenirs stacked floor to ceiling in the pantry and packed down the side of the basement stairs. Hardly room to walk better yet stand and kiss somebody. Harlow pestering me to schedule Goose's surgery (*yes, now*) and worry about the money later. *Trust me*, she says. So when the diner window says 66 days, I schedule the appointment.

A week passes without me noticing. More than that. Suddenly I'm painting a 58 in the diner window. This day stands out from the others because when the usual blocks of cheddar cheese and onions are delivered, ten boxes of screen-printed T-shirts arrive with them. Mom's are navy blue with a smiling yellow lobster and a cursive "West Finch, Maine" spiraling over its tail; Dad's are gray with light yellow text. Don't know why I thought they'd agree on a single design. Of course they couldn't place just one order.

"Which ones are we selling?" I ask, holding up a tee in either hand for their consideration.

Naturally the answer is both.

By the time the diner window says 54 days I'm giving both my parents T-shirt sale updates at the end of each day. Dad slips me a twenty to show him Mom's log. She's consistently outselling him by five. The tourists can make a selection based on their own personal styles and the merits of each design, but for locals, the purchase implies an alignment. Most everyone buys one of each to be safe.

Days at a time I get to work early, leave late. Sometimes on purpose. When I get an hour for just Harlow and me, it's walking Goose in the dark, sitting in damp sand watching the piping plover chicks motor across the beach.

I tell her things I don't believe. The world isn't ending. Things don't always get worse. She drapes my arm across her shoulders but I hardly feel it. She asks, "Where are you?" because I'm staring at nothing again. I give her a smile that won't reach my eyes no matter how wide it stretches.

And me: tired but not sleeping. Meeting the golden lobster's unblinking gaze and wondering if I've made up yet for even a quarter of the pain I caused Cliff. Sketching the seawall's fractures and crags in dense lines on a piece of scrap paper though there's no way to give it to him now. Almost too tired to think, *is this all?* To stroke the silver hairs on Goose's brow and imagine her better. But what will I do then?

Too busy to feel down. Postponing therapy one week at a time for a whole month. My life too perfect to need the meds rattling around my backpack and then, when I worry someone will notice, wedging the full bottle I pick up from the pharmacy at the beginning of July onto the messiest of shelves below Dad's register.

Too busy to see the piping plovers fly away. Only hearing from Harlow after and letting her take me to the beach. Standing in the rain as Jules and Skye roll up the chicken wire that saved those birds' lives.

"Are you okay?" asks Harlow, slipping my hand into her raincoat's pocket.

"Does it really matter?" I answer without thinking. Like a dumbass. The pretending always hardest in front of her. I fantasize about letting go of her hand. Walking into the water. Not to die this time, but to feel the salt water do the excruciating work of holding me up. Floating just five minutes.

Later when that pit does yawn open inside me and I start to sink under the utter pointlessness of it all—how even if I save Goose now, she's six years old, and will probably get sick again; how Harlow and I see each other even less now that we're not a secret—then I go to the diner's chest freezer and take too long to find nothing. I let the ache spread up my fingers, through my arms and shoulders until my nerves trick themselves and my skin grows warm. Or if I'm home I take a shower, as cold as I can stand, until my brain erases itself.

I know how it sounds. But doesn't everyone feel down sometimes?

Staying busy. Getting sun. Talking to people. Snapping out of it.

Pulling myself together one day at a time.

Forty-Two
ELLIS

A universe where I ignore every instinct and give her a month to set things right.

Organize paperwork for her parents the day after the funeral. Begin weekly physical therapy for my hamstring the day after that, and actually do the home exercises I'm assigned. Pick up shifts at the diner to help with golden lobster mania. Try to be as good to Jules as he is to me. Buy Dad's T-shirt, not Mom's, when I feel like if I don't get to fight with someone soon I'll say something I won't be able to take back.

Above all, spend whatever time with Tommy I can get. Forget checking his room, which clearly wasn't helping. Try somehow to make up for the months and years I wasn't paying attention. Show him I'm worried without saying so, with words I don't have.

We converse instead with the rhythm of stacking. He places a rock; I place a rock. Every afternoon for a week I come out from the diner's back entrance, following the path through the rotting garbage breeze and sand speckled with spent cigarettes. The path runs mostly straight between the gravel parking lot on one side and the dune grass on the other. Worn smooth and baked hard. Standing in a litter of pebbles and dust from the granite, he's fitting two of the rocks back together. They're all from the same quarry in New Hampshire, and he's found two that fit together before getting blasted out of the earth. He holds the pair on top of the wall we've been working, now navel-high, and he kneels and squints along the edge of them before laying a precise smear of concrete their exact length so there will be nothing extra to dry out and crumble.

I expect the Harlow problem to come up right away, but that first week the wall gets taller and we settle deeper into its slate-sheet rhythm. And the next week, when her name does cross my lips and feels like swearing? The sky's so blue and his face so gray that I stop short of ruining her for him. Perhaps if the right time never comes that means nothing needs to be said. So I let myself linger in this temporary space where walls and aching muscles represent an accomplishment. Ignore leg cramps and aches that aren't there.

A universe where I pull him aside and lay her worst deeds on the table. Another where I bargain with her: offer her something she can't resist in exchange for never touching my brother again. A prize only I can give.

One month of making myself miserable just in case he feels it. Skip lunch so he'll be short with her. Stay up too late and watch purple bloom under his eyes. Convince myself Jules isn't sweet, he's boring. We kiss and I can feel the expiration date in it, those first notes of sour before the whole thing turns.

If Tommy feels what I'm doing he doesn't say so.

But Jules does. We're in the room at the B and B he shares with the other guy, Hunter, only Hunter's down the hall hooking up with Zoe in the room she shares with Skye, and Skye's on a grocery run. They've really embraced the West Finch way of life.

"This isn't working," Jules whispers into my neck, sounding a bit strangled as he grabs my wrist and guides it away from him—far, far away, until I'm cupping the quilt instead.

"Oh." All my blood reroutes itself to my burning face.

"No, *that* was fine," he clarifies. (Just fine!) "It just doesn't seem like you're into this."

My hands have been all over his body. He's wearing my teeth marks on his shoulder. I look him in the eye and lie, "Jules. I'm into this."

He pats my head like I'm some annoying kid. Rolls off the bed. "It's all good."

It's not. This is the night before my brother's dog probably dies in surgery and I'm hiding out here so I don't have to look at him with nothing comforting to say. I need this.

Jules steps into his pants. Shrugs on his shirt. "You have an open invitation to Montana, you know."

"But you're not leaving until next week," I say slowly. The piping plovers and their chicks flew away four days ago, but his crew is sticking around a bit longer to hammer out final plover protection stuff with Mr. Albertson.

"I didn't want to forget to tell you," he replies.

The air conditioner kicks on and I realize I'm actually cold. Also that Jules is fully clothed and I'm very not.

I can take a hint. But I'm starting to think I should ask people stuff instead of pretending I know what they're thinking.

"Am I not going to see you?"

He gives me a sad smile, perfect eyebrows peaked. "I guess that's up to you."

———

When I picture home the night before Goose's surgery, I expect to find Tommy eating crap and watching bad TV. Maybe having a little cry. Not Harlow next to Goose on the dog bed, reading her old picture books from the living room bookshelf. Goose never sleeps in her own bed anyway, so Harlow's taken to dragging the dog bed everywhere Goose goes during the day. It's always somewhere I don't expect, and I'm always tripping on it.

I remind myself it was a good day before Jules. I finally got a haircut and my arms are achy from work on the wall. My lips feel swollen from being kissed. I hope she notices.

Harlow looks up at me and chokes out a single laugh. "Too short," she says.

I scrub a hand through my hair. The strands stop sooner than I expect.

Fingers close on nothing. Is she saying that to annoy me, or does she actually think it? Used to be I could tell quick as looking at her. Now I squint my eyes until she's no bigger than my thumbnail.

I try to make her leave before Tommy gets home, but she slams the picture book shut and picks up another.

The front door sucks open. "Hello?" Tommy calls.

"In here!" we chorus, then glare, mostly at ourselves for matching. Neither of us wants to show our claws in front of him.

He walks in looking like pipe cleaners are holding him upright, the tips of his fingers pink and raw.

"You worked on the wall?" I ask.

"Just one layer."

Harlow pouts. "I thought you were bringing home dinner. We were going to hang out, remember?" This last part is for me.

He doesn't have the energy to look annoyed. How he's survived the past month attached to her I'll never know. "Okay. Let me clean up and I'll figure something out."

While he's upstairs, she wanders to the fridge and rifles through the Gatorades and yogurts and oranges—everything at the diner's so rich that, at home, Mom makes it a point to stock the kitchen with healthy food that none of us will eat—and unearths an unmarked mason jar full of a thick black liquid that turns out to be homemade hot fudge sauce. She spoons it over saltine crackers and shatters one after another between her teeth until there are speckles of dandruff-looking crumbs on her collar. I'm not going to tell her.

She sees me looking, and after a moment of hesitation, offers me a cracker. I wonder if there's a universe where the three of us could be friends. I suppose the laws of physics say yes, sure.

I wrinkle my nose in disgust. I do not want to visit that universe.

Tommy comes back wearing a T-shirt and sweatpants. He takes in the scene: Harlow at the open refrigerator with her gross snack; Goose begging at her feet; me with my arms crossed on the other side of the room. As always, he looks like he's about to sigh.

Harlow holds up her concoction. "Cracker?"

His face doesn't move. "Please let me cook you some real food."

Her shorts are cutoffs. I try to work out if she bought them that way or created them herself. They don't sell them that short, do they? I blink. Try to get my head on straight. I'm only looking because Tommy is looking. I fight the urge to cuff him around the back of his bald head.

I only get my attention span back when he leans his forehead against his arm on the pantry door. His fingers walk along the shelves, picking out ingredients like books from a bookshelf.

"You missed pancakes this morning, right?" he says.

"Yes," we answer in unison, again. Two-way dagger glare. Not even Mom's pancakes are enough to make me sit in the same room as her.

He doesn't need a recipe, just a giant bowl, a rubber spatula, and the metal measuring cups on their ring. He melts an admirable quantity of butter in a large cast-iron skillet. Harlow and I look on in awe, accidentally meet each other's eyes. A whole month and it still kills me to see the hurt in her gaze. The hurt in me, too, remembering she's not mine anymore.

I quickly examine the tanned backs of my arms as she sidles up to Tommy, head on his shoulder, one hand absently (or, knowing Harlow, not so absently) touching his lower back. He doesn't look at her but he smiles down at the frying pan. "What?"

"I forgot you could actually cook."

He rolls his eyes. Still smiling, though. That's the kind of power she has over him. I think I'm going to puke.

"Did you finish that eastern section of the wall?" I cut in, just for a topic she can't participate in. "Dad said if we need more supplies he'll go with us."

Harlow coughs into his shoulder.

"I think we're almost done, though," I add.

Harlow hacks up a lung.

"Need a tissue?" I ask. "No? And there's still a pile of rubble at the Ocean Drive place."

She scratches Tommy's back and my skin prickles. "That's like cannibalism," she says.

I sneer. "Survival of the fittest, my little piping plover."

She shows me her middle finger.

But it doesn't have the same zing it would've a couple weeks ago. Mr. Albertson already announced the jetty demolition, and as soon as the negotiations with the protestors are over, I'll lose Jules for good. If I haven't driven him away already. The one person left who belonged to just me.

There's an envelope in Harlow's hand that came from nowhere. Whatever's in it, she's excited about it. But Tommy takes his time, swirling the pan so the raw batter in the middle runs to the edges where butter foams. So she hasn't completely brainwashed him yet.

"What is it?" he asks.

"Just open it, silly."

I can feel myself turn into woodwork, wallpaper, drywall. No, the wood the drywall hangs on. Do I exist at all?

Screw this. I'm not sitting here while they eye-bang each other.

I hop down from the counter and grab the envelope. "Careful!" Harlow yelps as I rip it open. I'm not, but the check still comes out intact. Five thousand dollars and sixty cents.

Ears: pounding with blood. Stomach: like it went through a cheese grater. I knew she was collecting money from people in town but still, I should've thought of it first.

When I finally hand it over, he puts two fingers in the envelope's opening and peeks without removing it. Opens his mouth. Shuts it.

"Is it enough?" she asks. Like there's any way that girl didn't memorize the number.

All she gets is a mute nod.

Oh boy. He is *pissed.* Of course he doesn't want her charity. He wouldn't even take Mom and Dad's loan! I must've subconsciously sensed he'd react this way. That's why I didn't think of it first.

The pancake on the stove is massive, the size of a plate, just like at the diner. He holds the spatula in one hand and searches for a clean plate with the other, and I pass him one, all while Harlow gulps and turns to stone.

"Fuck," he says.

"The first one's always the worst," I say quickly.

But when he turns and holds up the plate, it's perfect.

He shoves the plate down the counter toward Harlow, who only stops its progress by getting in front of it. He doesn't just hate her gift. He hates her for giving it to him, and hates himself for needing it. This is it. He's done with her!

Or maybe that's just wishful thinking on my part. Because he doesn't say anything else to either of us, good or bad, before pouring more batter into the pan. Harlow and I involuntarily exchange another look.

Help! her look says.

I hope you choke on that pancake, says mine.

When she gets ready to leave, there's a long production of saying goodbye to Goose, then re-lacing her combat boots. Finally she says, "Okay. Thanks for dinner." Touches Tommy's arm. Tries to untouch it by wiping her hand on her bare leg. "I'll pick you up at seven?"

My head snaps up. "I'm going to the surgery with him. We already decided."

She goes a little pink. "I've been going all summer. Tommy needs my notes on Goose's medical history."

We both look at Tommy to decide which of us he loves more.

He sighs, exhausted. "You can both come."

Harlow throws a look over her shoulder at me, like, *now see what you made him do?* But I'm not bothered. Eventually there will be just one winner—and I don't do participation trophies.

July

Forty-Three

TOMMY

Thursday, July 20

At 6:50 a.m., Goose and I sit in the mudroom. Only ones in the house.

At 6:59, Harlow's dad drops her off with a cardboard castle full of doughnut holes and a tray of slushy-looking coffee drinks with pink and orange straws. She dumps the doughnut carton into my arms and pats Goose tenderly on the head.

At 7:01, Ellis lopes up the driveway with his own cardboard tray of hot coffees and a squished paper bag full of Mom's chocolate-chocolate muffins.

They glare at each other. Offer everything to me. I take a coffee from Ellis and one of Harlow's powdered doughnut holes even though I don't trust myself to keep anything down.

While I buckle Goose into her car seat:

"You can sit in the front," Harlow says graciously.

Ellis halts. "No, go ahead."

"You're taller."

"Well, you're older."

A tense silence. I press my forehead against Goose's and stay there until the doors around me open. Ellis throws himself into the front seat and takes a gigantic bite of a muffin while Harlow slides into the back on Goose's other side. She smiles and puts an arm around Goose's shoulders. The two of them side by side. Staring at me. Three brown eyes and one blue and I can't make my face move to smile back.

It's kind of becoming a problem. When Harlow gave me that check last night for example. Not my finest. But if I'd opened my mouth I don't know what I might've said. Like now, as Harlow kicks the back of Ellis's seat. And he grabs the bar underneath and slides back into her face.

I can count on one hand the moments the three of us have been together like this. Making pancakes last night. Handing out flyers at the beach. Car rides to school. The weekend before the SATs in March—the only time they invited me to study with them. I said no because I'd already promised that day to Cliff. But I'd wanted to. Would've canceled my plans without a second thought if Cliff and I weren't leaving in five minutes.

At the vet I push the check—already made out, in cursive—across the counter. That thing was with me less than twelve hours. I almost dive back down the rabbit hole I tunneled last night wondering who contributed to Harlow's fund. Were the Samuelses part of it? Was this all back when Cliff was alive, did he wonder why I didn't ask for money if I needed it, why I never let him—

Enough.

It doesn't feel real that now I have thousands of dollars in my bank account earmarked for nothing. I should make a list. Ten things I want to do with this money. There should be something else I care about after Goose. Why isn't there anything else?

Meanwhile Goose leads Harlow in two laps around the room while Ellis chases alongside them, even taking off his sweatshirt and spreading it on the ground to tempt her into plopping down on it. I should soothe Goose. I should laugh. I shouldn't balance on a single square tile like it's the roof of a tall building, waiting for the room to stop spinning. Shouldn't think: Maybe I'll just jump.

And then they come for Goose. The vet who tells me every single time that Goose takes chemo like a champ. Harlow hands over her leash and

Goose is looking up at me like she always does, nervous but trusting, more than I deserve, and I can't stand that, either. I pat her head once then retreat several feet so that I don't fly apart.

After they take Goose away from me, there's Harlow holding her stomach because she drank her coffee too fast and Ellis pacing around the waiting room. It's the TV on the wall full of bad news.

"Clueless," she mutters, shaking her head at the fourteen-day forecast, then marching up to the front desk.

The TV shows footage from the June storm. When Cliff. Green-gray waves, driftwood city on the beach after, a gale swirling around the Mac-Queen's sign. August third, the anchor promises.

The third is when Ellis is cleared to run away again. The other reason we have to finish the seawall. We're the closest now we've been since we were kids, so I feel his restlessness. Like insects crawling all over my legs. I can't compete with conditioning and tempo runs.

"Enough doom and gloom." Harlow aims a remote and the TV goes dark. "What's the first thing you're going to do when you hand in your apron?"

I look at my brother who looks back at me.

"Tommy?" Harlow says. "You're quitting, right?"

We haven't talked about this. Not because I can't quit but because it's none of her damn business. Just like the check last night. Except this isn't about the money.

It's that she brings up these topics even though she's seen how this place makes me, and sure enough, I'm angry again in a way I can't explain.

It's that without Goose's bills I'm out of clear-cut, visible-in-the-light-of-day-type problems to solve. There's nothing I'm allowed to feel down about after this.

It's that she waited until the night before. For my brother to be there. Handed me an envelope, then stood there like I was going to pull a sticker sheet of gold stars from my back pocket. How Ellis asked me about the seawall the moment Harlow pressed her face against my arm and sighed happily.

It's that I don't know who I'm supposed to be loyal to, the girl who bullied me into seeing beautiful things or the brother who abandoned me, then built me back up again.

It's the realization that they'll always love me best in front of each other.

So it's kind of about the money. But does it matter why she did it? She did it.

"C'mon, man. Are you going to say something for yourself?"

No, I'm not. All I'm going to do is sit right here and try not to think about them opening Goose's belly easy as gutting a fish.

"He needs a break," Harlow decides.

"No, he likes being busy. Stop trying to micromanage," Ellis says.

She looks at me. "Am I micromanaging?" Without waiting for an answer, pointing at Ellis: "Why are you even here? Isn't your boyfriend leaving soon?"

"In a week."

"A week!"

The percentage of dogs that die under anesthesia. The odds of a six-year-old mutt dying of cancer. The kind of useless trivia Harlow could whip out like a pistol if I asked to be shot.

"Maybe with this weather they'll get stuck here." He grins not nicely, nodding at the TV.

Harlow scoots her chair closer and hooks her arm around mine. "Six more days together," she says to him. "Sweet. Maybe after that, you can see if Olivia's still desperate. I mean free."

He moves his jaw around. A vein in his forehead glistening. "Fuck you too."

It's not about the money.

It's that they are so obviously not here for me and Goose. Not here for anyone's benefit but their own.

"Just go." My shaky voice cuts through their chatter. "I'll call you when I'm done."

Harlow barnacles herself more tightly to my arm. Ellis looks at her and laughs.

"Both of you," I add sharply, letting my words smack the laughter off his face.

His mouth hangs open, but his reluctance stirs Harlow to life beside me.

"If Tommy wants time to himself, we should respect that." She gets up and carefully brushes dog fur off her black leggings. Avoids my eyes.

"C'mon, man." Ellis still looking at me. "What'd I do?"

I stare back at him. I should feel exhilarated or ashamed, instead of what I feel, which is that the line of confusion between his eyebrows is really something. Does my face get like that? I make a quick sketch of it on my pant leg but only get halfway done before he turns and leaves.

I sink low in my chair. Lose a staring contest with the cat in the carrier on the other side of the waiting room. Wonder if Goose is asleep yet. Have they already cut her open. Will she wake up. It's so quiet without them. Maybe it was better to listen to that than my own thoughts.

When my phone vibrates minutes later, my money's on Ellis. A rambling text. How sorry he is, *man*, and let's not let Harlow Goddamn Prout come between us.

I check my phone and it's not a text at all. It's an email from Ruby.

If I come see this lobster next week, will you be there?

With a link to the diner's website. One of the illustrations I made for Mom and Dad's T-shirts in the header.

School hangs like a curtain over the end of summer. Can't see past it. I'm nervous for everything that goes with being back. Small talk. Classwork. Expectations. But I'd be lying if I say Ruby doesn't take up a bigger chunk of my worries than most. I wonder if things can be normal enough between us that I could sign up for an art class in the fall and not have to drop it if she's there. That thing Ellis said about needing more friends than just Harlow. Maybe he'd get off her back if he thinks I'm taking his advice.

Cliff would've liked Ruby. They never met, though I thought about inviting her on our museum trips a dozen times, even after she quit speaking to me. Almost did it too. That weekend before the SATs in March. I couldn't risk her *no*, though—not that day, when my lungs finally had air in them again—so Cliff and I embarked on our art trek alone.

The South Solon Meeting House was a two-hour drive north, snaking up the coast and then forking toward the woods. The trees multiplied and crept closer to the road with every mile, and my ribs tightened across my lungs to match them, and I was glad. Off my meds five days already just so I could feel what it was like living in my own body.

The meetinghouse sat at an unmarked intersection across from an overgrown field. On the outside it looked like the same white clapboard chapel you'd find on any New England postcard. To walk through the door, though, was to rethink what it meant to have a religious experience.

Frescoes floor-to-ceiling. *On* the ceiling. Layers of paint laid down by dozens of hands. The place hummed. And *I could feel it.*

Cliff and I split up—as much as we could in such a tiny space—and each absorbed the paintings. It was dusty in there, a little too quiet, and as I peered through the gloom, something about the frescoes put me on edge. Maybe the imagery, Biblical and kind of frightening. Or maybe just that frescoes were usually viewed from farther away than this. Surely we shouldn't be allowed to get so close. I closed myself into one of the boxy pews and opened my sketchbook. It'd be the first time I drew since quitting my antidepressants. I felt a blaze of excitement so bright and fast it was almost like panic.

The first line didn't come out right, and that was okay. But neither did the next. I looked at my pencil, my hand. Why wasn't this working? Had the meds permanently changed my brain chemistry? What if I'd never been any good at all?

Shaking, I flipped back through my sketchbook. Incorrect proportions. Poor use of space. Pages of crap. I needed to go home and check the others on my shelves, the books from last year and before it, though I knew they'd be just as irredeemable. I stumbled out of the pew. Tapped Cliff on the shoulder.

"I'm done," I told him, not bothering to hide the emotion in my voice. The lines near his eyes crinkled with sympathy.

"Already?" he said.

A pang of guilt. But not enough to stay.

That's why Goose's surgery won't go well today. It's what I deserve. Otherwise what kind of world is this, if I treat Cliff like that but he's the one who dies? I lose him but he loses everything. It's not fair.

But in case her fate isn't sealed I make bargains. If Goose survives I'll take my meds. Write Ruby back. Do all my homework next year. Hug my mom. Let Dad help with the wall. Stop getting angry at Harlow. At my brother for doing the same thing. Don't be what comes between them.

I must nod off because next thing I know it's three hours later and the vet is touching my arm and telling me, "Goose was a champ."

I stare at her because I still don't believe it. Goose was going to die in there. I could feel it. Now the light's coming through the windows from a strange angle and the waiting room's filled with pets that aren't mine and I feel well-rested for the first time in weeks.

While I wait for Goose to wake up from her anesthesia, I walk outside. Close my eyes. Point my face toward the sun and feel its warmth cascade down my spine, so hot, so quick, that I shiver. When I squint my eyes open I see my brother holding the top of a push-up in the parking lot. Arms quivering. Harlow sitting on the curb with her elbows on her knees not far away.

I sit down between them.

I write Ruby back yes.

Forty-Four
HARLOW

Wednesday, July 26

"We'll be fine," I say, though we might not be.

"I know," Tommy says, but he doesn't.

I've seen hardly any of him since Goose's surgery last week. It went well, but he's still working, so at most I glimpse his elbow as he disappears into the kitchen, or his strained-looking smile from across the countertop.

Right now he's all blue: blue MacQueen's shirt and well-worn jeans and pale blue skin from the it's-too-early-for-this light filtered through the blinds on his bedroom window. It makes me want to stall and keep him here an hour, two, longer for the private show of yellows, reds, and oranges coming back into his face. I would've agreed a long time ago to this first shift of keeping Goose company if I knew I'd get to see him like this.

He kisses my lips, knuckles Goose's head, leaves for work.

Goose stares up at me standing in the doorway, blinks a couple times, then waddles across the room to Tommy's bed, where she jumps up and spirals herself until she's half-hidden by the covers. It's not the first time I've come over to dog-sit, but it's the longest, and I have this unshakable feeling I'm going to let Tommy down. Discover she's allergic to bees and we don't have an EpiPen (do those work on dogs?). The chocolate chip disaster all over again. She gets lost, or heatstroke, or a sudden case of rabies and bites a small child on vacation from Montreal. There's yelling. In French.

No. Goose is a good dog, despite that she destroyed her cone of shame as soon as she got home from the vet. So today I'm going to treat Goose to the best day of her life, and when Tommy gets home from work tonight, I'm giving him all the beach treasure left in West Finch. It won't be like the surgery check, either. I'll do it in private. Everything will be perfect.

Through the wall, a mighty snore. In me, a déjà vu feeling of being on one side of the boys' shared bathroom, unable to think of a good excuse to cross over to the other. I don't have enough good karma for a fight today. Better if he doesn't know I'm here at all.

I tiptoe across the carpet and snuggle into bed beside Goose. My head rests on Tommy's pillow, her head on my arm. I pull a handful of his comforter to my face and breathe it into my mouth and nose at the same time. Bodywash and frying oil and even the smell of Goose, and under all that just an essential Tommy-ness. Something tight in me loosens.

I put on a dog movie (one where the dog doesn't die) and angle the screen toward Goose. It's not the most thrilling of tales, and soon my attention wanders. His room looks so different from that time I came in here after Ellis crashed my car. Now it feels lived in. The large clasp-top jar winks at me from the shelf over the desk.

I pop the lid, close my eyes, and let my hand close over something that feels right. Since it was my suggestion he save Cliff's gifts like this, I don't think this counts as trespassing, but I turn my back so Goose can't see just in case. When I look down, I'm holding a long, black rock smooth as porcelain. I rub the smoothest, flattest edge across my lower lip while we watch.

It's a good rock. Different from the kind I've found. Maybe too different. A whole month I've been gathering things for him, weighing down my pockets every dog-walk. I collected only the most perfect examples of sand dollars, starfish, New England Neptunes with delicate pointed spirals.

On the desk next to the treasures there are sketchbooks labeled by year—and, impossibly, one with a piece of tape down the side and this year's dates on it. Clean white edges. Sharp corners, not banged and bruised from being carried around in a backpack.

I used to live in fear of catching a glimpse of my likeness in one of these books, certain if Tommy turned his artist's eye to me, he'd draw me with my insides on my outsides, and everyone would recognize the rot and the decay: *Yes, that's Harlow. That's her exactly.*

As I pull this sketchbook toward me, I find I'm hoping for something else. To catch just a glimpse of myself and how he sees me now. A girl in whose care he'd leave his dog. Again, not trespassing. He did tell me at his Dad's that I could look at them.

The sketchbook's pages are blank, but there are loose, mismatched scraps of paper tucked inside, each labeled in clear script at the top.

Harlow's Laugh

A plastic cup of pink lemonade done in colored pencil, the sides dimpled and foggy like the real thing.

March

A gray puff of smoke. No, a storm cloud. A bad one.

Brothers Talking

A diagram of what is unmistakably the wall.

And the dates on each page—some of these are months old. All while he's been on his meds. Because he can't not. When he says he isn't doing art anymore, he means not for other people to see. Not yet. I close the sketchbook and slide it back into its place, dreaming of a moment when its pages are filled and he asks me to take a look.

—

Goose kicks me in her sleep and wakes me from my own nap. I find the credits of the dog movie scrolling by and the rustling of a burglar in Tommy's closet. A Tommy-shaped burglar. No. An Ellis-shaped one.

"What are you doing?" I stick my nose out of my blanket nest.

Ellis jumps, smacking his head on the closet's doorknob. For a moment he looks so entirely undone by this scene: me in Tommy's room, without Tommy. It doesn't escape my notice that, even though both of us have been quietly skipping pancake days, we've still ended up in the same place on a Wednesday morning.

His expression turns stony. "Checking."

I'm surprised he's here. It must be his last day with Jules. Mom messaged me that Bea saw the protestors lugging stuff out to their car, and Jeanie Albertson confirmed they're checking out of their room at the B and B tonight.

"This is what you meant when you said you're keeping an eye on him?" While I've been checking for signs I've been helping Tommy feel better, Ellis is looking for proof I'm making things worse.

He nods once, mostly to himself, then goes back to pawing through Tommy's possessions as though I'm not here. Goose's eyes are open, eyebrows raised. I'm not sure we're supposed to tolerate this.

Ellis makes "checking" sound as much like "banging pots and pans together" as he can manage. I think of the drawing in Tommy's sketchbook called *Brothers Talking*. A wall so impermeable not even his pencil could do it justice. If they could just treat each other like human beings with their own brains and feelings and ask each other how they're doing, they wouldn't have to build a tipping hazard of a seawall or dig through each other's closets.

"Will this take long?" I ask after a bout of newspaper crumpling that seems to go on forever.

"Probably," Ellis calls without lifting his head from the closet.

I allow myself a groan and settle back in the blankets. If he's not leaving, neither am I. I carefully pick a piece of fuzz off one of Goose's eyebrow whiskers and start the dog-lives movie again, but we haven't even seen the dog yet when my phone vibrates with a call from Helen. I fumble to answer before she has time to wonder where I am, what I'm doing, if I've maimed her son's dog.

"I'm putting Chloe on." Before I can protest, the receiver is handed off, and Mrs. Samuels's much quieter voice says good morning.

Mrs. Samuels and I haven't spoken since Clifford Samuels died. I don't even know how she feels about Tommy and me. Tommy says she's happy for us, but we all know people tell him what they think he wants to hear.

I face the wall for privacy and mumble, "Hi, Mrs. Samuels."

Ellis's movements by the bureau stutter. Then he goes faster than before to prove just how much he doesn't care about this conversation.

"Helen and I are cleaning out the house and I found . . . well, it's part of the collection he and Tommy shared. I think you better come over."

I haven't gone near the Samuelses' house in seven years. I don't even visit that road they live on. She knows that.

On the other end of the phone, Mrs. Samuels says my name.

"Sorry. I'm here. Um, what do they look like? Could you describe them?"

Through the phone, a sound like stones cascading in a tumbler.

"Oh, they're all shapes and sizes." A pause. "I could send you some pictures if you'd like."

Goose raises an eyebrow again. She's right. No way am I going to make sweet Mrs. Samuels take photos of this thing between her husband and Tommy and send them to me one by one.

"I'll come over. See you soon."

There's nothing so scary about a house full of a dead man's things. I grab Goose's booties and her harness.

"You're going to the Samuelses'?" Ellis lifts his head from his snooping.

"It's actually just Mrs. Samuels's now," I say snottily. His face darkens.

The booties are too ridiculous for Goose to wear on their own—she deserves more style than that. So I untie the bandana on my own head. Ellis takes one look, snorts, returns to his noisy task, but I won't let him make me feel bad. I feel bad for *him*.

"I know what you're doing," he says from halfway inside Tommy's bottommost dresser drawer. "He only likes that shit when it's from Cliff."

I fluff the bandana on Goose's neck. We'll see about that.

To get to the Samuelses' without taking the road, we have to cut through several backyards before finally reaching their rear patio and circling to the front of the house. I loop Goose's leash around my hand an extra time and peer beyond the end of the driveway. That intersection at the end of the street, with the stop sign? That's where it happened. The bikes. The blood. I'm not afraid of it, exactly, but no good will come of making myself walk by.

Helen answers the door. Boxes and tote bags are piled in the entryway around her feet with labels like DONATE and KIDS, but the house itself is cozy and bright. I thought I'd never been inside, but now that I'm here, it feels familiar. Possible I came one afternoon that summer when we first moved here, before Ellis's accident. Or maybe my parents brought me here after, though I can't imagine them traumatizing me like that. The therapist I saw back then definitely wouldn't have encouraged any sort of big reckoning. She said time was the only way to heal. Act like my world was normal and it would be. Well. I'm sure that works for some people.

Helen raises an eyebrow at Goose's new look. "*Fetching*, right?" I barely keep myself from quipping, but I know my audience.

"We're celebrating his life. Not mourning his death," she says with a wry expression, so I don't know whether I'm supposed to laugh or what. When I still look confused, she adds, "That means big smiles."

"Smiles. Got it."

"And when she offers you lemonade, take it." Like I have to be told twice.

"Is that her?" Mrs. Samuels's calls from a different part of the house.

"It's me!" I call back, chipper and not at all terrified.

I walk into the kitchen and stop just this side of gasping aloud.

First there's the fridge covered with a retrospective of Tommy's art. Looks like a piece for each year, even before the art classes he began when we were nine. Near the cold black wood stove in the living room, a framed line drawing of a lobster, so delicate it's hard to see. A blotchy ink portrait of Goose in a frame on the windowsill over the sink.

Mrs. Samuels isn't in here after all, which means I can stare openmouthed at all the art she's lucky enough to just have in her home. This is beyond pretending-to-be-Tommy's-grandparents. It's a freaking museum, all of it work I've never seen before or only caught sight of as the pages disappeared into the trash. Some of the pieces on the fridge are stuck down with a starburst of seven, ten magnets to straighten out the creases.

I pause in front of a drawing of the Samuelses' house in colored pencil, and behind me, Helen stops too. The lines are sharp and exact, the colors vibrant. No beige or black. He's drawn this place not how it actually looks but how it feels to be inside it. Smiling, supported, smothered. How hard it must've been for the Samuelses when Tommy avoided them all that time. And yet, how could he come back here, with the pressure of his own past displayed on every wall?

His jagged signature's in the bottom corner. No date. But those colors. They look raw. Like they've sucked the life out of the other drawings around it.

"When Cliff was in the hospital," Helen says behind me, answering the question I haven't yet asked. "December."

"It's nice, isn't it?" Mrs. Samuels says as she rounds the corner into the kitchen.

I don't have a word for the feeling that drawing gives me, but *nice* isn't quite it.

Mrs. Samuels is slighter than ever before, her joints making sharp angles in her pastel-blue slacks and flowy blouse. Even her hair seems like a wisp of white smoke. The effect's magnified by the impossibly large clasp-top jar she clutches. It's a bigger version of Tommy's, filled about two thirds of the way with every kind of nature debris imaginable. She sets it gently on the kitchen table.

My tote bag chafes on my arm. They both know I've been scouring the beach for weeks, pocketing only the most unique pieces, but I'm positive I have nothing worth sharing now.

"Let's see," Helen says, summoning me to the table.

I clear my throat. "I didn't know what was right." Pull out handfuls of crumpled *Herald* pages and then the large, dingy, zip-top plastic bag they're all rolling around in. There are rocks and shells, sea glass and sand dollars, bits of life lost or forgotten. The pieces send up a billowing cloud of dust, and the top of the table goes gritty with a fine layer of sand. I adjust them into a tidy, even layer and ask, "Do these look okay?"

Mrs. Samuels appraises my display with the tips of her wrinkled fingers, turning the treasures this way and that. Her brown eyes are wet, but they kind of always look like that. Helen, meanwhile, looks without touching, her shrewd gaze flickering to me every other stone.

I should've asked these questions while Cliff was alive. They must both be thinking it. I don't know if it would've helped—possibly I'd have gotten too tongue-tied to let him impart any wisdom—but I might've understood Tommy a little better.

Mrs. Samuels taps the top of the massive jar she set on the table. "This is everything Tommy brought him, ever since he was just a boy," she says, which is not an answer exactly. She unhooks the clasp and scatters a handful of its contents across the table.

All of it *gorgeous*. There are shells with golden ratio spirals, rocks etched to look like mazes, star-shaped shells and shell-shaped stars, weathered driftwood in the shape of a fish, in the shape of a bird, a dried anemone that will pierce you if you let it.

"Let me get Cliff's."

At this rate, I expect her to come back with an even larger vessel. What she actually produces is a small mason jar, the lid already unscrewed. I hold it close.

The stuff Clifford saved to give to Tommy is so . . . ordinary. No other word for it. The rocks are dull gray. Some are symmetrical, but many more aren't. If I spotted any of these on the beach, I wouldn't even think to pick them up. Maybe he hadn't given them to Tommy yet for a reason, and these were the bottom of the barrel? But with the way Mrs. Samuels affectionately pats the jar's belly when I hand it back, that can't be right. I look up at her for some explanation.

"Now seems like the time for a glass of lemonade," she says.

Helen brings her coffee mug to her face and holds it there without sipping. I can't see her mouth, and her eyebrows are as furrowed as ever, so it's hard to know how she feels about my project. But I came all the way here, didn't I?

Feeling silly at first, I hold up each of my treasures one at a time and compare them with the contents of the glass jars. I begin sorting the trinkets I brought into piles without much conviction.

Helen gently picks up the item closest to her. A fragment of shell that looks a bit like the porcelain teacup I discovered at the Ocean Drive house so many months ago. Without speaking, she sets it on the pile of beautiful things.

We work silently like this until Mrs. Samuels returns with a fresh batch of her famous lemonade. And Helen didn't need to worry about me saying no. It's *good*. Only after tasting the bitter zest, how a little salt brings out the sweet, do I recognize how fake my favorite pink version is.

I look again at the jar of things Cliff meant to give to Tommy. I see the man who walked along Ocean Drive to the marina every day watching the way the tides shifted against beachfront homes. Who saw the story in half an ordinary mussel shell. Who put a golden lobster in his bathtub. Things were special because he said they were. Because everything was. Somehow I think I already knew this answer. It doesn't really matter which of these pieces I give Tommy as long as I make them mean something.

I finish my lemonade, then pack up all my treasures and say goodbye. Goose and I let ourselves out the front door and pause on the porch. A sea glass wind chime flutters overhead.

The street Mrs. Samuels lives on *looks* okay. Meaning, just as dangerous as every other street. I wrap Goose's leash tightly around my hand again, thinking how this road made both of us. Tommy wouldn't have needed Goose so badly without it, and I could have been different in any number of ways. Brave and lucky. Kind and true.

If I'd pedaled faster or slower. Taken a wrong turn. Stopped when the red sign told me to. Let Ellis win.

Here's something brave and true: This road is just as unspecial as the items weighing down my tote bag. It's a frost-cracked road in a village of frost-cracked roads, meaningful only because I think it is. I hitch my tote bag up on my shoulder and go down the porch stairs.

I focus on the pavement. On counting the houses. There's Bea and Yvette's, a patch of wild-looking flowers by the mailbox. Dewdrops caught in cobwebs in the short grass. The rustle of purple tassels on bike handles. Goose's leash in my hand. The smell of heat rising off the pavement in waves. A sign that says STOP. Goose politely averts her gaze as I wipe my right eye with my palm, then dry it on my shirt. I bend down, tighten her harness, and let her lead the way home.

Forty-Five

TOMMY

First thing Ruby does is hug me.

Second thing she does is lie and say I look good.

Third thing is spin in place in the middle of MacQueen's like it's Disney World or an old chapel where you can tell everyone from the mason to the carpenter to the person who crafted the stained-glass windows believed in God.

I take in her taking it all in, hair shorter than when I last saw her and lips painted vibrant coral, and remember she's never been here before. Unlike the tourists, I know she catches the little details, like the sparkle of sugar crystals on the blueberry muffins and the pop of color from Cliff's buoys hanging on the back wall. She'll be able to paint this from memory a day, month, year from now.

Harlow's watching Goose back at home. Mom's with Mrs. Samuels. All I need to get Ruby and me a half hour to ourselves is Ellis covering my shift. There's a lot less work to do now that the piping plovers are gone and the crowds have thinned, so he says yes before I reach the question mark.

"But only if you come to the protestors' goodbye party at the B and B," he adds after I pass him my apron.

I don't know why he wants me there. Why I'm flattered. "Sure," I say.

Now he waves at Ruby. Raises his eyebrows at me. Jules is leaving tonight, and I feel his desperation when I look at him. Like I'm about to lose something too.

Ruby slides onto the red vinyl stool closest to the lobster tank and I take the one beside her. The golden lobster lounges inside the tank. Claws banded blue. Black eyes watchful. There's nothing wrong with meeting Ruby though. We can be friends. I know Harlow won't mind when I tell her. If I tell her.

I trace a dull scratch in the glossy countertop. Glance at the ceiling tiles. Back to my fingernails.

"So . . . ," Ruby says to fill my awkward silence. "Do you have your sketch pad?"

Our old routine. I'd almost forgotten. Before I can stop her, she tears a chunk of pages from her own sketchbook and floats them in front of me. Damn good paper. It'd be a crime to waste it. The 6B pencil she passes me is my favorite too. Heavy. Smudgeable. Every time you make a line you're saying something.

"Five minutes," she says as she punches the time into her phone. "Ready . . . go!"

My first sketch is stiff like after a long car ride. So is the second. Next to me Ruby curls over her paper. Drawing with her whole arm. Using all of the space. She goes through page after page. But I focus back on the lobster, and once I warm up, my body takes over. I remember to look past the precious golden shell and go deeper. The primitive nervous system that's not supposed to feel pain. The way their claws beat the boiling pot anyway. Maybe the lobsters in that tank look out at us and think we must not feel things either.

I don't disappear into the page like I used to. I'm still aware of the seats we're taking from paying customers, and how the lines don't look on the page the way they do in my head. But when the timer rings I actually want to keep going.

"Hey, so." Ruby uses the end of her pencil to scratch a spot on her temple. "I'm just going to ask. Are you and Harlow Prout a thing now?"

The way she says it. Peeking up at me through her dark lashes. I *know* that's not everything she wants to say. There's a piece she's holding back. Part of me thinks I should suck it up and ask what. I already know the worst thing Harlow's ever done. Love her anyway. How can this be worse? But I'm not curious about the details anymore. Just afraid.

Using one finger I drag my topmost drawing toward me and dip my pencil back in. Even though I know better. That first impression's usually the right one, and if you don't like where you landed, you should start a fresh sketch.

"Yeah, we're together," I confirm.

"Oh. Wow! I didn't believe it when I heard, but congrats. Really." It's too much. All smiles, but something else underneath. She hesitates. "I guess that means you know everything now?"

Shut the fuck up.

It startles me, this harsh thought flashing through my head, almost slipping out. I have to calm down. Now. If I reveal just how clueless I am, she'll tell me for sure.

"Yeah," I lie. I put her pencil behind my ear for safekeeping. "She told me all of it."

"Oh thank god." Ruby slumps in her stool, relieved. "I kind of got in my head? I didn't really know you before and then we were hanging out so much. But I never should've believed her. I knew you weren't a stalker."

A swell of pressure in my face. Vision blurred. Then I'm rising like a balloon until I bump the diner's ceiling. I can see the top of my own head. I can see the gold on my left cheek from the lobster's reflection and the blue on the other from the window painting.

"Her 'proof' should've given it away. Like, you deleted other guys' numbers off her phone? Who *does* that?"

A guy who doesn't realize she'll just memorize his brother's number instead.

"She's convincing," I say, voice hoarse.

"And then when you were in the hospital she came back and was, like,

Ruby, what do you think about trying things with Tommy again. That's when I realized she'd lied. I was *pissed*." Without warning, a switch flips and Ruby's back to smiles, pulling me into a hug. "But I guess this story has a happy ending!"

———

After she's gone I do as many normal things as I can think of. Refill the salt-shakers. Brew coffee. Find my pages from earlier and color in the lobster's feet, dragging Ruby's graphite over the same spot until there's a noticeable dent in the page. Vow to take my meds right after this shift. Yes. Think this over with a level head. Because you can't do all that to a person and then fall in love with them, give them five thousand dollars and let them make pancakes as they promise you the world won't end.

Outside Harlow's sitting at the picnic table pouring a trickle of water from her reusable bottle and letting Goose lap up the stream. I have the urge to knock the bottle from her hand.

Did she see Ruby come out of the diner? Does she know we met? I'm not going to mention it if she doesn't.

"You." She kisses my cheek when I sit down. Goose snuffles at my palm. "I have a surprise for you tonight."

I bury my face in her neck. Orange blossom and honey. Can a lie smell this good?

Ruby doesn't know what she's talking about, and if she does, I can pretend otherwise. It's part of loving someone. Taking the bad with the good.

"What's this?" She slides Ruby's pencil from behind my ear.

I thought I wouldn't be able to look at her but I can. I totally can. I pull the pages torn from Ruby's sketchbook out of my back pocket and lay them on the picnic table, drawn sides down. "Pretend I'm not here," I say. She points her face away from me like an arrow.

I draw what I see. Her chin a horizontal line. Her hair a cloud. The peels of paint and wood grain around her hands. The awkward way she leans to give Goose shade from the sun. Sea foam on her sneakers. A girl who's mine. A beach that goes for miles. Now that I've drawn it, all of it true.

——

I want to wear all blue. Wake up at six on the dot without setting an alarm. Take something Harlow cares about and smash it at her feet. Re-shave my head, stare at the sea, no one coming to save me, scream until my voice leaves my body and I'm too hoarse to say my own name. And it's all Ellis's fault. He's a mess of emotions on the way to say goodbye to Jules, and walking next to him makes me want to skydive. Blow something up.

Does he know what Harlow did? Her silent co-conspirator.

All summer Ruby's been texting me, Ellis bothering me about it until I had to say yes just to shut him up. Did he put her up to this? Did he tell her about Harlow, did he say *ruin them*? Was Ruby happy to oblige?

Inside the Albertsons' B and B, Ellis and I follow the snorts of laughter coming from the sitting room and find Skye, Jules, Zoe, and Hunter sprawled on the mismatched couches. The ends of several sleeves of crackers and hunks of cheese on the antique table between them. There's a burst of cheers when we round the corner.

"Didn't I promise a going-away present?" my brother says with a flourish of his arm.

The cheers. For me. Skye even runs over to give me a hug and sits me down next to her. I smile back the best I can, considering, and remember that time Harlow got so jealous over Skye having my number.

Harlow. Jealous.

When she asked how many other girls first before settling for me herself? Walking down the hallway at school, I bet. Banging on lockers. Asking one by one.

Ellis lands next to Jules on the couch and I look at them in love or on their way to it and damn. That's the way to do it. Find a random stranger who will let you put your mouth on theirs. Make them work to learn how to hurt you.

But Jules barely looks at him.

It's awkward, all of us feel it, and especially me. My brother's chest tightens and my teeth clench and he just wanted me happy. That's why he talked up Ruby. He didn't want my first girlfriend to be a person who seems one way when they're actually a backstabbing, lying—

"We thought maybe you weren't allowed to talk to us anymore," Skye teases, interrupting my spiral.

"Huh?"

"You and Harlow!"

Jesus. Why does everyone want to talk about her today? I grab several crackers and shove them in my mouth, wash them down with a swig of water, realize I forgot my antidepressants at the diner. But there's still time to go back. I can take them tonight. I have a month and a half's worth in the cubby under Dad's register and a refill ready to pick up next week. I'm going to think all this through and not do anything rash. I'm going to sleep for a year.

"You *are* the hotter twin. Clearly she has taste," Zoe toasts me with her apple juice flute.

"Hey!" Jules says, more reflex than anything.

Ellis springs up from the couch. To defend his honor, I think. Because if I want to get in a fight that means he does too. I hold my breath. Wait for him to say something that leaves a mark.

But my brother is out of here.

After all the barbs he's tossed at Harlow and me these past few weeks. Jules stands to go after him but I shake my head until he sits back down.

I follow Ellis outside, down the street, until he reaches the wall. As far as he can go before he gets wet. He hooks his fingers behind his neck and bows his head and I watch his shoulders rise because there's not enough space for his lungs. I know the feeling.

"It was a joke," I tell him.

He paces. Angrily searching for an extra piece of granite to cement to the wall or hurl through a window or swallow whole. But we've laid every stone. Patched every seam.

"You're better at everything. That's why it's funny."

He whirls around. "Do you really think she loves you?"

This morning I would've said yeah. Pretty sure she does. She's probably snuggled in my bed with my dog right now. And I would've shrugged humbly as I said it, so I don't hurt his feelings.

"I know I'm her project, if that's what you're worried about." My face hot and wet but I swear his was first. "You've always been her project and you're doing fine."

"You don't get it." He pushes his hand through his hair and yanks on the short strands. "She doesn't care about you. She only cares about herself."

A missed-step feeling that he's right. And Ruby. Every nice thing Harlow's said and done just another phase in a scheme to make her own life better. But if she's so terrible, why does he want her back so damn bad?

I sneer. "Are you saying that you're perfect for each other?"

If Ruby's right so what? The girl she described is the one I've known seven years. Hypocrite. Manipulator. But everything else I've learned about Harlow—that her loyalty and logic are unmatched, that she can scold and motivate in one breath, that she *gets me*—is still true. If that makes me pathetic then I guess he is too.

"She has to fix everything, even if it makes it worse. And then she tries to fix what she breaks." He looks up. Eyes black. "That's why she's still with you. She'll never run out of things to fix."

———

I run until I'm around the corner, and when I stop, it's only because my legs and lungs make me. I would go and go if my body were in any kind of shape.

Luckily my shadow isn't allowed to chase me. Doctor's orders.

I haul myself up the front steps and kick off my shoes. A low murmur inside. They're sitting in a cloud of fur on Goose's blanket in the living room. Goose's head in Harlow's lap. She's reading a picture book aloud. *Goodnight Moon*. The sad, blue I'll-love-you-forever one on deck.

Goose, wearing Harlow's bandana around her neck, tries to roll onto her back for a belly rub without leaving Harlow's lap. Like her old self, except for the black stitches showing. Harlow contorting herself to accommodate all the splayed dog limbs, looking up at me with a laugh in her eyes.

She loves me.

She squeezes my hand. "Ready for your surprise?"

She has to.

I think but don't say that I've had enough surprises for today. Goose leads the way to my bedroom.

Or more accurately: my shipwreck.

My bedroom has been transformed into a tidy re-creation of the ocean floor. Everything everywhere but also in a place of honor. Sand dollars with sand dollars. Black and purple mussel shells arranged like a flower. It's the Samuelses' house. It's Cliff. All my furniture's covered. Can't move without breaking something.

I pick them up one at a time. Shells and glass and how many things are there? Could it be a thousand? I find two stones that fit perfectly in my palms and hold them until they warm up to where I can't feel them.

"I know it's not the same," she says, still hovering in the doorway. "Mrs. Samuels showed me the stuff you gave Cliff and it was so *perfect*, and then the things he saved to give you were perfect in their own way. I was going to throw all the stuff I'd gathered away but then I thought—"

I lean her back against the doorjamb with the tips of my fingers. I press the stones in my hands into her palms.

"Do you like it?" she whispers into my jaw, lacing her fingers through mine around the stones as she pulls me closer.

It's like she ripped me in half but not all the way. My exposed, frayed edge. How good it would feel to let her keep tearing.

Goose barks once and nudges her head into my leg. I gently shepherd her into the hallway, and Harlow closes and locks my door. Goose keeps barking from the other side.

As if we've done this a hundred times before, we cross the minefield of my floor. Harlow pulls her shirt over her head and I hear the crack of a shell under my heel as I stumble. She's wearing this bra speckled with blue stars, and this she leaves on, though I want to ask her not to. I don't think I've had a chance to look at her in the daylight. Stripes of sunlight coming through the blinds and no one banging down the door. I don't think I ever noticed the dimples on either side of her spine, just above the waistband of her cutoffs. Before I can touch more than her hip, she's pinning me down on my sea-glass-studded bed and pulling my shirt over my head too.

She loves me. But all I feel is the familiar sinkhole open up in me, one I'd fill with just about anything.

I let the sea glass's worn, rounded corners bite the skin on my back as I slide my hands around her thighs and pull her against me. She fingers the waistband of my shorts. Her hand moves lower. *That* I feel. My breath hitches. Without thinking I whisper, "I have condoms," into her neck. But it feels totally right. Inevitable.

"HARLOW!"

She freezes in my hands as Ellis slams the front door.

We can hear everything: the sharp *ping* of his keys as they miss their bowl and crash to the floor. His footsteps through the living room and into the kitchen. He pounds up the staircase hard enough that the water glass on my bedside table quakes. She's still straddling me. Legs tense on either side of my hips. Hasn't answered yes or no or maybe or never or can you repeat the question please. Her skin has goose bumps above the cups of her bra.

His steps end in the hallway. I know he's staring at my locked door.

Harlow looks at it too. Maybe they both have X-ray vision. Maybe she conjured him here just in time because she doesn't want to have sex with me.

When she turns back to me, the skin around her eyes is tight.

She whispers, "Are you taking your meds?"

I can't believe she's saying this right now. Searching my face the way Mom does and looking for the broken piece she can pop back in place, when I have the ammo Ruby gave me. A few weeks' missed doses versus screwing with someone's life. Really? She wants to have *this* conversation?

She swings her leg over and is gone. Eyeing my desk one moment, yanking open drawers the next. "Where are they?" Pebbles in her hands. Pushing aside the spirals of stones she carefully arranged. "Have you taken them *at all*?"

I haven't admitted shit but she's *so sure*. Because I wanted to have sex? It was months ago I told her how my meds mess me up. Of all the things for her to remember. Of all the things for me to forget.

I prop myself up to watch her, hands strangling my comforter in bunches, imagining the shelves over my desk raining all her wannabe treasures down on her own head. She lied to me. She ruined my life. It's none of her goddamn business. Suddenly the comforter and the garbage that was on it is on the floor, not in my hands. I think I threw it. And she's watching me realize. *She knows.*

I need to calm down before she thinks this is because of the meds. I breathe out hard. Lungs empty. Nothing I want less than to admit she's right, but it'll be worse if I lie.

"I was going to start them again tonight," I confess. "I'd already decided. I swear."

Her fists around rocks against her forehead. Ellis calling her name from the hall. "What were you thinking?" She groans. "I can't believe you'd do this to me."

The sinkhole in me yawns wide enough to swallow this whole house. Every painting I've ever made and all the ones I could make still. The ugly jar she made me get to keep Cliff's gifts neat, tidy, out of sight.

"You can't believe *I'd* do this to *you?*"

"It's probably a good sign." Talking more to herself than me. "You felt so good on them you thought you didn't need them. But you can't just stop without telling anyone. Think about the last time you—"

"I know about Ruby."

Her lips part. The mask of her face, the one she wears outside to fit in with the world of normal people and nice things, slips away. I'd expect this to make her look strange, but instead, I recognize her more easily than ever.

"What do you know?" A flicker of fear in her eyes.

Finally.

I'm running this show now. Me. We're done ransacking my room and pretending I'm the one with something to hide. Ellis is yelling both our names and Goose is barking right along with him. My fist aches. He's going to break the door in.

"Apparently I stalked you." I flatten my hand against my chest. My collarbone. Once I say this next part, it's out there. She can tell me it's true. "And you couldn't convince her to give me a shot so you did it yourself."

She stands like the miniature wooden mannequins we used for figure drawing in class. Perfect posture. Arms hanging at her sides.

Deny it, I think. Explain it away. But she gulps and lets her gaze flit to the rattling doorknob.

"Don't tell him," I say. With my hand I crush a corner of my pillow.

Her face is surprised, then not. I make sense to her again. My puzzle pieces are everywhere but she's pretty sure she has them all now, knows which are the edges and corners.

"Okay," she says slowly. "I won't."

She's lying. I squeeze harder. Feel my fingernails through the pillow, digging into my palm.

"I'm not joking," I say. "You tell him and I spill every bad thing you've done to him that he doesn't know or doesn't want to remember. I've got a fucking list." I tap my forehead.

"I said I won't." She swallows. "But you're making me wonder if I should."

She loves West Finch because Ellis is in it. She loves the diner because it's why he hasn't moved somewhere else. She loves the ocean because it binds him on one side and she loves Mom for forbidding him to drive and blocking the other. Can't love me because I'm part of the reason he doesn't want to stay. They'll always pick each other.

"I'll tell him about Ruby."

She presses her lips together hard enough to disappear them. "He already knows."

If your brother kept a secret, would you?

"I'll tell him about the accident."

Harlow's palms open, the stones she was holding fall, and at last the earth sucks us in.

Forty-Six

HARLOW

Here is what Tommy Knows.

While Clifford Samuels was gearshifting from near–vehicular manslaughter to hero, I was running as hard as I could. Past Fran tending the flowers in her front yard and Jeanie Albertson checking her mailbox. Past the diner. Past my own house, where Mom was working from home. The whole time Clifford Samuels's phone getting slipperier in my hand because if I'd called 9-1-1 like he told me to, they'd ask what happened. I ended up at Ellis's house because it was the opposite side of the town. The farthest I could get.

Then while I was getting sick all over the roses that haven't grown back since, *What's wrong? Where's Ellis?* And I said—

"I haven't seen Ellis all day." Sixteen-year-old Tommy does an impression of nine-year-old me as Leaky Pipe does its thing and my chest fills. "Isn't that what you said? I want to get it right."

I feel like I'm seeing him for the first time in months. Not liking what I see. The floor's not any better, littered with the garbage I thought would level the canyon of us. Like anything could ever change.

"I don't need my meds anymore. I've never felt better," he says as a constellation of fear explodes across his face. There a rigid jaw. There an eyebrow, arched and quivering. Like his skin is wearing him. "But I'll take them again. For you."

If. He forgot to finish.

If I do what I'm good at and keep my mouth shut.

I can't believe five minutes ago I was on top of him, wondering if making someone happy was a good reason to have sex with them. A couple months ago, just his hands under my shirt would've been hot. A couple months before that, unthinkable.

I cross the room, lean over the bed, and kiss him. Memorize his lips and the taste of his mouth, the smell of his neck, how it feels in this moment when the odds stacked against us come true. Trying as he kisses me back to think of a way I don't have to open that door. But I can't picture myself melting into his arms the rest of the night, promising we'll figure this out together. Can't say okay and pick up where Goose and I left off in *Love You Forever* and live with myself.

I wipe my lips on the back of my hand and think of all the secrets that will escape if I move now, his and mine. He smiles at me. Maybe for the last time.

I turn away.

"You'll regret this," he says as I slip on my shirt.

Probably.

I open the door. Ellis and Goose are inches away. Goose barks one extra time to express her frustration, then trots past me into the room.

Ellis is harder to look at. Anger rolls off him in impressive waves. No, not anger. Loneliness. I'm afraid to touch him—that same old fear that, skin to skin, he'll feel what I've done. So I step back and wave him into his brother's room.

He takes in the rocks. Tommy's missing shirt. He's lying on his back with his arms crossed over his chest like he's practicing being dead. I don't know how I didn't see it before. Except I do know: I didn't want to. Goose licks his elbows, trying to wake him.

"Tell him," I croak.

Tommy slowly turns his head in my direction but otherwise doesn't move. "You tell him." Nothing at all behind his eyes.

"Someone tell me," Ellis says, using his foot to sweep a patch of my sea glass and shell mosaic away with a crunch.

"He's not taking his meds."

Ellis whirls to face his brother, still lying on the bed. "Is that true?"

Goose and I disappear from the room and for a moment it's just the boys looking into this cruel mirror of how they've each gone wrong.

"I was going to start again tonight." All the heat gone out of him. He glances at me, maybe to see if now I believe him. "They're at the diner."

Ellis's eyes dart toward me too and I can't move, can't breathe. What if he thinks I told Tommy to ditch his pills? But this isn't about me. The only thing I can do now is make sure Ellis doesn't run like last time.

"What do you want to do?" Ellis asks, steady and clear, not running anywhere. He could fly a plane with that voice. Negotiate world peace.

Tommy blinks at him.

"I can call Mom. I can call your therapist. Or we can drive over and pick them up now." He jerks his thumb toward the window. Casual. Like he's been waiting for this moment to come and already had three backup plans at the ready.

"The last one." Tommy's voice is as flat and emotionless as his face. Goose noses her way into his lap and he rubs her neck absently. Pulls on his shirt.

They leave the room one after the other without looking at me. A boy and his shadow. I don't know who's who. Goose watches from her cozy spot on the bed for a moment, then makes up her mind and jumps down. She waits at the top of the steps as they put on their shoes, open and lock the door, all without saying anything to either of us. She stares after them in disbelief, thunders down the stairs, whines at the injustice of it all.

I'm full of snakes. No, I *am* snakes. They make up my intestines, small and large, plus my spinal cord and brain stem and even tiny ones for each blood vessel and vein, the capillaries thin as hairs and crimson straight through. I'm still taking on water but these snakes can swim.

The one time I do the right thing.

I lie down next to Goose. She's by the front door. Won't be moved. The doormat is rough and I let the bristles press into my cheek. My arm. When one patch of skin gets used to the feeling I roll over and punish a new section.

Nothing I told Ruby was strictly a lie. But it wasn't the truth, either. Tommy did delete Ellis's number off my phone—so many times I finally memorized it. He did follow me home from school that time, but only because we live in the same direction. He did make me uncomfortable, but maybe now I get why. I don't even know why I did it, except that back then I thought if I couldn't have what I wanted, then he shouldn't either.

Out there they're turning down Main Street. Tommy's taking him seven years back and Ellis is listening, brow furrowed. After weeks believing there's no one more selfish than me, he'll understand at once that Tommy's telling the truth. They're never going to talk to me again.

And the worst part? If Tommy tells Ellis everything he knows, that's barely half of it.

August

Forty-Seven
TOMMY

Thursday, August 3

On the car ride to the diner I could have told him all of it.

The roses and vomit I've smelled every time I go up our front steps for the last seven years. How far Harlow ran when she left him to die. Past the diner, which was closer, all the way to our house where, for all she knew, no one was home. Cliff's phone was in the dirt under a nearby rosebush. We didn't find it until days later.

What I told him instead: "I saw you the day of my swim."

His hands on the steering wheel went from ten and two to eleven and one.

A tumble of excuses held behind my lips—*you didn't know what you were seeing, there was nothing you could've said*—but I didn't think the thin air in that car could stand even a stretched truth.

My brother worked this over in his shoulders, in a vein above his eyebrow while I held my breath. Flutter-kicked my legs. By the time he answered me I'd be on the Atlantic's other shore.

"I saw you too," he said.

We sat there in the truth of that. My rage streaming through the air vents and the choking air of his disappointment in me, no, in himself most of all, and the sharp points in my shoulders shame about making him feel this way. The grooves of the steering wheel on his fingers, on mine, the air-conditioning blasting and coughing on itself, blowing in my face, and he felt the wetness on his eyes too. The thoughts running around Ellis's head and now bruising my skull: *should've counted the pills should've looked for the bottle should've* when he shouldn't have felt any guiltier than me.

Sadness like a drain that'd suddenly been unplugged and was never going to stop, and I knew it wasn't mine. Its edges didn't feel the way mine do. But I sat in it with him and gave him some of my nothing to balance it out. And under it all, so slight it could've been a memory, a wave of relief that wasn't mine either.

He pulled us into the diner's parking lot, facing the seawall but there was nothing to do. No holes left to patch, and if there were, we wouldn't see them until it was too late anyway. I got my pills. We drove back home.

———

A week later I'm up early. Before anyone misses me. Before Goose. Heart leaping like I've been waiting a long time except I just got the idea this morning.

It's only now that I'm back on my meds that I feel how bad things got. But this new normal is strange and empty in its own way, like the day after a bit lip heals, when your tongue keeps searching for the wound. My sinkhole not just filled with dirt but gone. I'm glad to see it go. I miss it. Both true.

I smear gray concrete along the crevice where two rocks meet and press in: a smooth white stone that looks how it feels to stare at the moon on a cold night. A line of miniature sand dollars. Dad stands in the back door to his kitchen just watching, all devastated and hopeful and trying, and when he sees me wave him over he grins like Ellis, like me. We work side by side placing alternating shells and glass.

"Ain't that something to look at." He whistles and passes me a treasure.

My grip tightens around the perfect cupped shell for a second.

"Something good from something bad," I say back, and press the shell into the concrete. Who knows if the wall will last but it feels worth it for the way it catches the light.

Even if she doesn't see it.

She was still there when we got home from picking up my meds. I already regretted everything. Didn't know where to begin. Ellis told her to leave and I didn't stop him.

Tonight she's staying with us during the storm. Mom asked to make sure it's okay before she offered. After the week of meds, of not getting any replies to my messages and trying to be okay with it, therapy twice, I said yes.

I wonder if she's there already. I've been drawing nonstop to make up for the time I lost believing art and misery were two sides of the same coin, where if you're looking at one, you can't see the other. I'm not miserable or happy now, just somewhere in between, and my left hand's raw from scraping against the paper. I have so much to show her.

Then something jigsaws me from the inside out. A terrible, thrilling idea that vanishes as soon as I try to let it take shape in my mind. I search my bag for something that might tape me back together—blushing starfish, leathery seaweed cord, no, this one, a piece of glass the water hasn't dulled yet—and after I press it into the cement I can't remember what was the matter.

The concrete will take too long to set. The waves will reach higher still. But no matter how thick the salt crust that forms, this seawall will gleam through it. It will right shipwrecks. It will turn tides.

I can't wait for her to see it.

Forty-Eight

ELLIS

When Mom sees me prop my running blade next to my bed for tomorrow, I think she'll disown me. But I need to run like those astronauts training for a one-way shuttle to Mars have to go to space. Because someone told me I was good at it, once.

I wake while it's still dark. Head out without saying goodbye, without checking if I'm first gone or last. The feeling of something I forgot but I don't know what. It comes to me a half mile later that there are loose ends to be tied. A goodbye text sent a week too late. A trip to Montana I won't take.

It's not raining yet, but it's trying to. Cold mist on my shoulders and a sizzle of steam as it hits the baked asphalt. A sense that I've been here before, will be again. I could take any street at any intersection and still land on the same solution. A plan only I can set in motion but no one—not even me—can stop. Dream team. It's always been us.

There's a universe where I stand still. Get good at it. And the things people would say about me: Ellis can be happy through anything. What a lucky guy. On the road there are no brothers, no friends between their sheets, no dogs that still die one day, no boys out west, no to-do list beyond heel-striking and springing forward.

I could apply to only out-of-state schools and leave this all behind.

I could wait for the summer-fling flames to snuff themselves out.

But I've never been much good at waiting. And this is my most brilliant idea yet.

Forty-Nine

HARLOW

There's a tiny dent in the MacQueen + Bell front door. A mark like someone had been very mad at it, or more likely, something bigger than it, but the door was here so the door got kicked.

I didn't tell him.

I never could've guessed there'd come a time when that's the worst thing Tommy could tell me, until he did.

Eight days ago I left their house in knots. Couldn't eat, couldn't sleep kind of night—*Ellis knows now he knows now he knows*—but I still woke up the next morning. Brushed my teeth and took my vitamin and when I inhaled, my lungs filled completely for once.

If I could survive Ellis knowing, maybe I could also do every other thing I'd told myself I couldn't.

One whole day I thought that.

Tommy's text sucked me under, back to how things were before. Shallow breaths and shame. But also nothing like it was before, because I can't forget what Tommy's capable of. I've tried.

I stare at the little spot on the door. Rub it with my finger. I'm sure the key is still inside the flowerpot, but what if it isn't?

Ellis hasn't reached out at all. It hurts, but it's okay. I decided I'm not waiting anymore. I'm done keeping secrets, even the ones that are mine. Especially those.

This tiny dent, for example. Does anyone else know it was the careful work of several years?

Once: slamming the door behind me and feeling like that wasn't good enough. Kicking it for good measure before stomping down the concrete steps, glad to feel the shudder up my legs.

Another: the time the key was gone. Banging on the door with both fists. Every expletive in my vocabulary, not that there are many. Kicking the door. Ellis's words from the day before boomeranging back to me. *He wouldn't do it if it didn't bother you so much.* A second time, watching the door quake on its frame. *Why do you let it bother you?*

I don't usually have to stand here long enough to remember that.

Helen opens the door now. Instead of letting me in, she steps out to meet me. She's wearing a roomy sweatshirt, and her hair nest is not a nest but a neat ballerina bun, only a couple loose strands blowing around her face in the earliest hints of what the meteorologists claim will become a hellish storm. Perhaps this is how her hair always looks at the beginning of a day and I just never see it.

We're standing on the same rectangle of welcome mat, close enough that I smell the jasmine of her perfume. My parents are riding out the storm from a news office in Biddeford for the next several hours, some tasteless, premature news segment about the "tragedy of West Finch." They didn't want me home alone during the storm, and apparently Helen insisted I stay with them, but it sure doesn't feel like it. I take a quick step back.

Helen leans forward and wraps me in a hug.

"Tommy told me what you did." Her voice sounds like it's been folded over on itself many times. "Thank you."

I feel a flutter of pride, like, if it weren't for me last week, he wouldn't have started taking his meds again. Then I remind myself: If it weren't for me, he might not have stopped.

"I should've noticed sooner," I whisper. My hands clutch the extra fabric of her sweatshirt. I squeeze my eyes shut and keep squeezing.

"*We.* Not just you." She pets my hair. Must be something about this welcome mat. I don't want to move from it.

Goose has been waiting for us on the other side of the door. She makes right for me, tail going, which is flattering. At least I know I still have one friend. I scratch her neck until I find a spot that makes her hold still and hang her head sideways, and I only stop when Helen takes my backpack and leads us down the hall.

"I strongly recommend the upstairs bathroom instead of this one," she says, raising her eyebrows and frowning, and I'm relieved for this expression I know well. "We have another guest."

She opens the bathroom door just long enough for a fishy smell to waft out and for me to see the big clear plastic bin in the middle of the floor, filled with water, glowing yellow, the kind of container you shove your winter clothes into when it warms up in the spring. The Helen I know would never let a lobster crawl around her bathtub, so it's comforting to see that hasn't changed.

She sets my backpack down in the living room. I'll be sleeping on the couch, which I expected, but it's still strange not to go straight up to Ellis's room and drop off my stuff on my own.

"It's just us for now, but they shouldn't be long," she says.

As if the boys will talk to me at all. I almost ask where they are, automatic, but just like it didn't feel right to let myself in the front door, I don't think this is any of my business, either. I stand awkwardly in the middle of the living room, sensing it wouldn't be okay to belly flop on the sofa and burn through their DVR. Goose circles me, then sits on my left foot, tail hitting my shins. I pet her over and over.

"Do you want water? Something to eat?"

"No, thank you." I've never felt like such a stranger.

"All right, well. You know where everything is."

The wind sighs again, papers in a locker at the end of the school year, a sketchbook with its glued seam broken, and Helen and I both look. Through the window, sunlight dapples through the green leaves and shows off their veins, their caterpillar holes, but the leaves don't seem to care.

"Forecast said it will blow over by this time tomorrow," Helen says softly. I'd thought she was looking out the window, like I was, but she's actually looking at me.

"I'm not worried."

If I were worried, it'd mean I believe the forecasts, which means I'd have to believe the predicted wind speeds and tide levels, and I can't do that.

"I told them to be back before the rain. Shouldn't be long," she says again.

They're not back before the rain.

But Tommy's close. His backpack and the shoulders of his white T-shirt are only wet with a spare smattering of raindrops when he gets in. Goose ditches me at once and toenail clicks to his side, one happy bark before he shushes her and she listens. He already looks better than he did a week ago, like there's some padding between his skin and bones, and the bags under his eyes aren't as gray.

He stops short at the end of the hall toward the mudroom when he sees me. His hand half reaches for his neck.

"Hi." I swallow nothing. I should've taken Helen up on the water.

He nods once. "I'm glad you're here."

I don't say anything. I'm not sure I'm glad yet. Goose circles his legs. His hand does find the back of his neck then. He drags it across the skin. Lets it fall. That gesture's so him, it kind of makes my heart break all over again.

"I have to take Goose out. Want to come?"

He's being so careful around me. And while I haven't forgotten what he did last week, I can't stand pretending we're strangers all weekend. I tie my raincoat around my waist just in case and he fastens Goose's harness.

"Come back right away if there's thunder," Helen says.

Tommy nods. "Five minutes."

Is that all it will take to figure out if we can ever trust each other again? But even as I think that I know the answer: Yes. And I know it again when he grabs my hand with his free one and holds Goose with the other, and his finger touches the life line or the love line on my palm. I can never remember one from the other.

It's the most beautiful day outside: the temperature so perfect it doesn't feel any different from your body's. It should be impossible for anything bad to happen on a day like this.

We reach the stop sign at the two-minute mark. Goose squats and we wait, then turn back around. The clouds aren't even dark yet. I half expect my parents to be there waiting for me when we get back because clearly everyone was wrong about this storm.

"I was at the diner," he says.

I haven't been since last week. But I know from Dad who knows from Bea that they took Cliff's truck and hauled away all the furniture, anything that could be moved, just in case. I wanted to swing by and make sure they didn't forget anything important, but I had to hope they know what to do by now.

"You should see the wall," he says.

"Sure."

"I mean I want to show you. I'll take you after the storm."

Our eyes connect, then glance away at our respective pairs of shoes. We both know that, same as the diner, the seawall may not be there.

"We boarded up the windows. There are sandbags along the back wall and in the basement in case it floods. We turned off the utilities this morning." His expression softens. He touches my cheek. "Did I remember everything?"

I nod. His eyes are kind of swimmy, but he moves his hand up and drags his thumb under my left eye, like I'm the one about to cry.

"I'm sorry I fucked everything up," he whispers.

"You didn't," I say. He squints at me, tentative but hopeful, and I bite my lip. "I mean, it wasn't nice. But you weren't exactly feeling like yourself."

He rubs his arms. Stares down the street at something I can't see. "That doesn't excuse being an asshole."

This surprises me a little. Because if that doesn't excuse assholery, what does? Besides, he was only mad because I'd ruined everything first. Same as always.

"What about Ruby?" I ask.

I don't mean it like, aren't you in love with her, though I guess that too. I mean what about the thing I did in October. How he was right about me all along.

He shakes his head, frowning. "You're not that person anymore."

He's sweet, but I haven't changed. I'm still bursting with secrets he doesn't know the half of, and it's not quite his turn to hear them yet.

He shoves a mess of papers at me. "To start your collection."

I look down at myself.

Me on the picnic table. No, not me. The picnic table is there, drawn in simple lines, and the waves behind me, the seawall and a vanishing shape that must be the jetty. An outline of me that I recognize from my hair, and where my insides should be: tiny seashells stacked and jigsawed together in a hectic pattern. I flip to the next one. *Harlow and Goose, 2 min.* What must be a contour drawing of me and Goose from the back, my head transposed onto her shoulder, my hand dark with lines on her back. *The Beach.* Ink on thick paper: two figures watching a house face down a wave five times its size.

It begins to rain.

I didn't tell him, Tommy's text said. But god I wish he had.

The idea hisses like a freshly struck match in the living room's jumbled-limb darkness as, in the hallway, the stairs creak.

Tommy dreaming in his sleeping bag on the floor beside me. Goose with her chin on her dog bed and her butt on Tommy's shoulder. Me on the couch with a pillow and blanket that smell like him. I hear the stairs only because I'm listening for something I hope will never happen.

Or maybe that's what I'm telling myself, and I was waiting for exactly this: Ellis in the kitchen with his walking leg on. Gathering flashlights so big they have built-in handles, coats with hoods, courage. Goose watches silently as I shadow him into the mudroom and out the door.

He's standing on the porch just out of the rain, which is coming down in sheets. I step up next to him. He bumps his arm into mine.

I am so full of things to say to him, a month's worth of updates, a friendship's worth of confessions, that I forget most of the words I know.

"Dangerous," I say quietly.

"Probably," he agrees.

I bump him back.

The car rocks in the wind but his grip on the wheel is sure. He safely delivers us to the first streetlight, then the next, until we reach West Finch's single traffic light, a column of shuttered black eyes swinging on its wire that I imagine crashing down as we inch beneath it. As we get closer, he murmurs warnings I can barely hear over the never-ending drumroll on the roof.

We might not be able to get inside.

It could be gone already.

Then the road ends. Painted lines hidden somewhere under standing black water, streetlights out. He drives by memory. I close my eyes.

"It'll be there," he says. "Bet you anything."

He cuts the engine in the place where the diner's parking lot should be. Leaves the headlights on. Outside the car he stripes his flashlight back and forth a few times and the beam catches—for a split second each—a monster swell and a glint of the massive seawall the boys built, holding steady.

Ellis lets us in the diner. Inside it's like being in the hull of a ship. Doubly so because of the plywood hammered over the windows in preparation for the storm. The golden lobster signs Tommy painted lean against the dining room wall, but the space feels unfamiliar without the chairs and tables.

We scatter and gather trinkets no one will miss. In quick succession, Ellis lifts a yellow plastic pen with a lobster on the top and sticks it behind his ear, then helps himself to one of the cellophane-wrapped mints in the bowl by his dad's register. I trace my fingers along the glass of the drained lobster tank, the stacks of menus in their cubbies. We don't have long. Too slow and one of us will get hurt, and then won't that be silly? Risking bodily injury for treasures that already belong to us. But I would settle for a generic plastic cup. A counter stool if they weren't bolted to the floor.

I look around the room and picture it warm with light, loud with laughter. The rush of looking to the table by the window and seeing Ellis already saved it for us. The tug of my stomach when Tommy's behind the counter, and he looks up when I walk in. I don't take anything I can see. But I take this.

Back in the car, Ellis cuts the lights and the rain disappears. The diner shimmers through the gloom. I tell myself I'm the only thing keeping it standing. If I look away for even a second, it will go.

"Tommy says you two made up."

I barely register what he's saying because I'm so focused on the tiny flame of my idea as it gutters, grows hotter. I'm going to tell him. I can feel it. Here, in this car. Sifting through silent confessions to the shower drain, to my reflection as I avoided meeting my own eyes. Carefully gathered over the years. I won't leave out a single detail.

The sea takes everything. After a storm you hear it bubble in the gutters and grates. The people with houses near the ocean know better than to park in their driveways. On trash day they clip their garbage cans to their mailbox posts with rope and carabiners.

No one wants to talk about the inconvenience of it, the expense. Instead they'll tell you about the pump the town bought five years ago. I guess it's helped some. But no one is saying now, this is the way West Finch is meant to be.

Things will never change. But they have to.

"Ellis."

"Harlow."

"I have to tell you something," I say.

"Can I go first?"

I glance out of the corner of my eye and he's a little ill-looking. A little excited.

I nod.

"Jules and I broke up."

I know. Jeanie told Bea told Fran told my mom. I consider putting a comforting hand on his arm but stop myself, remembering the electricity I used to feel lying beside him in his bed. The last thing I need right now. "You'd hate long distance," I say.

"I think so too." He gives me a sideways look I can't quite decipher. "He was a wreck without you, you know."

"Tommy?" I think of him today, showing me his art in the rain. I don't want him to be sad but still, a wreck. For me.

To my surprise, Ellis loses his face in his hands.

"You don't even know the effect you have on people," he says. "You look at him like he's cured and he thinks you must be right. You know how dangerous that is?"

I don't know if I'm supposed to disagree or reassure him, but my idea is going to burn me down if I don't move. I'll choke on the fumes. Still Ellis stares through the rain-soaked windshield. I'm always waiting for him like this: He washes off whatever bad things he's done while mine build up, layers of grime so thick that when I touch the skin on the back of my arm, I can't feel it.

He takes my hands. His are cold.

"I practiced this whole speech but I just really fucking miss you."

How strange that I know his body, the way it moves when he runs, the way he sprawls in sleep like he's jumped from a plane, but that his hands aren't familiar. For the first time since we came out here, I'm scared.

He brings both my hands to his face.

Presses his lips to where my left knuckles meet my right.

I don't know how I escape the car without opening the door, but I do it. I'm outside and the whole passenger side, door and window, remain shut tight behind me. Maybe I slipped through the heat vents. Maybe I changed states, solid to something—anything—else.

The sea is vicious liquid steel and I'm glad for it. I want to watch something I love get torn apart. It could be rain or sea salt pelting my face. Don't know, don't care. Ellis is out of the car too. Headlights a column at his back, standing before me with his arms outstretched.

"Haven't you ever wondered what if?" he yells over the downpour.

I'm too furious to speak. He *knows* I have.

"This summer was miserable without you. I know it took me too long to figure that out."

Rain courses down the fine planes of his face so fast it carves him a new one. An Ellis who's unknowable. Wild and bright.

"But this is what it's supposed to be. You and me. Saving the world and taking names. Everyone knows it. Tommy knows it."

He doesn't want this. Not this, not me. He doesn't think of me like that. How many times have I heard him say it? At least as many times as I've given up waiting for his apologies and forgiven him anyway.

I guess now I'm supposed to swoon and fall into his arms. Tell him I'd wait seven more years if he asked because, damn, he's just that worth it.

"I'm not going to be with you just because you don't like that I'm with him." My voice shakes through my clenched teeth.

"Why? Because it will ruin our friendship?" He howls with laughter. "*Fuck that.*"

A wave swells and crashes not over their seawall, but through it: water exploding on all sides, a spray I feel on my face from here, distinct from the rain overhead. There it is again: a sparkle all along the rocks, like it's studded with moonlight, waterlogged, glistening.

"Don't say no." A finger against my lips. Salty and calloused in a way mine aren't. "Think about it on the drive home. Will you give me that?"

I turn my head to the side. Still taste salt. "I need to tell you my thing now," I say.

He throws up his hands as another wave crashes over the wall behind him.

I tell him: This will be bad.

Crashed-your-car-into-a-tree, made-out-with-your-brother, tore-down-a-wall, chose-him-not-you-level bad. I take the pieces from each boy and, for the first time, knit them together out loud.

"I bet you a dollar I could beat you in a race to the end of the street."

A long street. Five stop signs at least. The roads around here so dead we don't have sidewalks.

"We were wearing helmets, but we weren't scared of anything."

Bumping your back tire with my front. Standing to pedal. Look, Ma, no hands.

"I saw a car coming and knew it was Cliff's. I thought he would stop. I thought you would."

Most of all I knew I'd make it through the intersection and win.

After, wiping out in the grass on Bea and Yvette's front lawn because of the sound. Not loud, but unexpected. Brushing blades of grass off my shirt. Not even a scuffed knee.

Then your blood.

"I didn't try to find anybody. Threw Cliff's phone away. Told Tommy I hadn't seen you all day. And when your mom told mine not to bother visiting you in the hospital, I was relieved."

Finally I'm quiet. I've said all of it I know how to say, and even now the details sound sad and small. But sometimes it's the tiniest things. Rain and sand. Wind and salt.

Ellis's head bows toward mine until our foreheads touch. "When's the part where you tell me something I don't know?"

I wipe the storm and the sea from my eyes so I can look at him. There's no trace of his usual bravado. Hair plastered to his head, eyelashes clumped together, he just looks like a boy in the rain.

"I saw his car coming too." He counts on his fingers. "I know about Cliff's phone because my mom told my dad. That's why she wouldn't let you visit." He pauses, bites his lower lip. "I found out you'd told Tommy you hadn't seen me all day when I was outside his room last week and heard you two fighting. And you've never been a fan of hospitals." He shows me his handful of extended fingers. Gives me an almost-embarrassed shrug. "Nothing stays secret in West Finch for long."

Seven years, seven years, the only two words my brain wants to sing.

"You never said anything. Even when we were up on the roof of that house. You never—"

"I told you. It's no one's fault."

All this time I've been doing whatever I could think of to prove to Ellis I'm worthy of him. All this time he's known I'm not—but been mine anyway.

We hear the first crack, distinct from the groaning we heard inside. Nothing changes on the exterior but I imagine a beam weakening in the basement, another spot in the foundation, as the salt water begins to pour in. He curls his arm around my shoulders.

The sea takes everything—except this.

"What do you say? You and me. Just like you've always wanted." He smiles with one corner of his mouth higher than the other. Like together, we could do anything. "I'm in if you are."

August 4

The taste of salt in the girl's mouth like she's drowning.

The next morning, a single sleeping bag like a spent chrysalis on the living room floor. She checks one messy bedroom, which contains only a sweet, sleepy dog with mismatched eyes and a scar on her belly, then crosses through the bathroom into a second empty room. She lies on the mattress and reaches in all directions. The bed where they don't fit together anymore fits her.

In the kitchen she discovers precut orange slices in the fridge, an unbreakable plate covered in plastic wrap. She looks out the window with the sting of citrus on her tongue. There's nothing yet to suggest anything more terrible than usual has happened. Downed branches and leaves so sodden they look like garbage. Rivers where the streets should be. That sort of tired thing. A scribbled note tells her where she'll find them.

She pulls on rain boots and picks her way past things dead and on their way to it, severed tree limbs, decapitated street signs. Seaweed on trees, on front steps, draped over a child's bike abandoned on the side of the road.

The diner cracking away from its foundation sounds like the creak of a hardwood floor, but it may as well be the earth splitting open. Because it's eight in the morning, and because of the storm, there's no horizon separating sea from sky. One boy waits on shore while the other pushes to waist-deep in the ocean, the current so frigid that after a couple minutes, the August water must feel as cold as if it were March or January. The boy's fingers must be pink with cold as they grasp each new floorboard and ceiling rafter that floats by. Splinters wedge into the open palms of his hands as he lifts the planks from the water and throws them to his brother, who stands on the beach and catches them.

They're different in a million ways, except for their faces, which slip into identical raw expressions following the best or worst news. Except for the list of people they love, which is the same. Except for this synchronized skimming of planks off the high tide.

A seawall too big to be believed cuts through the mist. The girl has to take the long way around it. She trails her fingers along the stones as she does. It's the first time she's laid hands on it. It's smoother than it looks, even with the glittering sea glass and shells embedded in the masonry, like victims of a landslide or works of art, depending on how you look at it.

The girl sidesteps piles of knotted black seaweed and sits in the sand. One of them gives her a half-wave, and maybe the other boy just doesn't see her yet. Maybe he'll never look happy to see her again.

There are no tears. This is a community of people who can no longer be shocked, whose capacity for outrage has emptied down some drain they didn't know was left open. No one is surprised the building was here yesterday and today isn't. Theirs is not the first to fall into the ocean with the black jetty still winking, extending a quarter mile into the sea like a rocky arm. They've seen bathroom floors washed with waves and living rooms where the water stands still.

One boy presses deeper into the water and one stays on shore. One tosses the boards like they're fish and the other catches and heaves them into a pile on the dune grass. There's a three-thousand-dollar fine for killing that grass, but nobody will have the heart to make them pay it.

Board by board, they pile their family's restaurant into a loose pyramid of soaking-dark logs only a few hundred feet from the leveled dirt where it once stood. The waves wash away everything except the straining sound the wading boy's throat makes when he throws planks toward shore, and the plunk as they hit the other's flat, open hands. The one on shore tries to catch his brother's eye but he won't look back. Only out. The remainder of the wood is beyond his reach now. His fingers close on nothing.

"Leave it!" the boy on land calls.

The other steps farther out. He's in up to his armpits, and the curve of his shoulders and back of his head rock with the waves.

The girl stands beside the boy on land with her fists on her hips. He takes a step away from her, into the cold wash of the Atlantic.

"We've got enough!" he yells. Saying so makes it seem true.

The boy in the water swims. At first, they can see the flash of his arm every time he reaches for a board and cradles it against his body. After that he's too far. What looks like the crown of his head could also be the ridge of a wave.

When he's visible again, it's not because he's coming back. Rather, he's amassed so many boards that he lies across them like a raft, holding tight as the planks pitch on the waves. He flutter-kicks and steers himself toward the next bit of drifting wood.

"Go help him," the girl almost says. Not long ago, an order like that would have had the boy beside her swimming until she told him to stop. She's afraid if she says it, he will. She's afraid he won't.

The girl, she is already building castles in her head, rearranging the diner like a jigsaw, brick by brick.

AUTHOR'S NOTE

I don't remember much of high school (a defense mechanism, probably), but I do remember the summer I started writing this novel. Harlow and Ellis were in the very first pages, riding their bikes, and there was a terrible accident, but they had different names, and their town wasn't washing away. Tommy and Goose didn't even exist yet.

That was 2009, and in the years that followed, I tried to write this story every which way, always focused on those pieces that were there at the beginning: a friendship that felt as necessary as breathing. Shame. Forgiveness. But it wasn't until the following stuff happened that the story started to become itself.

(1) I remembered the field trip I took to Ferry Beach Ecology School, when I stepped onto the jetty in Camp Ellis, Maine, and saw a row of houses that had only the ocean for backyards.

(2) Mental illness became not just a thing I read about in books or on the internet, but a forever part of my life and the lives of those closest to me. Just saying the word "depression" felt scary, let alone writing about it.

Here's where I hit you with the "these characters are fictional but the problems they face aren't" stuff, okay?

West Finch isn't a real place, but the eroding beaches of Camp Ellis, Maine; the twin villages of Newtok, Alaska, and its replacement, Mertarvik; and the countless other communities already experiencing the very real effects of climate change are.

Tommy's chapters were sometimes hard to write, but only because his experiences are so familiar. An estimated half of young people in the United

States have experienced mental illness, and over 13 percent have experienced major depression. So if this is your experience, too, then bear with me for a cliché here and remember that, though your head might tell you otherwise, you're not alone by a long shot.

If you're struggling with your mental health or having thoughts of suicide, please talk to someone you trust—a friend, a family member, a teacher. There are people ready to listen and help.

Crisis Text Line
Text HOME to 741741

National Suicide Prevention Lifeline
1-800-273-8255

Trans Lifeline
1-877-565-8860

TrevorLifeline for LGBTQ+ youth
1-866-488-7386
Or text START to 678678

ACKNOWLEDGMENTS

When you work on a project for as long as I worked on this one, you end up with a small army of people to thank.

My agent, the indomitable Jen Rofé. I'm still in awe that so much editorial prowess and business savvy live inside a single person. Thank you for seeing the potential in the rough (rough, *rough*) version of this story that landed in your inbox and pushing me to let my characters have emotions, dammit! Kayla Cichello, for your editorial notes, cheerleading before and after we sold this book, introducing me to *Dawson's Creek*, and spot-on fancasting for the miniseries of our dreams. The entire Andrea Brown Literary Agency, for building such a strong support network for your writers and illustrators.

Kate Meltzer, my champion, brainstorm partner, no-you-don't-have-to-rewrite-the-book-to-fix-this-plot-problem counselor, and yes, editor: You of all people know how different this book would be without you. Thank you for your patience at every stage, for letting revisions take the time they take, for Getting It. Thanks as well to the Roaring Brook and Macmillan teams, especially Jennifer Besser, Avia Perez, Anne Heausler, Kelsey Marrujo, Katie Quinn, Olivia Oleck, Susan Doran, Kristin Dulaney, Jordan Winch, Molly Ellis, Allison Verost, Connie Hsu, Veronica Ambrose, and the many others who helped transform a too-long Word doc into a physical object I can and will carry on my person at all times. Aurora Parlagreco and Jessica Cruickshank, thank you for making the outside of this book match its insides in the most gorgeous way possible. My immense gratitude also goes to the Estate of James Schuyler, for granting permission to quote from "The Crystal Lithium" from *Collected Poems* in both the epigraph and title of this book.

Sensitivity readers are the often-invisible heroes of publishing, but these folks do the critical work of ensuring that when characters jump from authors' to readers' heads, their experiences of the world are depicted as accurately and complexly as possible. Thank you to Mark O'Brien, Caitlin Conner, and Alex Schwartz, among others, for being so generous with your time and feedback. Anything I got right is thanks to you; any mistakes are mine.

This story wouldn't exist without the time and care shown to me by a number of fantastic English lit teachers and writing professors. Dennis Harrington, Kim Shell, Christine Gangemi, Joanne Contois, and Tommy O'Malley, I'm so fortunate to have had the opportunity to learn from each of you. To my mentor, Catherine Tudish: You'll know I'm not exaggerating when I say I would've given up on this story several times over if not for your encouragement. You read this during the long, brutal phase when it had no plot, yet you still regularly asked if I was working on the story about the diner and the kids on the bikes. Thank you for asking.

Thanks also to the #queerever21s and #the21ders for the community and thoughtful conversations. I'm honored to be part of such a talented debut group. Tess Canfield, Marguerite Croft, Julie Zigoris, Lisa Manterfield, Evangeline McMullen, for the talks about craft, weekly write-ins, and generous critiques. Y'all are the real deal. Jeremiah, for AIM roleplays with Sebastian and being my first fan. Krisha, Kathleen, Hannah, Amanda, Devin, Erik, and Talia, for your friendship. Huan He, for being able to talk as deeply about American studies and ethnicity as you can about *Drag Race*, and for feeding me whenever I'm in LA. Renee Lai, for the long talks about creativity and existential crises, and for being a fellow reformed overachiever. Thanks also for being my unofficial consultant on all things art, even though I completely ignored some of your advice (like, "no, high school art students don't use turpentine"). Let's call it artistic license?

Kissan, Nisha, and Alita, for your love and support, especially when I did that one endless revision over Thanksgiving. Ezra, for your tireless enthusiasm and pep talks, and for showing me what self-care and being gentle with myself should look like.

Marisa, for letting yourself be forced to read early chapters of this story. Mom and Dad, for the summer writing programs, unconditional love, and freedom to hog the family computer so I could read and write fan fiction.

And lastly, Dravid. Not just my rock; my boulder! Thank you for keeping our lives running smoothly whenever I disappeared into my revision cave. At least you don't have to hear me gripe that I don't know how to tell this story anymore. You get to hear me gripe about not knowing how to tell the next one!